D1598116

THE LATE BREAKFASTERS
and other strange stories

ROBERT AICKMAN was born in 1914 in London. Aickman is remembered today for two very different accomplishments: as the co-founder of the Inland Waterways Association he played an instrumental role in preserving and restoring England's canal system, and as an author and editor he established himself as one of the most important figures in the history of weird fiction.

His earliest stories were published in *We Are for the Dark* (1951), which featured three tales by Aickman and three by Elizabeth Jane Howard. His first solo collection would not come until *Dark Entries* (1964), a volume that would be followed over the next twenty-one years by six more original collections of tales that rank among the finest and most influential in the genre. Aickman was also the author of two volumes of autobiography, including the fascinating *The Attempted Rescue* (1966), as well as the novel *The Late Breakfasters* (1964). A novella, *The Model*, was published posthumously in 1987. Aickman also edited eight books in the *Fontana Books of Great Ghost Stories* series between 1964 and 1972.

Aickman was a recipient of the World Fantasy Award and the British Fantasy Award, though in his lifetime he did not receive all the recognition he was due, particularly in the United States, where most of his works were never published. Since his death in 1981, however, his reputation has continued to grow, and in recent years he has been praised by Neil Gaiman, Ramsey Campbell, Victoria Nelson, and Peter Straub, among many others.

PHILIP CHALLINOR was born in 1969 and lives in London, England. His critical studies of Robert Aickman's stories have appeared in *Studies in Weird Fiction*, *All Hallows* and *Wormwood*, and some have been collected in the Gothic Press chapbooks *Akin to Poetry* and *Insufficient Answers*. He also posts fiction, verse and assorted grumbles on a weblog, The Curmudgeon, and publishes his longer fiction at Lulu.com.

Books by Robert Aickman

Collections
We Are for the Dark (1951) (with Elizabeth Jane Howard)
Dark Entries (1964)
Powers of Darkness (1966)
Sub Rosa (1968)
Cold Hand in Mine (1975)
Tales of Love and Death (1977)
Intrusions (1980)
Night Voices (1985)

Novels
The Late Breakfasters (1964)
The Model (1987)

Autobiography
The Attempted Rescue (1966)
The River Runs Uphill (1986)

Nonfiction
Know Your Waterways (1955)
The Story of Our Inland Waterways (1955)

ROBERT AICKMAN

THE LATE
BREAKFASTERS

and other strange stories

VALANCOURT BOOKS

The Late Breakfasters and Other Strange Stories by Robert Aickman
First Valancourt Books edition 2016

The Late Breakfasters was originally published by Gollancz in 1964
'My Poor Friend', 'The Visiting Star', 'Larger Than Oneself' and 'A
Roman Question' originally appeared in *Powers of Darkness*, published
by Collins in 1966
'Mark Ingestre: The Customer's Tale' originally appeared in *Dark
Voices*, edited by Kirby McCauley, published by Viking in 1980
'Rosamund's Bower' originally appeared in *Night Voices: Strange
Stories*, published by Gollancz in 1985

Published by Valancourt Books, Richmond, Virginia
http://www.valancourtbooks.com

ISBN 978-1-943910-45-8 (trade paperback)
ISBN 978-1-943910-46-5 (hardcover)
Also available as an electronic book.

All Valancourt Books publications are printed on acid free paper that
meets all ANSI standards for archival quality paper.

Cover by M. S. Corley
Set in Dante MT

Contents

INTRODUCTION

A few weeks after Robert Aickman's birth, the end of the world began. He never stopped mourning its demise: the sense of loss is central to his fiction, along with the sense of a vast immanent reality full of deathly, dehumanising peril – and, for an ambiguously lucky few, erotic or awe-inspiring mystery.

"I do not regard my work as 'fantasy' at all, except, perhaps, for commercial purposes," Aickman wrote. "I try to depict the world as I see it; sometimes artistically exaggerating no doubt." His style is a model of clarity, elegance and understated wit, but his plots often operate on a level that confounds common sense. He can glide over what most of us would consider major points, or skip them altogether for his readers to contrive as best they can, while dwelling on seemingly incidental details that are home, as it eventually turns out, to some rather powerful devils.

He was born in June 1914 on the fringes of the English aristocracy, to hopelessly mismatched parents: "the doomed couple" he calls them in his autobiography. At the time of their marriage, Aickman's father was a spoilt child of fifty-three; his mother, thirty years younger, discovered her husband's age only at the signing of the register. Impractical, inconsiderate, utterly self-centred and prone to daily tantrums, the father was an object of dread to his son and festering resentment from his wife. The specific doom in question was the consummation, at which Robert Aickman was presumably conceived, since his mother hinted strongly that the ordeal was never repeated.

In August the Great War broke out: "Nothing that has happened in modern history, perhaps in all history," asserted Aickman, "has approached in importance the strange débâcle of 1914, when man ceased to run his own world." Whatever the traumas of his childhood, Aickman believed that he had lived through the end of a golden age, and that the mechanisation and social levelling of twentieth-century Britain represented a disastrous shrinking and coarsening of everything he valued most. Many of his stories, and almost every page of his autobiography, resound with lamentations for the solidity and largeness of the world that was lost, and the hollowed-out pettiness of the one he was forced to inhabit. His characters lose their innocence, their illusions, their dreams, their realities and, not infrequently, themselves; only a select few are able to fill the resulting void with a larger and deeper reality.

Aickman published reviews and magazine articles from the mid-1940s, but he emerged as a fiction writer relatively late in life, and the style and quality of his work remain remarkably consistent throughout his career. Three stories appeared in a 1951 collection, *We Are for the Dark*, alongside three by Elizabeth Jane Howard; Aickman's first solo collection, *Dark Entries*, did not come out until thirteen years later. It included one of his early masterpieces, "Ringing the Changes", which had so impressed a literary agent and publishing executive named Herbert van Thal that he wrote to Aickman asking to see more. With van Thal's encouragement, Aickman also produced his only published full-length novel, *The Late Breakfasters* (1964), which for many years has been virtually impossible to obtain. Four of the stories in the present book appeared in Aickman's next collection, *Powers of Darkness* (1966); the other two are from the posthumous *Night Voices* (1985). Between 1968 and his death in 1981, Aickman produced five more collections, almost all subtitled "Strange Stories" or "Strange Tales": one comprising reprinted and revised stories and the rest made up of original works. A short novel, *The Model*, appeared in 1987.

To those who have read his stories and novellas, Aickman's novel may seem a bit anomalous. *The Late Breakfasters* begins as a rather old-fashioned comedy of manners featuring eight or ten vivid eccentrics in a country house, and develops into a largely amiable *Bildungsroman* with an undertone of grief, a few hints of the fantastic and various side-swipes at the minions of modernity. Despite his otherworldly reputation, Aickman's dislike of his times often makes for direct and pungent social comment: his narrative voice and his characters' remarks frequently express the author's own opinions as set forth in his essays and autobiography, and *The Late Breakfasters* repeatedly contrasts the carefree, whimsically kindly upper classes with the coarse common ruck, who substitute resentment for generosity and sloganeering for conversation. The novel shares with Aickman's other work his urbane and brilliantly suggestive style, his typically comic or symbolic character names, and the exemplary strangeness of such episodes as the lovers' separation at the end of Part One, and the old aristocrat's death in Part Two. At the old aristocrat's mansion, the product of a mute dwarf's labours echoes the name of the hostess at the house-party which opens the book; and, in accordance with the best Aickman logic, it is at this mansion that the heroine at last discovers someone who may have knowledge of her lost true love.

Aickman's satire is often delightfully on target. The passage of half a century has done little to dull his dissection of Britain's political administration in the early pages of "My Poor Friend", whatever one may think about the suggested solution of a return to hereditary aristocracy. Presumably drawn from long and tedious experience as chair of the Inland Waterways Association, a society which he helped to found for the preservation of Britain's canals, Aickman's tale conveys the grinding futility of parliamentary procedure – verbose, labyrinthine and interminable – without once becoming boring to read. Meanwhile, behind the ludicrous and frustrating foreground, the narrator glimpses the half-visible horrors of a father haunted and humiliated by the little angels he has spawned. Although he proclaimed that the ghost story "need offer neither logic nor moral", Aickman's best tales operate according to a precise and intricate logic of poetic symbolism; and he certainly was not afraid to moralise. "Rosamund's Bower" offers two morals, one at the beginning and one at the end; although it's debatable how seriously either is meant. Still, for a writer whose subtlety and indirection are deservedly renowned and occasionally denounced, Aickman can also be remarkably heavy-handed. *"Bowel Discipline*, by a prominent member of the Labour party," a throw-away line from "Larger Than Oneself", is doubtless a concise expression of his gut feelings about the political left, but indirect and subtle it is not. More fruitfully, the story attacks the varieties of ersatz spirituality, which are so grindingly trivial and mundane that not even the Devil's own wife – herself the very soul of banality – can put up with them for long. But mystery and awe sit alongside the comedy: like several other Aickman stories, "Larger Than Oneself" climaxes in a transcendent illumination, accessible to a select few among the characters and comprehensible to even fewer.

Aickman was an erudite and conscientious student of the weird tale, although his work is quite free of the genre box-ticking and name-dropping that now beset us. Between 1964 and 1972 he edited the first eight volumes in the paperback anthology series *The Fontana Book of Great Ghost Stories*, selecting seventy-six tales by seventy-six different authors without ever relaxing his exacting standards of quality, and providing incisive and provocative introductions. He is capable of using the hoariest genre tropes, from vampires to country-house hauntings to "midnight callers" on the telephone; but always in a style uniquely his own. "Mark Ingestre: The Customer's Tale", one of Aickman's last stories, employs the penny-dreadful myth of Sweeney Todd to flash a brief, sharp light on the murky sub-cellars of the brashly commercial English consciousness. "A Roman Question", perhaps the nearest thing to a conventional ghost story in this book, is full of characteristic touches: the precise and poetic depiction of "uniform houses in dark red brick: quite large, solidly built, sparsely adorned, blackened by Birmingham"; the séance carried out with the perfectly logical aid of sugar lumps; the apparently extraneous oddity (in this case, the dead body of a horse), which later takes on a new and chilling significance.

Besides his work for the Inland Waterways Association, Aickman chaired the London Opera Society and Balmain Productions, which administered a ballet company; he also worked as a theatre critic for a monthly journal, *The Nineteenth Century and After*. His fiction contains many cultural allusions, drawn not only from English and other literatures but from painting, theatre, music and architecture. Ironically enough considering Aickman's likely opinion of the internet, such references are easier to decode today than ever before. If you don't know your Plutarch, or have never heard of Hero and Leander, or haven't a clue why people would joke about Griselda de Reptonville being patient, it is the work of a few minutes to find out. Aickman would almost certainly not approve – there are, he would affirm, several worlds of difference between worthwhile knowledge and Wikipedia – but it does make the textual richness of his work more accessible for those who are interested.

Aickman claimed that "The Visiting Star" is "closely based on fact, whatever else may be surmised". In the same essay, he wrote that a good ghost story, by transcending mechanical modernity, "can bring real joy. The reader may actually depart from it singing." Having enticed the narrator under the earth and lost their only light, the title character in "The Visiting Star" reveals the secret of her Faustian existence and ghostly allure "because I wanted you to stop being frightened". Her creator conceived the weird tale to be an art form related to poetry; and his own best fictions are less stories of supernatural events than stories which induce a sense of the supernatural, whether threatening, transcendental or both. Anyone can write about a ghost, but with Aickman's work it is the tales themselves that haunt. Like all the best ghosts (and some of the best comedy), they violate the normal rules while obeying laws of their own: elusive and rigorous and infinitely strange.

Philip Challinor
April 2016

THE LATE BREAKFASTERS

I dedicate this book to
HERBERT VAN THAL
Magician

PART ONE

CHAPTER I

Griselda de Reptonville did not know what love was until she joined one of Mrs. Hatch's famous house parties at Beams, and there met Leander. Her brief and blighted association with Leander led rapidly, as a reaction, to her marrying the unsatisfactory Geoffrey Kynaston. After Kynaston's death, she took up with an unpopular baronet, and lived with him very happily. There may have been one or two earlier episodes, none of them important. She is now twenty-five and has never wholly forgotten Leander; their ecstatic community of thought and feeling is something she fears she has lost for ever. She knew its worth at the time; she never for a single moment doubted it: but society was inevitably too strong for her, and ate her improper passion at a gulp. Leander doubtless never expected anything else, and therefore possibly suffered less, but of this there is little record.

A woman of less spirit would have blushed at being named de Reptonville; wearied of being called patient, and of the remarkably general assumption that by reason of her name she would always be so. De Reptonville, when Mr. Repton assumed the name (early in the nineteenth century), was quizzed as the apogee of unwarranted pretentiousness; now it is written off as a meaningless relic of conquest feudalism. Griselda, however, merely smiled sometimes when she looked at her visiting card, newly printed in flawless italics by Parkin and Gotto. The repetitive jokes about her patience only led her to think that in the absurdity of human nature lies much of its charm.

Beams was not an enormous house but it was approached from the insanely noisy main road through Hodley village by a drive two miles long. There had been a car to meet her and the other guests at Hodley railway station; but the season had called to Griselda, and the other guests alarmed her. She had sent on her suitcase, and was now following on foot. As the weather looked settled for an hour or so, her jacket and handbag had gone on with the luggage: she was now wonderfully unencumbered. She wore a white silk blouse, a short skirt of black linen, and substantial shoes. She walked fast, swinging her arms and singing "Now that I have springtime." This song came from "The Three Sisters" by Hammerstein and Kern, which she had seen at Drury Lane the previous evening with a girl whom she had known since childhood. The drive was lined with poplars, slightly discoloured with dust from the new works of the North Downs Cement Company, which now gave good employment to the village.

Beams had a glorious situation (once or twice a year it was possible to see the English Channel from the top of the tower); but as architecture it was unremarkable. Run up by the Duke of St. Helens, owner at that time of Hodley Park (since demolished), to provide accommodation for a great Belgian actress named Stephanie des Bourges, whom he had loved frenziedly until her premature death, it was soon acquired by Mrs. Hatch's grandfather, a rising merchant banker, called Eleutherios Procopius. His son John Procopius represented the Division in Parliament for the remarkable period of sixty-one years. At his death he left Beams to his only child Melanie, together with more than three million pounds, which would at that time have enabled either of them to live in something larger. The Procopiuses had never, it seemed, been lucky in love: of Mrs. Eleutherios there is no record at all; Mrs. John died in childbirth the year after her marriage to a man aged nearly sixty; Melanie married during the Boer War a certain Captain Hatch of the C.I.V.s, who almost immediately proceeded to drift away from her and in one way and another to resist recapture during a period of time not expired at the date now under construction. Beams, none the less, had eighteen reasonable bedrooms and was a wonderfully comfortable place to visit. It was, however, haunted: quite seriously, even, on occasion, dangerously, by the apparition of Mademoiselle des Bourges, beautiful even in death.

After glancing at the view, which only burst upon the visitor as he or she reached the lovely gravel waste before the house,

Griselda pulled the elaborate bell handle. Though apparently designed to operate an old-fashioned bell wire, the handle proved, in fact, to have been connected with a modern electric system. Before the servant could reach the door, it opened and an elderly gentleman passed out of the house into the garden. He was wearing rather shabby tweeds, leggings, and a black homburg hat. On seeing Griselda he jumped considerably, and nervously raised his black hat; then, without a word, linked hands behind his back and shambled off towards the rose garden. Griselda noticed that he was still shaking perceptibly with the shock of their encounter. By now a middle-aged footman had arrived. Griselda had never before seen a servant in appropriate livery except in musical comedy.

"Good afternoon, miss."

"Good afternoon. I'm Miss de Reptonville. Mrs. Hatch is expecting me."

"I'm sorry to have kept you waiting, miss. It's the new bells. The Prime Minister got to the door first, I'm afraid."

"Was that Mr. Leech?" Griselda had thought there was something familiar about the quivering figure.

"Regular visitor, miss. In office or out. Mrs. Hatch makes no distinction. Would you care for me to show you to your room?"

"Thank you." The front door closed behind her. "I sent on my luggage in the car. Also my handbag and jacket." After the spring sunshine, the house seemed cold.

"They have been taken to your room, miss. This way please."

The large hall, though filled with comfortable armchairs and sofas (a little like a furniture shop window, Griselda thought), was completely empty. She followed the footman up the wide staircase. A royal blue carpet completely covered the shallow risers. The mahogany balusters were expensively hand-carved. After the soft spring tumult outside, the house seemed silent.

"We've only just ceased the central heat," remarked the footman over his shoulder as he trudged before Griselda down one of the passages which radiated from the gallery encircling the hall.

Griselda noticed the gilded pipes at frequent intervals.

"You've got the Newman Room, miss." He opened the door.

"Why is it called that?"

"Cardinal Newman used to sleep here when he came to stay."

"Was that often?"

"Often, they say. To write his books and that. Mr. Cork's got many tales of him. He's our Head Gardener. You must get him to tell you."

"I'll remember. Thank you."

"Thank *you*, miss." He withdrew.

The Newman Room was large, square, well-lighted by windows in two walls, well-heated by a coal fire in a modern grate of patented design. Neither beautiful nor particularly ugly, it had recently been entirely refurnished by a contractor. It had no atmosphere whatever; of its eminent former occupant, or of anybody or anything else.

Griselda began to unpack. The drawers slid on stainless steel runners; the innumerable hangers in the wardrobe rattled together like the bones of a dancing skeleton. In the corner of the room was a cabinet, which proved to contain a shower, with a bath adjoining. Griselda turned the tap: the water cascaded downwards with terrifying force, far exceeding the capacity of the wastepipe in the floor. It was difficult to imagine anyone standing beneath that cataract and emerging undrowned. The water began to flow out of the cabinet and soak the bedroom carpet in a rapidly expanding black blot. Griselda rotated the tap (it seemed to be geared very low, she thought); but all that happened was that the downpour suddenly became scalding hot. A great cloud of steam filled the bedroom, like a geyser suddenly blowing off.

"Don't mind my interrupting your bath," said a firm voice behind Griselda's back.

Griselda rapidly rotated the tap in the opposite direction. It was difficult to see who had entered the room.

"I'm Melanie Hatch. Just thought I'd say How d'you do?" With a spasmodic crash of plumbing, the water stopped. It was as if it had been intercepted in the pipe.

"How d'you do? I've heard so much about you from Mother."

"How is she?"

"Still suffering rather a lot, I'm afraid."

"Bad business about your father."

"Yes."

Mrs. Hatch was a woman of middle height, considerably more than broad in proportion, but very healthy and active. Her chestnut hair was excellently dyed; but it had never been very beautiful hair. She was the kind of woman whose appearance, for better or for worse, changes surprisingly little with the years. Her expression indicated that a deficiency in imaginative understanding of the problems with which she had been faced, was so far as possible made good by conscious will to face them. She wore an extremely well-cut and expensive tweed coat and skirt; finely made woollen stockings; and a grey sweater with a polo collar enclosing her large neck.

"Do go on with your bath."

"I wasn't really having a bath. It was just curiosity."

"Well, have one now."

"I don't think I want one. I might have one tonight." Griselda, as in the matter of her name, never lacked for spirit to resist attempts to order her doings.

"I shan't be here then to talk to you."

"I can't talk and scrub at the same time," said Griselda smiling. "I'm a perfect simpleton by your standards."

Mrs. Hatch looked at her. "Do you mind if I sit down?"

"Please do." Mrs. Hatch seated herself in a large Parker-Knoll armchair at the foot of the bed, and watched Griselda putting away her stockings and underclothes in the ample drawers all lined with paper which smelt of a specially perfumed disinfectant.

"You know your Mother fagged for me at Wollstonecroft?"

"She has always told me how fond she was of you. I hope you'll go and see her one day."

"Poor old Millie," said Mrs. Hatch crossing her legs. "I easily might. In the meantime I expect to prefer your company."

"Thank you," said Griselda, hanging up her mackintosh. "It is very kind of you to ask me."

"Not really. I can always do with young girls about the house. The great men who visit me expect it. It helps them to relax. I'm very calculating."

"I see. I'll try and do what is expected of me. It's nice of you to ask me."

"I've got Austin Barnes here this weekend. In fact he should have come on your train. You must have met him in the car."

"I walked from the station. I couldn't resist the weather."

"So you like walking?"

"I love it. Particularly by myself."

"You must come for a walk with Austin and me. We're both good for twenty or thirty miles still. Austin's an old flame of mine, you know."

"I only know about his public life. And not very much about that. I didn't know that Cabinet Ministers had any other kind of life nowadays."

"As far as I'm concerned, Austin hasn't. Though he's still game enough, I believe, when circumstances are more propitious. But let me see your dress. The one you've brought for tomorrow night."

"I haven't brought any particular dress for tomorrow night. Should I have done?"

"Didn't your mother tell you?"

"I don't think so."

"My dear. Millie must have told you about the All Party Dance tomorrow. It's the main reason I asked you—asked you now, I mean."

Griselda had not been told and the reason was clear. Griselda so detested dancing that, had she been told, she would have declined Mrs. Hatch's invitation altogether, thus possible alienating a friend from whom Mrs. de Reptonville hoped for much.

"I'm terribly sorry. I don't dance."

"Why not? Are you crippled?"

Griselda felt disinclined to explain.

"Shall I go home?"

Mrs. Hatch considered the proposal for a moment. Clearly she was much disturbed. "No, no . . . No, of course not." Then, taking control of the situation, she returned to her previous demand: "Let me see your dress." She added: "I do think Millie might have warned me."

With some reluctance Griselda took from the mechanized wardrobe one of the two evening dresses she had brought. "I must clearly tell you: I won't dance." The dress was made of coffee coloured taffeta and very simple. She held it up.

Mrs. Hatch seemed surprised. "It's far too old for you, of course, but delightful. Where did you get it, if I may ask a plain question?"

"Nothing very distinguished. A friend of mine works in a dress shop. I think she has very good taste."

"Improbably enough, she has. My friend Louise will help you put it on."

"Thank you very much, but I don't need help."

"You don't know how much Louise will do for you. I'll send her along. Now then." Unexpectedly Mrs. Hatch smiled.

"Yes?" said Griselda, unexpectedly smiling back.

"Before tomorrow night you must learn to dance. Oh yes you must. I positively owe it to Millie. In the meantime I'm glad to have met you, Griselda, and tea will be ready when you are. In the Hall then."

And suddenly she had left the room, leaving Griselda rehanging her dress.

CHAPTER II

The party in the Hall had grouped themselves round an electrical space-heater, which raised the temperature of the atmosphere without anybody becoming aware of the fact. Mrs. Hatch was manipulating a vast and heavy teapot, apparently without effort. As Griselda descended the stairs, two men rose to their feet.

"This is Griselda de Reptonville," said Mrs. Hatch, recharging the teapot from a silver kettle which must have held at least a gallon. "Her mother used to be my greatest friend at school. Griselda, let me introduce you: Pamela Anslack, you two should be great friends; George Goss; Edwin Polegate-Hampden, he runs the St. James's News-Letter, which tells us what is really happening in the world; and Doris Ditton, who lives in Hodley. Now let me give you a crumpet. There's room for you on the sofa next to Pamela. You two must make friends."

Griselda was rather regretting she had not put on her cardigan, but Pamela was wearing a slight (though obviously exorbitant) afternoon model and seemed perfectly warm enough. A wide diamond bracelet encircled her left wrist; a diamond watch, her right. She was indeed about Griselda's age, but her perfectly made-up face was singularly expressionless, her dark hair like a photograph in "Vogue."

She said nothing at all: not even How do you do?; and Griselda biting into her crumpet, stared with furtive curiosity at George Goss. The famous painter looked much older than he did in the newspapers; but his hair and beard, though now more grey than black, were impressively unkempt, his face exceedingly rubicund, and his general bulk prodigious (though augmented by his unyielding green tweeds). He drank, not tea, Griselda noticed, but something in a glass; probably brandy and soda, she thought, as it sparkled energetically. He drank it noisily; and even more noisily devoured huge sections from a lump of rich cake which lay on the plate before him; while he stared back at Griselda, delighting massively in the thrill his presence gave her. He was like a very famous hippopotamus.

Edwin Polegate-Hampden was discoursing upon the inside politics of Morocco. He had paused to greet Griselda with significant courtesy, even, it seemed, cordiality. About thirty-five, and beautifully preserved for his age, he was dressed equally beautifully in a black jacket, cut rather fancifully after a bygone sporting original, yellow trousers, a mauve shirt, a silk tie with large spots, and a beautiful rose from Mr. Cork's smallest and private conservatory. His hair was treated with a preservative pomade from a shop in New York.

He resumed.

"But all I have been saying is of secondary importance. Quite secondary. What really matters is that the Atlas Mountains are entirely made of tin. You appreciate what that means in the modern world?"

George Goss nodded heavily, as painters do when interesting themselves in politics or sociology. Griselda looked bright and interested. Mrs. Hatch looked from Pamela to Griselda, and back to Pamela. Doris Ditton continued looking into her empty teacup. Possibly she was reading her life's pattern in the leaves.

"The Sultan himself told me the inside story of the concessionaires. I won't tell you the full details, but it comes down to a fight between Meyer Preyserling of Wall Street and a London firm of bankers whose name I can't pass on. I've known Meyer for years, of course, and when I heard that he was interested, I at once flew over and had a talk with him. As a matter of fact, I stayed with him a week. To cut a long story short, he told me that Washington is behind him—secretly, of course, but up to the hilt; so that he has all the gold in Fort Knox to play with. Naturally the London people can't compete with that. So you can take it that all the tin will go to America, as they can exchange it for gold. And that will mean new labour troubles in Bolivia, possibly even a revolution."

George Goss nodded again. Mrs. Hatch was lighting a cigarette. Pamela, Griselda noticed, was one of those girls whose mouth is seldom entirely closed.

"So if you have any Bolivian investments, you'd better think carefully what to do. Of course, it may all blow over. The output from the Bolivian tin mines largely goes to Germany anyway, and I think the market may hold up for some time yet. But we must find out what the French are going to do about it all."

"Why the French?" asked George Goss. His voice reminded Griselda of a porpoise.

"Morocco."

"Oh yes," said George Goss like an undergraduate convicted of inattention. Noticing that his glass was empty, Mrs. Hatch passed him a bottle, and added soda from a syphon behind him.

"I've an engagement to talk matters over with Derrière in Paris next week." Edwin's French accent was incredibly good. "Derrière is the one man who really counts in France at the moment, and, after all, the Moroccan business may easily end in a world war." He subsided affably.

"Have some of our fruit cake, Griselda?" said Mrs. Hatch. "It's one of our traditions. No other cake for tea but our very special fruit cake."

"Thank you very much."

"Have some more tea, Pamela?"

Pamela merely shook her head.

"You're not sulking are you?"

Pamela shook her head again.

"What about you, Doris?"

"Thanks, Mrs. Hatch." Pamela looked at Doris scornfully; Griselda with some curiosity. Edwin handed her cup with precise courtesy.

"You've had five cups already."

"I'm afraid I'd lost count, Mrs. Hatch." Doris was a pale little creature, with intermediate hair and wearing a cotton frock, obviously her best but somewhat crumpled.

"I just thought I'd tell you." Mrs. Hatch had refilled the cup and Edwin returned it to Doris with pale hands.

"The arranging must have made me thirsty."

"Doris has been helping with the preparations for tomorrow night," explained Mrs. Hatch to Griselda. "The balloons haven't been used for some time and a lot of dust had been allowed to collect. And that," she continued firmly, "reminds me."

"Must I?" asked Griselda, rather charmingly, as she thought.

"Would you believe it, Edwin? Griselda thought we could do without her at the dance."

Pamela's mouth opened another half-inch.

Edwin replied: "I do hope not."

"I can't dance," cried Griselda a little desperately.

Pamela's large eyes opened to their utmost.

"Please permit me to teach you," said Edwin. "It would be delightful."

"Thank you. But, as I've explained to Mrs. Hatch, I don't really like dancing."

"Let me teach you," suddenly roared George Goss. "You'd like it well enough then."

"Neither of you will teach Griselda," said Mrs. Hatch. "It's much too important a thing to be left to amateurs. You'd be certain to start her on entirely the wrong lines. She's a job for Kynaston."

"Who's Kynaston?" asked Griselda fearfully.

"He's a somewhat neurotic young man who none the less dances like a faun. He makes a living teaching dancing in Hodley."

"Only until he establishes himself as a poet," unexpectedly interjected Doris.

"Doris is in love with Mr. Kynaston," explained Mrs. Hatch. "But it's quite true that he writes poetry as well. Very good poetry too. If you spend the whole day with him tomorrow you should pass muster as a dancer by the evening."

The project appalled Griselda, but to continue in her refusal seemed somehow gauche, and not only in the eyes of her hostess.

"Doris will speak to Mr. Kynaston tonight and you can go down in the car at ten o'clock tomorrow morning."

"And I very much hope," added Edwin as epilogue, "that when the time comes you will give your first dance to me."

Griselda smiled at him rather uncertainly.

"I wish Leech would come in. The tea's cold."

"Let me go and look for him, Mrs. Hatch." Edwin had sprung to his feet and was making for the door.

Pamela was staring at Griselda's uncoloured finger nails.

"And where's Austin and the Ellensteins?"

Griselda supposed these to be the terrifying figures whose company she had evaded in the car from the station.

"Send Monk upstairs," said George Goss. "Don't look at me."

"Doris," said Mrs. Hatch, "would you mind ringing for Monk?"

Doris rose and rang. The footman appeared who had shown Griselda to her room. Mrs. Hatch despatched him to enquire after the missing guests. Soon he was back.

"Mr. Barnes asks you to excuse him, ma'am. He is lying down in his room. Their Highnesses are coming directly."

"Thank you. We'd better have some more hot water. I don't imagine their Highnesses will require crumpets, or Mr. Leech either. Though you never know."

"No ma'am." Monk departed with the vast kettle.

A fat elderly man was descending the stairs, followed by an equally fat woman of similar age. Both were immaculate; she in a dress younger than her years, in which, oddly enough, she looked much more attractive than she would have done in a more appropriate garment.

"This is Griselda de Reptonville," said Mrs. Hatch. "The Duke and Duchess of Ellenstein."

The Duke clicked his heels and kissed Griselda's hand; the Duchess, even more to her surprise, kissed her lips.

"You two are late," said George Goss. "Tea's over."

"For some time now it is during the afternoon that I make Odile mine," explained the Duke, in a high gentle voice with only the slightest of accents, and that adding greatly to his charm. "We both of us find it best at nights to sleep."

"I'll look in tonight and see if Odile will change her mind."

"We make love while the sun shines, George," said the Duchess.

"Only during the wretched war have we missed a single day," said the Duke, putting a piece of cake on his wife's plate, and then taking a larger piece himself.

Monk returned with the recharged kettle, sustaining with difficulty his dignity and its weight.

"Bring Miss Ditton's bicycle round to the front door, will you, Monk?" said Mrs. Hatch. "Now Doris, don't forget. Mr. Kynaston is to set aside the whole of tomorrow for Miss de Reptonville's tuition."

"Tuition?" said the Duchess. "In what, my dear?"

"Griselda is learning to dance, Odile."

"But that is impossible in England. I learned for years when I was a girl and not till I met Gottfried was I anything but a cart-horse. Believe me, my dear, I was mad to dance, just like you, but you cannot dance until you love."

Monk's liveried figure passed the window pushing Doris's rattling bicycle. She slipped away.

"It would be a weight off all our minds if Doris married Geoffrey Kynaston," observed Mrs. Hatch.

Pamela took the opportunity to retire upstairs. The Ellensteins, George Goss, and Mrs. Hatch were engaged in animated conversation about experiences they had shared in the past. Their memories seemed excellent; their relish for detail almost unlimited. No reason was apparent why they should not continue for days or weeks; and then start again at the beginning like a film programme. Necessarily, little attempt could be made to include Griselda. Though she did not much care for George Goss, she noticed even that he had ceased to look at her and was gazing instead at the Duchess's fat but still not ill-proportioned legs. (He resembled, she thought, an inquisitive elephant.)

After about an hour and a half of it, Edwin returned and said that he had been having a really valuable talk with the Prime Minister upon the Indo-Chinese problem; and that Mr. Leech had made his tea of a biscuit or two he had brought from his pocket. "I'm so sorry, Mrs. Hatch," concluded Edwin. "I just couldn't persuade him to leave his beloved roses."

There were a number of cold dead crumpets on the occasional table in their midst, and some dregs of tea in the cups; but, Griselda noticed, the Ellensteins and George Goss had eaten the entire famous fruit cake among them.

"Thank you, Edwin," said Mrs. Hatch. "I quite understand. You'd better go back and pump the old man until dinner time. We're perfectly happy without you."

"I'm sure you're divinely happy every single hour of the day, Mrs. Hatch," replied Edwin. "But I must admit I should be glad to have the true story of the railway strike. I have a great responsibility to my readers. They do trust me so completely."

He was gone.

"Is there a railway strike?" asked Griselda. "I didn't notice it."

But the Duchess was recalling the night the four of them (and several others) started a bonfire in Leicester Square.

"Do you remember?" said the Duchess. "It was Austin Barnes's idea."

CHAPTER III

Dinner was not until 8.30; but Pamela gave the impression of having spent the entire interminable interim changing for it. Griselda, plainly debarred for tonight from the coffee-coloured taffeta, had put on her other dress, of pinkish organdie and very nice too; only for Pamela to make it immediately though silently obvious to her that the proper style for the occasion was that followed by herself, a blouse and long skirt. Mrs. Hatch, when she appeared was similarly dressed; as, to Griselda's complete dejection, was the Duchess, who came down last, skilfully made-up, with the Duke in a beautifully fitting dinner jacket. Edwin's dinner jacket was of very dark red velvet; and his rose had been

changed by Mr. Cork for an even larger one in a more suitable
colour. Mr. Leech looked rather nondescript by comparison.

"Where is Mr. Barnes?" asked Mrs. Hatch when they were
seated.

"Mr. Barnes asks me to present his compliments," replied
Monk, "and to say that he is so fatigued that he has thought it best
to retire completely to bed. I am to bring him a boiled egg later."

"There is nothing the matter with Mr. Barnes, I hope?" asked
the Duke anxiously.

"I understand nothing, your Highness. Mr. Barnes did mention to me that his present condition was nothing out of the
ordinary. Shall I request Mr. Brundrit, ma'am, to serve Dinner?"

"Please do," said Mrs. Hatch; and under the superintendence
of a tall, wasted-looking butler, Monk and a pretty parlourmaid
called Stainer served the most portentous meal Griselda had ever
attended. There was paté; there were truffles; there was a sorbet.
There was a blanc-mange-like pudding with angelica and an
undertone of rum insufficient to offset the otherwise total lack
of flavour; which in turn was followed by a savoury (called Tails
in the Air), and a choice of stilton cheese or dessert, or both for
those (like the Duke and Duchess and George Goss) who wished.
There had been no alcoholic preliminary, but, accompanying
the food, four successive wines and a liqueur with the wonderful
strong coffee. Mr. Leech ate very little, but at the end brightened
up enough to express a preference for brandy if any was available,
and Mrs. Hatch joined him. Pamela found tongue enough to indicate her various gustatory preferences; though even then appearing to force out words like stones from her mouth, and as if each
single word was a disgusting thing to be shunned when uttered.
Griselda did the best she could, seated between the Duke, who
occasionally said something paternal to her, and Mr. Leech, who
showed little sign of the taste for young girls which Mrs. Hatch
had plainly implied to be his; but by the end she felt a little sick.

During dinner there were more reminiscences. Griselda
noticed that the endless stories tended to begin admirably and to
hold out real promise; but after a time it always became apparent
that there was to be no climax, point, or even real conclusion. The
stories were simply long rakes, designed to turn over as many

memories as possible. There was little nostalgia, however, about the reminiscing quartet, Griselda observed with pleasure; they all in their different ways seemed as full of gusto as ever, especially the Duchess, in whom gaiety seemed positively a normal mood.

Replete, they migrated to the Drawing Room; an apartment of which the faultless and spotless comfort fell just short of elegance. There were a rosewood grand piano of German make; a white mantel some way after the Adam Brothers; and a number of French eighteenth century pictures, well and harmoniously selected. The general colouration was pink; which, as it happened, excellently set off Griselda's dress. There was a real Aubusson carpet, like the cloths of heaven to walk upon. All that fell short was individuality, and perhaps vitality, however controlled.

Edwin at once suggested bridge. Mrs. Hatch agreed with appetite; and the Ellensteins also volunteered. Mr. Leech asked if anyone would mind his sitting quietly in a corner with an excellent book he had found in the library. He then half sank into an elaborate illustrated manual of horticulture, sitting semi-submerged for hours, every now and then turning the volume round and round on his knees the better to penetrate the botanical detail. Griselda noticed, however, that much of the time his mind seemed to be wandering and his expression strangely blank. He turned the pages much too infrequently and irregularly. Occasionally he could be heard sighing, almost groaning. It was remarkable how little any part of him moved: even the occasional blink of his eyelids seemed consciously decided upon and consciously executed.

The Duchess being occupied, George Goss seated himself on a sofa upholstered in couleur de rose flowered silk, beside Pamela. Pamela immediately moved to an armchair next to Griselda; whereupon George Goss making the best even of adversity, placed his feet on the sofa where Pamela had been seated, and lay bundled together like a giant chimpanzee in a dinner jacket. He continued smiling blandly before him, and soon, without asking Mrs. Hatch's permission, fired and began to draw on a huge inefficient pipe which had recently been presented to him by an admiring young woman. Later, again without enquiry of his hostess, he managed to reach a bell with his long arm, thick as the branch of a tree; and, when Monk answered, ordered a bottle of brandy to be brought to him with a syphon. Having appeased his thirst, he fell asleep and began to snore. Bridge had gripped the players into its own distinctive delirium; so that none of them noticed George Goss, still less Griselda and Pamela.

To Griselda's surprise, Pamela, upon escaping from George Goss, spoke to her.

"Are my eyes all right?"

Griselda looked at them with conscientious care. As well as being large, they were yellowy-green and ichthyological.

"I think so. They're lovely."

Irritated with the familiar compliment, Pamela replied: "The mascara, I mean. It's new stuff. Daddy brought it back from B.A."

Griselda looked again. "It looks all right to me." A question seemed expected. "What was your Father doing in South America?"

"You know that Daddy's Chairman of Argentine Utilities. We practically own the country. You don't use mascara much, do you?"

"Not much," said Griselda.

"I can tell by the look of the lashes. You're probably very wise." The tone of the last observation suggested that the speaker thought the opposite. "Mascara's frightfully bad for the eyes."

"Like staring too long at me," said George Goss.

"Shall we look at this together?" said Pamela to Griselda, ignoring George Goss, who continued smiling all over his face.

It was the latest issue of "The Sketch." Griselda was not particularly interested, but something had to be done to pass the time, and Mrs. Hatch had told her to make friends with Pamela. Moreover, Pamela was used to getting her way.

"Where do you live, by the way?" asked Pamela.

"About twenty miles outside London."

"I thought I was the only one to do that. But perhaps *you* don't mind?"

"I haven't much choice really."

"Daddy thinks the country air's good for me and Mummy. It's hell having to motor out after parties and having no friends."

"It's surely easier to make friends in the country than in London?"

"It depends what you mean by friends."

Pamela began to explain the scandalous circumstances and backgrounds of the various people whose photographs appeared in "The Sketch." The explanations were rendered lengthy by Pamela's lack of vocabulary; and complex by her lack of all standards of references beyond her own changing impulses. Griselda noticed however, that Pamela was as much interested in the financial as in the sexual history of her friends, and as well informed upon it; also that she appeared as strongly to disapprove of homosexuality as if she had been an elderly pillar of some Watch Committee.

When they had finished "The Sketch," Pamela produced "The Tatler" from the same heap; and before she had finished explaining "The Tatler" (her opinions of various current plays and films being now involved, and of certain recent Rugby football matches at Twickenham), George Goss had ordered his bottle and fallen into a slumber, and the bridge players had entered upon their inevitable row. It seemed to be mainly Mrs. Hatch setting upon the Duchess (her partner). The Duke (though, of course, on the other side) loyally backed his wife (to whom, indeed, he seemed utterly devoted in every way), wheezing with exasperation and becoming much more Teutonic in delivery. Edwin was trying very hard indeed to smooth things over, so that the game could be resumed. When one expedient or line of argument was obviously unavailing, he never failed to produce another, surprisingly different. Griselda had noticed for some time that the partnership of which Edwin was one, seemed usually to win. The combatants stabbed their fingers at selected cards among the litter on the green topped walnut table.

Absorbed in an account of how well she knew Gladys Cooper, Pamela ignored the row as long as possible. When it became necessary almost to shout above the raised voices, she switched to details of the similar scenes which commonly attended the frequent bridge parties organised by her parents. "I can't be bothered with the game myself," said Pamela, "though I've quite broken Daddy's heart by not playing with him." An achievement of some sort seemed implicit in her words; a triumph of right-eousness in some inner conflict. George Goss's mouth had fallen wide open, but he was snoring less loudly in consequence.

Griselda looked at her wrist-watch.

Suddenly with a high-pitched squeal, the Duke had over-turned the card-table, the top of which struck Mrs. Hatch sharply on the ankle. "We are misbehaving ourselves," cried the Duke, "let us kiss and once more be friends. I appeal to your warm heart, Melanie."

"I really think that would be better." It was Mr. Leech who spoke. "Of course I take no sides in the matter under dispute. But I do warmly endorse the Duke's appeal." His finger remained fixed to a point in a large diagram of corolla structure.

Mrs. Hatch had lifted her long skirt above her knees, and was rubbing her ankle while the blood rushed to her head. "I think you've broken a bone, Gottfried," was all she said. She certainly seemed more chastened than aggressive.

Griselda hurried forward. "Perhaps I can help. I've had a little first-aid training."

The Duchess, absolved from offering succour beyond her competence, smiled gratefully at Griselda, and began carefully to attend to her heavy make-up. Edwin rushed to bring a cushion to support Mrs. Hatch's back.

Griselda began to take charge. "May I remove your stock-ing?"

"Please do."

Griselda undid the suspenders and rolled off the stocking.

"Nothing's broken. But it's an exceedingly nasty bruise." The swollen place was already turning the colour of cuttlefish ink.

"If that's all, I'll say no more about it," said Mrs. Hatch.

"Melanie, you are magnanimous," exclaimed the Duke. "I knew you had a great heart."

"You'd better put your leg up, and not take much exercise for a day or two." Griselda placed the injured foot on the chair vacated by Edwin, who immediately ran to fetch another cushion, to place beneath the foot.

"My dear Griselda, what about the dance? What about the preparations for the dance?"

Griselda felt most strongly tempted to reply that the dance might have to be cancelled, when George Goss, whom she had not seen wake up, cried out:

"Melanie won't miss the dance. Melanie won't miss a dance when she's in her grave."

In some ways it seems uncharacteristic that Mrs. Hatch should be so fond of dancing; but all the evidence seemed to suggest that such was the case.

"I'll be there, George," said Mrs. Hatch. "Gottfried has failed to break my leg."

"The idea!" said the Duke tearfully. "It was only a gesture for peace between us. My very dear friend." He placed a plump hand on the shoulder of Mrs. Hatch's evening blouse.

Pamela was reading about Longchamps in "The Bystander."

George Goss lumbered round to look at the bruise. "It's like the night Austin Barnes gave Margot two black eyes." They laughed. George Goss subsided on a Pompeian red pouffe and sat leering at Mrs. Hatch's expensive underclothes still visible inside her lifted skirt.

"Have you any liniment?" enquired Griselda.

"You shall apply it in my bedroom," said Mrs. Hatch, rising to her feet and letting her skirt drop. She staggered and Edwin supported her. "You and Pamela shall help me to undress. The rest of you can stay here if you want to. Monk has gone to bed, but you're at liberty to forage if you wish, so long as you conceal the traces from Brundrit and Cook, and don't leave messes about for the mice. Come along, Pamela, you can't read all night." Reluctantly Pamela let "The Bystander" fall upon the floor. George Goss remained seated, but the others grouped themselves solicitously. "Good night," said Mrs. Hatch.

The Duke clicked his heels. Edwin said: "There must be something I can get for you." Mr. Leech said: "I am so relieved that things are not worse." The Duchess kissed Mrs. Hatch on the mouth; then said to Griselda and Pamela: "I suppose I shan't be seeing you two again tonight either," and kissed them also. At the moment of Mrs. Hatch's departure, George Goss floundered vaguely upwards; but his intentions had not been made clear before she had left the room with one arm round Griselda's neck, and the other round Pamela's. Edwin went before them and opened the door of Mrs. Hatch's bedroom.

"Good night, Edwin," said Mrs. Hatch, and he retired downstairs, having said Good-night to the girls in a tone which at once commended their charitable helpfulness and conveyed his own deep regard for them.

The bedroom was stuffed with clothes and lined with photographs, many of them signed ones of celebrities, with pleasant words of gratitude adjoined. A real fire burned in the grate, making the room close (the Dining Room and Drawing Room had been impalpably warmed by further space heaters). The single bed was white and simple. In the corner of the room was a large green safe.

Pamela's assistance proved fairly useless. Not only had she become silent once more, but she more than once knocked something over, and even tore Mrs. Hatch's slip while trying to extricate her from the garment. Not unreasonably, Pamela seemed to fear the effect of the heat upon her complexion, and carefully kept away from the large fire. Griselda could have wished for the presence of Louise, that expert in putting on clothes: but in the end, and despite Pamela, inserted Mrs. Hatch, masterful to the last, into her pyjamas, and was rubbing her leg as she lay sprawled on the bed. Pamela was now yawning ostentatiously.

Griselda rubbed diligently for what seemed at least ten minutes.

"That'll do," suddenly said Mrs. Hatch, and began to roll down her pyjama leg. But I may want you to do it again tomorrow."

"I shall be dancing," said Griselda, almost maliciously. The exertion and the rubbing against the bed had not improved her beautiful fragile dress.

"So you will. But I expect you'll be back for tea. People usually are. Tea at Beams is a daily event, you know. You can massage me, if necessary, between tea and dinner. I usually lie down before a dance anyway."

"I'm not really a masseuse, you know. It's quite easy to do the wrong thing, I believe."

"You won't do the wrong thing. Would you please give me my book? Over there on the banker."

In the corner of the room was a big cabinet, with long shallow drawers.

Griselda brought the book. It was entitled "Warlock on Comparative Agriculture." Mrs. Hatch was hanging from the other side of the bed and opening the door of the commode, apparently to confirm the presence of its contents. It was a distance to stretch and Mrs. Hatch, at the very end of her reach, had to shut the door with a slam.

"Thank you, my dear Griselda, for all your help."

Griselda smiled.

Mrs. Hatch opened the book at page 601. Griselda was about to say good-night and depart, when Mrs. Hatch looked up.

"Pamela is very pretty isn't she?"

Griselda started. It was an extraordinary thing but she had not noticed Pamela's departure.

"Where is Pamela?" Griselda felt she must be very tired to be so unobservant.

"She slipped out while you were kindly attending to my injury. Never mind. She's in the room next to yours. The Livingstone Room, we call it."

A big brass clock above the large fire struck two. Griselda was surprised it was not later.

CHAPTER IV

Trouble began almost as soon as Griselda was back in her bedroom.

The house, formerly so quiet, not unlike a specialist's waiting-room, now seemed full of noises. Nor was it only the noise of Pamela snoring like an ox and perfectly audible through the substantial wall, or that of some unknown making periodical clattering trips down a distant passage (could it be Austin Barnes? Griselda wondered). There were constant small disturbances which seemed in her own room, or at least only just outside the door: creaks and jars, of course; but also sudden sussurations, in among the window curtains, near the cabinet containing the shower, or under the bed. To Griselda, overtired as the incident in Mrs. Hatch's room had suggested she must be, it was almost as if some small animal were loose in the apartment. Rats and mice seemed extremely improbable in such a carefully ordered house. Griselda, used to living out of London, wondered whether some small creature could have entered during the day. She had removed her charming dress and was vaguely endeavouring to fluff up the organdie, flattened and pulled while she had worked on her hostess's leg: it was certainly true that the garment no longer looked new, as it had looked so far every time she had worn it. Laying down the dress, she began to investigate the room, half-heartedly examining corners and peering into the angles of the ceiling, not very well illuminated by the concealed lighting. Even a small bird was not out of the question, she thought. As the idea came to her, a screech owl cried very loudly outside her window. Griselda found that she was shivering, slightly clad as she was, and away from the excessive heat of Mrs. Hatch's bedroom. She drew her dressing-gown from the wardrobe and put it on. It had once been the colour of dying peonies, but Griselda had owned it since her last disastrous year at school.

Griselda hung up her dress, assumed her pyjamas, and faithfully removed her make-up. She cleaned her teeth, carefully and thoroughly as always, for she regarded her teeth as attractive. Then, still shivering excessively, she drew back the curtains, opened the window at top and bottom, and leaped from her familiar dressing-gown into her unfamiliar bed. Outside there was a misty moon, predicting, as usual, a change for the worse in the weather. Inside, the little noises had not abated, but Griselda resolved to ignore them.

The noises were difficult to define. Nor was it easy to know whether or not any particular one of them was a new noise. One of the worst, and surely a new one, however, was like that of voices muttering. It came and went like a radio set out of order and turned very low; with long pauses of silence. Another was like long nails destructively scratching at smooth hard paintwork. Once a silent bird struck the window very hard, so that Griselda felt surer than ever that another had flown in during the day and was now in the room with her, probably lying exhausted behind a piece of furniture. The sussurating noise was still audible from time to time: it rustled for seconds or minutes in one place, then was long silent before starting elsewhere.

Griselda slept intermittently until she reached a condition of uncertainty whether she slept or waked. She continued disagreeably cold until she was merely shivering without any distinctive consciousness of being cold at all. At one moment when she was nearer waking than sleeping, she heard the sound of tears, a high-pitched sobbing, somewhat petulant it seemed, but distant and subdued. It was possible, she thought, that Pamela wept in her sleep. Before long the noise, which from the time she first heard it had been growing less and less, died away.

Several times during the later part of the night Griselda woke from nightmare; but not a detail could she remember even in the first moments of consciousness. She might have been dreaming of things so horrible that the mechanism of repression was forced to clamp down once more on her consciousness in the very instant of waking. But the nightmare had each time seized and penetrated her whole body and mind; it was as if she had been twisted into another identity, mysterious and horrible, which, when she returned, there could be no question of remembering since the two beings had no capacity for memory in common. She shuddered to reflect that this second identity, totally unreachable, lay always behind her face and beneath her thoughts. The strain of having perpetually to maintain the ascendancy over it weighed upon her. Now that she no longer loved her Mother, perhaps it was getting possession of her mind and affecting her gait. In the end none the less, she returned to slumber.

The worst occurrence of the night was perfectly natural and commonplace. Griselda woke to hear a dog howling. It howled on an unusually shrill whining note. It continued howling for a very long time; for long after Griselda was fully and entirely awake. She lay with her back towards the window listening to the distressing sound and unavailingly searching her memory for a dog in the house. In the end, she was almost reduced to leaving her bed and investigating; but desisted when she saw that the dawn was near. This circumstance, she felt, might be related in some way to the unknown dog's behaviour; moreover, she had once more started to shiver and shunned the silent chill of the large room. She was uncertain whether the dog had ceased to give tongue before she once more fell asleep.

With the first symptoms of daylight, the tension in the room melted into appeasement. Griselda subsided into deep quiet sleep, the little noises ebbed, a measure of warmth returned.

Griselda slept steadily for the time which remained. At the last moment before waking, she seemed to have a dream of a different order. The earlier dreams she never remembered; this one she never forgot. She dreamed of a strange perfect love; a great good, unknown to the waking world; an impossibly beautiful happiness. The rapture of her dream was something new to her. It stayed with her while she rose to wash and dress; and longer.

CHAPTER V

A housemaid brought her tea and two rusks on a tray.

"Pity it's raining. It'll spoil tonight."

Filled with her dream, Griselda felt happily combative.

"I don't see why it should."

"All the lovely dresses'll get sopping wet. And lots won't come at all if it's raining."

"Perhaps it'll stop. Rain before seven. Fine before eleven."

The housemaid laughed. "Not round 'ere." Then, looking at Griselda accusingly, she said, "Will I run a bath for you?"

"No, thank you. I'll manage it myself if I want it."

"The shower's tricky."

"I'll risk it."

"Just as you say." She went.

Without resorting to the shower, for she hated getting her head wet, Griselda washed carefully all over. She felt that there was no knowing where the day's events might take her. To meet the changed weather, she put on her coat and skirt, and a woollen jumper.

Mrs. Hatch was already seated at the head of the breakfast table, dressed precisely as on the day before; but there was no sign of any of her other guests. Monk and Stainer were both in attendance. Before Mrs. Hatch was an enormous congregation of eggs, all so green that they looked as if disease had struck them.

"Good girl," said Mrs. Hatch. "Up in proper time and prepared for the weather, I see. You sit next to me. Pamela can sit the other side of me when she chooses to appear. Have some eggs? At Beams we have duck eggs every morning for breakfast. It's one of our traditions. Take as many as you like. And have some cocoa. We don't rot our guests with tannin or caffeine until later in the day."

"Thank you," said Griselda. "I'm hungry. May I take two?"

"For breakfast at Beams no one ever takes fewer than four. Except Mr. Leech, perhaps. I'm sure you don't want to follow after him. Take another two."

Monk raised a huge bowl-like cup containing about half-a-pint of cocoa and conveyed it to Griselda.

"I think I'll eat these two first, if I may."

"Afraid for your liver?" enquired Mrs. Hatch. "You needn't be, you know, if you make sure of enough exercise. That reminds me, I plan to take Austin for one of our walks tomorrow. It'll set him up and blow away all the fug from the dance as well. As you're a walker too, I'm sure you'd like to join us."

"Thank you," replied Griselda, battering her second egg. "If I'm not too tired after dancing."

Mrs. Hatch glanced at her, but at that moment one of the windows was raised from the outside, and Mr. Leech entered over the sill. He looked very tired and dingy.

"Good morning. I trust I'm not late. I've been trying out my old limbs on the trapeze in the garden."

"Fine exercise for men," said Mrs. Hatch. "Useless for women, unfortunately. Help yourself to eggs."

With a hand which trembled slightly, Mr. Leech took a single egg.

Monk, who had departed for the toast, now returned bearing also an armful of mail. He proceeded to sort it and to distribute it among the various places. Most of it seemed to be for Edwin: a vast heap of letters in flimsy envelopes with foreign stamps, and large official packets. The correspondence for the Ellensteins seemed mostly to bear penny and halfpenny stamps. George Goss received a single letter: in a very thick violet envelope, bigger and more massive than usual, and threaded down one side with a fragment of carmine ribbon. The handwriting of the superscription, Griselda could not but observe, was proportionate in size to the envelope. Mrs. Hatch received a few nondescript items, all of which she opened voraciously with the bread-knife before reading any. Griselda, to her surprise, received a letter from the girl she had known since childhood, and who liked to write to someone sojourning at so distinguished an address as Beams. She had nothing to say and Griselda felt faintly bored by the obligation to reply. Pamela received nothing. Probably, Griselda felt, Pamela never replied to letters, so that people gave up writing. More surprisingly, Mr. Leech seemed to receive nothing either.

"Mullet is taking Mr. Barnes's letters up to his room," remarked Monk.

Mrs. Hatch said nothing.

Soon Edwin appeared full of apologies and newspapers. At least six of the latter were under his arm in various stages of mutilation and decomposition.

"I do hope you will also forgive my taking the liberty of cutting up all your morning papers. I shall, of course, replace the copies later, but Miss Van Bush, my secretary, will be calling immediately after breakfast, and it is best if I can pass the really relevant items on to her right away." He flourished a little packet with a large red seal. "Clippings. The result of my labours before breakfast. Ah, how really wonderful to see a Beams breakfast again. There is nothing quite like it anywhere else." Edwin wore a brand-new light grey suit, a dark grey silk shirt, and Old Etonian tie, and an orchid. He began to wade through the expected clutch of eggs.

George Goss entered in his hairy green tweeds.

"Good morning, Melanie. Gottfried and Odile ask me to tell you they won't be down until later."

He put his letter to one side unopened, and began to smash away at a bevy of eggs. Immediately he had entered, Monk, Griselda noticed, had slipped away.

"George," said Mrs. Hatch. "Would you please put that billet-doux in your pocket or somewhere? No one cares for a good scent more than I do, but that isn't a good scent. It makes the whole room stink."

"The poor little thing hasn't the cash for the sort of stuff you'd go in for," remarked George. Inserting a thick finger, he rather clumsily ripped open the envelope.

Monk returned with a bottle of brandy, about two-thirds full, which he passed on to Mrs. Hatch. Taking a syphon from the sideboard, he placed it on the table next to George. This seemed the usual method, Griselda observed: Mrs. Hatch normally maintained control of the bottle.

"Why do you keep her so short?"

"My dear Melanie, now that I've got on in the world, so to speak, I don't have to *keep* anyone. There's always a long line eager to take care of me."

He began to read the letter, looking, Griselda thought, like a monstrous sheep which had been dyed green.

Edwin was working methodically through his heap, opening the letters neatly with an ivory and gold paper-knife which had been given him by the King of Roumania, and making three piles, one of matter to be handed over to Miss Van Bush, one of items to be answered in his own holograph, and one of empty envelopes.

A number of the packets containing whole newspapers, often with marked passages. Glancing at one of these, Edwin suddenly rose, and saying to Mrs. Hatch, "Excuse me. Something rather unexpected," bore it round the table to Mr. Leech, pointed out the significant passage, and said something quietly in Mr. Leech's left ear. The Prime Minister, who had apparently sunk into a light coma (he had not even finished his egg), stirred very slightly and began to read. After some time had passed with Mr. Leech staring unwinkingly at the paper, Edwin spoke again in his ear.

At last Mr. Leech slowly nodded twice. "I suppose there's no help for it," he said.

"I imagine that a couple of divisions would suffice, sir," said Edwin. His voice was still low, but this time fully audible. All of them could appreciate the urgency of the matter.

"I don't really know," said Mr. Leech, still without blinking.

"Better make it three, perhaps," said Edwin as before.

"I'll consult Mr. Barnes," said Mr. Leech almost in the tone of one nearing a decision. "Can't be swayed by the press, you know," he added roguishly.

Edwin returned to his place, looking as if a weight had been lifted off his mind. "Sorry Mrs. Hatch," he said. "So many things happen at the most inconvenient moment." He began to assault his fourth egg.

"Melanie," said George Goss. "Could I have a drink?" He was still less than half way through the prodigious letter. Mrs. Hatch passed him the bottle. He looked round for a tumbler, and, when Monk had brought him one, filled it liberally, passing back the bottle. He resumed reading the love letter, belching every now and then as food reached his empty stomach.

"Do have some more to eat, Griselda?" said Mrs. Hatch.

"No thank you very much."

"How is Barnes this morning, Mrs. Hatch?" enquired Mr. Leech.

Mrs. Hatch looked at Monk.

"Mr. Barnes asked for his breakfast to be taken to his room as you know, madam. Also his letters. Beyond that I know nothing, madam. Shall Stainer ask Mullet?"

The parlour-maid glowered. Mrs. Hatch turned to the Prime Minister.

"Would you like that to be done, Mr. Leech?"

"Please do not go to any trouble," replied Mr. Leech. "I'll find my way to his room and enquire myself later. I must consult him on some business; urgent, alas!"

George Goss looked up. "Never could see why Austin gave his time to politics at all. Should have thought he had too much red blood in his veins if you know what I mean."

Mr. Leech stared at him. "That is just why, Mr. Goss," he said with unusual fire. "I believe you once painted Barnes's portrait. You cannot have overlooked the main fact about your sitter: that he is a patriot."

George Goss chuckled gutturally. "Poor old Austin," he said.

"Austin Barnes is also a magnificent administrator," said Edwin reprovingly. "A first class man to put in charge of any Department in the Government; is he not, Mr. Prime Minister?"

"A leader," replied Mr. Leech. "Certainly a natural leader of men." He discarded the remains of his egg and began to look round for the marmalade.

Pamela arrived. She was wearing a simple white silk nightdress and a lilac satin wrapper. The large yawn with which she entered suggested, however, that this costume implied less of coquetry than of the possibility that she had only just awakened. Then Griselda noticed that Pamela was made up with her usual time-consuming elaboration. At her entrance George Goss had actually dropped the letter (he was still far from having completed reading it). Mrs. Hatch was also staring at Pamela, though less noticeably. "Don't want anything to eat. Just a cup of coffee."

Mrs. Hatch seemed alarmed. "Are you ill?"

"Slept too long. I'm always doing it."

George Goss guffawed.

"Sit in your place," said Mrs. Hatch, "and see what you can manage."

Pamela subsided into her seat and silence. Monk brought her the usual bowl of cocoa. Edwin began to converse with her on subjects suitable to one who has overslept.

There was a knock at the door which gave access to the kitchen, and the head was poked in of the housemaid who had awakened Griselda.

"What is it, Mullet?"

"Maghull waiting for 'is orders."

"Good gracious!" cried Mr. Leech. "It's no business of mine, I know, but I do think it rash of you still to retain in your employ a man who played such a catastrophic part in the Irish disorders. You will recall that I thought it my duty to warn you on a previous occasion."

Edwin tried to indicate that this topic should perhaps be left until the servants were absent.

"Common enough knowledge," muttered Mr. Leech, subsiding considerably, however. "But no business of mine, I know."

"Tell Maghull," said Mrs. Hatch, "that he is to take Miss de Reptonville to Hodley immediately, to Mr. Kynaston's. Then he is to return for further orders. I expect we shall all be very quiet today, preparing for the dance."

Mullet went.

George Goss flipped a fragment of eggshell across the table to Pamela, who was looking particularly disagreeable.

CHAPTER VI

It was an unremarkable speculative builder's two-bedroom bungalow; one of about a dozen lined up along the fiendishly noisy main road through Hodley. Geoffrey Kynaston himself opened the door, explaining that though he called upon a certain amount of casual assistance, it had at the moment all failed him, so that he was alone in the house. He closed the front door, thin, narrow, ugly, and with small panes of glass at the top to light the little hall; and suggested coffee. It was early and Griselda had just swallowed an excessive quantity of cocoa; but she offered to make it. Kynaston thanked her pleasantly, but said that that would be unnecessary as he had some just off the boil awaiting her arrival. This statement did not increase Griselda's inclination.

"Come into the studio."

It was what the builder of the bungalow would have called the lounge: in fact, the only sitting-room. Now the floor was bare; a bar extended round the walls; and there were photographs of Karsavina, Lifar, and Genée. There was also a rather larger photograph of Doris Ditton in a white shirt and black tie, the walking-out uniform of some women's organization.

"It's not very much," said Kynaston, glancing round. "I'll talk about myself over our coffee."

"It looks very interesting."

"Sit down." With his foot he pushed towards her a small round stool covered in scarlet artificial leather. He departed for the coffee.

Griselda soon rose and began to examine the photographs. Lifar, every feather in position as the male Blue Bird, particularly took her fancy. Doris Ditton also, she thought, looked more self-sufficient than at the tea party the previous day. There was a heap of copies of a paper she had not previously heard of. It was called "The Dancing Times."

"Do you read poetry?"

This was something Griselda had forgotten about her teacher.

"Not as much as I should."

Kynaston had returned with two large mugs and a small dun-coloured book:

"I don't know about that. But some of these might amuse you while I fill the jug."

He departed once more. The book was entitled "Days of Delinquency" by Geoffrey Kynaston. It contained about thirty short poems. Somewhat to her surprise, Griselda seemed quite able to understand them.

Incubus

Can you hear my feet approaching?
Can you bear my heart encroaching?
No hope to hide when I am coming
Straight into your soul I'm homing.

There were about twenty more lines but Kynaston had returned with a steaming jug and a milk bottle.

"White, I imagine?"

"Please."

The mug was very heavy and very hot. It was in peasant ware and bore an inscription in Breton.

"What are you making of your own life?" He sat on the floor at her feet.

"Very little."

"Good. I dislike womanly women. They're the only ones who make a success of it. Of being a woman I mean. It's hell, isn't it?"

"It varies."

"Do you read Rilke?"

"Yes."

"I don't altogether care for his work but he had a lot in common with me as a man. I have the same utter dependence on a strong woman."

Griselda looked up at Doris's photograph.

"I didn't mean Doris. Though she can look rather splendid, don't you think?"

"Very attractive."

"It's only skin deep, though, or clothes deep. She lacks guts, little Doris."

"I rather liked her." This was not true, but Griselda disapproved of Kynaston's comment.

"Of course. Don't misunderstand me. I adore Doris. She's the sweetest girl in Hodley."

"How long have you lived in Hodley?"

"Eighteen months. Ever since I left the Shephard's Market Ballet. They chucked me, you know. After that I was done. You don't get another shop when you've been chucked for the reason I was."

Griselda thought enquiry was unnecessary.

"I refused to go to bed with Frankie Litmus."

"Oh." Griselda took a resolute pull at the interminable coffee.

"I'm not that way at all, believe it or not. And look what's become of me in consequence! Let that be a lesson to you. Ditched in this pigstye teaching the lads of the village to caper. Have some more coffee? It's actually Nescafé, as you doubtless perceive."

"No thank you." The vast mug was still more than half full.

"Pupils like you are rare. Do you mind if I make the most of you?"

"I hope you will."

"We've got all day. Will you come for a picnic with me?"

"I'm under orders to learn to dance."

"That won't take you all day. By the way, why can't you dance?"

There was something about him which enabled her to tell him.

"I dislike being held."

He rose dangling his empty mug.

"Even by someone you're fond of?"

"I've never been fond enough of anyone."

He considered. "In that case clearly, I must first win your confidence."

She smiled.

"More coffee?"

"No thank you."

"Do you think the preparations for a picnic are the best or

the worst part? Cutting the sandwiches. Filling the thermoses. Counting the knives."

"The worst part."

"In that case we'd better not set about it until later. I haven't told you much about myself yet. That'll fill the gap. Or better still I'll read you some of my poems. I've given up serious dancing you know and am trying to establish myself as a poet." Griselda noticed it was the phrase Doris had employed the day before.

"I shall be sent home if I don't dance."

"If they are cruel to you at home, you can always come and live here. But more of that later. And, by the way, I'm coming to the Ball myself, you know."

"Mrs. Hatch didn't mention that."

"I'll be able to keep an eye on you. And hands off you, so to speak. Other hands than mine, of course. Apropos of which—" He began to read aloud.

> "*Disclaimer*
> Other loves than mine may kill you;
> Other hates than mine fulfill you;
> Other saints through grief atone you;
> Other sinners crowd to stone you——"

He continued through the poem, then read several others. Griselda, a fair judge of verse, was not very much impressed by Kynaston's poesy, but more than a little charmed by his excellent delivery. His attractive voice and skilful accentuation made far more emerge from the verses than had ever entered into them.

"I won't ask you what you think," he said at the end. "A poet I believe must heed only his inner voice."

This, on the whole, was a relief.

"May I say," enquired Griselda, "how very much I enjoyed the way you read?"

"I was taught by Moissi," replied Kynaston. "And much good has it done me."

"That was before you took up dancing?"

"I have many gifts," he answered, "but none of them has come to anything at all. I need a suitable woman to manage my life for me. Without that, even my poetry will be still another dreariness and misery."

"You've at least achieved publication. Many poets don't."

"True. And against really passionate opposition by Herbert Read. Still, fewer than a hundred copies have sold. Well, well. Before we pack the picnic basket, will you help me with the washing up?"

There were not only the coffee adjuncts, but the remains of Kynaston's breakfast and of another vague meal which had seemingly involved the consumption of some very fat ham or boiled bacon. Griselda hung her jacket on the door of the little kitchenette and applied herself, while Kynaston dried on a small, discoloured tea-cloth. The tiny room became hot and steamy.

When it was all over, Kynaston, from a box-like cupboard in the hall, produced a large wicker picnic-basket.

"Now for the awful preliminaries."

"Must we have the basket? Are there going to be enough of us?"

"If we don't take the basket, the picnic will turn into a walk, and with you, I couldn't stand that."

From the dilapidated meat-safe he produced the knuckle end of a Bath chap, a bottle of French mustard, and half a stale loaf. "Better than no bread," he remarked. "Will you please do your very best with the ingredients provided? Here's a knife. I'm going to pack the tinned apricots and the opener."

Griselda began to make sandwiches. Kynaston hurried about packing the basket with heavy, and, in Griselda's view, superfluous objects. "I'll just get the stove for coffee," he said.

"What does Doris do?" enquired Griselda at one point, for something to say, and in the capricious and destructive spirit in which women ask such questions at such times.

"Part time nursing," replied Kynaston, packing plates. "She's no use at the bedside, but the clothes are good. Mostly, she's waiting, of course. Waiting for experience of the male. Shall I put in some bottles of beer?"

"I dislike beer."

"You sound as if you dislike me too? Would you rather not come on the picnic? I can always go unaccompanied."

"I have to stay here until it is time for tea. You're supposed to be teaching me dancing, which I don't want to learn. We'd better use up the time somehow."

"Yes," he said, lining up the cutlery they were to take. "You're at my mercy, aren't you? I should so much prefer the situation to be reversed."

After a round of complicated preparations, remarkably oner-ous in view of the smallness alike of the bungalow and of the undertaking before them, they at last found themselves on the doorstep.

"Forgive me if I double-lock the front door," said Kynaston. Griselda reflected that the whole woodwork would yield like cardboard to any housebreaker.

They set out along the distractingly noisy main road through Hodley, carrying the ponderous basket between them. The traffic made conversation impossible, and the preservation of life, weighed down as they were, a matter calling for constant attention. After about a hundred yards Griselda wished she could change hands with their burden. After about a hundred and twenty-five yards she arranged with Kynaston to do so. After about a quarter of a mile Kynaston shouted: "Up there for the Woods. Up the steps to your left."

Griselda was realizing that her left arm was by no means as strong as her right, and she transferred the basket once more as she struggled up the steps ahead of Kynaston. Hodley Woods, though a well-known beauty spot, were neither as extensive nor as dense as Griselda had expected from the descriptions she had often read of them in advertisements; but they appeared unpopulated, it being a time of the day and week when all but the anti-social were at work. The road now ran in a cutting which much diminished its uproar. The sun, moreover, had begun to shine, falsifying Mullet's forecast; and among the undergrowth Griselda noticed a yellow-hammer.

"Places like this are only beautiful when they're near a town," remarked Kynaston.

"I don't think I follow."

"When there's no town, the landscape should be more star-tling. Miles of this sort of thing and nothing else, would be intol-erable."

"It's what I'm used to. I haven't travelled much. Where do we settle?"

"What about here? You can just see the main line through that gap in the trees. At least you will be able to, when there's a train. I like trains."

It was a spot where several trees had been cut down. Generations of pine needles warmed and cushioned the dead roots. Griselda began to convert one of the stumps into a table. Kynaston lay on his back.

"I suppose you work."

"Not at the moment. Or not in the way you mean. I had to give it up owing to troubles at home."

"You mean they took exception to the nature of your employment?"

"No. I had to return home and help."

"Why? What happened?"

"Things went wrong. Have a sandwich?"

Still regarding the tree-tops he reached about with his arm. "You're not very informative. Never mind. It's unlikely that I'd be able to assist much. Even with advice." His hand, roving through the air, struck the arm of her jacket. He took her arm between his fingers and thumb and followed it down to the wrist. Then he took the sandwich. "I detest mustard, by the way. I should have mentioned that."

"There's no mustard. I forgot to ask you. I don't like it either."

He began to drop bits of the sandwich into his upturned mouth.

"As we've carried plates all this way, perhaps we'd better use them," said Griselda.

"Am I eating swinishly? After all, it's swine I'm eating."

"Here you are," said Griselda firmly. "Take it." She held a plate before his face.

Kynaston sat up. He placed the remains of the decomposing sandwich on the plate. "I am a creature of moods," he said. "As you see. But I like women to know their own minds."

For the remainder of the meal his behaviour was irreproachable.

After they had consumed the final tinned apricot, Kynaston

busied himself making Nescafé on the little stove. The stove was slow to light and laborious to sustain. "It's getting old," he remarked. "I've had it since I was at school. I was at Stowe, you know," he added, as if alluding to a matter of very common knowledge. "It's supposed to be better than the usual reformatory. We were allowed to have a few possessions of our own. This was mine. I used to make Bantam in the grounds. Nescafé hadn't been invented, I think, at that time." He was striking matches and blowing the minute flame. "Don't get me wrong all the same," he went on. "At the best Stowe's only a vulgar makeshift. It was built for another purpose."

"Wasn't it the house of the Duke of Buckingham?"

"It was, Griselda. May I call you Griselda? I think one should ask. Oh, curse." He had burned himself rather badly.

"You may call me Griselda. I like you to ask. Can I do anything helpful?"

"Nothing."

"Cold tea would be good for that burn."

"We've only got Nescafé. . . . How did you know about the Buckingham's?"

"I read."

"About the history of architecture?"

"Family histories."

"What else?"

"Almost everything else. You can't define. You know that."

"I know that. I was trying to trap you into an admission." The stove was now flaming merrily; almost hysterically, Griselda thought. "I was trying to trap you into an admission of anything."

"I have little to conceal."

"Are you awakened? I think not."

"You think the same of others, I notice."

"Doris, you mean? It's true. Have you read Casanova?"

"Yes."

"Oh. You have. Then you'll recall his remark to the effect that most people never receive the initial jolt which is required to bring the mind to consciousness." The water boiled over, extinguishing the long yellow flames. There had been a good blaze and little of the water was left.

But they made the best of it and somehow began a conversation about books and the psyche which continued until Griselda noticed that her wrist-watch showed half-past three.

"What about my lessons?"

"You've too many brains to make a good dancer, but I'll do what I can in the time."

"Whose fault is it about the time?"

"Blame it on life. It's hard to know where to begin else. Living in Hodley I cannot be expected to regard someone like you only as a source of income."

Griselda wondered what there was about her to elicit a compliment from a man who, however irritating in his habits, yet undoubtedly had seen much of the world. She wondered but smiled. Then she thought of the ordeal before her.

They returned with the picnic basket to the bungalow. Entering the studio immediately, Kynaston put a record on the gramophone.

"Leave that outside," he said, referring to the basket. "Anywhere." Soft music trickled forth.

"There's a note for you," cried Griselda, staving off events. "It was behind the front door."

"Read it. Out loud."

" 'I have put your shirt in the top left hand drawer on top of the others.' "

"For tonight. Doris has been washing it. She has to wash her own shirts the whole time and she's become very good at it."

"I'm looking forward to meeting her again tonight." This remark could hardly do more than gain time.

"Doris won't be coming. I'm asked only for professional reasons." The music was murmuring on. Kynaston was in the centre of the room. He spoke with a touch of impatience. "I'm ready."

There seemed no help for it.

CHAPTER VII

Immediately Griselda re-entered Beams, the Duchess clutched her by the arm.

"You have returned at the right moment, my dear," she said. "I have something I want to ask you. Tell me the truth. Did you hear Fritzi last night? Were you awakened?"

This last question seemed to recur.

"I don't think so," replied Griselda, courteously but cautiously. Could the Duchess be referring to the noisy frequenter of the distant passage?

"I am so very glad to hear it. The lovely Pamela was not awakened either, and, of course, George it is always utterly impossible to awake. But everyone else, it seems. Even that Irish assassin, who sleeps outside above the motor-cars. And poor little Fritzi he could not at all explain to me what was the matter with him."

Griselda realized that Fritzi was the Duchess's dog. She remembered. She was a little frightened.

"Have you no idea yourself?"

"No idea at all. Gottfried and I woke up together. There was little Fritzi crying his poor heart out. We could not see him as there was no light. Gottfried, you know, will never allow there to be a crack of light in the room when we are in bed. I clutched Gottfried very tightly. What could it be? Gottfried kissed and caressed me. Then he got out of bed and turned on the light. Fritzi was standing up in his basket, quite erect and stiff as a statue. I got out of bed too. I went to Fritzi and asked him why he was crying. And do you know, my dear, what happened then? He growled at me as if he didn't know me. Fritzi has never growled at Gottfried or me in all the eleven years we have had him. But Gottfried made it better for me again and in the end Fritzi stopped crying and fell asleep quite suddenly. I asked him again in the morning but he couldn't tell me what it all meant."

Palpably the Duchess had related the story many times, presumably at intervals throughout the day. None the less, Griselda for some reason was not surprised that she still seemed much upset. The Duke came to her, and, saying nothing, put his arm round her shoulder. Suddenly Griselda realized that the dog was dead. She recalled that the Ellensteins had not appeared for breakfast; and, with unreasonable shame, her own confident inner explanation of their absence.

"How perfectly dreadful!" she said to the Duchess. "I am so very sorry."

The Duchess kissed her gratefully. "Thank you, Griselda," she said. "Fritzi was only an animal, but the death even of an animal that has been a long time——" She left the sentence unfinished, as the Duke led her to a sofa. She looked up brightly, and the more engagingly for what had gone before. "I am absolutely determined not to spoil the dance." The Duke kissed her left hand. Griselda was pleased that the Duchess had remembered her Christian name aright and called her by it.

The others present, Mrs. Hatch and Mr. Leech, had doubtless, with the rest of the house, expressed their grief already. Mr. Leech none the less looked exceedingly distressed as he nibbled at a chunk of the unique cake.

"Come and have your tea, Griselda," said Mrs. Hatch. "I shan't require massage, after all, but I daresay you could do with a short rest before you change. Pamela has gone up already."

Griselda advanced and sat down with an enquiry after her hostess's affliction.

"I've been so busy all day that I've not had time to think of it. In consequence it has now quite ceased to trouble me."

"How splendid!" said Mr. Leech quietly. "Would that all our ills could be cured so readily." He sighed.

"Several men have already asked me for dances with you," remarked Mrs. Hatch to Griselda, "and I've booked some of them on this card." She took a dance programme from her handbag. "Only some of them, of course." She passed the programme to Griselda. "I won't ask whether Geoffrey Kynaston was pleased with your progress; but I'll ask whether you were. Were you?"

To her alarm and mortification Griselda felt that her brow and neck were hot.

"I did my best," she answered. "But Geoffrey tells me I'm too much of a bluestocking to make a dancer."

"You're starting late. But you're starting under excellent auspices. It's much too soon to despair."

"Of course it is," said the Duchess. "Griselda may meet her affinity this very night. Then she'll dance better than all of us."

"I don't know about that," said Mrs. Hatch. "But the All Party Dance is certainly going to be an occasion. We shall be making history tonight."

Griselda felt very ignorant. "Is it such a very special dance?"

Mrs. Hatch looked at her. "You cannot have been reading the newspapers lately."

"Not very much, I'm afraid. I prefer books."

"Good thing too. Provided you choose the right books. Millie always had dreadful tastes: Tolstoy, von Hügel, and rubbish like that. Still you ought to know about tonight." Mr. Leech nodded gravely several times.

"The country's on the rocks," continued Mrs. Hatch. "That I'm sure you *must* know."

"More than usual?" asked Griselda.

"Much more. You've heard about the Roller Report?"

"I've seen the name on the newsbills."

"The Roller Committee has presented a Report showing that we're bankrupt."

"And after sitting for only six months," interpolated Mr. Leech. "That's where much of the seriousness lies, you know, Mrs. Hatch. Things are really urgent."

"Well, you know what that means?"

"Not a revolution?" This was the Duke.

"I suppose it means we must all make some more money," suggested Griselda rather wildly.

"It means a coalition."

Mr. Leech nodded again more gloomily than ever.

"I see. The dance is to celebrate?"

"Certainly not." Mr. Leech almost snatched the words from his hostess's mouth. "I will explain." It was clear that his life mainly consisted in explaining the same thing to a succession of careless audiences. "When Lord Roller came to me, my first thought, after consulting my colleagues, was to get in touch with Mr. Minnit, though it's never pleasant to have to ask favours of the Leader of the Opposition. Still one must put the country first, of course. After we had talked things over, Minnit said that he and some of his people would come in with us; but we both thought that something more was needed than a merely administrative change of that kind. After all, Miss de Reptonville, not everybody nowadays even knows who is or who is not in the Cabinet at any particular moment." He smiled. There was a complete silence. Mrs. Hatch was wriggling her foot in the thick carpet. The Duke's arm was still round his wife's shoulders, his hand on her breast. "Something more seemed to us to be needed," repeated the Prime Minister, blinking. "Something more—so to speak—emotional. In a popular sort of way. Something which appealed to the underlying unity of the nation, the readiness of the people to make sacrifices for patriotic reasons. For sacrifices will certainly be called for. A heavy burden. Oh yes——" He paused again, then pulled himself together. "My first thought was a Mass Meeting in some suitable place, to be addressed by Minnit and myself in turn. Considering the country's need, I thought we might prevail upon the L.C.C.——"

"Then fortunately Mr. Leech consulted me," interrupted Mrs. Hatch. "I happened to be calling in at Downing Street for tea. I saw the answer at once. I offered Beams for an All Party Dance. The press response has shown how right the idea was. Everyone is coming. Not only Minnit and all of them, but representatives of the splinter parties too. Half way through the evening Mr. Leech and Mr. Minnit are going to make their speeches—short speeches, of course—as hostess I insist on that; and everyone will think well of the coalition from the outset, instead of the whole thing falling flat."

"Will there be enough people to listen to the speeches?" asked Griselda. "I don't mean to be rude. I'm sure there'll be everyone there's room for. But will there be quite enough to achieve national unity?"

"People don't actually need to *hear* the speeches on these occasions," replied Mrs. Hatch. "In many cases it is better if they do not. All the press will be coming, and, of course, the speeches will be broadcast. Those are the things which matter nowadays."

"I was more than a little doubtful myself at first," remarked Mr. Leech, "whether we should avail ourselves of Mrs. Hatch's wonderfully generous offer. But she soon quite won me over."

"Melanie," observed the Duke, tightening his hold upon his wife, "will persuade the Recording Angel to let her organize a dance at the Day of Judgement."

Monk entered and began to pound with a gong in the sight of them all.

"The dressing gong," said Mrs. Hatch, rising smartly. "Dinner will be in exactly an hour."

CHAPTER VIII

In her bedroom Griselda found a tall thin girl seated in one of the armchairs, who rose as she entered.

"Who are you?"

"Louise. If you like, I'll help you to dress."

She was wearing a costly dress of pale grey silk, which tightly fitted her long neck up to her chin and ears, and was buttoned with many small buttons from the waist to the top of the collar, and girdled with a shiny black belt. Her long hair, the colour of smooth water under a grey sky, was drawn into a tight ballet-dancer's bun. Her face was exceedingly pale, and made paler with a suggestion of powder almost green in tinge; but her features made an unusual blend of resolution and sensibility, a large nose and small firm chin combining with a slightly sensual mouth and huge dark-brown eyes, full of life and beauty, behind very large and expensive black-rimmed glasses. Her voice and accent were contralto and cultivated.

Griselda recalled her hostess's words: "You don't know how much Louise will do for you." To have Louise about one, would, she thought, be charming and beautiful. It was the first luxury she had really desired.

"Hadn't you better help Mrs. Hatch first? She'll have to be down to receive people, I expect."

"No one outside the house party will be here until nine.

Mrs. Hatch particularly wanted me to help you." Louise smiled delightfully.

"Thank you." There was a silly pause. Griselda had placed her handbag on the bed. "I must tell you I've never met a lady's maid."

"I'm not *exactly* a lady's maid."

Griselda blushed. "I'm so sorry. Mrs. Hatch——"

Louise waved away her apologies. "We'll have to learn from one another. About each other, I mean."

They were standing in the middle of the floor, looking at each other, about three feet apart.

"Are you coming to the dance?"

Louise shook her head. "Political dances are not my thing. Not that kind of dance. Therefore I'm not asked."

"What do you do?"

"Various things. But now it is time that I help people to dress."

"For dances you don't go to?"

"And for some I do."

"Do you like the work?"

"I have a certain natural aptitude, I think," Louise answered solemnly. "And little alternative. I am destitute and unqualified. But I don't give satisfaction, I'm afraid."

"I think that Mrs. Hatch might be hard to please. From what little I've seen of her, of course."

"It's I who am hard to please. At least, harder to please than Mrs. Hatch." Again she smiled.

"I see."

"Shall we begin?"

Louise helped Griselda remove her jacket, and pulled her jumper swiftly over her head.

"I expect you would like a bath?"

"I'm afraid of the machine."

"I'll try to protect you from it." Louise began to operate the formidable equipment, while Griselda removed her remaining garments.

In a remarkably short space of time Louise was announcing that the bath was ready. "Hot," she added. "And deep. We've won. It's a beautiful bath." She stared for a moment at Griselda's naked body. The steam of the bathroom had made her face glisten very slightly, despite the careful make-up. "Given the right dress, you will be the belle of the ball," she said.

For the second time that evening Griselda felt herself blush; this time, it seemed, all over her body, making her look absurd.

"Fortunately," she replied, "I have exactly the right dress."

Likewise the bath was the right temperature, the right depth, accompanied with the right accessories, a new cake of heavily scented soap and a huge white bath towel. Griselda entered it, letting the water rise above her shoulders.

"Which dress?"

Griselda shouted back. "The taffeta." It was wonderful.

Louise appeared in the bathroom door, which Griselda had left open. "Your dress is good. Really good." Griselda felt flattered and pleased that Louise did not seem surprised, she whose taste, it was obvious, was unapproachably high.

"I told you it was."

Louise was withdrawing to the bedroom, but Griselda stopped her.

"Come and talk to me." She had never spoken like that before. "Or is it too hot and steamy?"

Louise shook her head and sat on the bath stool, an inappropriate throne.

"Undo the collar of your dress. Make yourself comfortable."

Louise shook her head again. "My dress must be worn severely."

"It becomes you."

"I have no wish to look like everyone else. It is one thing about my life here that it enables me not to. Soon even nuns and nurses will be wearing little cotton frocks from Marks and Spencer."

Griselda remembered what Kynaston had said about the photograph of Doris. She thought for a moment.

"Cotton frocks are comfortable."

"But do they appeal to the senses? Are those who wear them satisfied?"

"Does what one wears affect that?"

"Very much indeed. One's body needs to be always conscious of its clothes. One reason why there are so many more unsatisfied women than there used to be, is that they have forgotten that."

"I fear my clothes are very commonplace. Except that dress."

"I will help you to do better if you like."

"Thank you. But I have very little money."

"That matters more than it should, but less than you think."

"Then I should like you to help me."

"Of course there are limits to what I can do. But if you are seriously interested, I might later introduce you to Hugo Raunds. He lives entirely for clothes. He designed this dress. You've probably heard of him. As it happens, his father, Sir Travis, is coming tonight. Not that all this matters much, as I'll be leaving here at any moment, and that will be that."

"Where will you go?"

"I shall try to find someone amenable to my ways."

Griselda began to fill the bath with strongly smelling soap.

"I know so little of life. Oh, curse."

A sud had entered one of her eyes. Louise rose and carefully removed it with a handkerchief, which she took from a pocket in the skirt of her dress. It was a silk handkerchief and soothing: though the pain remained, therapeutic in sensation, but curing nothing; probably, in fact, Griselda feared, damaging slightly the conjunctiva. Louise had resumed her seat. She was wiping her large glasses on the handkerchief.

After thanking Louise, Griselda continued: "All I know comes from books. It's a wonder I keep my end up as well as I do."

"Books are better, I think, most of the time," replied Louise. "The more you know of life outside them, the less it's like them. But there's one problem that you have to solve if you're to go on profiting from books, and books won't help you much to solve it."

"And that is?"

"The problem of finding someone, even one single person, you can endure life with. To me it's acute."

Inadvertently Griselda knocked the large slippery cake of soap on to the floor, where it slid out of sight.

"I always thought *that* difficulty was peculiar to me," said Griselda.

Louise had laid her glasses on the stool and was groping for the soap.

"Please stop," cried Griselda. "I should be getting out anyway. It was selfish of me to ask you to sit in all this steam."

Louise returned the soap to its lair and resumed her glasses.

"I'm not all that short-sighted," she remarked. "Though I am, of course, a little short-sighted I don't have to wear glasses. It's just that glasses suit me. We may as well get *something* from modern inventions."

Griselda was out and towelling.

She found that Louise had laid out new underclothes for her.

She submitted to being dressed by Louise, to having Louise brush her short hair, even to being made up by Louise; all with a strange remote pleasure, possibly recalled from childhood, though certainly not consciously, for Griselda could recall little of her childhood that was pleasant, except books.

It all took a long time, and as they worked, they talked.

The remarks they exchanged became shorter and rapider; varied with occasional longer passages such as in normal converse no one listens to. They began, without any feeling of guilt, to talk about the people in the house.

"Have you ever set eyes on the mysterious Austin Barnes?"

"No."

"Why does he never appear?"

"The coalition. He hates it."

"Oh yes. I heard about the coalition during Tea."

"Also he thinks he ought to be Prime Minister and not Leech."

"I see."

"Also he's afraid of Mrs. Hatch."

"I like the Ellensteins."

"Yes," said Louise. "The Ellensteins are good. One could not endure living with them, but they are really good. And that is most unusual."

"What about the Duchess's dog?"

"It was Stephanie."

"Who's Stephanie?"

"Stephanie des Bourges. She's a ghost."

"So the house is haunted?"

"Only occasionally. Stephanie comes only at certain times."

"I could wish the times weren't the present."

"I could not. Stephanie was my only friend until you came." This now seemed to Griselda not even to call for acknowledgement. "In fact she came because I was here."

"Do you talk to her?"

"Oh yes, often. She's a lonely ghost."

"When did you last talk to her? Last night?"

"This afternoon."

"Where?"

"Here. I was talking to Stephanie just before you came in. I talked to her here yesterday too."

"Do you mean that I've been given the haunted room?"

"Dear Griselda, you couldn't expect a beautiful woman like Stephanie—for she *is* beautiful, fortunately—to come to my little turret and probably wake up the servants below into the bargain? Now could you?"

"I suppose not," said Griselda. "But it explains why I slept badly last night."

"I don't think so," said Louise. She was drawing on one of Griselda's stockings and now paused for a moment, kneeling at her feet. "It is not that this is the haunted room or anything so vulgar, if you will forgive me putting it so. You think of it like that because you think a ghost must be bad. This is merely the room where Stephanie and I meet because, being at the end of the corridor and usually unoccupied, it is quiet and seldom disturbed. And you mustn't think of poor Stephanie as bad either. Ghosts only harm those who fear them. Stephanie is one whom I find it easy to love. And you must do the same, Griselda."

"I'll try." Louise began attaching the stocking to its suspender. Griselda felt curious. "Do you *see* her by daylight?"

"No. It is true that you can only see her at night. But I can talk to her sometimes by day."

"Could I?"

"I don't know. It depends."

"On what?"

But Louise was reflecting and did not answer directly. "Yes, Griselda," she said. "I think that *you* could see and talk to Stephanie. It occurs to me that it may have been because you also were here that she has come at this time. She hadn't been seen or heard of before, they tell me, for more than twenty years. Not since the time something happened during that bloody silly war. I don't precisely know what." She was on her feet again.

"I'm afraid," said Griselda, "that nothing you say makes me very much less frightened of Stephanie. I'm not sure that I shall find thought very enjoyable—I mean, even after the dance, to which I'm not looking forward at all. She was even responsible for the poor Duchess losing her dog," added Griselda as an after-thought.

"It's difficult about animals," replied Louise. "But you can't say that ghosts really treat them worse than we do."

"What colour is her hair?" asked Griselda.

"A gorgeous golden red," answered Louise. "And her eyes are, of course, green."

"I have never seen really green eyes outside a book."

"I think that Stephanie must be a mixture of races," said Louise. "Probably she has some Jewish blood. I should say quite a lot."

She lifted Griselda's dress from the bed where she had laid it. "Now for it," she said.

It was done.

"You are truly beautiful," said Louise.

"The girl who designed the dress should get most of the credit," said Griselda, looking away from Louise, and into the mirror.

"What was her name?"

Griselda told her.

"I might have known it," said Louise. "In fact, I really did know it. One of Hugo's."

"I haven't heard her mention him."

"No. Hugo is a very secret man."

"Oh. Anyway I don't know her very well. I wish I were a better dancer."

"Don't worry about that."

"I wish something else. I so much wish, Louise, that you were coming to the political dance with me."

Stretching out her hand, she touched Louise's grey silk neck.

"Yes," said Louise gravely. "To my utter surprise, I wish that too."

CHAPTER IX

"We mustn't let things go to our heads," remarked Mrs. Hatch as she seated herself at the dinner table. They settled to a substantial meal.

Griselda, for some reason, had come down rather late, and Mrs. Hatch, whose practice as hostess it was always to appear for dinner last, had entered the dining room only just behind her. The absence of Louise might in any case have retarded her preparations.

Griselda, to whom Louise's good opinion of her dress had given more confidence, carefully examined the company. The Duchess, in a very tight dress which, it had to be admitted, suited her much better than something looser would have done, was certainly the most striking; but Mrs. Hatch, in a sense (not a sense that Griselda particularly cared for), ran her close, wearing a dress after the style favoured by Madame Récamier, but dark blue, and elaborated, perhaps somewhat inappropriately, with a full display of the famous Procopius jewellery, a fabulous, multi-coloured mêlée. Pamela, in one of the quieter garments approved by "Vogue", seemed slightly outshone by her seniors; and to be in a state of sulky suspicion, though her appetite remained good. Altogether Griselda felt rather pleased.

With the men it was simple: the Duke (bearing on his dress coat a tiny but conspicuous token of some ancient chivalrous Order particularized in the Almanach de Gotha), and Edwin (in a dress suit the colour of night on the Côte d'Azur, and wearing a rare flower in his buttonhole, which Mr. Cork said grew only on the island of Tahiti and in his conservatory at Beams) were well-dressed; Mr. Leech and George Goss were not. George Goss had not even brought a tail coat.

There was soup with wine in it; a large, but excellent, sole; roast duck, with apple sauce, and salad; a confused but rather rich

concoction described as "Summer Pudding" (though, as someone pointed out, it was not yet quite summer); mushrooms on
toast; and dessert. "No cheese tonight," announced Mrs. Hatch,
"in view of what is before us. Those who are still hungry must
make do with nuts; or go and see Brundrit privately in his pantry."

Pamela had refused to take duck on the ground that her Father
had always said that ducks were garbage eaters; and had had to
have a small exquisite point steak specially cooked for her. When
it came, she ate it, without a word, almost in a couple of mouthfuls.

It was not the gayest of meals. The Duchess, upon whom so
much depended in that direction, was cast down by the death of
Fritzi, though she struggled pathetically hard with her feelings,
and though the slight air of grief (like most things) distinctly
became her. The Duke, though he did all that could be expected
of him with Griselda, complimenting her upon her dress and
describing clothes worn by beautiful women he had met at
now extinct German courts, was concerned about the Duchess. Mr. Leech was concerned about his speech, apologizing to
Griselda for his inattention to her remarks, apologizing to his
hostess for making notes during dinner, dropping his food on
his clothes, and from time to time muttering a possible rhetori-
cal effect under his breath, then changing it with a stub of pencil
and muttering it again. Edwin seemed almost more concerned
than the Prime Minister, and his concern seemed more active or
transitive; it was not that he deflected in the slightest from his
habitual perfection of appearance and behaviour, but that a score
of unconscious details disclosed his inner distress, and made him
less than a contributor to the sodality of the occasion. Once even
he had to ask for a second access to the salad, being unable to eat
any more duck. Pamela was as negative as usual; and even Mrs.
Hatch seemed strung up, in her not very suitable dress and dangerously valuable jewels. It hung over all of them, perhaps, even
over Mrs. Hatch, dearly though she appeared to love a dance, that
the gaiety ahead had an ulterior, and presumably important, end.
George Goss merely leered at the Duchess's bare bosom and ate,
crouched over his plate like an octopus.

Mrs. Hatch left the table early in order to receive the first

guests, commanding the others to remain and give their diges-
tions time to work. Edwin, however, sprang up, and, exclaiming
"I am sure there must be something I can do," followed his hostess, having bestowed a final uncertain glance upon Mr. Leech.

"It's bad news about our friend Austin," remarked the Duke,
after a pause.

"I hadn't heard, darling," said the Duchess.

"Same old trouble," grunted George Goss.

Griselda had meant to enquire further of the Duke, but after
George Goss's remark, felt quite unlike doing so.

"I hope we have a schottische," said the Duchess, brightly
making conversation. "Mentioning Austin made me think of it."

"I doubt whether the younger generation have ever heard of
it," said Mr. Leech. He was at his very gloomiest.

Griselda had to admit that she had not.

"I've heard of it," said Pamela, gnawing round an imported
nectarine. "All those Victorian things are coming back in, you
know. Chaperones, petticoats, and all that."

For Pamela it was quite a speech.

CHAPTER X

"Hallo, Griselda. What a dress!"

The first person she had met was Kynaston, and she was not as
pleased as immediately after she had last left him, she would have
expected to be.

"Hullo, Geoffrey. Don't think me rude, but I'm on my way
upstairs."

Probably it was rude, but she could not help it. Her mood was
expansive, something she could not recall having previously felt;
and about Geoffrey there seemed an enclosed and private air
unsuited to a large convivial gathering. Though, she recollected,
she did not know him very well; so that possibly this was wrong.

Approaching her room she felt unreasonably agitated; and
entering it, much more unreasonably disappointed. The room
was empty. From one of the dressing-table drawers she took the
dance programme Mrs. Hatch had given her; and looked at it for

the first time. There were three names inserted in Mrs. Hatch's clear handwriting (one of them twice), none of them known to Griselda, except that of Edwin Polegate-Hampden, inserted not, as he had hoped, for the first but for the supper dance. There were no names inserted after supper. Griselda was wholly ignorant of the procedure on these occasions, but had thought that dance programmes were obsolete. She wondered whether it was usual for the hostess, unasked, to arrange in this way partners for her guests. It might be important to ascertain whether it was the custom or merely a peculiarity of Mrs. Hatch's. Then Griselda thought of Stephanie des Bourges and hurried from the room, her final preparations abbreviated. This, she felt, was no time to meet a ghost. She wondered where Louise was; and shivered slightly.

Suddenly hundreds of people had arrived. The hall was full and quite a queue extended down the long passage, lined with palms and baskets of flowers, which extended to the resuscitated ball-room, recently the scene of Doris's dusty labours. At the entrance to the ballroom Mrs. Hatch was shaking hands with people, and introducing them to Mr. Leech, who stood on her right, himself looking rather in need of a dust, and to another man, standing on her left, whom Griselda divined to be Mr. Minnit, the Leader of the Opposition. Mr. Minnit was a determined-looking elderly man with sparse black hair and a raucous penetrating voice. His evening suit made an even poorer impression than Mr. Leech's, because, besides having been worn for longer, it had cost less in the first place. Grouped round the trio were a number of men whom Griselda, identifying one or two of them, took to be some of the new Cabinet. Few of them made a more favourable impression than did either of their leaders.

"I've been waiting for you to come down." It was Kynaston again. "I'm quite as terrified by all this as you are."

Griselda realized that she wasn't terrified at all. She considered herself much better dressed than most of the other women; and, quite possibly, no less generally attractive. Looking round her, she even began to wonder whether she would show herself much inferior as a dancer. She smiled at Kynaston to give him confidence, and because she still felt she might have been rude to him.

Just then the band struck up. "You hear that?" said Kynaston. "You'd better get your hostess's moneysworth."

They began to make their way along the crowded passage. Kynston shook hands with Mrs. Hatch, who asked after his poetry. Then they entered the ballroom.

It was a fine large room, though not very inspired architecturally, and expensively decorated not only with vegetation of various kinds but also with a number of patriotic motifs. At one end of the rectangle, the platform occupied by the band was banked with hundreds of carnations which pleasantly perfumed the otherwise already slightly smoky air. At the other end was another, smaller platform, now unoccupied but the purpose of which was clear, as it was swathed in red, white, and blue fabric, and bore an ominous green baize-topped table, with three hard chairs. Above this platform were two oval plaques, edged with laurel, and bearing lively messages from Lord Beaconsfield and John Burns. Presumably many of the guests were not expected to take the floor, as round the walls was ranged a triple rank of gilt chairs with crimson seats, their thin red line becoming disordered as people sat upon them; but already the enthusiastic and the impetuous were in action, their faces settling down to ecstasy or boredom. The long far wall of the room contained a line of big French windows, uncurtained against the chance that later the growing heat might require them to be opened. Griselda wondered who might be without these windows, unseen but all-seeing.

As Kynaston led Griselda on to the floor, they encountered Edwin with a fascinatingly beautiful young partner. Briefly he introduced her as the Marchioness of Wolverhampton. "See you later," he said to Griselda, in an accent of warm significance. Griselda watched them glide away. Obviously Edwin's dancing was as flawless as everything else about him. Griselda wondered why he should elect to sup with her instead of with the incomparable Marchioness; or whether this also was Mrs. Hatch's doing.

Griselda danced three times with Kynaston, not precisely with elation, but certainly with competence. Her ancient inhibition against being intimately clasped by a little-known male had not disappeared, but was perhaps in abeyance. In practice, the whole curious transaction seemed, at least with Kynaston, unexpectedly impersonal. They said little, the monotonous music thrummed in Griselda's brain, and she felt completely mistress of the situation, while still unclear why such store was commonly set by the pastime. Possibly things would be different in the circumstances advocated by the Duchess; but surely it must be only occasionally that the habitual dancer could dance with a partner whose body inspired to passion? Griselda wondered whether possibly she suffered from some physiological deficiency akin to tone-deafness. She then listened with her conscious ear to the music, and deemed that the matter was not worth undue concern.

The business had its social problems, however. Griselda's fourth dance had been allocated by Mrs. Hatch to an unknown named Mr. Coote. She did not know who Mr. Coote was, but when she announced his imminence to Kynaston, she was startled to learn that Kynaston had taken it for granted that she would be dancing with him (Kynaston) throughout the evening.

"You said you wanted me to ward off other males."

"Not exactly."

"You couldn't abide being pawed."

"Mrs. Hatch has arranged the next dance for me."

"What do you think I'm going to do? I don't know a soul here—if anybody here has a soul; and they're not the kind of people I *want* to know. Not that I'm likely to be introduced. I'm a mixture of a poor relation and the local tradesman."

"What would you have done, if you hadn't met me?"

"Contrived to bring Doris. Of course, I much prefer you, but I've made a very fair dancer out of Doris, and she's vastly better than having to talk about the state of the nation with a string of politicians."

The situation was dissolved by Mrs. Hatch appearing with Mr. Coote.

"Let me introduce Mr. Coote, Griselda; your next partner. This is Griselda de Reptonville. I told Mr. Coote about you while you were out of the house and he asked me for a dance with you."

"The reality exceeds the description," said Mr. Coote.

It was a waltz and Mr. Coote was heavy on other people's feet. While dancing, however, he maintained a steady flow of conven-

tionally complimentary verbiage, of a type which Griselda was
surprised to find still existed, but which began heavily to pall in
an astonishingly short period of time. Griselda had always understood that men preferred to talk about themselves and tried to
direct the conversation in that likely direction. But Mr. Coote was
unexpectedly reticent. Griselda could only gather that though
not in the political limelight, he occupied an entirely indispensable position far behind the scenes.

"Sort of Chief Foreman, you know. The chap who sees that
the roundabout is oiled. Poor sort of job at times, I find it. Let's
talk about something pleasanter. Our excellent hostess told me
you had short hair but I never knew short hair could be so attractive."

Suddenly Griselda noticed something odd. Mrs. Hatch was
dancing with (and much better than) Pamela.

Mr. Coote was, Griselda recollected, the one of her three
allotted partners who recurred. He was due to reappear for the
next dance but one. Apart from anything else, it seemed poor
planning, like selling all the adjoining seats in a theatre, instead of
spacing the audience about.

This little trouble solved itself, however, in the very instant
that Griselda had thought of it.

As the dance number (it was a bagatelle entitled "Mooning
with the Moon") neared its point of cessation, Mr. Coote suddenly crumpled up in the most dramatic possible way. He dropped
his partner, clutched the lower part of his belly with both hands,
became instantly green in the face, and lurched groaning to one
of the gilt chairs which had strayed out among the dancers. There
he sat, odd pairs of dancers occasionally navigating round the
back of him, until two muscular and efficient footmen assisted
him away, their hands under his armpits. Now that the music
had stopped, his dreadful groans were clearly audible above the
hubbub of talk; but so expertly was the incident disposed of, that
few were clearly aware of what had happened, and none sus-
tained any notable setback in jollity.

Griselda had been left isolated not far from the centre of the
floor, and, so thick were the dancers, could not reach Mr. Coote
before he was whisked away.

"If that doesn't teach you, I cannot imagine what will. You see what happens when you try to fraternize with the people." It it was, of course, Kynaston. Griselda could have struck him. Then she saw the large shape of George Goss coming towards her, solitary and menacing.

"Better me, don't you think, after all?" said Kynaston, comprehending the entire situation. Griselda, really furious at his deliberate or careless misunderstanding of the need for her to dance with Mr. Coote, placed her hand on his arm; and the music started once more, this time a number entitled "You Twisted Me Before I Twisted You."

"You don't have to do this the whole time, of course," said Kynaston.

"Indeed no. Later I am partnering a Mr. Mackintosh, and after that Edwin Polegate-Hampden for the supper dance."

"To hell with them. I didn't mean that. I meant that we could sit out sometimes."

Absurdly, Griselda had overlooked this possibility.

Out of the corner of her eye she observed George Goss lumber off the floor disappointed.

"Don't I seem to know your unlucky friend?"

"George Goss," said Griselda.

"I'm flattered that you prefer me. George Goss is the only really first-rank painter now alive in England. Probably in the world. When I looked at his Holy Family at the Leicester Gallery last autumn, I cried like a child."

It was by no means the end of George Goss, for immediately the dance was over, there he was again.

"Could we please do what you said," appealed Griselda to Kynaston, "and sit this one out?" It was to have been Mr. Coote's second dance, and Griselda considered that even he would have been preferable to George Goss.

"Let's look for the refreshments," said Kynaston. "I expect there are some." He put his arm round her waist to lead her away. It was hard on George Goss and Griselda smiled at him as she departed. He stood looking after her, fixed like a toad.

But it was not to be. Mrs. Hatch appeared.

"As Mr. Coote has been taken away, I should like you to meet

Lord Roller." Mrs. Hatch's memory for the details she herself had organized, was appalling.

The great Lord Roller, whose revelations had just shaken the entire world and lay behind the present festivity, was tall and stout, though dignified and wearing the most perfectly cut clothes.

"Melanie suggests that we should dance," he said in an attractive cultivated voice. "But I should prefer to sit and talk for just the few minutes allotted to me."

Griselda consented with relief. Kynaston prowled away, presumably after liquor.

"It's not that I never dance. On the contrary, twenty years ago I used to be considered rather good. But I've been having a tiring time lately and this evening, as you know, is rather a strain on some of us."

Griselda said she could well understand. They sat. They had moved round the perimeter of the dance floor looking for two empty chairs and had reached the comparatively inaccessible and deserted window side of the room.

"However, no more of that. Let us talk of something else. What do you do in the world?"

"Very little. For various reasons it's difficult for me to leave home."

"That's bad. The days when women stayed at home are over. For better or for worse. But over, I assure you. What are the reasons, or ought I not to ask?"

Griselda hesitated. But Lord Roller had achieved his position in the world by being under all circumstances unfailingly reassuring.

"My Mother, mainly."

"Illness?"

"Not exactly. Though she suffers a lot."

"I won't enquire further." Changing the subject, he said kindly, pointing out a well-known figure: "You know that's George Goss the painter?"

"Yes. He's staying in the house."

"I've known him since we were at Winchester together. Then he was a splendid young chap. Full of life. Quite irresistible. He did a drawing of me a year or two ago and I must say I thought he'd become something of an ox. When I saw the drawing I realized that he thought the same of me."

"You're not at all like him," said Griselda.

"Our lives have been different. Mine has been spent in the City, like the rest of my family. I haven't been able to let myself go in the way a great painter can. Despite appearances, I suspect I'm very much the man I was when I was at school. I observe that the Prime Minister hasn't been provided with a water bottle." He pointed to the bare green table at the end of the room. "That's bad. Later I'll have to see that something is done about it."

The Duchess passed dancing with Edwin. Seeing Lord Roller, she smiled radiantly; then, observing that he was in conversation with Griselda, smiled again, a little ruefully.

"I've been in love with Odile for twenty years," said Lord Roller. "To attempt concealment would be quite unavailing."

"You know you said you wouldn't enquire further?"

"Yes. I said that. Do you want me to enquire further? If so, I shall."

"Am I a pest? I should like advice."

"I know very little about the world outside business and politics. For that reason I should be honoured to advise you. I have all the confidence of ignorance. What is it about?"

It was the next dance and Griselda looked round for Kynaston, but there was no sign of him. She and Lord Roller went on talking.

"I have decided to leave home. My Mother will have to get on as best she can."

"I can see that this is an entirely new resolution. I hope it is not based on what I just said. You must not take an old man, ignorant of life, too literally."

"No, Lord Roller. It *is* a new resolution, but I made it before I met you. The question is what best to do afterwards."

"I hardly know you well enough to advise you upon that. In any case, it is the most useless thing it is possible to advise upon. If you have no clear and conscious vocation in life, I advise you to marry and have children as soon as possible. Of course, I speak as a bachelor."

"I want your advice on something much more definite. I have few claims to a job of any kind, and, of course, a job I must have. A friend of mine has offered me one in the Secretariat of Sociology. It sounds pretty dull, because all the good jobs go to people with degrees, and I have no degree; but I have to promise to stick to it for three years. I don't want to do that unless the result amounts to something, however small my contribution. I am sure you know all about the Secretariat of Sociology. Does it amount to anything?"

"To save a young woman from the Secretariat of Sociology," replied Lord Roller, "I would offer her a job myself. With all the new regulations the coalition will introduce, we shall be able to carry more passengers in the business. I quite understand that you wish not to be a passenger, but that is unusual, and you can take over the work of someone on our staff who does. If you care to write to me, I'll see what can be done. It will at least be somewhere near productive employment."

"But I have no capacity. I cannot even type."

"If typing is necessary and you do not learn to type within a month of our engaging you, we shall, of course, engage you no longer. You said you wanted to do work which amounted to something. That is the sort of obligation which work amounting to something involves."

Griselda said: "Naturally."

He rose.

"I have enjoyed our talk. Now I must see that the Prime Minister is given his water-bottle, because the speeches will be soon, I regret to say. Have you a partner for the next dance?"

It was Mr. Mackintosh's turn.

"Please do not wait, Lord Roller, if time is getting on. I'll find him myself."

"We may meet again."

"Thank you for your advice."

He bowed and departed. His gait was full of distinction, his expression of confidence. As he passed through the throng, he nodded affably from time to time.

There was still no sign of Mr. Mackintosh, and Griselda, feeling isolated, and still fearing George Goss, began, faute de mieux, to look round for Kynaston. Almost at once, she saw him. He was dancing with Pamela. Where previously Griselda had resented his attaching himself so calmly and firmly to her, she now resented his having anything to do with Pamela. In both cases resentment was only one of many feelings jumping about in Griselda's mind, most of them without rising to consciousness; and in both cases she felt that resentment was unreasonable.

Not wishing Kynaston, or Pamela either, to see her sitting by herself, she removed to a less conspicuous chair in the back row near a window. She recalled the term "wallflower" and wished someone nice would speak to her. She still thought her appearance compared favourably with the appearance of the other women present, but all her immediate neighbours were dull looking people seated in small groups, indifferent to the dancing, but talking among themselves, sometimes acrimoniously. Griselda desperately wished that Louise could be there.

She began to study the scene impersonally. Though there were some beautiful women and distinguished looking men, the majority impressed as rowdy but dreary. They had, of course, Griselda recalled, been largely assembled for political rather than social reasons. There had been no sign of Mr. Leech since the fun began and Mrs. Hatch had now also disappeared, after a sequence of strenuous dances, doubtless in order to settle final details of the feast of rhetoric which impended. Mr. Minnit, on the other hand, was dancing energetically with, as Griselda supposed, his wife. The Duke was now partnering the ravishing Lady Wolverhampton; and the Duchess one of the better dressed among the new Cabinet Ministers. In one corner there had been a minor disturbance for some time. Griselda had been only vaguely aware of the turmoil; now she perceived that it arose from attempts to prevent one of the splinter parties from posting propaganda bills on the ballroom wall. Mercifully George Goss was not to be seen. Possibly he was gone for a drink.

"Do you think it was wise of us to exclude the Communists?"

One of the group around Griselda had dried up conversationally and a member on the outskirts of it addressed her. He was elderly in the extreme and resembled a distinguished nonconformist dignitary.

Griselda considered the question.

"I don't see what else we could have done."

"I think our appeal should be to *all* groups in the nation: to forget the past and think only of the future." The speaker's voice and accents were great-grandpaternal. "I've always been a radical; and what are the Communists but today's radicals? I'd be a Communist myself if I were still a young man."

"Hardly Zec. Not with your collection of fine old stocks and shares," said a hard-faced woman in his group, almost Zec's contemporary.

"It's Travis Raunds who's responsible for their not being invited," Zec grumbled on. "The man's nothing but a despot. What do you think, young woman? Let us heed the voice of youth."

"I'd rather leave it," replied Griselda prudently, "to whoever issued the invitations. But tell me about Sir Travis Raunds. Is he here?"

"Over there," said Zec stabbing a desiccated forefinger towards the opposite side of the room. "The old deathshead to the right of the centre mirror. Most reactionary man in the country. I've fought him all my life and he's fought me."

"You flatter yourself," said the hard-faced woman.

Griselda stared at the man mentioned by Louise, father of Louise's friend, Hugo Raunds. Though obviously very old, Griselda found him the most striking-looking man in the room. He had a considerable quantity of white hair, fine aristocratic bones, and a yellowish skin. Despite his years, he sat very upright and his expression was that of a censorious Buddha. His long mouth had finely shaped lips, his nose was magnificently powerful, he was clean shaven, and his eyes, Griselda, whose sight was excellent, could see across the room, were a clear yellow.

"Is his son Hugo here too?" asked Griselda.

The effect was unexpected. Zec stared into Griselda's eyes, his own the colour of granite setts and as unyielding, then said: "Young woman, it is time you learned that to shock and insult your elders is never amusing."

"I'm sorry," said Griselda calmly. "Hugo Raunds is only a name to me. I know nothing whatever about him."

"I think," said the hard-faced woman, "that you'd be well advised to leave it at the apology." Clearly she supported Zec in aggression though in however little else.

Griselda was about to rise from her chair and walk away when she became aware of tapping on the high French window behind her.

"I *told* you Hugo was a very secret man," said the voice of Louise.

Griselda nearly fell off her chair with surprise.

The window had been opened and stood slightly ajar. Louise's pale face and large glasses were just visible through the gap.

"Have you got a partner?"

"No. I'm a wallflower."

"Come away."

Louise's hand entered through the gap, took Griselda by the wrist, and with unexpected strength drew her outside into the garden before she had time to consider. Louise shut the window and fastened it as easily as she had opened it. The two of them looked through the glass at the disgusted faces of Zec and his friends. A few of the other guests had noticed the brief draught; and it was clear that already, seconds later, they had forgotten it. Even Zec did not consider the incident worth rising from his seat to investigate.

"Louise, I'll be cold."

"I think not. If you are, there's a cloak."

"Where?"

"In the Temple of Venus."

"What's that?"

"One of the Duke of St. Helens's follies. We're going there." Indeed it was one of those precocious spring days which anticipate or excel Midsummer. There were stars and a moon. How very wrong Mullet had been!

Louise had changed into a simple but elegant black coat and skirt and a white silk shirt. The night was full of her perfume.

"You can see the Temple of Venus at the end of the vista. But the Water of Circe lies between us and it; so, as we have to go round it, the walk's longer than it looks."

"Circe lived on an island."

"There is an island. In the middle of the lake. It's where she's buried."

"Circe?"

"No. Not Circe."

"Stephanie?" Griselda almost whispered.

"Of course."

They set out. It was a broad grassy way, cut wonderfully short. In lines parallel with the grass were beds of flowers just coming into bloom, but drained of what colour was theirs by the moon.

"What about the dew?" Griselda's shoes were for dancing.

"There is no dew. That means it will probably rain tomorrow. We must make the most of tonight."

"Yes, you can smell in the flowers that rain's coming."

"This morning's rain also."

"It would be nice if it sometimes stayed fine for longer on end," said Griselda.

"Nice. But, like most nice things, probably unnatural," replied Louise. "What do you think of dancing?"

"I've never danced before tonight—or rather today."

"I know."

"Was it so obvious?"

"It came out. Never mind. How do you like it?"

"I think that much depends on one's partner."

"When does it not?"

They walked in silence the few more steps which brought them to the edge of the lake.

"Don't look back till we're round the other side and have the lake between us and the house," said Louise; and Griselda never thought of disobeying.

"Give me your hand," continued Louise. "The path round the lake is wooded and much rougher. There are roots." Griselda placed her warm right hand in Louise's chilly left one.

As soon as they had entered the trees the music from the house rapidly faded away.

"The path twists," said Griselda.

"The Duke did not intend the shortest way between two points."

"But the trees grow very regularly."

"They do not grow. They were planted. This is called the Grove of the Hamamelids because every tree bears a fruit."

Griselda did not know what Hamamelids were or had been, but the new blossom was ubiquitous, claiming alike the senses of sight, smell, hearing, and touch.

"It's an orchard."

"No, Griselda, it's a grove. It's believed to be the only grove of its kind anywhere."

After many swift sinuosities the path reached and crossed a wooden bridge in what appeared to be the Chinese style. The blossom, the moon, and the bridge compounded a scene very like to the Orient before one got there, thought Griselda.

"This is the stream which feeds the lake," said Louise.

"Where's the path?" asked Griselda, looking round. Beyond the bridge it appeared simply to stop, although hitherto it had been wide enough for the two of them abreast.

"The path ends here. After they crossed this bridge, the Duke and Stephanie had no need of it; nor were others desired to follow them."

Griselda and Louise found their way hand in hand among the trees along the edge of the lake until they rediscovered the vista.

"Now you can look back."

Across the water and up the other half of the vista the house, normally a trifle obvious in aspect, appeared unbelievably mysterious. The misty moonlight blurred all detail, but across the line of long lighted windows the keen eyes of Griselda could see the moving figures metamorphosed into beauty by night and distance. Looking at them as they danced, it was impossible to believe they were the people Griselda had just left. At that distance she could imagine herself longing to join them.

"If it were all like that," she said, "we would neither of us ever wish to leave."

Now they were out of the grove, the music just reached them.

Turning their backs on the sound and once more retreating from the populous house, they continued towards the Temple of Venus, now black before them at the other end of the vista.

"I want to see you again, Louise," said Griselda. "After I leave Beams."

"We will talk about that when we get to the Temple. It may not be possible, Griselda."

If there was any doubt, Griselda did not want to talk about it. She changed the subject.

"Do you often come to the Temple?"

"Only at night, when I can't be seen. I wear black and it is not difficult to remain unobserved."

"Did the Duke build the Temple for Stephanie?"

"Yes. She lived in the house, but she was happiest in the Temple. She was seldom happy, poor Stephanie."

"Like you, poor Louise."

"Like us, poor Griselda."

"I'm happy tonight."

Louise did not reply.

They walked the short distance remaining in silence.

At first sight in the darkness the Temple seemed to consist of a portico, surprisingly lofty, and with Ionic columns. Up three broad steps was a chamber open to the garden and appearing semi-circular in the moonlight.

"Before you enter," said Louise, stopping Griselda at the foot of the steps, "I think you had better put on this mask." She produced a black velvet domino from a pocket of her jacket. Griselda was about to demur or enquire further, but thought better of it, and consented without a word to Louise putting the mask round her eyes and tying it tightly at the back of her head. Louise knew how to do this so that the wearer had no uncomfortable sensation that the mask was about to slip.

"I like it," said Griselda; and immediately ascended the steps.

Inside, a seat ran the length of the curved back wall, broken only by a large door in the centre, which gave access to an inner apartment of the Temple. In the middle of the floor was a huge marble bench, wide and long, and curving up at both ends into Ionic flutings. On the Bench were a number of large cushions, looking darkly purple; over which was spread a huge black cloak.

"Put it on," said Louise. "Put it on and sit down."

Griselda again did as she was told. The cloak seemed the right length, and was a businesslike garment with simple black buttons, which Louise proceeded to fasten, shutting Griselda in.

Griselda realized that she was now nearly invisible. For no clear reason she felt a sudden palpitating rush of excitement, bereaving her of all reasonable thoughts.

"Now sit down."

Griselda's normally strong legs were weak and she was glad to obey. Louise sat at the other end of the bench, her beautiful neck whiter in the smoky moonlight than her white shirt.

"What about *you*?"

"*What* about me?" Louise's tone was warm but enigmatic.

"You'll be cold."

"Oh . . . No, I shan't be cold. But we'd better speak softly."

"Why?" This question Griselda knew to be absurd, but her excitement was such that she had no difficulty in restraining a wild hilarity.

"It's better." Louise paused, then again began to speak, very low. "I've kidnapped you and brought you here so that we can make some plans. It was necessary that we could be sure of being alone, and also this is the best place."

"The best place in which to plan?" enquired Griselda, equally softly. She had either to shout or to whisper. She felt she might easily faint.

"Yes, Griselda. If you wish to plan. I don't know whether you do or not. You said you did, but perhaps it was only the beauty of the night or a reaction from other people."

"Will it be difficult?" Griselda's voice was barely audible.

"It will be very difficult, Griselda. I love you."

Immediately Griselda felt completely calm; an entirely and absolutely different person. She would never be the same person again.

"I love you, Louise," she replied in a level voice, still pitched low.

After a moment's silence, Louise said, "It's a pity that the world instead of being at our feet, has to be about our ears."

Griselda replied: "As I said in my bath, I know very little about the world."

"That, though a good thing," said Louise, "is also a bad thing. It makes the next step difficult."

"No," said Griselda. "I think it makes the next step easy. I'm so innocent that whatever the next step is, I'll take it without a second thought."

"Will you live with me?"

"I've decided to leave home. Where else should I go?"

"We could share a loft."

"That would be rather expensive for us. I've very little money. At least until I get a job."

"What sort of job?"

"Lord Roller offered me something."

"Are you going to take it?"

"If it would enable us to share a loft."

Louise looked her in the face. Louise's smile was full of tears and anguish; she took Griselda's hand.

"The air is, I am sure, full of nightingales," she said, "if only we could hear them."

"This is their night," said Griselda. "Tomorrow it's going to rain."

"Does that stop them singing?"

"Unless they are very imprudent nightingales."

"I can't see your face," said Louise. "It is entirely overshadowed by a column."

"Of course you can't. Am I not totally invisible?"

Griselda thought that when she said this Louise looked round the Temple in a way more anxious than she cared for. Then Louise said: "For my part I have no money at all. And not only that but I hate work of any kind. I hate not to be free."

"I've never yet had a real job," replied Griselda. "I am not looking forward to that particular part of it at all."

"I wonder if Hugo would give us an allowance? He understands people like us."

But Griselda noticed something.

"Look Louise. That door's open. It was shut when we came in."

Louise started up. The black door interfered with the columnar pattern on the carpet of moonlight.

"And there's someone coming."

Louise's perfume was suddenly heavy on the air. Louise stood quite upright, her back to the garden and the moon, her eyes on the open door. There were undoubtedly footsteps.

But it became clear that the steps were outside the temple. A figure appeared between the columns.

"What's going on in there?"

It was a policeman. He flashed his lamp, ineffective in the moonlight, upon Griselda's dark figure.

Louise wheeled round.

"Officer," she said, "please return to your fireside. No one is in need of help."

"Sorry miss," the policeman replied. "I thought you might be reds."

"You can see at a glance," said Louise, "that we're not."

"Yes miss," said the policeman.

"I don't know so much," cried Griselda, rising to her feet. "Look at me." Cloaked and masked, she was the perfect operatic conspirator.

"I can see you're nothing you shouldn't be, miss," replied the officer. "Just like the lady said. Still we have to be careful. The whole house and garden's surrounded."

"Surrounded by what?" asked Griselda.

"By the force, miss. We have our orders. There've been half a dozen of us on duty all the evening not a quarter of a mile from this outhouse. Spread about of course. Well, I must be getting back to them. Good night, ladies."

At this moment the door of the inner apartment of the Temple banged shut as unaccountably as it had opened. The policeman jumped.

"I'd better have a look round." The beam of his lamp made a dim circle on the heavy painted woodwork of the door.

"There's no one there," said Louise. "It often happens."

"If you say so, miss—" He thought for a moment, then looked at Louise searchingly. "Quite sure, miss?"

"Quite sure, officer. I often come here at night." Her tone was unbelievably patrician.

"Very well."

Again he bade them Good-night. They reciprocated; and this time he departed.

"We must go back," said Louise. "Soon they'll be looking for you."

"Shall I leave my cloak?"

"No. When we reach the house I'll take it."

Silently they returned upon their tracks.

They were only a few paces from the shore of the lake.

Louise remarked, "I don't know how Stephanie is going to behave about this. She is, after all, a Belgian."

Griselda shivered inside her warm cloak, but said nothing. They entered the Grove of the Hamamelids.

"You know," said Louise after a while, "you know that Stephanie was at the Temple?"

"Yes," said Griselda. "I know."

"It was a mistake. I didn't expect her tonight. But I knew she was there even before we got there ourselves. Her scent is the same as mine. I fear she may go after revenge. Though that would be rather absurd of her."

"Revengeful people don't think of that."

"Poor Stephanie! But, after all, Griselda, she *is* only a ghost." Louise suddenly laughed very musically.

"I don't want at all to be gloomy, but do you think I shall be all right alone in the haunted room?"

Immediately she had spoken, she jumped violently. They had crossed the wooden bridge. The figure of a man was visible among the trees. His back was towards the two women and he appeared much occupied at some labour.

The women stopped for a moment; then Louise held Griselda's hand very tightly and they advanced together. Not until they were right up to the man, did he learn of their presence.

"Good evening, miss," he said, seeing Griselda's long cloak. "Didn't expect any of the guests to walk this far from the house." His voice was sombre.

"Good evening," said Griselda.

He was leaning on a spade. He was elderly and enormous.

"For her Highness's dog." He indicated a pit he had dug. "The best place for 'im on the 'ole property. And if you listen you can 'ear 'em knocking up the little chap's coffin."

Through the still moonlight night came indeed a very distant hammering.

"Poor little Fritzi," said Griselda. Louise was lurking indistinctly among the foliage.

"Dunno about that, miss," said the Gravedigger. "Reckon 'e

was ripe." Lifting his spade he plunged it up to the haft into the soft black earth. Though hideous, he was still hale in the extreme.

"Good night," said Griselda, who found the subject distasteful.

Louise drew further into the bushes.

"Goodnight, miss. I must get on with things." He was again digging rhythmically.

Louise rejoined Griselda as if she had been her shadow. The coffin makers appeared to be working somewhere in the Grove itself.

"The policeman began it," said Louise. "Now the whole garden is polluted. Let's get back as quickly as possible." She walked faster.

"But before they came," said Griselda, "we were happy." She remembered her unforgettable dream of the night before.

Worse was upon them. As they left the Grove they saw that the vista up to the house was spotted with guests. Several of the long windows had been thrown open. Through them came a certain sound, not of music Griselda realized. The speeches were afoot and most of the guests had left the ballroom. It was incredible that it was not later and the speeches over. But then she had no idea how long they had been continuing, despite Mrs. Hatch's injunction of brevity. After all, she recollected, it was a turning point in history, and enthusiasm might well have carried the orators much beyond the dictates of deference to their hostess.

A man in evening dress seemed in hopeful spirit to be approaching the two lone women.

"The cloak," said Louise brusquely. "I shall need it to get away in." Unbuttoning it, she had it off Griselda's and about her own shoulders before Griselda could utter the enquiry of all lovers.

"When shall I see you?"

The man in evening dress was near.

"I'll contrive. Bless you." On the words, Louise was gone. Her black figure flitted for a second in the moonlight and had vanished.

"Good evening," said the man. "You look very romantic. Can we go further away from the sound of the human voice?" He tried to take Griselda's arm.

"Thank you," said Griselda. "But I want to hear the speech."

"Then what are you doing out here?" Frustration made his tone didactic and patronizing.

"I felt faint and needed some air." No excuse could be too conventional for the commonplace creature.

"Minnit's hour-long pronouncement of his own righteousness had that effect upon many of us. His objective, you know, was to cut Leech out of his broadcasting time." Presumably the man now hoped to gain his end through general conversation. "Pretty low trick, don't you think? Or are you perchance one of Minnit's supporters?" He smiled; and his tone again reminded Griselda of Stephenson's remark that foremost in the character of every man is the schoolmaster.

"No," said Griselda. "I have no politics. Will you please excuse me? I must go back to the house."

He was so startled by the failure of his charms that, writing Griselda off as in some way peculiar, he did not even propose to escort her. Griselda could not feel that his observations boded well for the new coalition government. But possibly he was unrepresentative. Soon she would see. She crept in at the window through which she had joined Louise in the garden.

The scene was transformed. Most of the gilt chairs were ranged in irregular rows across the dance floor in front of the speakers' platform. Though by no means all the chairs were occupied, many of the remaining audience were drooping packed together on their feet behind the backmost row. The emptiness of the chairs and the crowd standing behind them combined to make an effect of desolation. Many of the women looked bored. Many of the men looked aggressive. It was plain why Mrs. Hatch had demanded brevity. Amplifiers had been lowered from the ceiling and every now and then emitted a resonant croak as the technicians dismantled the broadcasting apparatus, the end of the time allotted to the feature being long past. Each time the amplifiers croaked, Mr. Leech stopped short in his flow of words and glowered momentarily upwards before resuming. Often this resulted in his losing the place in his notes.

Even without foreknowledge, it would have been obvious that the Prime Minister had been speaking for some time. His sparse colourless hair stood straight on end, his face was the colour of cheese, and he was thumping continuously when he had a hand free, in the effort to awake from slumber the long defunct interest of his auditory. "Time presses," he cried, "and the festivities offered by our splendid hostess will soon once more be calling us. We have already addressed you for far too long." Mr. Leech, while one eye roamed from table-top to audience, glared momentarily with the other at Mr. Minnit, who sat slumped forward upon the green baize, his head upon his arms. As with Lady Macbeth, it was impossible to deduce from Mr. Minnit's eyes whether he slept or waked. He was, Griselda realized, a man of very unusual appearance. "But," continued Mr. Leech, "it would be improper indeed were I, for any reason whatever, to bring these remarks to an end before coming to the dire and daunting circumstances which have prompted me to begin them." This time Mr. Leech did not thump, but it made little difference.

"I have spoken," he continued, "of our great traditions, our unique heritage, of literature, art, and science, of our public school system, our mercantile genius, our sportsmanship, our village hostelries, our ancient monuments, Magna Carta, the noble City of London, the late terrible world conflict, our aircraft and balloons, our love of animals, and the faith we repose in our young folk. Shining through and igniting the whole splendidly coloured picture is one theme peculiar to our people alone: the theme of initial failure transmuted into ultimate success, immediate disaster into final victory." There was an unexpected burst of cheering. Not even the prevailing need for food could wholly deaden so conditioned a reflex.

"And what has been the philosopher's stone which has wrought the miracle? Always it has been one thing only: our readiness for sacrifice." Some of the older people nodded their agreement. "I venture to say before you all, that no other people has so often had demanded of it so many sacrifices. As page follows page of history we read the same story: the story of final ruin averted by ruinous sacrifice. And on too many of those pages we see that the writing was in sacrificial blood. Tonight it may appear that the need is less: not for blood, but for toil and taxes and toil again, to rebuild the sinews of greatness."

But, if so, it appeared wrongly. For when Mr. Leech came to

these words, there was a flash and a detonation; and the ballroom momentarily took on the aspect of a battlefield. The Communists had contrived to throw a bomb.

A group of about a dozen classless figures had appeared from nowhere, screaming slogans and distributing leaflets. One of them even had a banner, bearing a highly coloured portrait of Engels on one side, and a quotation in German on the other (the article having been salvaged from a sympathetic foreign organization recently dissolved by the authorities).

Griselda, whose first political meeting this was, looked around terrified. Fortunately, however, there appeared to have been no loss of life, or even major injury, and what blood the historian could have drawn upon, had come mainly from noses. There was, however, a terrible smell of poor quality chemicals and burnt cardboard. The victims of the outrage were setting themselves and their chairs upon their feet, adjusting their garments and calling for redress. Those who had not been bowled over, were even more belligerent, having more available energy.

Immediately a flood of policemen armed with batons poured through the french windows, and made a series of arrests. The Communists were borne off into the scented night, twisting and biting. One of them had been standing close to Griselda, screeching out vilifications, his face that of a modern gargoyle. In the rough and tumble with the police he was knocked out and dragged from the ballroom by the legs.

"Ladies and gentlemen. Supper is served."

Mrs. Hatch had resumed control. Griselda was startled by the volume of the cadaverous Brundrit's voice, as he stood at the other side of the ballroom, just inside the door from the passage.

For the most part, the guests pulled themselves together smartly, and another long queue began to form. The Communists had provided everyone with something to talk about. A small group, however, remained round the platform, and between the heads Griselda could see that both Mr. Leech and Mr. Minnit lay recumbent in their chairs. Recalling for the second time during the visit her slight knowledge of first-aid, she was about to go forward and offer assistance, when a handsome figure detached itself from the group and approached. It was Edwin.

"How entirely that mask becomes you."

Griselda had forgotten. She groped at the knot behind her head.

"No. Don't take it off. Unless, of course, you wish; in which case you must allow me to assist."

"Clearly it is no disguise."

"Were you seeking to escape supper?"

Griselda remembered. It was appalling.

"I went out in the garden. I am dreadfully rude."

"Not at all. The speeches, you know, were to have been *after* supper. The broadcasting arrangements were responsible for the change. It's late, but at least we've now nothing to do but enjoy ourselves." He offered Griselda his arm. They moved towards the tail of the queue.

"What about poor Mr. Leech?" Edwin's lack of concern seemed inconsistent with his usual attitude to Cabinet Ministers.

"He'll be better soon. One becomes used to these things in politics."

"I didn't know that."

"They're all to the good really. They bring the sediment to the surface so that it can be skimmed off instead of seeping all through society."

"How did they get in?"

"In the B.B.C. van. This is going to take a long time." The queue was advancing at a pace so irksome to the ravening guests that, here and there, some of them had to recall to others the conventions of behaviour. "If you'll excuse me for just a single minute, I'll see if something can be done."

With a precise movement Edwin replaced Griselda's arm by her side, then disappeared out of the ballroom and into the passage, leaving her alone in the queue. Shortly afterwards he returned.

"I've made arrangements."

Ignoring the queue, he took Griselda into a little book-lined study, where the Duke and Duchess, together with a group of elegant people Griselda had not met, were eating and drinking in privacy. Everybody was speaking German, in which language Edwin immediately gave every appearance of being word-perfect, though Griselda could not be sure. He conversed animatedly with her, every now and then throwing out a remark in German to the others; and looked after her needs with delightful punctiliousness. She was introduced to the strangers, who made her welcome in broken English, and complimented her upon her mask. The Duchess, radiant in her tight dress, kept a kindly eye upon her welfare. Though Griselda understood little of the general conversation (Edwin was discussing the year's books with her), the atmosphere was friendly and delightful. Griselda had become very hungry in the night air. She ate happily, and drank luxuriously from a glass with a hollow stem.

Suddenly the Duchess cried out in her attractive voice, "Shall we have a game?" She had been speaking German so much as a German does, and now spoke English so much as does an Englishwoman long married to a foreigner and resident abroad, that Griselda was at a loss to decide her nationality, whether English, German, or Ruritanian.

Conversation ceased and there were guttural cries of assent. They all seated themselves round a large polished table and the Duchess explained to Griselda the rules of an extremely simple card game. They began to play. The game was neither dependant on chance nor exigent of skill: it demanded a degree of intelligence which Griselda, in the circumstances, found perfectly appropriate and delightful. The language difficulty seemed strangely to vanish once they were all immersed, giving Griselda a dreamy illusion of brilliant communicativeness. Small sums of money continually passed, the women every now and then turning out their gay evening handbags for change. Edwin continued to ply Griselda with champagne, nor were the other players backward in drinking. From time to time Griselda wondered what was becoming of the dance, but decided that if the others were unconcerned, she would be unconcerned also. It had been obvious that the main business of the evening was over by the time she had left the ballroom.

No one had interrupted them, but, at the end of a round, suddenly one of the men, a fair youth, resembling Lohengrin, said something in German, and, rising, locked the door. Several of the women (whose ages were unusually disparate), thereupon embarked on motions apparently preliminary to removing their clothes.

Griselda was a little drunk, but not too drunk to observe that her new friends seemed unanimously to turn to some new pursuit upon a word from one of them.

The women were wearing little and the present process could not last long. Almost before it started, however, the Duchess realized that Griselda, as a stranger among them and of a different nation from the majority, might wish to leave. Probably the young man, in making his proposal, had forgotten about her. But at a word, he unlocked the door, they all ceremoniously bade her Good-night, and Edwin escorted her into the hall. The door shut behind them.

Outside the little room it was cool and quiet. Griselda found that all the other guests had apparently departed.

"I expect," said Edwin, "that you must be ready for bed. Or can I do anything further?"

"Nothing, thank you," said Griselda, drowsy with drink. "You have been really very kind to me. I enjoyed the Duchess's card game."

"I think the others have gone up already." Edwin and Griselda were drifting towards the staircase.

"I am sure they have. Good night. And thank you again."

"Good night, Griselda." It was obvious that, in the most considerate possible way, he wished to be rid of her. She ascended.

Even at this distance the air was loaded with the smell of the banked carnations in the ballroom. It had long since overpowered the smell of cordite.

CHAPTER XI

Griselda did not again see or hear of Louise until the following evening. It was a desert of time; and a desert with few oases. However, she had happy thoughts and bright, vague prospects: things often preferable to the presence of the being who inspires them.

Back in her room she felt tired and contented, though her mask would not slip over the top of her head and the untying

of the knot proved tedious. In the end, however, the labour was
accomplished and the velvet strip lay on the dressing-table before
her, loading the air with the smell of Louise. Griselda sat resting
her arms, looking at the mask, and thinking. How and when, she
wondered, would the late guests return to their homes? How had
Edwin, although still quite young, achieved welcome ingress into
every single one of the world's innumerable diverse sodalities?
Was Mr. Leech alive or dead? What would become of her and
Louise, once they had left Beams? Louise's scent wafted strongly
to her brain: more strongly than the faint vapours from the mask
could account for. Either it was Stephanie; or it was Griselda's first
experience of a lover's hallucination of the sense of smell. The
memory of her ecstacy in the garden swept even fear from her.

She put the mask in a drawer and soon she was in bed. Immediately she slept. There was no other sign of Stephanie; and the
room and the night were quiet. Griselda dreamed of a posse of
policemen dancing rapturously with the late guests.

In the morning it was again raining. In the muddy light water
slapped against the glass of the windows in frequent protracted
spasms. Griselda looked at the wrist-watch on the table beside
her bed. Despite appearances, it was half-past nine. There was no
evidence that she had been called, but clearly it was time to rise.
She lay for a moment remembering her happiness. She saw that
there was a puddle on the carpet. The rain had been entering for
hours through the window she had carefully opened the night
before.

She shut the window and dressed. She put on the clothes in
which she had arrived, because she imagined that Louise would
prefer them to the only other day clothes she had, those she had
worn the day before. The silk blouse and linen skirt, though white
and black respectively, which Griselda was sure would be taken
as progress in the right direction, were far from warm. It was
remarkable that such a morning could follow such a night. But
the weather would surely deter Mrs. Hatch from the proposed
walk of which Griselda retained an indistinct though menacing
recollection. Griselda decided to put appearance before comfort
for as long as the circulation of her blood permitted. She was sure
that Louise would approve of this.

Exactly as on the previous morning, Mrs. Hatch was seated at the breakfast table alone. She wore the same grey sweater. She was talking in an unusually low voice to Brundrit and Monk, both of whom were stooping towards her, one on each side of her chair.

"Excellent," said Mrs. Hatch, as Griselda entered. "You're first again. Sit down and take some eggs." She went on murmuring to her retainers. Griselda could catch only parts of sentences and thought it would be impolite to occupy her former breakfast seat next to her hostess. Taking two eggs, she proceeded towards the other end of the table.

The conference ended with the retainers straightening up and walking away, one on each side of the long table, looking remarkably gloomy, which came easily to Brundrit, but to Monk only with effort.

"Whatever happens," called Mrs. Hatch in her usual clear tones, "I cannot be kept hanging about in the house after half-past-eleven. Everybody concerned must clearly realize that this is Sunday." It was a fact Griselda had forgotten. Tomorrow she was to return.

"I perfectly understand, madam," said Brundrit, in his reverberating croak. "We shall see to it that everyone is apprised."

"Do," said Mrs. Hatch. They departed. The room, for the first time in Griselda's experience, was without a domestic to assist with the eating.

"Good morning, Griselda," continued Mrs. Hatch. "I should have said that before. Please forgive me and have some cocoa."

"Good morning, Mrs. Hatch."

"You are somewhat distant."

Griselda started; then realized that the allusion was spatial.

"Shall I move?"

"I think that would be better. Come and sit next to me, as you did yesterday, and tell me what you thought about the dance. Politics apart, I fancy everything went like a circus, do not you?" Griselda was transporting two eggs, one of them opened and liquid, a plate bearing a slice of bread and butter, and a heavy bowl of cocoa. Before she had time effectively to reply Mrs. Hatch continued: "You're not very appropriately dressed. The clothes you were wearing yesterday would have been more suitable. You don't mind my speaking practically? Your Mother wouldn't be pleased with me if you were to go home with a streaming cold after our walk."

Griselda looked at the windows. A curtain of water cataracted down the glass, completely isolating the room from the grey world outside.

"Are we walking in weather like this?"

Seated next to her hostess, Griselda saw that today Mrs. Hatch was wearing a pair of waterproof trousers from Burberry's and knew that the game was up.

"You won't take any harm if you wrap up, and if you've never walked in the rain you should take this opportunity of making a start. It's enjoyable. But naturally you must not come if you would prefer not to." Mrs. Hatch said this perfectly kindly, and without any intent to shame; and Griselda responded accordingly. She never had walked in the rain except reluctantly, uncomfortably, and under the stress of need; but at Beams she had already liked a number of things which she had not thought to like or had never liked before.

"I'll come if I can borrow some suitable clothes. When do we start?"

"I usually start at half-past ten. But today we're burying Odile's dog first. I've just been settling the arrangements with Brundrit and Monk. I don't think we'll get away much before an hour after the proper time. Still we must think of Odile's feelings. We don't usually call our guests on Sunday. As I'm not prepared to stay at home and entertain them, I think it's only fair to let them sleep if they can. But today everyone's coming to the ceremony. Except, unfortunately, Austin Barnes, who has been really not at all himself after last night's incident. I have reluctantly come to the conclusion that Austin is no longer the man he was. It's a pity, because otherwise he'd be coming with us. Many's the hard tramp I've taken with Austin Barnes during the last thirty years. I cannot believe he'll be much further use to the country if he's really leaving me to go alone." Mrs. Hatch seemed genuinely upset by the Cabinet Minister's defection.

"I expect he's run down," said Griselda sympathetically. "Perhaps he's been in office too long."

"I'm very fond of Austin," replied Mrs. Hatch after a moment's thought, and gulping a draught of cocoa. "I've always been his inspiration, I believe; and through him I've inspired the course of events from time to time. Otherwise I prefer the company of women, in the main. They both feel more and have more common sense. So you gain both ways."

Yet again Griselda felt herself blushing; this time darkly and hatefully.

"Though it's rarely enough I find myself having anything much in common with anybody. Another egg?"

"No thank you. I've had enough." But suddenly Mrs. Hatch's character had been enlightened to Griselda, far beyond anything Mrs. Hatch had actually said; and Griselda, to her surprise, did not dislike what she saw. It had been the same with some others at Beams, she realized. The dreadfulness of people was possibly a product not only of their isolation, but also of their community and likeness to one another. Griselda, while pitying and even liking Mrs. Hatch, felt curiously superior to her.

No one else appeared for breakfast.

"I'll lend you a waterproof. A proper one," said Mrs. Hatch, as she wiped her mouth. "I'll send Mullet. The funeral's arranged for eleven. In the shrubbery down by the large pond. Among the fruit trees. You'd better meet me in the hall, and we'll go together."

It was sad to miss a possible chance of seeing Louise. But in a short time Mullet appeared in Griselda's room with an enormous mackintosh and a pair of dark brown boots lacing to the knee.

"Mrs. Hatch says will you try these for size."

Griselda inserted her feet.

"Mrs. Hatch keeps all sizes for her Sunday walkers. But she's good at guessing people's feet."

"They fit perfectly."

"Will I help you lace them?"

"I'll be lacing all day if you don't."

The boots were wonderfully warm. They supported Griselda's calves in a manner which was new and unbelievably comfortable. She donned the vast mackintosh and drew the hood over her head.

Mrs. Hatch awaited her in the hall, wearing a tunic and beret matching her trousers. Most of the other guests were also assembled, unbreakfasted and varyingly ill-prepared against the climate. George Goss, who apparently had a really dangerous hangover, wore a shaggy dingy ulster, the bottom edge of which varied greatly in its distance from the ground. Pamela wore an allegedly protective garment more calculated to seduce the eye than to resist the rainfall. Even Mr. Leech was there, looking little worse than usual. There was a group of servants attired like refugees, and no more enlivened by the project before them than anybody else. Only the Duke and Duchess were missing.

"Shall I go up and offer a word of encouragement?" asked Edwin.

But as he spoke the bereaved couple appeared at the head of the staircase, contained in elegant waterproofs of Continental cut. The Duchess wore a small black velvet hat with a large black feather, a purple silk mackintosh and black Russian boots. A veil was drawn tightly across her face and knotted behind her head. Through it her features appeared completely white and her eyes very large. Altogether she looked most striking. Griselda recalled her very different aspect on the last occasion she had seen her. Clearly the Duchess responded with a whole heart to all life's different occasions, however contrarily they might succeed one another. The Duke carried a cherrywood box under his left arm, presumably containing the deceased.

"It will be a shorter walk in the rain for those of us who dislike getting wet, if we go through the ballroom," said Mrs. Hatch in a loud firm voice before the Duke and Duchess had reached the bottom of the staircase. Possibly she wished to save her guests from having to grope for further unconvincing commiserations. She began to marshall the cortège.

"Griselda and I will lead the way. Edwin and Pamela had better come next. Then will you, Mr. Leech, follow with George? Then Gottfried and Odile. The rest of you can follow after. Would you like Monk to carry Fritzi?"

"Thank you, Melanie. He is light as feathers."

"Very well. Then I think we had better go at once."

They set off down the passage to the ballroom, their mackintoshes rustling in the silence, otherwise broken only by George Goss's heavy breathing. Griselda noticed that the Prime Minister was carrying a club-like walking stick. In the ballroom, which now looked depressing in the extreme, the Duchess, who was bearing up wonderfully, broke step and, crossing to the platform occupied the night before by the band, bore back a vast armful of carnations, not as fresh as they had been but still far from dead, which she proceeded to carry in the little procession like a prima donna, her head sunk among the petals. Mrs. Hatch had opened one of the french windows, and the party entered the garden.

It was indeed a dispiriting day: one on which it was equally difficult to believe that things had ever been otherwise or that they would ever be otherwise again. The party advanced up the soaking wet lawn and entered the group of trees. Griselda was surprised that the distance was not greater before they reached a large hole, surrounded with adhesive black earth rapidly turning to mud, beside which stood her elderly gravedigger of the night before, leaning on his enormous spade.

"Is everything prepared, Hammersmith?" enquired Mrs. Hatch.

"Ready it is, mum," replied Hammersmith. "Ready since midnight it's been. Ready and waitin' for yer."

"Never mind about that now. Though it's always best to do things in good time, of course." She addressed the others. "There's going to be a short ceremony. Will you all please gather round the grave? You too, Hammersmith. Don't you go."

Griselda, encased against the elements, glanced round her fellow guests. Pamela's teeth were chattering rather audibly. George Goss, who had augmented his horrible ulster with an antique cloth cap, resembled a dyspeptic bison. Mr. Leech wore an expression of extreme resignation. Edwin looked as if his mind were on other things. Mrs. Hatch, impervious to the rain and efficient as ever, looked trim and attractive by contrast with the rest. The aspect of the Duke and Duchess, as chief mourners, was such as to touch the heart of any statue. The aspect of Hammersmith, his vast muscles outlined by his soaking shirt, his redbrown eyes glaring at the coffin, was likely to unman any young woman less resolute than Griselda in her new boots.

"Proceed," said Mrs. Hatch. Griselda, whose Mother went regularly to church, gravely doubted the canonicity of the whole affair.

The Duke pulled his wide-brimmed homburg hat further over his eyes and made a short speech. On his wife's behalf he thanked them all for their attendance and even for their existence. When setting out for a weekend of joy with a lady beloved by all of them, their dear Melanie, they were unlikely to have foreseen an occasion to tragic as the present, and made so much worse by the weather. (At this point Mr. Leech was seized with a spasm of sneezing, which continued to the end of the Duke's remarks. He sneezed inefficiently; giving on each occasion the effect of unsuccessfully attempted suppression leading to rising inner dementia.) Though only a dog the one they mourned was as dear to those who loved him as any prodigal son. He had been with them eleven years and now he was gone away. (Here Griselda heard the terrifying Hammersmith vigorously expectorate.) Where he had gone or whether dogs had souls like the rest of them, it was useless to speculate. In gratitude to them all for their sympathy, however, in particular to their dear Melanie for her gift of so sentimental a resting place, he had prepared a poem, such being the custom of his country, which he would like to read to them. He had to apologize for the poem being in German, but his Muse, not very ready even in her native tongue, was dumb in another. He hoped that most of them would have enough German at least to follow the general theme; and that the rest would appreciate that he was speaking from the heart. Here was the poem.

The Duke produced a fair-sized wad of paper from the pocket of his waterproof, and, at a sign from Mrs. Hatch, Monk raised an umbrella. Pamela, who disliked poetry, had seated herself upon a wheelbarrow, where she rocked backwards and forwards quietly moaning. George Goss simply walked off towards the house. Shortly they all heard him being sick among the bushes. The Duke took a step forward as from a line of Imperial Guards; Monk followed him with the umbrella; and the Duke began. Fortunately Mr. Leech had stopped sneezing, though he was beginning to look very wet.

Before the poem was far advanced, indeed during the first five minutes, the Duchess was weeping fluently; and by the time the final antistrophe was due, she was in an appalling state of dampness, though Griselda had been offering what comfort she could. Edwin, who clearly appreciated every word and nuance of the poem, listened throughout alertly, like one assessing its merits in a competition. Mrs. Hatch stood as to the National Anthem. The Duke read remarkably well, in full and expressive accents of passion and woe. Griselda wondered whether he too had been trained by Moissi. At the end there was an extremely long silence, though Pamela could be heard grunting miserably in the rear. The heavy rain was making the vapours rise from the newly strewn manure.

Now it was time for the committal. The Duke clicked his heels and passed the coffin to Edwin, who, his features distraught with fellow feeling, transferred it to Hammersmith. The hole was very much too big (it was impossible to resist the idea that Hammersmith had postulated some larger occupant); and had been filling for hours with surface water. Before Mrs. Hatch could stop him, however, Hammersmith had hurled the coffin into the grave, splashing and muddying the mourners from their hats to their shoes; and had raised his left arm, bare from the bole-like-elbow, towards the sky in a cosmic Niebelungenliedlike gesture. Instantly there was a thunderous salute, as a maroon, released at the signal by the garden boy (hidden behind some laurels for the purpose), tore apart the hopeless clouds until it vanished into the empyrean. Hammersmith's face, neck, and shirt had been plastered with yellow subsoil from the grave, making him look more primeval than ever; but as Griselda averted her eyes, she saw that Mr. Leech had fainted. He was not so used to loud bangs as Edwin the night before had implied.

They returned to the house: Edwin carrying Pamela in his arms; and Mrs. Hatch and the Duke bearing Mr. Leech (fortunately a lightweight) between them, as Mrs. Hatch considered that Hammersmith had better fill in the vast grave before someone fell into it and damaged himself. The Duchess, distinctly more buoyant now that all was over, scattered the carnations in a wide circle round Fritzi's resting place; to which Hammersmith returned a grimly abrupt acknowledgement, his rufous eyes rolling, his ropey muscles extending and contracting all over him as he shovelled.

"Now that little Fritzi has been laid to rest, can we not once more be gay?" enquired the Duchess in her curious interglossal accent. It was nearly 11.30. Edwin had carried Pamela upstairs; and Mr. Leech, his sensibilities revived by Monk, sat quietly in a corner drinking, at his own request, a tumbler of warm water laced with a dessertspoonful of brandy.

Mrs. Hatch was seen to hesitate.

"I usually tramp until dusk," she said. "But today for your sake, Odile, I shall make an exception. I shall return for a late luncheon, if all of you are prepared to wait, and after luncheon we'll play games. If that is agreed, perhaps, Odile, you'd be so good as to order luncheon for 2.15. Mr. Leech had better only have arrowroot. Come, Griselda; let us return to our elements."

Though Mrs. Hatch walked very fast, Griselda, used to long lonely walks almost since childhood (for conditions at home had tended both to drive her afield and to compel her to solitude), was perfectly able to keep pace with her. Mrs. Hatch, moreover, had been right about walking in the rain. A proper costume made all the difference (just as Louise had said). Whatever else Griselda thought of her hostess, she would always owe to her the introduction to a new pleasure, which was more than was usually owed to anyone. As they walk through the lanes (some of them in process of development into the avenues of a new housing estate), Mrs. Hatch cross-examined Griselda about her life and Griselda schemed to find out more about Mrs. Hatch. Neither was particularly successful, but each returned home with increased respect for the other, and a glow of joyous struggle. Griselda re-entered the house warm and dry, hungry and happy; also muddy to the tops of her boots, and healthy to the roots of her hair. She felt equal to anything: to Louise's love; or, contrariwise, even to an afternoon of organized playfulness.

On the doorstep they met George Goss, still wearing his horrid blanket and untidy bonnet, but green as a chameleon on a faded billiard-table.

"I say, Melanie, will there be a chemist in Hodley who's open on Sunday?"

Mrs. Hatch, pushing out health and unbuttoning her tunic, took in the seedy figure of her distinguished guest.

"Nonsense, George, you don't want a chemist. Six or seven mugs of cold water will flush you much more cleanly. Besides how are you going to reach Hodley? If you walk it, you won't need any other remedy."

George Goss shuddered all over. Then he said, "I was going in Leech's car."

"I didn't know that Leech was leaving us?"

"Cabinet Meeting or something. As if I care. But his car's due any minute." He spoke quasi-sotto-voce.

Lurking about the hall were four strange doughty-looking men in ready-made tweeds. Mr. Leech, wearing an overcoat and hat of the type favoured by important public figures, was seated on a hard chair in their midst, his official despatch-case, his botanical vade-mecum, and a large Gladstone bag on the floor at his feet. As Mrs. Hatch entered, he rose and came towards her, looking his most imposing.

"It is as Mr. Goss says, Mrs. Hatch. My hand is immediately and unexpectedly needed on the rudder of state. Now that we are subject to a Coalition, such sudden calls must, I daresay, be expected of us all."

"Who are these men?" asked Mrs. Hatch in a loud undertone.

"A foolish precaution deemed necessary by our new Home Secretary," replied Mr. Leech. "One of Minnit's people, as you will recall. For my own part I should not only have preferred to take my chance, but should have insisted upon doing so. But it is necessary to tread softly in these early days, so I have subdued my natural inclinations." None the less, Griselda thought, the Prime Minister appeared distinctly to have gathered confidence from some source or other.

"What about lunch before you go? Your arrowroot? After your misadventure, it would hardly be prudent to travel under-fed."

"Thank you, Brundrit was good enough to lay me out some brawn," replied the Prime Minister a little stiffly, "and I helped

myself to a couple of Abernethy biscuits. I am too old a campaigner, you know, to require more."

A large black car had driven up outside. It was visible through
the open front door. A footman dismounted and stood in the
doorway holding a camel-hair rug. Griselda noticed that he carried two pistols in holsters attached to his belt. The pistols were
large and old-fashioned, and made him look like a pirate.

"I'm sorry you have to leave so suddenly," said Mrs. Hatch,
"but Griselda and I will see you off. As for you, George, you'd
better go and lie down."

"Lying down only makes me vomit," said George. "I'd have
you know I've a headache."

"Griselda knows about those things and may be able to help
you," said Mrs. Hatch. "All in good time. Do you think you have
everything, Mr. Leech?"

Griselda liked as little as ever the look on George Goss's face;
and she turned to bid the Prime Minister adieu. Mr. Leech had
made for the door with an unusually determined step, almost
amounting, indeed, to a stride. In many ways he seemed a
changed man. His henchmen had taken up positions from which
the entire scene could instantly be raked with gun-fire.

"Good-bye," said Mr. Leech, smiling gravely. "And thank you.
I know nowhere which offers such peace as the rose garden at
Beams."

"My roses are sensible of your devotion, Mr. Leech." At this
point Griselda noticed the barrel of a musket projecting from the
rear window of the Daimler.

"It is ever and again to the ample silent things of life that we
return for renewal," continued Mr. Leech, his eye searching the
watery clouds from under the brim of his important-looking hat.
"But too soon we are recalled by the reveille of duty." A few big
drops of rain fell from his hat on to the astrakhan of his lapels.

"Too soon, indeed," replied Mrs. Hatch. She began to rebut-
ton her tunic. There seemed no knowing how long this might
continue.

Griselda realized that she had greatly grown since she had first
set eyes on Mr. Leech two days before.

"Good-bye," said Mr. Leech again, suddenly pulling himself

together and smartly returning the chauffeur's salute. "Good-bye, Miss de Reptonville." Griselda remembered that success in public life is dependant upon remembering people's names.

"Good-bye, Mr. Leech."

The Prime Minister set aside the proffered camel-hair rug.

"Thank you, no. Not on this occasion." The atmosphere was heavy with the crisis and the coalition as well as with the damp.

Mr. Leech took his place beside the musket; the footman beside the driver. There was a moment's uncertain silence as the four bodyguards whispered among themselves, in the manner of Becket's murderers. Then one of them without a word opened the car door and, seating himself next to Mr. Leech, manned the lethal object. He fiddled about with the mechanism like a wood-wind player tuning his instrument. The weapon still pointed directly at Griselda.

In the moment the car started Mrs. Hatch cried out, "What shall I do about Austin Barnes?"

It was no good. Already the Prime Minister's eyelids were drooping into slumber. Mr. Leech had been having a strenuous time of it.

"It's all very well, but what *am* I to do about Austin?" Mrs. Hatch seemed seriously to be seeking Griselda's advice.

"Everything's in order, Mrs. Hatch," said Edwin's voice in the doorway. "I deeply regret to say that Austin Barnes has felt it his duty to offer the Prime Minister his resignation." The moist air wafted the distinctive perfume of Pamela, heavy on Edwin's black suit, the very essence of fashionable mourning.

"Resigned?" It was a cry from Mrs. Hatch's heart.

"Quite resigned."

"I must go to him."

"I think that would be best. The Prime Minister asked me to tell you after he had gone; and to apologize on his behalf for his inability to tell you himself. He was sure you would understand that the emotion involved was too much for him at the present time."

Without a word, Mrs. Hatch had re-entered the house.

"Permit me to escort you." Edwin, who had not risked getting wet a second time in the same morning, also disappeared into

the gloom within. The three surviving murderers had previously
likewise vanished, their grim countenances set for food from
Mrs. Hatch's groaning granaries.

Griselda was left by herself waiting for luncheon in the rain
she had learnt to love. Before going in, she put back her hood and
raised her face towards the discouraging heavens. She was startled to see the head and shoulders of Louise projecting from an
upstairs window. She was wearing a perfectly white mackintosh.
There was no knowing how long she had been there. She threw
Griselda a kiss with one hand and a letter with the other. Then
she withdrew indoors, shutting the sash window with a marked
slam.

Overwhelmed, Griselda looked at the letter. On a thick sheet
of deckle-edged hand-made writing paper, it had been folded and
sealed, in the fashion of the days before Sir Rowland Hill, with a
big medallion of bright yellow wax. It was superscribed simply
"Griselda" in black ink and a large well-proportioned hand artistically simplified. Letting the heavy rain uncurl her hair, Griselda
split the seal and unfolded the letter. In such a hand there was not
room for many words upon a single side of a sheet of handmade
paper.

"Never forget, dear dove, that the sky into which you soar is
full of falcons and that falcons fly higher than doves. As I listen,
your heart is softening towards the falcons. Beware of the falcons!
They not only kill: they disfigure. Their nests are matted with
blood. The streets and fields are filled with bodies whose vitals
the falcons have eaten. The falcons eat only the hearts, the brains,
and the livers of their prey; whom, bored, they then return, like
bottles, Empty. The Empties clutter our lives: they break easily,
and becoming worthless become also dangerous."

The letter ended with a single tender sentence which made
Griselda very happy. Though dated it was unsigned. Raindrops,
like tears, were beginning to spoil it. Griselda put it into a pocket
of her borrowed mackintosh.

"We are waiting."

Mrs. Hatch had reappeared in the doorway. Some time must
have passed, for she had changed into a skirt. Griselda, though
extremely hungry after her walk, had forgotten about luncheon.

There was no knowing how long Mrs. Hatch had been standing there.

"I'm so sorry. You've taught me to enjoy rain. I've been enjoying it."

She thought that Mrs. Hatch's expression was equivocal and, for some reason, not very likeable.

"You need to take proper precautions." Griselda raised her hand to her head and realized that her hair had become very wet. "If you don't mind us starting to eat without you, I think you'd better go upstairs and dry yourself."

Griselda entered the house. She opened the collar of her mackintosh. "How is Mr. Barnes?"

Mrs. Hatch glanced at her sharply. "I'm finished with Austin Barnes." Something was obviously wrong with her: and presumably this was it.

Griselda wondered what to say.

"One of your oldest friends? Surely not?"

"Old and new, the world's much of a piece," replied Mrs. Hatch with intense bitterness. She turned from Griselda and entered the dining-room.

Upstairs, Griselda removed the heavy mackintosh and suspended it in the bathroom to drip and dry. After hours of it, she felt so underclad without it that she more clearly understood how little related to any consideration of utility is the quantity of clothes people wear. She towelled her short curly hair into a bewitching disarray. She put on a red pullover. She would have liked to remove her boots, but time pressed.

She descended to an extremely late luncheon. From inside George Goss's bedroom came an intermittent soft mooing as of a cow in her last labour before retirement from maternity. Griselda realized that her period of communion with the rainfall had among other things spared her from having to hold George Goss's sick head and necessary basin.

The party for luncheon was indeed depleted, in spirit more than in number. George Goss and Mr. Leech were absent; and Pamela should have been, for she had contrived to contract a most unpleasant cold. Despite this malady and the inappropriate weather, she had refused in any way to wrap up, but sat sniffing and sneezing in a delicate eau-de-nil crepe-de-chine blouse, sleeveless and conspicuously open at the throat. It was noticeable that Mrs. Hatch had apparently now washed her hands of all responsibility for Pamela's welfare and happiness. Even Edwin had seated himself as far as possible from the source of infection, where he was discoursing, as Griselda entered, upon the subject of the main item in the next St. James's News-Letter.

"We all found ourselves in complete agreement," said Edwin, "that an attempt must be made—on a world scale, needless to say—to vitalize the inner life of the working man. Happily the means came at once to hand. That very same evening I spoke of the need to the wife of a certain Polish Prince, a woman having great wealth of her own—invested outside Poland, of course: who at once suggested that the answer was a film, but of an entirely new type, not a specifically religious film, you understand, but a film aiming in the same general direction though stated in contemporary terms, a film that would really penetrate through the top-dressing of propaganda and take root in the wholesome soil beneath."

"So to speak, a non-religious religious film?" suggested the Duchess helpfully.

Mrs. Hatch, Griselda noticed, was really looking very sour indeed: almost baleful.

"You might, I suppose, put it like that," said Edwin rather doubtfully. "At least in sophisticated society such as this. Anyway, the Princess (I am sorry I cannot tell you her name, but she particularly wishes to remain entirely nameless in this matter, which she conceives in the light of a high spiritual duty), the Princess is not only prepared to arrange finance for the whole project, but actually has access to an entirely suitable director for the film, a man who treats the cinema almost as if it were a true medium for art. The Princess has assisted in the birth of many of his past productions, and has often been very close to him in a number of different ways. She told me that the two of them together could do things that neither of them could do apart. It is true that the man's a Galician Jew, but the Princess says he has more of the real thing in him than any other Christian she's ever met. And, after all, it's her money," concluded Edwin, descending to the world of fact.

The trouble was that no one seemed sufficiently interested, though the Duke and Duchess followed up politely.

"Who is he?" enquired Pamela, the resonating chambers of her (never very resonant) voice clotted with mucus.

"I beg your pardon?" enquired Edwin courteously.

"The director. What's his name? Or is that a whimsey little secret too?" Pamela was unused to not being answered first time.

"The director's name is not actually a secret, but I doubt whether any of you would know it."

"Thought he was world famous," persisted Pamela spitefully. Probably she had by now something against Edwin. She added with unwelcome acumen: "How's he to reach the masses now if he hasn't done it already?"

"I don't think I actually described him as world-famous: only in certain informed circles." It was the first time Griselda had ever seen Edwin reduced to the defensive. His entire narrative, moreover, seemed to her less impressive than some of its glittering predecessors.

"I see," said Pamela, "high hat. Tell your Princess she'd do better with Punch and Judy. More to remould society, I mean, if that's the idea, as you say it is." Pamela seemed to doubt whether it was the idea. She tried to sniff, but her nose was so blocked that she failed to do so, which was much more distressing than even success would have been. The zymosis which choked her tubes seemed, none the less, somehow to have cleared her brain. She applied a minute hard ball of a handkerchief and began with the other hand to release drops from a bottle of bitters on to her pancake.

Griselda noticed that Mrs. Hatch was barely even eating.

Real trouble broke out only when Brundrit brought in a large dish of medlars.

The trouble was that no one seemed to want medlars: no one except perhaps Mrs. Hatch, and even she, like most people in such cases, seemed more concerned that the others should like medlars than happy that she liked them herself. She implied, with the faintest undertone of pugnacity, that these particular medlars had been preserved in exactly the recommended state of decomposition since the previous autumn, an undertaking involving much skill and difficulty, of which the present company were privileged to enjoy the benefit.

To begin with, the Duke and Duchess did not know what medlars were, and fogged themselves worse and worse with obscure Germanic polysyllables, cooing together like puzzled budgerigars. Then Edwin seemed afraid that the deliquescent fibres would damage his suit. And Griselda had experienced medlars in the past.

Pamela merely said, "They look rotten."

The Duke, speaking German, made some reference to their smell.

"Not rotten at all," said Mrs. Hatch. "The fruit is in the finest possible condition for eating. It is properly bletted."

"What is bletted, Melanie?" asked the Duchess.

"Medlars cannot be eaten, Odile, until they mature. Then they are the most delicious of all fruit. Try one and see for yourself."

The Duke and Duchess took one medlar each.

"Griselda?"

"No thank you."

"Don't be narrow. Have you any first-hand experience of medlars?" This question clearly, in the grammarians' phrase, expected the answer No.

"Yes. I'm afraid I don't like them."

"Then you're a silly girl. Pamela."

"I'm only allowed to eat food which is perfectly fresh."

"What about you, Edwin? You may use the table implements if you wish to preserve your appearance."

"Please excuse me on this occasion, Mrs. Hatch. I always lunch very lightly, you know. Usually only a single quail brought to my office from the Express Dairy or somewhere like that." Edwin had begun to doubt whether the proposed film would regenerate the proletariat after all. This made even so perfectly balanced a man as Edwin a little standoffish. Perceiving the fact, Griselda wanted to restore his confidence, as he was so much more agreeable when confident.

But before she could think of anything to say, the Duke and Duchess had begun to misbehave. The rearrangement of the table consequent upon the departure of Mr. Leech, the absence

of George Goss, and the reluctance of Edwin to risk contracting a nasty cold, had brought the Duke and Duchess against all
custom to adjoining seats; and the difficulty they had experienced
in identifying the strange foodstuff in the Duke's language, had
amplified into intermittent and giggling exchanges of pleasant-
ries in German. Suddenly the Duke said something very quickly
to his wife under his breath; and the two of them burst into explo-
sions of unsuitable mirth. They tilted back their chairs, roared at
the ceiling, nudged one another, and gasped out confirmations of
the joke which were strangled by new attacks of laughter beyond
all control. It was plain what they thought of medlars, even when
properly bletted.

Mrs. Hatch said nothing at all, but piled up a heap of medlars
on her plate, and began to devour them displaying much more
appetite than earlier in the meal, and sucking rather noisily.

The Duke and Duchess went on laughing in an uncontrolled
Germanic way. At first they were oblivious of their isolation;
then suddenly they became over-sensitive to it and began long-
windedly to apologize. The single medlars, still almost intact,
were evidence of their good intentions.

"It was something of which Gottfried said they reminded
him," concluded the Duchess not very happily; especially as they
then began both to laugh again.

"I was spending a night once inside the Great Pyramid,"
began Edwin. He had overheard and understood the Duke's
simile and was fearful of its disclosure. "We had nothing to eat
but dates. Not the artificially nurtured Tunis dates we buy in
boxes, but the real native dates, small and packed into blocks and
not very clean. The dogs, you know. Not to mention the heat and
the native children. We had a little camel's milk too in a gourd. It
would have been most unwise to introduce any Western food,
as we were entirely in the power of the group we had gone to
meet."

"Was it a pleasant meeting?" asked Griselda.

"Very profitable indeed. It enabled me precisely to foretell the
date of the rebuilding of the Temple."

"Which Temple?"

"The Temple of Jerusalem. As you probably know, I adhere to

British-Israel. It is to my mind the only conceivable explanation of modern British history. We are mere tools."

"Shall I serve coffee, madam?" asked Monk. Mrs. Hatch who was still silently assimilating the putrescent-looking heap, merely nodded.

Griselda tried to talk intelligently about the Glastonbury Thorn and to discuss the question of whether or not the Prophet Jeremiah was buried on an island off the coast of Scotland, only to be reborn as General Booth; but it was difficult going. Edwin, naturally, was eager and convincing, politely countering possible objections and clarifying dark places; but the Duke and Duchess had sunk into a state of guilty abashment, quite unlike their usual mood, and sat drinking cup after cup of café au lait and wringing their hands under the tablecloth; while Mrs. Hatch continued simply to sulk. She had been so agreeable on and before their walk that Griselda was unable fully to understand what was the matter with her, though Austin Barnes, shaker of nations and breaker of lives, almost certainly had something to do with it, she supposed.

Ultimately the house party fell to pieces like the ten little nigger boys. Two were already missing. Then, as Edwin was explaining the mystical status of the Union Jack, Pamela abruptly remarked that her Father always insisted upon her going straight home when she was ill, and proceeded upstairs to pack, Mrs. Hatch offering singularly little resistance. Five minutes later, by which time Edwin had arrived at the Biblical appointment of the site of Balmoral Castle, the Duchess, with exquisite anguish, observed that if there were to be no games in which all of them could join, she and Gottfried would like to retire for their usual afternoon rest, and departed easing the belt of her dress (she was a little flushed) and followed by her husband hard on her heels. Again Mrs. Hatch stonily acquiesced, and sat glaring at the épergne. Suddenly Edwin stopped in the middle of sentence and, exclaiming "The Aga Khan. I must, if you will forgive me," hastened away. "I wonder if the lines to that part of India are busy at this hour?" he enquired absently as he carefully closed the door.

Left alone with Griselda, Mrs. Hatch was clearly about to say something of the utmost significance. Her mien was almost frightening with import. But Monk entered and asked if he could clear; and once more Mrs. Hatch wearily acquiesced.

"Shall Stainer serve tea, ma'am? It's the usual time."

"Do you want any tea, Griselda?"

"Yes, please," said Griselda stoutly. "If I could first remove your boots."

"Remove what you like," said Mrs. Hatch; then, addressing Monk, added "Tea for Miss de Reptonville. And I suppose we may have visitors. Tea for five or six. Nothing for me."

Griselda began to realize that few things are so important in any kind of shared life as the moods of the person it is shared with. Mrs. Hatch was being quite unlike herself. Griselda recalled Louise's words about the difficulty of living with anyone, and that even Louise had shown signs of a moodiness which would doubtless wax on longer and less desperate acquaintanceship.

To judge by her past experience, she suspected that so many medlars had made matters worse by giving Mrs. Hatch colic.

It took Griselda twenty minutes to remove the boots, and to oil and part her hair; and when she again descended it was to find that Mrs. Hatch's single visitor that Sunday had arrived, a certain Mrs. Cramp, the wife of a neighbouring landowner. It was still raining hard.

"Bitches," cried out Mrs. Cramp in a loud harsh voice like a police whistle, "have two or three times the staying power of dogs. If not more."

A fire had been lighted and the scene offered all the cosiness of an English country house at Sunday tea time; though none of the other guests seemed eager to partake. Griselda soon learnt that Pamela had already left without saying Goodbye to anyone, even to her hostess. In the end, however, George Goss clumped down the stairs.

"Think I've thrown up the worst by now, Melanie," he announced. But he seemed too dispirited even to pester Griselda. He sat by himself crumbling a lump of the famous cake and casting round the furniture for the alcoholic provision normally made for him.

"Melanie," he said at last. "Could I have a drink?"

This time Mrs. Hatch did not even answer; and George Goss

continued to sit feebly opening and closing his fingers, like a frustrated crustacean.

Nor did Edwin fare better. When he reappeared from the telephone room (it had been converted from its previous function of downstairs lavatory), Griselda was startled to notice that his face was pale and his hair almost dishevelled round the ears. Manifestly he was using all his worldly knowledge and resource to conceal that anything was wrong. He accepted tea and cake; but every now and then Griselda heard him whispering to himself between mouthfuls. The words sounded like "It can't be. It can't be." The crisis came quite suddenly: Edwin sat up straight in his chair, and, returning his cup, from which he had been drinking, to his saucer, cried out: "The Pope must intervene." After that he seemed to recover rapidly, and to return to his normal, exceptionally well-adjusted frame of mind; but not before Mrs. Hatch had said in the rudest possible way, "Edwin Polegate-Hampden, you bore me." It was proof how hard to disturb was Edwin's fundamental equilibrium that he was able to smile and reply, "The ex-Empress used to say exactly the same." Edwin then munched briskly and began to draft a long sequence of telegrams for Monk to spell out as best he could to a country telephone operator on a Sunday evening. Mrs. Hatch even seemed almost to demur at Monk being given this employment.

Dinner was worse. The Duke and Duchess made a belated reappearance, the Duchess, evening dress being inconsistent with the Sabbath, in a short gown of olive-coloured satin, rather more shiny than would have best suited any other wearer but exactly right for her; and Edwin seemed entirely restored to cheerfulness by the knowledge that Monk was still faithfully at work on his behalf and on behalf of enduring humanity. But George Goss was still rather ill, and also empty, as the rattlings and roarings of his intestines bore witness whenever conviviality ebbed, which was frequently. For Mrs. Hatch's mien had by now become such as almost to cancel all faintest prospect of the jovial. Griselda sincerely wondered what could be the matter with her.

It was unfortunate that none of the company, pleasant people though they all were, really appealed to Griselda as a sympathetic conversationalist. After all, it was her last evening as a guest at

Beams. Did most house parties deflate in this way? she wondered. She tried to place in her mind the exact time when the gaiety had been at its height, the social balloon most stuffed with gas. She was unable to settle this time. She could only think of Louise, who seemed in no way whatever a part of her surroundings. This, however Griselda reflected, was probably wrong: one had to put up with George Goss belching and with hours of wasted living if one was to have any hope of minutes with such as Louise.

"The thing I can least abide in life," announced Mrs. Hatch, apropos of some behind-the-scenes domesticity, "is deceit. Did you know, Stainer, that my grandfather in Greece once strangled with his own hands a servant who deceived him?"

"No, mum," said Stainer, shaking all over, and beginning to snivel.

"It was only a small matter. It was the principle my grandfather cared about. And I feel precisely the same as my grandfather. Do you understand what I say?"

Stainer was now speechless.

"Answer me, please. Do you understand?"

"Yes, mum." The words were hardly audible in the unpleasant hush that had fallen upon all present. Griselda reflected upon the fact that, unlike most domestic servants she had encountered, Stainer seemed to contemplate neither cheeking Mrs. Hatch nor leaving her employ.

"Then you will never attempt to deceive me again?"

"No, mum."

"Very well then. Serve the ortolans."

Griselda thought not of ortolans, but of falcons: of a sky full of falcons and herself a dove amongst them. She was frightened.

Their spirits temporarily broken, the Duchess did not suggest games, nor Edwin bridge. Instead, Mrs. Hatch, apologizing perfunctorily to her guests and referring them to their own devices, ordered Monk, by now as one shellshocked with telephoning, to bring her the big ledger, and settled down to an evening of entering up accounts, which she did with no small dexterity. The full deployment of her powers required concentration, however; and it was soon to be made clear to the luckless company that the continuum was readily disturbed. Edwin who would probably have liked to attempt flirtation with Griselda, or something tending in the same direction with the Duchess, was reduced to drafting a study for "The Times Literary Supplement" to be entitled "A Case for Holy Living." The Ellensteins and Griselda felt remarkably bored, and began, in their different ways, to think of bed, although it was not yet half-past nine.

Suddenly George Goss roared out "In Christ's name, Melanie, what's the matter with you?" Griselda realized that he was crazed from lack of liquor.

Mrs. Hatch who was adding an entire long column, made a small tight gesture of exasperation, utterly murderous, but said or did nothing further. George Goss began to stagger away, questing for a drink, a lion at last.

The Duke and Duchess excused themselves. Mrs. Hatch could not have seemed more indifferent. They ascended the staircase, a little shakily, Griselda thought. Nerviness riddled the entire community. Then Griselda decided to snap the link herself. After all, she had Sir Osbert Sitwell's "Winters of Content" to read; and her bedroom was just the place for such a book.

"If you can spare me, Mrs. Hatch, I think I'll go to bed too. Our walk must have tired me." This last statement was untrue, but something of the kind seemed to be required.

Mrs. Hatch was glaring at an invoice, seeking to pluck out the heart of its mystery. She said nothing.

"Well—Good night."

Mrs. Hatch still did not look up, but she said "Good night." Her tone baffled Griselda completely. It was certainly not noticeably pleasant. Griselda could not recall her Mother, or any of her Mother's circle, behaving like this in the capacity of hostess. But her Mother was limited, and her circle small. Nine-thirty struck in the hall as Griselda entered her room, leaving Mrs. Hatch in malign solitude with her sums. It was raining harder than ever.

CHAPTER XII

The room was filled not with damp night, but with Louise's perfume.

Griselda softly cried out, "Louise!"

Then again she recalled that the perfume was Stephanie's also. But as apparently only Louise could see and converse with Stephanie, it was difficult to know what to do, except be frightened once more. More than ever, Griselda wanted Louise to be with her. But she had no idea where Louise was.

Griselda tentatively removed her wrist watch and laid it on the dressing table. A gust of wind, weighted with rain, so jarred the window that Griselda thought she would investigate. There was nothing to be done about that either: though the water was seeping into the room at many points between the well-made sashes and frames, and though it would clearly be a troubled night for any sleeper not enamoured of a storm. Fortunately, Griselda was not such a sleeper. She was simply a sleeper not enamoured of a ghost.

For when she returned to the dressing table, though her back had been turned upon it for only seconds, a strange object had appeared, and lay beside her familiar efficient wrist watch. It was a tiny knife: almost a dagger; conceivably a stiletto. The silvery blade, as if daily used and polished for generations, reflected a great bar of light across the ceiling. The ivory hilt was inlaid with purple amethyst, spiralling round it like the pattern on a Byzantine column. From butt to tip the knife was about five inches long. Griselda picked it up and tried the blade. The two edges were so sharp that it was difficult not to cut off at least a finger. They converged to a tip like the sting of a glittering insect.

Again there was a disturbance at the window. Such noises were likely to continue throughout the night, and Griselda took no notice, but went on staring at the knife. But the disturbance took on definition. It seemed to be rapping and crying. Someone appeared to be seeking entrance through Griselda's first floor window.

Supposing that it might be Stephanie, Griselda felt utterly appalled. But the noises continued; and, as when a bird enters one's bedroom, it was impossible indefinitely to ignore them. In the end, Griselda took the little knife, crossed the room, and once more drew back the curtain. Crouched on the sill outside was indisputably a figure. After a moment's terror, Griselda realized that it was Louise. She opened the window.

"What's that you've got?"

"I thought *you* might know. I found it on the dressing-table. It seemed to appear when my back was turned."

Cascades of water were pouring through the open window, soaking everything. Louise's white mackintosh was the colour of clay; her long hair bedraggled like a corpse's.

She stood sniffing the charged air. "I wonder if it's a good sign or a bad one. Revenge or rescue. Pity it's so hard to know."

Griselda shut the window, becoming seriously wet in the process. She redrew the curtains and stood in the centre of the room.

"I'm so very glad to see you, Louise. On my last night."

"Did you think I wouldn't come?"

Griselda gently shook her head.

"Even if I had to swim the Hellespont like Leander visiting Hero."

"Dear Leander." Griselda put down the little knife. "As you've been so long in the sea, you'd better take off your wet clothes."

Louise began to remove her soaking mackintosh. She was wearing trousers like Mrs. Hatch's.

"Are you locked out?"

"No. I've been waiting in the Pavilion for your light to appear. I didn't want us to waste time and the house is swarming, which makes communication difficult. Everyone seems to have gone to bed very early tonight."

"Mrs. Hatch is doing sums, and didn't want us. You're soaked. Undress. I'll lend you some clothes."

Louise undressed. It took only a minute.

"Which clothes would you like? Which of my poor silly garments?"

Louise smiled. Then she crossed to the bed and put on Griselda's pyjamas, laid out by Mullet.

As Louise put on Griselda's pyjama's, a great wave of feeling swept through Griselda like a wall of flame. She was unable to doubt that this was passion. It left her muddled and stupid.

Louise sat down and dried her glasses on one of Griselda's handkerchiefs. Then she untied her hair and began to rub it. Seated in Griselda's pyjama's, and rubbing her long thick hair, she looked very beautiful.

"May I stay?" she asked, smiling like a representation of the Madonna, really the painter's mistress.

Griselda had herself begun to undress, but slowly. "Of course," she said. "But there is one thing . . . dear Leander. Mrs. Hatch said something at breakfast. . . ."

"This is true love, my Hero," replied Louise, rubbing her hair energetically. "Love is only possible where there is like feeling. Sometimes that can be found in a body which is unlike: more usually it cannot. Love without like feeling is something best left to little Fritzi. Do I make things reasonably clear to you?"

"Perfectly clear, darling. Not that it was really necessary."

"Then I may stay?"

Griselda shivered. "If you don't mind the haunted room." It was growing seriously cold; and she began to hasten the day's last rites.

"Really and truly I don't mind anything now."

The clock in the hall below struck ten. Louise was scenting herself with Griselda's scent, which made her smell very strange.

CHAPTER XIII

The clock in the hall below struck six.

Griselda, happier than she had ever been or would ever be again, heard it strike. Shortly afterwards there ensued, and quickly terminated, a train of events which she never in her life wholly understood; never, so to speak, got to the bottom of. Actual enquiry or close investigation were, in the nature of things, forever debarred to her. Later on in life she concluded that this applied to most mysteries she really cared about. This particular train of events took place, moreover, largely in silence, at least as far as concerned human utterance; and the crucial events largely in darkness also, as the bedroom curtains were still drawn, it was not yet fully daylight, and no one turned on the electric light until the crucial events were over.

There were steps outside, the bedroom door opened, and someone entered with a firm step in the uncertain light. Louise who was still asleep, was dragged from bed on to the floor, then hauled along the floor towards the door; all by the person with the firm step. On the way to the door, Louise, however, sufficiently realized the position to tear herself loose. There was a scuffle in the vicinity of the dressing table and a sharp groaning cry. Griselda guessed that one of the combatants had got hold of the dangerous little knife. At the cry a second intruder entered the room; and the two of them succeeded in dragging Louise away, still struggling valiantly but in utter silence. Griselda could hear the contest continuing down the passage outside. There was a lapse of time before courage enough came to enable her to leave the warm bed for the cold world, especially as, having brought only a single pair of pyjamas to Beams, she was naked. She put on her dressing-gown and went, trembling, to the open door. Outside all was now unexpectedly and frighteningly quiet. But suddenly the figure of Mrs. Hatch, in trousers and her usual heavy grey sweater, loomed up and came towards her.

"Get yourself dressed and packed immediately," said Mrs. Hatch in a voice of matter-of-fact command. "You will leave the house within half an hour: before anyone else is up. Maghull is already waiting with the car to take you to the station. When you have joined the train, he will drive to your Mother with a letter I have written her. She will have had time to read the letter carefully and, if necessary, repeatedly, before you arrive. I am sorry I cannot offer you breakfast, but the kitchen staff will not be down before you go. Hurry: or you will have to leave as you are."

She walked away.

It never occurred to Griselda not to do what Mrs. Hatch had ordered. She shut the door, turned on the light, and groped into her garments. Shaking all over, she packed. She packed Louise's letter. She noticed Louise's glasses, still on the bedside table. She wondered what had become of the little knife, and even perfunctorily searched for it. It was missing. Griselda recollected that she did not even known upon whom it had inflicted hurt. Whether the knife was meant to revenge or to rescue, remained unknown.

When, carrying her suitcase, she descended the familiar staircase to the hall, she saw that the front door stood open, the car waited outside, and that discoloured daylight was creeping into and around the house like mist. There was no sign of Mrs. Hatch, or of anyone else other than Maghull on his box; but upon the hall table the large ledger lay open, the final balance, reached at no one could tell what small hour, ruled off and repeatedly underlined in gay scarlet ink. Entering the lavish vehicle, Griselda noticed that Maghull's left hand was largely concealed by a newly tied bandage.

In the car Griselda wondered whether it would help Louise if she were to go to the Police. But she was not even sure whether her love for Louise might not be taken as an offence against the law. Griselda, in fact, felt at the moment too scared and ill to do anything effective. She began to weep, her tears spreading across the soft blue upholstery. She had to be assisted by Maghull into the railway compartment. He had the grip of a fanatic. No one asked to inspect the return half of her ticket.

It was only in the train that she clearly realized, in a series of horrifying shocks of perception, that neither she nor Louise had any means whatever of making contact with the other. Later it occurred to her that much trouble might have been saved, indeed two hearts from breaking and two lives from ruin, had either she or Louise thought to lock the bedroom door.

PART TWO

CHAPTER XIV

But it was useless to continue weeping after the train had passed
Clapham Junction. Not only was the compartment now filled
with early wage-earners, looking pugnacious and embittered
at their unjust destinies (one of them, a middle-aged woman,
shapeless and sagging with repeated mismanaged maternity,
stood for much of the journey upon the toe of one of Griselda's
shoes); but it had become clear to Griselda that a broken heart
does not annihilate routine necessities, but merely makes them
considerably more difficult to contend with.

Griselda's Mother being the woman she was, it was now out of
the question to return home, especially considering the trouble
which had attended Griselda's last year at school. This circumstance gave Griselda a marked feeling of relief. It was no comfort
at all for having lost Louise that she was also rid of her Mother;
but her new freedom from her Mother comforted her for much
else. As the train passed Queen's Road station, Griselda disen-
tangled her left arm, opened the purse in her handbag, and was
surprised to count three pounds, fourteen shillings, and sevenpence. Her Mother had made provision for her to tip: and she had
not tipped. She had not even tipped Maghull. On the other hand,
the clothes in her suitcase were appallingly inadequate as equipment for life: that is to say for what her Mother's brother, Uncle
Bear (his first name was Pelham, but he had never lived down a
hit he once made in a school play), for what Uncle Bear termed
"real life." On the other hand again, it was spring, and summer
stretched ahead, warm and endless.

By the time the train had passed Vauxhall and had settled
down for the wait common to all trains entering Waterloo, a
brief spell enabling the traveller the better to meet the massed

claims of the terminus, Griselda had resolved firstly to seek out
the Great Exhibition Hotel and secondly to seek out Lord Roller.
The Great Exhibition Hotel had been strongly recommended to
her by a schoolfriend who had the habit of spending odd nights in
Town. Lord Roller had offered employment.

At the other side of the compartment, four labourers, their
clothes smeared with yesterday's earth, were playing a simple
form of nap, easing the run of the cards with monosyllabic ob-
scenities. The train jerked into motion: as it racketed across the
barricade of points, every second, it seemed, about to be derailed,
the regular passengers rose to their feet and pressed towards the
doors, hypnotized by routine into an appearance of striving to
meet life halfway. Before the train had stopped, they were leaping
on to the platform and running towards the sliding iron gates.
The ticket collector had difficulty in controlling them. Until one
looked again at their faces, it was for all the world as if they had an
incentive in their existences.

Griselda, to whom the morning rush hour was a new experience, remained seated for a moment, fighting back the instinct
to run with the herd. Then she drew down her suitcase from the
rack and stepped from the train to find the platform deserted, and
the ticket collector, a few seconds ago flustered and perspiring
under the stampede, now irate and resentful of her dilatoriness.

"Come along there. You'll be late for work."

Having delivered up her ticket, Griselda sent her Mother a
telegram from the station telegraph office.

"Taking job in London please don't worry get better quickly
much love Griselda."

It seemed to be in the tradition of messages sent on these occasions, though it was Griselda's first of the kind.

She knew her Underground, and proceeded to South Kensing-
ton, changing at Charing Cross. Each train was again abominably
crowded; and the only excuse for a crowd, collective conviviality,
conspicuously absent. At every station men and women fought
in the doors and on the platforms. Between stations they joylessly
read newspapers. The whole grim business was utterly orderly.

The Great Exhibition Hotel proved larger than Griselda had
expected, and distinctly more pretentious. She booked a room

for a week, thereby (after some firm bargaining) incurring a liability of three pounds ten shillings, supposing she passed seven days without eating. A porter in his shirtsleeves took her in a tiny, slow lift to the fifth floor and to 79A.

"They knocked 79 in half," he explained, hanging about for recognition. Griselda gave him sixpence: which he regarded with a look which meant that women were all the same. The process of adaptation had proved fatal to the proportions; but the room was not exactly dirty, but offered a good view in the direction of Earl's, possibly even Baron's Court, the busy Inner Circle railway being in the foreground. The furniture was bright yellow but capacious. The bed bore a far-flung counterpane, hand-wrought in patterns of sheep-coloured wool, entirely different on the two faces. It was unbelievably heavy, the labour, obviously of years; superfluous labour Griselda thought. Beneath it was a flat and slithery eiderdown, covered in livid patchwork; and no fewer than four good blankets, tightly wrapped in on each side. Griselda deduced that many elderly ladies spent the evening of their days looking out towards the ghosts of old Earl's Court and its Great Wheel from the casements of the Great Exhibition Hotel: possibly, as they gazed, they matted coverlets heavy as lead sheeting, sewed gaudy scrap to gaudy scrap.

As in a royal palace, the water closet was of the gracious valve type. Small trays sprinkled with small breakfasts, were beginning to fidget towards the bedrooms as Griselda descended. In the Lounge sprawled several residents of a different type: one of them even whistled through his front teeth as Griselda passed. It was hard to believe that these residents needed bedrooms of their own: they seemed to live in the Lounge talking shop; and when they needed a bedroom, to have recourse, inevitably, to someone else's.

Griselda had noticed a Tariff in the Hotel which stated "Breakfast 3/6. With Meat 5/6. Preserves Extra"; and set out to look for a teashop. She found one open, and breakfasted excellently for one shilling and sevenpence plus twopence gratuity (forbidden but extracted). She then found that she lacked twopence with which to telephone Lord Roller, and had to return to the cash desk a suppliant. A further sixpence having been reluctantly converted into four pennies and four halfpennies (it was clear from her manner that the harridan in the little box lost hopelessly on the transaction), Griselda realized that she did not know the name of Lord Roller's firm. Nor was Lord Roller himself in the Telephone Directory, even at a private residence.

At a loss, Griselda peered through the glass of the telephone cabinet. The morning rush was over; the crowds had vanished into air. There were much refuse, two dogs, an ineffective cleaner, and a belated young man with a bowler hat and umbrella, obviously bound for the City.

"Excuse me," cried Griselda, breaking out from her place of confinement. "Could you very kindly tell me where I might find Lord Roller?"

The young man immediately stood quite still, staring round him, and blushing almost purple. "I—don't—know," he said after a long pause, forcing out the words through lips shuddering with embarrassment. "Sorry." He lifted his hat, looked at his wrist watch, and hastened on towards his world of familiar things.

The cleaner was also standing immobile, regarding. Suddenly she spoke: "You try Arkwright and Silverstein. That's where you'll find 'is lordship, dear. Arkwright and Silverstein. London Stone double two double two. You try and you'll find 'im."

"Thank you very much," said Griselda.

"Don't forget to remember me to 'is lordship." She gave a gurgling laugh and began to clatter furiously with her bucket. This made telephoning difficult, but Griselda did not care to complain.

Lord Roller had not yet arrived, but his secretary, on learning that Griselda had met him at the All Party Dance, made an appointment for her at ten forty-five.

"Ask for Miss Guthers," said the secretary.

The Inner Circle, which bore Griselda back to Charing Cross and then on to the Mansion House, was now almost deserted. Apart from a small intrusion of foreign tourists at Victoria, the clanking train had become a very fair place for hearkening to the inner voice. Griselda's inner voice remarked to her that she was wrongly dressed for seeking a job.

This contention received support when Griselda encountered Miss Guthers. Miss Guthers was dressed expensively and fashion-

ably, though she did not look expensive or fashionable owing
to years of overwork and the effort to control cheeky and lazy
subordinates upon always just too little authority for the purpose. She regarded Griselda kindly, and seated her in a minute
mahogany waiting-room like a large coffin, lined entirely with
bound volumes of "The Merchant Banker". A small table bore a
single newspaper, a copy of "The Times". Griselda opened it and
read the principle headline: "Aftermath Of The Roller Report".
She looked at the first leading article: "The Roller Report: What
Next?" She turned to the Court News: "Reception for Lord
Roller" (provided two nights previously, she read, by Edwin's dazzling friend, Lady Wolverhampton). The paper contained only
one photograph: a special study by a staff photographer of the
typical English village of Lydiard Bust, with an entirely new crop
of oats filling up the foreground, and much of the background
also. Griselda began to read Mr. Morgan's glittering comments
on last night's play.

"Lord Roller will see you now." Miss Guthers almost conveyed
concern that the interview should go well. There is no one it
is easier to like than a first class woman private secretary; and
Griselda liked Miss Guthers.

Lord Roller, however, wore an expression of extreme gravity.
He rose as Griselda entered, and personally offered her a mahogany chair.

"I must tell you quite frankly, Miss de Reptonville," he said,
"that I did not expect to see you quite so soon. That, none the
less, would have been entirely in order, and I should have been
pleased to assist you in your project of leaving the Secretariat of
Sociology. But under the circumstances which now obtain, you
will, I am sure, understand that any help from me is out of the
question. Please do not hesitate to smoke." He extended an open
cigarette case: it was made of gold and was one of a consignment
sent out the previous year as Christmas presents by the Ministry
of Mines.

"Thank you, Lord Roller," replied Griselda, "but I don't
smoke."

"An excellent thing. I wish my position allowed me to follow
your example." He sat back watching her; his fine head reflected

in the many photographs above the fireplace of past Permanent Secretaries to the Treasury, all of them signed, and many with warm words of greeting added.

"I have not actually got a job in the Secretariat of Sociology. I've merely been offered one. You very kindly advised me against taking it and said that you might be able to offer me something—something better, I think—yourself."

"I recall our conversation perfectly, I assure you, Miss de Reptonville. A good memory is unfortunately required by the nature of my work. I say 'unfortunately', because it is seldom that I have anything to remember which is so agreeable as was our little talk."

"That is charming of you, but I understood you to say just now that you were unable to help me? I gathered that you must have found me a pest, after all."

"Not in the least, Miss de Reptonville. I found you a most engaging young woman. I still find you a most engaging young woman." Lord Roller rotated his swivel chair and took a large cigar from a silver box on a table behind him. "Nor must you suppose, not for one moment, that I am passing any kind of judgment whatever. Not in the very least: I know much too little of the world to attempt any such thing." He took a match from a little ivory box on his desk, struck it, and drew heavily but gracefully on his cigar.

"But the offer of a job is closed?"

"It would be quite inconsistent with the obligations I have accepted. I know you will appreciate that. I do not have to say that the matter is entirely impersonal. I am subject to various duties, which take many decisions out of my hands. Very narrow lines of conduct are laid down. For better or worse. I frequently think for worse. But now let us say nothing more about these particular matters. I am sure you will agree. Let us discuss something else. I have no other engagement, I am delighted to say, for the next ten minutes." Lord Roller consulted his watch, a fine inherited repeater, and added: "Indeed, eleven minutes."

Griselda hesitated. Could her love for Louise be already such common knowledge? Had Lord Roller gone over to the side of her Mother? Was there a cabalistic communion, based presum-

ably upon telepathy, between such all eminent personages as
Mrs. Hatch and Lord Roller? Miss Guthers had seemed ignorant
of anything amiss. Or was it because of knowledge that she
had been so pleasant and agreeable? In any case a good private
secretary was supposed to differentiate in her reception of the
Recording Angel and of the man to read the gas meter, in degree
only, and not in kind. Griselda began seriously to worry about
her inexperience of Uncle Bear's "real life". But then her love
for Louise seemed much more "real" than her obligation to
Lord Roller. Repelling another onset of tears, Griselda reflected
that unless she had a reasonable job by the end of the week, she
would go to jail for debt, which would put society still more
against her.

"Lord Roller," she said bravely, "I need a job. Suddenly I need
a job badly. I have no right to bother you, but since we still have
eleven minutes, or perhaps ten by now, I wonder if you can suggest anything? Or must it be the Secretariat?" Griselda thought
of living in a loft with Louise. Tears, tears. Almost she wished
that she smoked. Lord Roller had already made the room like a
luxuriously aromatic engine house. The reek of his mammoth
cigar deadened the nerves of even non-smokers.

"It will not be easy," he said. His tone implied that his mag-
nanimity in offering to say no more about Griselda's offence (if
that was what he was offering to say no more about), was meeting with insufficient acknowledgement. But even now it was
uncertain whether his present remark alluded to more than the
depressed state of trade, so alarmingly revealed in the Report;
was more than an accepted and standard observation to job-
hunters. "You may have to enter the Secretariat after all." It was
as if Griselda had to enter a convent for a course of spiritual rec-
tification; even that being, all things considered, a lucky escape.

"I should so much rather not."

"Naturally. But it is not in every case possible to choose. Often
our present is decided for us by our past. I do not wish there to
be any misunderstanding, however; any doubt that I am anxious
to do everything possible. Though I should so much prefer to
talk about the daffodils I noticed growing in the Green Park this
morning, or the newest novel which I lack time to read, and can

only read about." He smiled: then expelled a cloud of smoke so dense and unexpected as to make Griselda cough.

"I *am* so sorry. Let me ring for a glass of water. And we might have the window a little open perhaps, just for a moment."

"Thank you. I'm perfectly all right." It was almost the sensation of crying again.

But Lord Roller had already rung. Miss Guthers appeared instantly.

"Could you possibly fetch a glass of water, Hazel? I have nearly choked Miss de Reptonville."

"Certainly, Lord Roller."

Again in an instant, Miss Guthers was back with a tumbler filled to the brim with water. Despite the speed of the transaction, not a drop was spilt; an achievement which Griselda found difficult to sustain.

"Could you open a window too?"

"The noise is rather bad today, Lord Roller. Now that it's almost summer, it's difficult to have the windows open. All the roads are coming up and the traffic's being diverted. You can hear the hooting."

"None the less, please open the window, Hazel. Miss de Reptonville requires air. The Ministry of Transport has no business to repair the roads anyway, with the country in the state it is. Write a letter to Leech pointing that out and I'll sign it. See that it catches the midday post or it'll never arrive with the posts as they are now. You might even send it to Number Ten by messenger."

"The messenger service isn't at all what it used to be, you know. Perhaps I'd better telephone Downing Street and ask *them* to send a messenger to collect."

"Please don't trouble," interjected Griselda.

"I beg your pardon?"

"The window. Please don't trouble, I'm perfectly all right."

"That's splendid." Miss Guthers smiled encouragingly. "What about some more water?"

"No, thank you. I still have more than half a glass. I wonder if we could possibly finish what we were saying, Lord Roller?"

"Of course we can. All right, Hazel. Just let me know when Sir George arrives."

"Yes, Lord Roller. Shall I take your glass?"

"Thank you so much for the water." It was probably wise to keep on the right side of Miss Guthers, especially as Griselda's last remark might have been interpreted as a dismissal and as presumption.

"Well, Miss de Reptonville, you want suitable employment." Lord Roller took a sheet of paper from a satinwood stationery stand which stood on the table with his cigars. He began to write. "An opportunity has occurred to me. It might prove to be the very thing." He scratched away. "You don't mind working out of London?"

"I should prefer London, but, obviously, I'm in no position to choose. How far away will this be?"

"Not far, you'll be pleased to hear. Not far at all. Just the other side of Seven Kings." He signed the document: a swift, driving, single name; then folded it and put it in an envelope. "No. On second thoughts, you'd better read it." He withdrew it from the envelope and passed it folded to Griselda.

The paper bore two or three sentences in a hand, dashing and sloping eagerly to the right, but not one word of which could Griselda read.

She stared at the indecipherable words while Lord Roller stood behind his desk watching her and waiting.

"I'm terribly sorry. I'm bad at handwriting. I can't read all of it."

"Doesn't matter in the least, Miss de Reptonville. Hardly worth showing you. Conventionality, simply; but I hope it does the trick. My fist's got worse and worse, I'm afraid, with increasing years of service. Give me the thing back and I'll pack it up again." Griselda gave it back. "Just find your way to this address and they'll take care of you." He was writing on the envelope. "I'll do it in capitals." He smiled again at Griselda.

"I feel I'm rather a fool, Lord Roller."

"Hardly worth employing, I'm sure." He said this with the kindliest of irony. "There." He returned the letter.

Miss Guthers was back in the room.

"Sir George, Lord Roller."

"Show him in, Hazel. And bring a lot of whisky. Better open a new bottle."

"Yes, Lord Roller."

"Good-bye, Miss de Reptonville. I do hope I've been of some small help. Your position is difficult." He extended his hand. "But whatever you do ... don't worry." It was the last word on the subject.

"Thank you for giving me so much of your time."

"I should so much have preferred to talk of the daffodils in the Park."

"Perhaps on another occasion."

He glanced at her.

"I hope so."

Miss Guthers had rather to rush Griselda's departure from the office, as Sir George could be distinctly overheard stamping like a thoroughbred in a loose box.

CHAPTER XV

Mr. Shooter, to whom Lord Roller's letter was addressed, hardly even attempted charm; nor did The Bedrock Accessories Supply Company, her prospective place of employment, impress Griselda much more favourably. Even when with the assistance of Messrs. Arkwright and Silverstein's outside porter, she had located Seven Kings, it seemed to take several hours to reach the place by train from Liverpool Street, so that on arrival she at least expected spring buds on the trees and skipping lambs. But Seven Kings seemed little different from the less attractive parts of London. It was now lunchtime but Griselda did not dare to eat; nor did there seem facilities, even had she dared.

Mr. Shooter worked in an untidy office entirely walled with a special kind of glass. Outside, a press of some sort was noisily making accessories. Every thirty seconds it stamped something out; so loudly that conversation above the concussions was difficult, and hardly easier between them. Grinding and rolling mills made up a background evocative of the nation's industrial effort. Mr. Shooter possibly found the general atmosphere of toil, stimulating; but as he was entirely bald, and rather yellow, it was not easy to say. The plywood door of his office bore the legend

"*Personnel* Manager. Do NOT Disturb" in ugly modern lettering. Above his electric heater was a large framed reproduction of de Laszlo's portrait of Lord Roller in the robes of a Baron.

Griselda was shown in by a sniffing child, fresh from some Essex hamlet.

"Maudie," screamed Mr. Shooter, as the infant was about to depart, "I want some real tea, not this stinking slops. Get busy, will you, and don't forget next time."

Maudie shuffled away.

"Take the tray with you."

Maudie returned for the tray. As she bore it towards the door, she winked at Griselda. It was impossible for Griselda to wink back, even if she felt so inclined. The office door rasped along the floor every time it was opened or shut.

"Well?"

Griselda handed Mr. Shooter the letter. Mr. Shooter really did not seem an easy man to talk to.

"May I sit down?"

"If you think it worth while. Bring that chair over from the window. You can put the box of samples on the floor under the dictaphone."

"Thank you." The box of samples was difficult to lift and tended to burst open.

"Sorry. Can't read this. What's it say?" Mr. Shooter tossed the letter back in the direction of Griselda, but it fell off his desk on to the floor. "Sorry. You read it."

"I can't read it." Griselda had succeeded in towing up the rickety little chair. "I'm sorry."

"It's from the great white chief isn't it?"

"From Lord Roller, yes. Is this *his* factory? I didn't know."

"One of his factories. He's got twelve in Canada alone. This one's only a sideline."

"What do you make?" enquired Griselda politely. "I'm afraid I'm very ignorant."

"Nothing but accessories," replied Mr. Shooter. The fact seemed to pain him; but it was as if the pain were something he had learned to bear. "Let's stick to you. What's it all about?"

"I understand from Lord Roller that you might be able to offer me a job. If you think I'm worth it, that is." Griselda was far from sure that, even desperate as she was, she wanted to devote herself to making merely accessories.

"You got that from the chief personally?" Mr. Shooter stared hard at Griselda. His eyes were like guns mounted behind slits in the yellow pillbox of his face.

"Certainly," said Griselda with hauteur.

"Well, there's one thing."

"What is it?"

"Welfare." Mr. Shooter's eyes were keeping Griselda covered more ruthlessly than ever.

"I might be able to help with that." Griselda saw herself dressed as a hospital sister and wondered whether she could call upon the required amount of saintliness. At once she doubted whether she could.

"Our last four welfare officers have had to leave us rather suddenly. Oh, personal reasons in each case. Quite sufficient. But now the job's going once more." He stared again at Lord Roller's letter, which Griselda had replaced upon his desk.

"Could you tell me a little more about it?"

"Knowledge of people, that's the main thing. Knowledge of the common people. The welfare officer must be guide, philosopher, and friend to every worker in the place. She must be able to get inside their minds. If she can do that, special qualifications are less important. There's a bit of simple nursing, of course, and first aid, naturally. Have you a first aid certificate?"

"Actually, yes."

"You have?" Mr. Shooter seemed surprised and impressed. He took a writing pad from the drawer of his desk and made a note.

"Then there's librarianship. Do you read?"

"It's my favourite thing."

"We don't want a bookworm, you know," replied Mr. Shooter, glowering. "Only the lighter stuff. Religious guidance is another side of the work; for those who want it. Mostly the young girls. You do that in co-operation with Mr. Cheddar, the priest-in-charge. What else is there? Oh yes, help with games of all sorts, and advice upon the food in the canteen. Mrs. Rufioli superintends the actual cooking, gives the kitchen girls hell and all that;

but the welfare officer has to see to it that the canteen expenditure doesn't exceed the firm's financial provision. I suppose you can keep simple accounts?"

The figure of Mrs. Hatch and her terrible ledger recurred in Griselda's imagination. "I think I can," she said faintly.

"The main thing is that the welfare officer must be on her toes morning, noon, and night. If she keeps on her toes all the time—and I mean *all* the time—the job's not difficult to hold down."

Griselda looked at her toes. Whatever Louise might imply, she thought her shoes were rather attractive. She wondered at what point the applicant introduced the matter of remuneration. Mr. Shooter, his oration finished, had produced a rectangle of madeira cake on a plate from another drawer in his desk, and now sat crumbling it into debris, and stuffing untidy briquettes of the debris into his small round mouth. It seemed to Griselda an inefficient way of eating madeira cake. Meanwhile, Mr. Shooter said nothing further.

"How much," enquired Griselda tentatively——

But Mr. Shooter cut her short. "The usual Rawnsley Committee rates," he said with his mouth full. There was little difference in hue, Griselda observed, between the cake and Mr. Shooter's complexion.

"And hours?"

"I think we're adopting the Giddens Council recommendations, but the whole subject's still in the melting-pot. You've nothing to worry about, though. This is a modern factory, based on efficient time and motion study." The banging press outside underlined his words. "Besides which, we go all out for welfare."

The door rasped and Maudie reappeared with her pale green plastic tray. The teapot was smeary; the cup, saucer, and milk jug discrepant. The sugar basin, however, was of the sanitary variety. Maudie had evidently resolved to seek re-entry to Mr. Shooter's favour by augmenting her allure: she had shaded her eyelids, cast off her cardigan, and assumed a mode of speech modelled upon that of Miss Myrna Loy.

"Your tea, Mr. Shooter," said Maudie, still sniffing. "Nice and strong."

Mr. Shooter looked up at her. "Thanks, Maudie," he said, in almost cowboy tones. "Sorry I was short with you."

"That's quite O.K., Mr. Shooter. We all know how hard you work." It was difficult to believe that Maudie would long continue an accessory. In two years time, when she would be fifteen or so, she would be conquering new and wider fields. Griselda suspected that Maudie was precisely the type which brought welfare workers into existence and rendered their existence unavailing.

"Now I must go into rather a lot of details," said Mr. Shooter, imbibing strong tea, to Griselda. "Some of them are pretty personal, but there's another lady present to see fair play." Maudie had seated herself on a stack of unopened parcels. They appeared to contain Government circulars upon questions of personnel management.

Griselda rose to her feet. "Please do not trouble," she said. "I don't think the position is quite what I am looking for." She felt entirely regal as she swept from the room; the regality being modified only temporarily by Maudie emitting a long squelching sound through her incorrectly painted lips.

CHAPTER XVI

After purchasing and eating four penny buns and drinking a mugful of Bovril, Griselda decided to seek a job by a different method. She took an omnibus from Liverpool Street to Piccadilly Circus, and rambled through the back streets north of Piccadilly and west of Regent Street, looking in the shops, and seeking also a place where she could possibly want to work. It was what her school had described as the Direct Method. On this occasion, the Direct Method proved immediately efficacious.

The aspect of a certain small bookshop appealed to her greatly. The window was stocked neither with Books of the Month nor with sombre ancients; but with a well chosen selection of books published during the preceding fifty years or thereabouts. Unfortunately for the enlightened management, the shop appeared to be empty. Above the window was the name "Tamburlane."

Griselda entered. A tall, well-made man, with a red face and white fluffy hair, emerged briskly from an inner room.

"I'm afraid we are out of Housman today," he said in a gentle cultivated voice.

"I already have him, thank you."

"Indeed? I must apologize for my precipitancy. I supposed that like my other customers today, you might have been guided here by that thing in 'The Times'."

"I'm afraid I missed that particular thing in 'The Times'."

"Just as well, really. At least in my opinion. Not that I've anything against the old man himself. But 'The Times' does rather dote, don't you think? On A.E.H. and J.M.B.?" His articulation of the word "dote" was pleasantly idiosyncratic.

"Yes," said Griselda. "Now you mention it, I really believe that 'The Times' does."

"Insufficient catholicity. Their enormous parsonical readership is at the back of it. It's useless attaching blame to the Editor. Quite a broad-minded well-read chap in his private life, I'm told. I wonder if you'd care for a small glass of port? I always indulge myself after luncheon and it's all too seldom I have a friend to indulge with me."

"There's nothing I'd like better."

"Delightful. You have spontaneity, the one real virtue. But I must not let myself stray into compliments. Please sit down." He indicated a Chinese Chippendale chair. Griselda saw that there were a number of them in the inner room.

"Are you Mr. Tamburlane?"

"Yes and no. But yes for present purposes. Certainly yes. And you?"

"Griselda de Reptonville."

He was filling two beautiful little glasses, from a beautiful little decanter, with assuredly most beautiful port.

"That is the most delightful name I have ever heard. In what is vulgarly known as 'real life', of course. I do hope I shall enrol you among my permanent customers."

Griselda swallowed half the contents of the glass at one unsuitable gulp.

"I really rather hope to be enrolled among your employees."

He was sipping like a rare and fastidious fowl.

"Well, nothing could be easier than that. Nothing at all. I take it you love books?"

"Perhaps I love them more than I know about them."

"Indeed I certainly hope so or you would stand little chance here. In view of what you say, you're engaged. Do you wish to start work now?"

"Would tomorrow suit you?"

"Excellently well. Naturally you will not be expected to lower the shutters. Ten o'clock I therefore suggest?"

He recharged the two glasses. The wine looked rich as Faust's blood.

"I think I should tell you of my qualifications. For working in a bookshop I have one or two."

"They are apparent to me. You have beauty and spontaneity, and you love books. Those things are rare and becoming daily rarer. They suffice. Indeed they suffice."

"I shall try very hard indeed," said Griselda.

"Never forget the words of the great Prince Talleyrand: 'Surtout, point de zèle.' That advice will carry you far in life. Though I am perfectly sure that you will be carried far in any case."

"I have made a sadly slow start."

" 'He tires betimes, who spurs too fast betimes.' I never can overcome my lust for Shakespeare. Can you?"

"I haven't tried. Should I try?"

"Peasant stuff much of it really; but none the less a genius. Indisputably a genius. I was speaking only figuratively. You mustn't take anything I say too literally."

Griselda looked up from her port.

"Oh, don't take alarm. My words are not serious, but my deeds move mountains. Or so I sometimes like to flatter myself."

A man entered the shop and began to explore the shelves. "Perhaps I should go," said Griselda. "Thank you very much indeed for the port. And for the job."

"It has been the greatest possible joy to me. Such a lovely head, such lustrous eyes: always about the shop. Blessedness, indeed: beata Beatrix, and all that. And don't misunderstand me in any particular. My homage is entirely aesthetic; wholly impersonal, so to speak. My eros veers almost entirely towards Adonis."

The customer looked up at these words, uttered in a voice like a ring of treble bells; and suddenly left the shop.

Griselda noticed the repeated claim of men to be regarding her impersonally. Their motives for this claim seemed as varied as their implication that the process ennobled them was consistent.

"I entirely understand," said Griselda. "Good-bye until tomorrow morning."

"Take something to read," cried Mr. Tamburlane. "Take this." It was 'Rupert of Hentzau'. "I presume you've read 'The Prisoner'?"

"I'm afraid that's one I've missed."

"Then take 'The Prisoner' too."

"You are most thoughtful. I'll return them very quickly."

"Indeed not. You'll read them for solace in years to come, most blessed damozel."

It was only later while eating an éclair in Fullers that Griselda realized that this time the matter of wages had not been mentioned at all.

CHAPTER XVII

But it settled itself quite suitably. As soon as Griselda diffidently raised the subject upon her arrival the next morning, Mr. Tamburlane cried out: "Please, please, please. No more holding back, I beg. Though alas, I cannot be prodigal. You will soon see for yourself the state of business, and I make it my policy to try to confine outgoings to a sum not exceeding takings. Would four pounds per week keep your slim gilt soul, if I may quote my old friend, within your rosy fingered body?"

"I believe that's about the market rate," replied Griselda, perhaps a little disappointed, however unreasonably. "Thank you very much." It would be necessary to depart from the Great Exhibition Hotel as soon as possible.

"The shop shuts at six o'clock, and at one on Saturdays. You will find that much of the business, such as it is, takes place each day during the general matutinal interregnum."

In many respects the job was an ideal one. The work was of the lightest and unfailingly interesting; and Mr. Tamburlane, apparently the only other person connected with the running of the business, became upon further acquaintance more and more likeable and sympathetic. The few customers were mainly artists, aristocrats, idlers, and scholars; persons bashed by life into extreme inoffensiveness, varied in certain cases by mild and appealing eccentricity. There was also a small number of exceedingly beautiful women customers, who lighted up the shop as with nimbuses. The main drawback, perceived by Griselda from the outset, was that the job entirely lacked what she believed to be termed "prospects". Until one knew him, it was difficult to understand what need Mr. Tamburlane had of an assistant. After one knew him, it was plain that his need could not truly be translated into financial terms.

Griselda also experienced much difficulty in finding a dwelling place. Having little idea how to set about this search, she attempted several unsuitable neighbourhoods, and a greater number of much more unsuitable landladies. She knew that she needed advice, but hesitated to apply for it to Mr. Tamburlane. By the end of her first week in the shop, she was still lodged at the Great Exhibition Hotel, and facing insolvency for lack of a few pounds.

In other ways, however, her acquaintanceship with her employer throve exceedingly. He proved a man precisely of his word: he complimented her ceaselessly and often imaginatively upon her appearance, her ideas, and even her work; but showed no sign at all of ever intending to go further. It seemed to Griselda an admirable attitude for an employer.

The real trouble, of course, was the loss of Louise. The extent and hopelessness of this loss, and also its unnecessariness, saturated Griselda's thoughts and feelings only by degrees. By Friday, however, she felt so despairing, and her acquaintanceship with Mr. Tamburlane had developed so warmly, that she resolved to confide in him, at least in part. It was necessary to confide in someone or die; and she could think of no other possible person among all her few friends and relatives, most of whom were, moreover, geographically unavailable. She was not sure that she would want to live in quarters found by Mr. Tamburlane; but in the matter of Louise, and Louise's disappearance, there might well be less suitable confidants. So early in the morning there was little risk of interruption by customers.

"Indeed I can help," cried Mr. Tamburlane, at the conclusion of the mournful tale. "You poor thing. And how fortunate today is Friday."

"I am glad that something about it is fortunate," said Griselda.

"Friday is the very day of the week for such a sad narration. Friday is the day Miss Otter calls."

"Who is Miss Otter?"

"I shall tell you. There is a certain weekly newspaper. It circulates only privately—to subscribers, you understand; only to subscribers. Not many people know about it, but it serves a variety of special and important purposes. There is no need for me to be more specific. I am sure I have said enough for you to take me?" Griselda thought of the "St. James's News-Letter"; wondered if Mr. Tamburlane were talking of something similar; and nodded. The drift of Mr. Tamburlane's words seemed utterly beside the point, and had Griselda spoken, she would have started to weep.

"The paper is generally known among its subscribers as 'The Otter'. It has, in fact, an entirely different, rather dull name, which is printed at the top of every copy; but 'The Otter' it has been for years, simply as a tribute to Miss Otter's personality. Miss Otter is the Editor, so to speak; certainly the entrepreneur. She visits me each week and we decide the contents of the next issue. I am proud to say that from time to time it has been owing to me that there has been a further issue. The sum involved is really very tiny. But as the unacknowledged offspring of a rich nobleman—rich even in these days—I happily have some very small resources of my own, with which I endeavour to add to the douceur of life."

"Unacknowledged, Mr. Tamburlane?"

"For good and obvious reasons, I'm afraid, Miss de Reptonville. Please don't think I'm the rightful heir deprived; or even a younger

son deprived. Nothing at all like that. I entirely uphold the strict-
est interpretation of the rules of blood and succession. Without
them the nobility would very soon become unfit to govern."

"I thought they'd ceased to govern anyway," said Griselda,
interested in spite of herself.

"Temporarily they have indeed. But you do not suppose that
the present political bacchanal will last many years, I take it? As a
wise and beautiful young woman, you cannot be deceived about
that?"

"You will remember that I attended the All Party Dance, Mr.
Tamburlane."

"I am answered as by an oracle. But to return to 'The Otter'.
It is fortunate indeed that you decided to confide in me. For 'The
Otter' exists largely in order to help with just such problems as
yours, Miss de Reptonville. But, as I live, here comes Miss Otter
in person." He dashed out of the little inner room where this conversation had taken place.

Griselda looked at the new arrival with much curiosity. Miss
Otter was a bent little woman, dressed, not very well, entirely
in black. She had a quantity of white hair, and a brown wrinkled
face, with a huge nose and enigmatic eyes. She wore no hat, but a
wide black velvet band across her white hair.

Mr. Tamburlane introduced Griselda. Miss Otter accepted the
introduction after the affable style of an important personage,
took Griselda by the hand, and remarked: "I perceive you are in
much distress of mind. I am grieved. Please accept my sympathy." The last request was delivered somewhat in the tone of a
dethroned Queen.

Griselda could only say: "Thank you very much."

"You are indeed right, Miss Otter," said Mr. Tamburlane, "as
always. Miss de Reptonville lives under a heavy burden. But fortunately you and I may be privileged to assist in lightening those
slender shoulders."

"It will not be our first such case," said Miss Otter, smiling
graciously.

"Nor yet our our one hundred and first, if it were possible
to keep a reckoning. Now, Miss de Reptonville, I leave the shop
entirely in your management. Miss Otter and I have affairs to dis-

cuss. If any problems arise, you must call upon your own good judgment to solve them. For Miss Otter and I must on no account be disturbed. Help yourself to sherry and biscuits if you require to relieve responsibility with refreshment. Miss Otter and I shall not emerge until teatime. When I am sure we shall all be very ready for crumpets and anchovy toast." He waved Miss Otter into the inner room and entering behind her, shut the door. Griselda noticed that Miss Otter carried a portfolio of papers and had a slight limp.

As usual there were few customers, though a young man who wanted a book on the botany of the Andes became quite offensive when Griselda, after much searching, was unable to find him one. A tired woman brought her son, aged about ten, to select his own birthday present. She seemed prepared to spend up to fifteen shillings, and urged the claims of a book of scientific wonders illustrated with many polychromatic plates, and acres of isonometry. The boy insisted on a copy of the Everyman Mabinogion. Despite the economy, his Mother seemed angry and disappointed. An elderly man prefaced his requirements by presenting Griselda with his card: Professor O. O. Gasteneetsia, F.R.S. The Professor then showed Griselda a minute cutting from a penny daily. It advised a book entitled "What About A Rumba?" Griselda offered to order it for him. But he kept saying "Tonight. I come again tonight" until drawn from the shop by a newsboy shouting about a crisis of some kind.

Griselda wondered whether she should procure crumpets and anchovies, but hesitated to leave the shop. The neighbourhood, moreover, seemed unpropitious, at least for crumpets. At about 5.15, however, when she had drunk all the sherry and eaten all the biscuits, and still felt exceedingly famished, a pleasing smell began to fill the shop. At 5.25, the inner door opened and Mr. Tamburlane called to her: "Enter, Miss de Reptonville. The fatted calf is dead. Alas! that Miss Otter has to leave us."

The room was full of blue smoke, the beautiful eighteenth century table spread with hot crumpets and buttered toast, a Wedgwood Chinese teapot, with cups and plates to match, an opened jar of anchovies, and a litter of papers in process of re-assembly by Miss Otter. Among the papers, Griselda noticed, seemed to be a number of very grimy and unpractised looking letters; others were inexplicable drawings in pompeian red on fresh white cartridge paper.

"All this clutter!" ejaculated Miss Otter, smilingly. "No, please don't help me. I am an untidy old woman. You sit down and eat your tea."

Griselda had never previously met with tea in the shop, or indeed, any other meal. It was true, however, that each day she left Mr. Tamburlane to provide for himself while she took lunch in a teashop. Today she was ready to tuck in.

"Good-bye, Mr. Tamburlane," said Miss Otter, strapping her portfolio. "I'll find my own way to the door. Good-bye, Miss de Reptonville. If you'll take an old woman's advice, you'll turn down the next proposal you receive. Come what may, you should turn it down. No matter how keen on you the other party seems to be. Feelings change, you know, with the passage of the years. Nor is that the only reason." She was on her way through the shop. "Don't forget what I say, Miss de Reptonville." The outer door shut.

"Don't you worry," said Mr. Tamburlane to Griselda, repeating Lord Roller's counsel. "I talked to Miss Otter very fully about your tragic misfortune. I think that together we shall have the great happiness of recapturing the lamb that has strayed. It is fortunate indeed that I was by when your need arose. Have a Bath Oliver?" He extended an exquisite Wedgwood biscuit box.

"Thank you. I'd like another piece of anchovy toast first."

"I imagine, Miss de Reptonville, that my words of cheer fill you with scepticism?"

"I'm afraid I'm not very hopeful that I shall find my friend. But it is very kind of you to concern yourself."

"You probably think that I am a crank and that Miss Otter is mad?" He was eating crumpet after crumpet.

"Certainly not."

"And that our weekly paper, if it exists at all, has less than no power in the land?"

"Not at all." Griselda began to wish she had never confided in Mr. Tamburlane.

"Yes, Miss de Reptonville, you certainly think all these things. How surprised you will be! That is all I care to say at the moment. How surprised you will be! How pleasantly and delicately surprised!"

"Would you let me see a copy of your paper?"

"Subscribers only, you will recall. I fear your sceptical attitude unfits you as yet to enter that charmed circle." He had begun to drink cups of tea in as quick succession as he had eaten crumpets.

"I see."

"Child of loveliness, yours but to reap where Miss Otter and I have sown."

He began to talk about books; and very shortly afterwards Griselda was engaged upon a dreary quest for lodgings in and around Ladbroke Grove.

CHAPTER XVIII

In the end, a decision being urgently necessary, she settled upon a small rectangular residence in a block of flats built for young, and presumably underpaid, office workers of her own sex, by a semi-charitable organization, The New Vista Apartments Trust. Situated just off the western side of that great dividing thoroughfare, the Edgware Road, Greenwood Tree House purported to improve upon such commercial lodgings as could be obtained for a like rental. Under the rules, tenants had to move out upon reaching the age of thirty; and were expected, though not compelled, to interest themselves in the work of the Y.W.C.A. or in some cognate organization approved by the Management Committee. The block was not an unreservedly first-class piece of construction, owing to shortage of funds; but it had been designed (for less than the rightful fee) by an eminent cathedral architect, and therefore reflected the very best in contemporary design.

In addition to her depression about Louise, Griselda now began to suffer from positive loneliness. Although Mr. Tamburlane's mysterious paper was stated to be issued weekly, he soon made it clear that nothing was likely to come of the quest for Louise for several months. Combined with the obscurity about how the paper in any way forwarded the quest, and Mr. Tamburlane's incommunicativeness upon matters of detail, this announcement confirmed Griselda's view that the whole episode was a dismal exercise in whimsicality, conducted at her expense, or possibly a patch of moonshine from the minds of two near-lunatics. Miss Otter visited Mr. Tamburlane regularly each Friday, but rarely remained closeted with him for so long as on that first occasion. Upon entering and leaving, she continued to favour Griselda with cryptic and prophetic observations: "Next time a title comes your way, Miss de Reptonville, I think you would be most unwise to lose your chance"; or simply "More friends are what you need most at the moment, my dear."

In three months of inner misery, Griselda made only a single friend, apart from Mr. Tamburlane, who continued as punctiliously complimentary as on the day she met him. The new friend was Peggy Potter, her neighbour in Greenwood Tree House. Peggy was a broad, well-built girl with a large bust; a little taller than Griselda, and with a quantity of more or less fair hair hanging to her shoulders. She wore woollen dresses, of which Griselda felt that Louise would have strongly disapproved; and had a reserved air derived, as Griselda soon discovered, from a conviction that she had little in common with her fellow inmates. This circumstance, combined with the fact that, before coming to London, she had passed her entire existence in Bodmin, where she had graduated at University College, made her as a friend for Griselda something of a cul-de-sac. None the less, Griselda found her very much better than nobody. Ultimately Griselda realized that inner misery was a positive handicap when seeking to extend a social circle.

It was the pipes in the passage which brought Peggy and Griselda together. Each apartment was equipped with an electric radiator dependant upon a shilling meter; but outside in the passages were occasional steam coils, installed to guard the cocoanut matting and other decorations from injury by damp. The flow of electricity was so costly that the tenants formed the habit of drying their stockings and underclothes on these pipes, which were kept hardly more than lukewarm. The practice was specifically forbidden in the Rules: but as the Rules in most cases failed to provide for sanctions (the Management Committee felt that small fines, for example, were anachronistic and reminiscent of the evil days before the Truck Act), this particular Rule was obeyed only by those who wore no stockings. The practice was to steal out after eleven o'clock and drape the coils: realistically, the difficulty was the insufficient number of the installations. Often there were grave friction and persisting feuds. Griselda and Peggy became friends upon Peggy suggesting that they sidetrack the general run of inmates by sharing the use and the cost of a single electric heater. This arrangement involved them in constant use of one another's rooms.

They began to drink tea together, and Griselda lent Peggy a packet of "Lux." In less than a week, Peggy suggested that Griselda accompany her to hear some music. It proved to be a recital of songs by Duparc, given by a rather elderly Belgian woman, retired some years previously from the provincial operatic stage of her country. The Wigmore Hall was almost empty, and Griselda was slightly scared by the unaccountable permanent decorations behind the platform; nor were the seats which Peggy and Griselda occupied, either very cosy or very close to the centre of interest: none the less Griselda enjoyed the evening because she was so glad to have a friend to share her enjoyment. During the interval, which was rather long, she gave expression to this feeling by offering to stand Peggy a cup of coffee: but the Wigmore Hall proved not to offer refreshments. Outside, at the end of the recital, a group of excitingly dressed women with collecting boxes and very little English beset the small audience for contributions to some continental charity. Griselda gathered that the charity had been founded to commemorate the recitalist's wonderful work for the Allies during the World War.

One thing followed another, and soon Griselda was accompanying Peggy to other entertainments: a production by students at the Rudolf Steiner Hall of a seldom performed Elizabethan tragedy; and a recital at Friends House of works by lesser members of the Bach family, the performers being partly professional and partly amateur. One Sunday afternoon they ambled round the Tate Gallery, where Peggy was much addicted to Mr. Graham Robertson's Blakes.

"Have you read that book of his? His reminiscences?"

"I found him an exhibitionist. He's not my period, of course."

"Shall we go and see the surrealists some time? At the Zwemmer? I'd like to."

"Once is enough for surrealism; just like Madame Tussaud. *You* go, Griselda, and you'll see what I mean."

"But the critics say that the surrealists are the modern equivalent of Blake, and you say you like Blake?"

"Blake had belief. The surrealists have no belief. Surely that is fundamental?"

"Have you belief, Peggy?"

"Not yet. But I am prepared to have."

They passed on to some water colours in the basement, with which Peggy was clearly well acquainted, as she discoursed upon them most convincingly and exhaustively, though water colour landscapes were not Griselda's favourite kind of picture.

Peggy seemed to live in a general condition of contingency: her prevailing attitude was the provisional. Thus although a permanent civil servant, and apparently well advanced in the service for her years (though remarkably ill paid, Griselda thought, considering her Honours Degree and years of youth devoted to passing difficult examinations), yet Peggy's attitude to her job was merely, as she put it, "marking time". Where she aimed to go when her march was resumed, was, however, indefinite. Equally her sojourn at Greenwood Tree House was described by her as a "passage through"; while even her health she referred to, upon Griselda once enquiring about it, as "under observation." She accumulated almost no possessions, and seemed content to have Griselda as her only friend. There were times when Griselda wondered whether Peggy was not in a state verging upon suspended animation.

One evening towards the end of June, they were seated in Hyde Park. Peggy was reading "The Listener"; Griselda a book from Mr. Tamburlane's stock. Peggy suddenly spoke.

"I'm taking some leave in August." It was the first time Griselda had heard the military term applied to civil life. "I'm going to

Italy. Not the big towns and tourist centres, of course; just some of the smaller places in the south. Right off the beaten track. I try to visit a new country each year. I suppose you wouldn't come with me?"

"I can't afford a holiday yet. Nor am I entitled to one, I think." It was difficult to imagine Mr. Tamburlane raising an objection; but, oddly enough, it was equally difficult to imagine the job being still there, or even the shop upon return from a holiday. "I'm terribly sorry. Of course I'd have loved to come." Griselda's regret was tempered inwardly by a distinct reservation in favour of the big towns and tourist centres; particularly, she felt, in Italy.

"I could find the money for both of us, if that's what it is. You could repay me later. Or not at all, if you couldn't."

"That's terribly generous. Thank you, Peggy." Griselda touched her hand, which Peggy slightly withdrew. "But as things are with me, I don't see how I could *ever* repay you."

"You needn't. I said that. Only if and when you can."

"I couldn't agree to that." Griselda knew that she could agree quite easily had she wanted to visit tiny poverty-stricken Italian villages with Peggy. "But thank you again. It is a very kind idea."

"Not particularly. I want you to come with me, Griselda. Do think it over. Believe me I'm quite good at digging out just the places no one else ever gets to."

"There are many better people than I am for that sort of holiday." But Griselda thought with guilt of her fondness for long walks, of how difficult she was to tire, her prima facie suitability for the undertaking. "What about the people you've gone with before?"

"I've usually gone alone. But I'd like *you* to come."

Griselda glanced at her: at her big bust, her rather dull hair, her indifferent clothes, her face already drawing on its iron mask of frustration, only to be removed by death.

"I'd like to come, Peggy. But I mustn't. I really mustn't. Please don't tempt me."

"I thought we could have a good time."

It occurred to Griselda as possible that Peggy, despite appearances, really cared for her: not in the least as Louise cared for her, and she cared for Louise, but in some other way, not necessarily the less authentic because probably approved by society or because completely unaccompanied by any display of feeling. Griselda was incapable of feeling very much without showing that she felt something; without tendering her affection. It seemed a simpler way than Peggy's.

"Next year, perhaps. Where do you plan to go next year?"

"Finland. I don't think you'd care for that."

Peggy resumed "The Listener". In the end they went to the Marble Arch Pavilion together, as if nothing had happened.

Later, while washing stockings in Peggy's room, Griselda said: "Would you like to borrow 'Old Calabria' before you go? Doesn't it deal with just the part you're visiting? It's a book Mr. Tamburlane always has in stock, and I could easily lend it to you for a week or two."

"Thank you, Griselda, but I think I'd rather form my own impressions. I don't know that I'd care to see things through Norman Douglas's eyes."

Griselda began to squeeze out a wet stocking. "Peggy," she said. "What do you want most in the world?"

Peggy looked faintly hostile, as in the Park.

"I don't think the question has much significance for me," she replied. "I don't think I see life in quite those terms." Then she added, obviously trying to please: "What do *you* want most in the world?"

But, contrary to Peggy's notion, Griselda had neither expected nor desired that the question should be thus lobbed back at her. She was merely trying to enter into a corner of Peggy's mind; fractionally to explore an outlook which she believed to be as habitual among her neighbours as it was alien to herself. "I want to know about *you*."

"Really I'm remarkably content as I am."

"I'm not content as I am."

"I know you're not. And of course I know why you're not."

"Why am I not?"

"Griselda, we're not schoolgirls. We don't have to go into all that at this hour of the night."

Her attitude was so impossibly aloof, that Griselda became

momentarily filled with a younger than schoolgirlish urge to shock. "What I want from life is ecstasy."

"What will you do when you've got it?" Peggy had taken off her dress and stood in her knickers and brassière. "I mean *after* you've got it?"

"I shall reconsider the whole subject," said Griselda.

Peggy smiled slightly, relieved that the conversation was apparently being dropped. By way of farewell gesture she said: "If you really want to know, Griselda, I'm not the marrying kind."

"*I'm* not. I rather thought *you* were."

"No, I'm not."

"I see." Not that she did. "Anyway you don't want to borrow 'Old Calabria'."

"Afterwards, perhaps. If I may?"

"Of course. If I'm still at the shop." Griselda gathered together four wet stockings, like bits of ghosts which had been out in the rain. "Good night, Peggy."

Peggy's preparations for bed had advanced no further. She jerked into speech. "Tell me something, Griselda."

"Yes."

"Is my bust too large?"

"Of course it isn't. It's much better than having too small a bust like me."

"Then it *is* too large?"

Peggy's face was white. She was very near tears.

"It's larger than most people's. I wish mine was. It's a good thing."

Peggy was visibly making a great effort. "I sometimes feel self-conscious about it. Not often."

Griselda kissed Peggy gently on each breast. Suddenly she felt a hundred years older than Peggy; and oddly enough, glad to be so. "Attractiveness is mainly a matter of thoughts."

Peggy had removed her last garments and was putting on her nightdress. "It's easy for someone as attractive as you to say that. Most men never get as far as a woman's mind."

Griselda recalled Louise's words about fellow feeling. "I expect not," she said sadly.

"I've decided to do without them. You can if you try. At least

I can. It's not even very difficult." Peggy began to brush her teeth.

"I need *someone* to love me."

"I'm glad to say I don't. It's extraordinary how well I do on my own."

"I can see there are advantages."

"Not that I'm bigoted about it. It's just what suits *me.*"

"I think you're very wise to do what suits you. But I still think you have a particularly attractive figure. Shall I turn out the light for you?"

"You're kind to me, Griselda." She was climbing into the divan bed.

"You're kind to *me.* Shall I open the window?"

"Please. Quite wide."

"The sky is full of stars."

"More rain, I'm afraid. July is often a wet month, though not so wet as August."

"Surely it would mean rain if there were *no* stars?"

"It depends. Often it means rain either way."

"What a pity! Good night, Peggy dear."

"Good night, Griselda."

Griselda returned to her own room, and, switching on the electric heater, began to dry the two pairs of stockings, to eat chocolate wafers, and to conclude her interesting book.

During the small hours she was awakened by screams and groans from the next room, and deduced that Peggy must be having a nightmare. She reflected that, as a friend, she should intervene; but before thought had turned to action, she was once more dreamlessly sleeping.

CHAPTER XIX

Griselda preferred a light luncheon at Fullers, comparatively dear at the price, to a cheaper and more substantial meal at Lyons or the Express Dairy. Some time after Peggy had invited her to Italy, she was making for Fullers' shop in Regent Street when she

encountered Geoffrey Kynaston. After several days of rain, it
had suddenly become humidly hot, and Kynaston was wearing
a white shirt, open at the neck, and grey flannel trousers, neither
garment being noticeably new, clean, or appealing.

"Hullo, you," he said in the most casual manner.

"Hullo."

"Still alive and kicking after the bust-up?"

"As you see."

"Got some new clothes too. A great improvement, if I may
say so."

Indeed it could not be said that Griselda was saving any money
at all. She was not even attempting to do so.

"Thank you."

"I didn't grasp that you were that way?"

"What way?"

"That way."

"I'm not. Or not entirely."

"I see. Thank you for clearing my mind. I'm not that way at all.
I think I told you."

"You did."

"In the light of your explanation, I'm glad to see you. More
glad, I mean, than had it been, as I supposed, otherwise."

"I'm glad."

"Perhaps we could start something up?"

"What?"

"Light refreshments first, I suppose. To judge by your air of
purpose. Can you pay for two?"

"With difficulty."

"If you can do it all, you're better placed than I am. Let's go."
There was a second's pause, and he added: "You don't mind do
you? I did feed you at Hodley."

"It's quite all right," said Griselda. "Come on." They advanced
up the hot busy pavement.

"You don't work, if I remember? I suppose you have an allowance?"

"No."

"Not a *job* after all?"

"Why not?"

"How grimly disillusioning."

"I'm sorry. How's dancing?"

"Packed up. What did you suppose?"

"It never occurred to me."

"It was on its last legs when you arrived. You could see the state of business for yourself."

"I'm sorry. What about poetry?"

"Same as before."

"That was better than nothing."

"Very little."

They reached and entered Fullers. Kynaston's costume was not precisely what the management was used to at that particular branch.

"What'll you have?" enquired Griselda, putting forward the menu.

"Just a large fruit salad," said Kynaston, without looking at it. "And a cup of Ovaltine or something like that." Seated opposite him, Griselda observed that he seemed really emaciated.

"Wouldn't you care for something more solid?"

"Not in this heat."

There was a pause.

"How's Doris?"

"Down with T.B. Never mind about her. I want to know about you. Or are you still uncommunicative? Of course, I see now that you had your reasons. Not that you need have had. I'm utterly sympathetic in principle. I hope you gather that?"

"Could we talk about something else?"

"I like masterful women—in fact, I direly need one myself to organize things for me."

"I remember."

"And, of course, that kind of woman often——"

"Please could we talk about something else?"

"I thought that perhaps you would be grateful for an utterly sympathetic listener?"

The arrival of the waitress spared Griselda an answer.

"There's no Ovaltine."

Griselda supposed that he would order Nescafé; but he said "A sundae will do. When I've finished the fruit."

"Which sort of sundae?"

"Any sort." Later he was brought a sundae costing 3/6. It was the biggest and best.

"Let's come to realities."

"Haven't we?" asked Griselda.

"I mean our joint future."

"I'm provided for. I've got a job in a bookshop."

"You can't be getting much?"

"No. But I like the job."

"Which shop?"

"It's called Tamburlane."

"Rather beyond the means of most people who can read. But reputable."

"You know it?"

"By reputation. Tamburlane was the son of pauper parents and raised in the East End. He always wanted to own a bookshop: a morbid respect for learning based on frustration. In the end he made a bit of money out of prospecting in Alaska and got his way. There! I feel well-informed."

"Better than I am."

"You pick up things like that from the sort of people I've mixed with. Where are you living?"

"Off the Edgware Road."

"Do you like it?"

"Not very much."

"Monica Paget-Barlow says there's a flat in Juvenal Court. It's not altogether an ideal home, but I expect it's better than what you've got. Possibly the two of us could afford it? That is if I could settle on something which brought in money steadily."

"I'm perfectly content where I am."

"You mean you've not yet had time to get round to the idea of living with me?"

"Not yet."

"You don't feel equal to organizing me?"

"Not even myself."

"I'm sorry, Griselda. I'm not really heartless."

At a neighbouring table, a child was sick on the floor. It was impossible to believe that so small a vessel could have held so much.

"I'm unhappy."

"Of course."

"I'm glad to have met you. I need a friend."

"I've always been fond of you, Griselda. You know that." He spoke as if his was a hopeless passion of many years standing.

"Where are you living now?"

"Friends house me for odd nights."

"Are you looking for a job?"

"The jobs available are mostly rather hell."

"I know."

"I'm trying to work up my plastic poses."

"Do they help?"

"It's an extension of Laban's teaching. But entirely original."

Across the room a waitress overturned a tray laden with portions of roast veal. She was a pretty girl and several men began to assist her with the re-assembly. But their efforts were competitive and helped very little.

"Now that I've met you I think I'll close with General Pampero."

"Who's he?"

"The Liberator of Orinoco. He spent most of his life in exile: naturally in London. The Orinocan Government have just bought the house he lived in. They want someone to curate. Very few Orinocans are allowed out of the country. I know a girl who works in the Embassy. She claimed I was a D.Litt. and got me the offer."

"Where's the house?"

"Somewhere the other side of Mecklenburgh Square. Quite a healthy neighbourhood."

"Why haven't you moved in already?"

"I'm afraid of acquiring roots."

"You had roots in Hodley."

Kynaston stopped eating and looked into Griselda's eyes.

"Griselda, I suppose you wouldn't marry me?"

"I'm in love with someone else."

"In love?"

"Certainly."

He continued to gaze at her.

"*I*'m in love with you."

"I doubt it."

"Of course I'm in love with you," he said with faint irritation. "You're unique."

Griselda said nothing.

"Let's stick to realities. Is there any *future* to this other business?"

Griselda still said nothing.

"I mean we've both made pretty good messes of our lives so far. I think we should cut our losses."

"I'm in love with someone else, Geoffrey."

"I have an intensely devoted nature. I could make you happy."

"Are you happy yourself?"

"*You* could make me."

"I expect most married couples have exactly those expectations of each other."

"They're perfectly reasonable expectations. People aren't designed to be happy in isolation like sentries in boxes."

He seemed startlingly in earnest.

"What about Doris?"

"I'm very fond of little Doris but I don't want to marry her. Besides, as I told you, she's got T.B."

"Does she want to marry you?"

"She can't marry anyone. She's very ill. I can only see her once a week."

"You do still see her?"

"Of course, I do. I'm very fond of her. I'm not a monster."

"I'd like to see her some time."

"I don't think you've much in common. But you can if you want to."

"I suppose we haven't really."

"I am glad you can see it. It'll save a lot of nervous tension and train fares. Will you come and look at this flat in Juvenal Court?"

"Won't you live where you work?"

"The Orinocans have sublet most of the house. The General's relics hardly fill two rooms. There'll be an Orinocan Enquiry Bureau in a third room. That's me too. An Orinocan trading concern have got the rest. But I can't afford Juvenal Court without you. It's quite amusing. Friends of mine live in the other flats.

Come and see it this evening. The flat won't stay empty for ever. I'll call for you."

"Geoffrey," said Griselda, "I must make it plain to you that the chance of my marrying you is entirely and absolutely nil."

CHAPTER XX

But when the shop shut, Kynaston was lurking outside.

"After all, I've nowhere else to go," he said.

He even assisted Mr. Tamburlane to put up the shutters; so that Griselda had to introduce him. Though he was reasonably good-looking by modern male standards, his clothes appeared as inappropriate as in Fullers.

Mr. Tamburlane seemed unperturbed. After they had stood about on the pavement outside the shop mumbling disconnected generalities, he said: "I wonder if the two of you would care to join me in a small repast? I usually go to Underwoods. They know my ways." It was the first such invitation Griselda had received from him.

Kynaston immediately accepted for himself and Griselda. They proceeded on foot to a restaurant near the Charing Cross Road. Mr. Tamburlane, although the hysteria of the evening rush hour was at its height, and tired workers were flickering and zig-zagging across the pavement like interweaving lightning, walked slowly and contemplatively, his eyes directed upwards to a group of swallows swirling after flies, his expression that favoured in coloured representations of the Blessed St. Francis.

"Sister, my sister, O soft light swallow," quoted Mr. Tamburlane, gazing upwards in a warm and gentle rapture, as the trio clove a passage through the toilers frenzied for the consolations of home.

"Sister, my sister, O soft light swallow,
Though all things feast in the spring's guest-chamber,
How hast thou heart to be glad thereof yet?
For where thou fliest I shall not follow,
Till life forget and death remember,
Till thou remember and I forget."

"There is no felicity," he continued, as they stood outside Swan and Edgars, waiting to cross the road, "exceeding that which can ensure upon utter disregard of the consanguineous prohibitions."

Underwoods claimed to combine the tradition of the English chop-house with that of the cosmopolitan restaurant-de-luxe. The tables were set in dark mahogany boxes, but there were attractive red-shaded lights, and the benches had been ameliorated with padded upholstery. The tablecloths were very white, the cutlery very glittering, and the menu cards large as barristers' briefs. There were dimly illuminated portraits of Daniel Mendoza and the Boy Roscius. There was a greeny-grey skull in a glass case bearing a silver plaque inscribed with the names "William Corder" in pleasantly extravagant Gothic script. Griselda thought it might well prove the most agreeable restaurant she had so far visited.

Mr. Tamburlane seemed to be exceedingly well known, both to the staff and to many of the other customers. Preceded by the head waiter, whom he had greeted with a quiet "Good evening, Andrews," he advanced between the lines of boxes, frequently acknowledging greetings. Griselda, following him, attracted almost as much interest; and Kynaston came last, looking more unsuitably dressed than ever. There were an unusual number of men in the restaurant; and few of the women but looked exceedingly striking. Under-waiters with long white aprons darted about like trolls.

Mr. Tamburlane was shown to a table near the back of the room. "I hope you will have no objection," he enquired of his guests, "to caviare, turtle soup, sole, a fillet steak, and a bird? I am becoming increasingly set in my ways."

Griselda noticed that Kynaston seemed entirely able to eat a normal meal provided that it was offered and organized by someone else.

As they ate, and drank the excellent and appropriate wines which their host ordered out of his head and without recourse to the Wine List, Mr. Tamburlane talked more and more expansively, breaking off every now and then to impart to an under-waiter a request for French Mustard or another baton. He called the underwaiters by their Christian names: Leslie, Frank, and

Noel. By the deference shown him in return Mr. Tamburlane might have been his namesake, the Scourge of God. It even seemed to Griselda a little exaggerated, like a caricature of good service.

"It gives me particular pleasure," said Mr. Tamburlane, "to meet another acolyte of the golden and gracious Miss de Reptonville, for another acolyte I readily perceive that you are. Miss de Reptonville has rapidly set up her own particular and especial altar in my soul. I am sure she has in yours also?"

"I proposed marriage to her today. During lunch."

"Then" cried Mr. Tamburlane, transfigured, "this little dinner is an agape, a love-feast, without my knowing it. How limited your news makes me feel, how squat and lacking in vision! We should have drunk from the fountain in the temple of Lantern-land, and the livers of young white peacocks should have been our sustenance. For, if I may for one single moment be personal, your youthful candour and clear brow give assurance of our goddess's response."

"Not quite," said Kynaston. "It's still an open question."

"You did not cry out and leap to his waiting arms," said Mr. Tamburlane in amazement to Griselda.

"We were lunching in Fullers at the time, Mr. Tamburlane."

"Do it now, Miss de Reptonville. They know me here and I can declare a plenary indulgence for all possible consequences. Take him and let us inaugurate a rite which shall last till Venus succumbs before the onrush of Apollo. On a later day, I shall myself take the bridegroom aside and, old man that I am, show him secrets of joy most germane to your bliss, Miss de Reptonville, most unknown to his heart." Mr. Tamburlane's fluffy white hair was moist with rapture, good wine, and the heat of the restaurant; his beaming face, the image of the Japanese ensign.

"I'm afraid I turned the offer down," said Griselda. "I'm very sorry to spoil things."

"But why, dear Anaxarete, make yourself stone?"

"You know very well, Mr. Tamburlane, that I have no inclination to marry anyone."

"But you could fall into no error more fundamental! If you wish to continue—if you hope to rediscover—" But suddenly, with a sound like the discharge of a cork, the excited Mr. Tamburlane, ignorant of the extent of Kynaston's knowledge, discontinued his observations. "Fear nothing," he said to Kynaston, his eyes still very bright, "nor let your night's rest be troubled unless with anticipation of raptures. I shall myself speak apart to our erring one during business hours tomorrow."

"It will make no difference," said Griselda, smiling sweetly. "I'm resolved to marry no one."

"Noel," exclaimed Mr. Tamburlane, "we're ready for the steak." It was exquisite; as was the ensuing bird, which Mr. Tamburlane carved personally, with a long thin knife, like a rapier, incredibly sharp, and a fork fiercer than Morton's. Afterwards came flaming pancakes, and rich Turkish coffee in cups bearing the insignia of the establishment, and two Benedictines each. Mr. Tamburlane completed the occasion by appending to the bill his curving, speckled, backward-sloping signature; and giving a pound in largesse. He then suddenly excused himself to Griselda and Kynaston, and rapidly disappeared through a little door beneath a reproduction of Winterhalter's portrait of the Duke of Sussex.

"Enjoy your dinner, miss?" enquired Noel.

"Very much indeed, thank you."

"Nice gentleman, Mr. Tamburlane."

"He comes here a lot?"

"Usually with his Indian friends."

"I don't know about them," said Griselda, her curiosity surmounting her manners.

"All in coloured robes and covered in diamonds and rubies." He placed his hands on the end of the table and sank his voice.

"I'm afraid we don't live up to that."

"No, miss," said the waiter, glancing at Kynaston's torn and dirty cricket shirt. "Of course, Mr. Tamburlane gets all his money from India."

"How?" asked Kynaston.

"Business with the rajahs and such like. They've all got as much money as a dog has fleas." He lowered his voice still further. "They say it's them who keep his account with us in order."

But Mr. Tamburlane was standing behind him.

"Beg pardon, sir. I was just asking the young lady whether she enjoyed her dinner."

"Of course, she enjoyed her dinner, Noel. This is the happiest day of her life."

Used to such situations in the course of his work, the waiter took Mr. Tamburlane's meaning immediately.

"My respectful congratulations to you, sir. And to you, madam."

"Thank you, Noel," said Kynaston calmly. "I've done nothing to deserve my good fortune."

"And what becomes of us now?" enquired Mr. Tamburlane, seating himself on the corner of the upholstered bench. "The night is still a virgin. All right, Noel. You can go."

"Thank you, sir. Good night sir. Good night madam. Good night sir."

"Tell me, young bridegroom," resumed Mr. Tamburlane, when the adieux to Noel were concluded, "what was your intention tonight in bearing off Miss de Reptonville? You must, I suppose, have had some intention. Or perhaps not; perhaps you thought merely to let the gale of love blow whither it listed? If so may I blow with it for a spell? May I savour, if only by proxy, le premier souvenir d'amour?"

"We were going to look at a flat."

"The hymeneal shrine! Nothing could more perfectly suit me. Let us go there at once. Frank," cried Mr. Tamburlane, "please ask the doorman to summon us a taxi. No, wait. Ours should be a ritual progress. Make it a hansom. There is always one stationed at the bottom of Piccadilly."

"There is one thing which is being overlooked," said Griselda when the flurry had subsided.

"Name it," said Mr. Tamburlane. "It shall be my privilege to provide it. Shall night-scented flowers be strewn before us as we pass through Leicester Square? I presume that is the direction?"

"Juvenal Court," replied Kynaston. "Just off Tottenham Court Road."

"Shall the fountains in Seven Dials run wine? Shall two white oxen be roasted whole in St. Giles's Circus?"

It occurred to Griselda that Mr. Tamburlane was a little drunk.

Possibly his meals when his Indian friends were actually present, were less far-reaching.

"The point we are overlooking," said Griselda, "is that I have no intention of marrying."

"Let us leave events to take their course," replied Mr. Tamburlane. "Indeed I have absolute faith that they will do so."

The doorman entered the restaurant and came to Mr. Tamburlane's table.

"Hansom, sir."

Mr. Tamburlane rose.

"Swift as the thoughts of love. We are grateful to our Hermes." Griselda's worst forebodings were confirmed when Mr. Tamburlane produced his wallet and found it empty. The pound he had given to the waiter must have been all it contained. He sought for change in his trousers pocket and produced sevenpence. This sum seemed far from satisfying the doorman, who, for one whom presumably he had regarded as a very special customer, must have run all the way to Piccadilly Circus.

"Blimey," said Hermes. "That all you've got?"

"The privilege of serving Eros must make up the balance."

"What's a ruddy statue got to do with it?"

"Come," cried Mr. Tamburlane, "let us mount the car of love."

"Bloody swindler," said Hermes. "Look at that!" He extended his hand bearing the seven coppers to Frank seeking sympathy.

"More fool you," said Frank. He added something which Griselda failed to hear, being now on her way out of the restaurant. She noticed, as she followed Mr. Tamburlane, who firmly took the lead, that his many acquaintances among the customers gave an impression of knowing him only by sight. They smiled and bowed as he passed, but said nothing. The doorman could still be heard execrating Mr. Tamburlane in the background. But Andrews, the head waiter, was as deferential as ever.

"Hope to see you again soon, sir."

"Tomorrow and tomorrow and tomorrow," replied Mr. Tamburlane.

"Would you care to book a table now, sir? Like yesterday?"

"All our yesterdays," said Mr. Tamburlane; and, suddenly

remembering the customary usage, stood aside for Griselda to precede him into the warm summer air. There could be little doubt that he was the worse for drink.

There was the appalling question of who could pay for the hansom; including, Griselda supposed, an extra passenger. Only one answer being possible, Griselda attempted to recall the total sum in her handbag. Did hansom cabs charge at the same rates as taxis, she wondered; and would there soon be a scene like the one with the doorman?

"Mount," said Mr. Tamburlane to Griselda.

The door of the cab hung back against the side, and Griselda put her foot on the little step and entered. She had never been in a hansom cab before. The vehicle, although astonishingly open to the air, somehow managed to retain a strong, utterly unknown smell.

"Mount," said Mr. Tamburlane to Kynaston.

Kynaston ascended and seated himself. He looked somewhat dishevelled with wine, though less so than Mr. Tamburlane.

Mr. Tamburlane's foot was on the step when the driver shouted down out of the sky "Two's the legal limit." He flourished his whip.

"Stuff," replied Mr. Tamburlane.

"I'll lose my licence."

"I'll buy you another one," said Mr. Tamburlane.

"Mind you do," said the driver. Mr. Tamburlane had looked like a tip of unprecedented size, and the driver was used to eccentrics who could pay for their indulgences. He flicked Mr. Tamburlane on the left ear.

Kynaston had moved close to Griselda, making a small amount of room for Mr. Tamburlane in the far corner. But Mr. Tamburlane ignored this provision and fell heavily into place between the two of them, sending Kynaston sliding away along the slippery leather.

"Permit me," he said, putting an arm round each of them. "For warmth."

Indeed it was surprisingly draughty for such a warm evening.

"Will you be cold?" said Griselda to Kynaston along the back of Mr. Tamburlane's neck. She had completed her mental arithmetic and a last desperate hope entered her mind. "Perhaps we'd better go by tube?"

As she spoke she felt through Mr. Tamburlane's body his other arm tightening on Kynaston.

"Thank you, Griselda," said Kynaston gulping. "I'll be warm enough. I loathe wrapping up." But his tones were soft. They expressed pathetic gratitude for what he took to be Griselda's first piece of solicitude for him, her first essay at managing his diffused and migrant life.

"Vile were it indeed," said Mr. Tamburlane, muscling in still further, "for the Lachender Held young Siegfried to mask his manhood with draperies."

There was a moment's silence while Mr. Tamburlane consolidated his grip, and Griselda looked up at the stars.

"Well?"

The cabman had lifted the little hatch in the roof.

"Advance," said Mr. Tamburlane.

"Once round the Park?" asked the cabman. "Or along the Victoria Embankment?"

"Juvenal Court," said Kynaston. "Just off Tottenham Court Road."

"It's not usual," said the cabman. "I don't cater for regular fares. Can't afford it. There's taxis for that. I've got my living to earn."

"We'll see that you don't lose by it," said Mr. Tamburlane, his voice full of banknotes.

"Take care that I don't."

"Young love is on the wing tonight," said Mr. Tamburlane.

"Honeymoon couple? O.K."

He shut the trap and they drove off. At the moment of departure the doorman appeared: "Watch out," he shrieked. "They'll welsh you."

"Lie down and cool off," rejoined the cabman ungratefully.

It was pleasant, though squashed. Griselda remembered Lord Beaconsfield's phrase "The gondola of London." To journey from one gilded hall to another by hansom cab alone with the person one truly loved must indeed have been heaven. As soon as the present journey started, however, Griselda realised the origin of the unusual smell. It came from the horse. The vehicle, moreover, lacked a jingling bell: that essential appurtenance for romance.

They clattered along swiftly. Pedestrians, habituated to vehicles equipped with audible warnings, were several times all but slaughtered, to the accompaniment of dreadful language from the cabman. Walking-out couples, glad of something to do, and parties up from the country, stood on the pavements sentimentally staring. Police constables were irritable or facetious. An elementary school child threw a fire-cracker, which fortunately failed to discharge. At Cambridge Circus an elderly woman shouted several times to the driver "It's unsafe. It's unsafe. It's unsafe"; at which the driver lifted the trap in the roof and bawled down "She's dead right", then went into roars of Mephistophilean laughter. Griselda wondered whether the fiery and erratic behaviour of the horse reflected some kind of incorrect feeding.

Juvenal Court appeared to be three adjoining mid-nineteenth century houses run together and converted into a rabbit warren. There were lights at every single window including one or two very small ones. A girl's head was projecting from one of the upper windows.

"Barney," she cried, "come to me." Presumably she was addressing an intimate on a lower floor.

Instantly a man looked out. "I'm tired," he shouted back in a cultivated accent. The street light showed that he had much smooth black hair and a large nose. The girl moaned and withdrew. Griselda had seen that she was wildly beautiful.

Kynaston had squeezed himself from Mr. Tamburlane's grasp and began to stand about ineffectively on the pavement. He seemed worried.

Mr. Tamburlane, though his eyes were open, indeed unusually wide open, continued supine.

"Well?" enquired the driver.

Griselda opened her purse. "How much?"

"I leave that to the party concerned, miss." The driver implied that the question was in curiously bad taste.

Griselda submitted two half-crowns. Instantly and wordlessly the driver hurled them on the granite setts of the gutter.

"It's all I can spare."

"Who's asking *you*?"

Kynaston had ascended the steps to the surviving front door and stood lurking in the shadows. The other two front doors had been superseded by kitchenettes.

"Come on, Mr. Tamburlane. We're there." Griselda dragged at his arm, but it merely came away as if it had dropped off his shoulder. Mr. Tamburlane continued to stare at the horse's tail out of unnaturally large white eyes.

The driver lifted his hatch. He addressed one word to his fare.

"Out."

Mr. Tamburlane hardly moved, but the horse swished his tail and whinnied. Kynaston was fidgeting. He seemed distinctly upset.

"Please, Mr. Tamburlane," cried Griselda weakly, but still, she thought, firmly.

Mr. Tamburlane turned a little away from her, groaned slightly, and addressed himself to the space formerly occupied by Kynaston. His voice was low and throbbing. "Γυγη. γυναικί κόσμον ή σιγη φέρει," said Mr. Tamburlane.

Griselda turned her back on him and called to Kynaston. "Can you come and help?"

"What do you suggest?" said Kynaston from the doorstep. He seemed almost shifty.

Griselda looked up at the cabman; who again lifted his little flap and in accents of deep distaste uttered another single word.

"Scram."

The effect was surprising. The horse reared a little, neighed noisily, and clattered away down the street. The tumult of his shoes on the granite setts was considerable. As the vehicle disappeared from sight it seemed for some reason to be swaying from one wheel to the other. The driver looked to have lost his reins and, at undoubted peril, to be erect on his perch expostulating. Soon, however, all was quiet once more and Kynaston was holding back the heavy front door, covered with letter-box flaps each with several names, for Griselda to enter.

"Thank God that's over," said Kynaston.

"I don't want Mr. Tamburlane to be hurt," said Griselda.

"I expect a policeman will pull them up soon. The police are always doing things like that. Anything rather than have him back. It's most unfortunate how strongly I attract that type of man. Young or old, it always happens. I regularly appeal to the wrong type in both sexes. I wish I attracted you, Griselda." He stopped groping for the switch and began to grope for Griselda.

"Let me advise you to recover the cash." A door had opened on to the dark hall and Barney was looking out. Kynaston saw the switch and turned on the light.

"Thank you very much," said Griselda. "I will." She had forgotten her two important half-crowns.

She returned to the gutter but the coins were not to be seen.

"Can't you find them?" It was Kynaston, once more at the top of the steps.

"Come and help to look for them."

He remained in the shadow. "I'm better at losing than finding."

"Let *me* look." It was Barney. He wore a check shirt and brown trousers. He descended to his hands and knees, and crawled along, striking matches.

"Please don't trouble."

"How much was it?"

"Five shillings."

"No trouble."

Kynaston was clearly bored. He still seemed uneasy.

"It's very good of you."

"Five shillings is five shillings." Barney groped along like a small brown bear taught to let off a train of tiny fireworks.

"Please stop now. It really doesn't matter."

Barney resumed the human posture. "The scum of the earth live round here. They wouldn't miss a chance like that." The street seemed deserted. "Would you allow me to reduce the loss? I imagine Geoffrey's in his usual condition." He put his hand in his trousers pocket and offered Griselda half-a-crown.

"Certainly not. I mean thank you very much; but No thank you. It really doesn't matter at all," Griselda added extenuatingly.

"Please yourself."

"I do mean thank you all the same."

"So long as you know what you mean."

Kynaston was looking embarrassed. He changed the subject.
"Is Dykes in?"

"I suppose so. Why?"

"We want to look at the empty flat."

"Empty what?"

"Empty room."

"We?"

"I'm going to marry Griselda. Griselda de Reptonville. Barney
Lazarus."

Griselda had heard of him. Paintings by Barney Lazarus were
sometimes mentioned by the Art Critics of "The Times". She
had understood that he painted mostly Mothers.

"How do you do?" said Barney. They shook hands on the pavement. "I cannot possibly congratulate you."

"It's the man you congratulate," said Kynaston.

"That remains to be seen," said Barney, looking Griselda up
and down. "I've known Geoffrey for years," he remarked to her,
"and I would rather marry King Kong."

"I don't know King Kong," remarked Griselda, smiling sweetly.

CHAPTER XXI

Dykes, who lived entirely in what had once been the larder of
the house (the other rooms in the basement being let to tenants),
proved to be wholly drunk. Roused by Kynaston, he stumbled
up the battered stair singing snatches of old songs. His memory
being ruined by the bottle, however, he was unable to recall
which room was to let. Furthermore, having forgotten all he
had ever learnt at school (if not more), he was incapable of dis-
tinguishing between the numbers on the different doors. The
three of them bounced and crashed from amorous routines to
solidary drudgeries until Kynaston asserted "I am sure Monica
said Number Thirteen."

He and Griselda climbed another flight; but Dykes said his
heart would carry him no higher. "We may not need a key," said
Kynaston. "I daresay it's lost."

Across the landing before them, a dark brown door was inscribed 13. Kynaston turned the elaborate brass handle and entered without obstacle (the key being on the inside); then sagged back, standing upon Griselda's toe.

"Good God, Lotus," he said faintly and peevishly, "this is really too much."

The room was medium sized, middlingly furnished in a style unexpectedly like Greenwood Tree House, painted in the same dark brown as the door, and with hideous paper leaving the walls and ceiling. Standing on the dust coloured carpet was the girl who had shouted from the upper window. At closer quarters, she was still wildly beautiful, with well kept golden-red hair, bright green eyes, a prominent somewhat Iberian nose, a large but well-shaped mouth, and a perfect skin. She wore crêpe-de-chine pyjamas, intended for parties. She was rather plump, though well-proportioned; and appeared to be expensively corsetted. Griselda found her age unusually difficult to guess.

She glared at Kynaston for a moment; then at Griselda.

"If you must be unfaithful to me, Geoffrey," she said in a voice as beautiful as her face, "then you need not insult me as well by always seducing an ingénue. There are other mondaine women in London."

Kynaston stood his ground remarkably well. "Lotus, I'm going to marry Griselda. Griselda de Reptonville. Mrs. Lamb."

"Are you insane, Geoffrey?"

"You can't look after me, Lotus. I thought you could, but I was wrong. I really believe Griselda can. And without bullying me, as you do. As well as being sensible, she is sweet and sympathetic. Besides you yourself refuse to marry me——"

"I am above such a thought!" she interrupted. Suddenly she extended her hand to Griselda. "Ignore my remark. It was intended only to hurt Geoffrey not you. As you love Geoffrey, you must forgive me for that also."

"I don't love Geoffrey," replied Griselda, smiling and shaking Lotus's hand.

"Perfect. That's the only possible basis for marriage."

"I'm not going to marry."

"Monica told me you'd gone away," said Kynaston interrupting.

"I've come back. I'm living with Barney now."

"I suppose that also is intended to hurt me."

"Certainly. And it's quite true."

"You've been quick enough."

"And you? Or is this merely another Doris Ditton?" Turning to Griselda she added: "Please don't think I mean anything personal."

"I'm going to marry Griselda."

"She says not."

"She'll be sorry for me in the end."

Lotus sat on the edge of the divan. "You know, Geoffrey," she said, "I'll take you back. This instant, if you like."

"I can't understand what you see in me, Lotus. I'm not your kind of man at all."

"What are you going to live on without me?"

"I've got a job. Anyway you've never supported me."

"Paid your debts. It's much the same. What sort of a job have you got?" She seemed genuinely to wonder; and remarked to Griselda: "Geoffrey's incapable of work of any kind." It was a simple statement of fact.

"I think we'd better face reality," replied Geoffrey.

"I inspired all his poetry too," continued Lotus to Griselda.

Suddenly she fell sideways on the divan and began to sob. She sobbed beautifully. Kynaston looked distracted.

"Good night," said Griselda.

"For God's sake," cried Kynaston clutching both her elbows and holding on.

"It's late. I really should go."

"I beg you," cried Kynaston. "You can see how utterly wrong for me she is and always has been."

"She's very beautiful," said Griselda falling into the new convention of speaking as if the person spoken about were not present.

"You're beautiful too, Griselda."

"Not in the same class."

Lotus looked up. "You are. You are. You know you are." Huge separate tears streamed down her lovely skin. "I love you Griselda. I need you. Please don't leave me now." He was still desperately gripping one of her elbows.

Lotus dropped off the bed and knelt on the floor crying her

heart out. "When you've married him, will you let me see him? Ever?"

But the door had opened and Barney entered. He spoke very quietly.

"I thought I heard Lotus crying. Silence, Kynaston, while I break every bone in your body." Barney was a painter of the traditional school. Griselda had never before seen anyone in so dreadful a rage.

His first blow laid Kynaston on the floor, where Barney began systematically to maul him.

Deeming explanation useless, Griselda began to drag at Barney's shoulders from behind. This was equally unavailing.

"Could you please help?" she said to the tear-stained Lotus. Even Lotus's pyjamas were becoming dark and saturated. Her beautiful tears were particularly wet.

Lotus rose from the floor and with a single kick from one of her attractive shoes, mastered the situation. Barney stopped half-murdering Kynaston, and looked up at her, all rage evaporated.

"I thought——"

"You thought wrong. Get out." She kicked him again, unexpectedly and maliciously.

"I wanted——"

"Go to bed, Barney. You said you were tired."

Once more his expression changed. "You'd made me desperate. I'm not a pekinese."

"You foul the air."

Barney flushed; rose to his feet; and took Lotus in his arms. Quite calmly, as it appeared, she bit deeply into his left cheek. Barney's blood on her big well-shaped mouth made her look like a beautiful vampire.

Barney felt in his trousers pocket for a handkerchief, but he was unprovided. Remembering the half-crown, Griselda extended her own handkerchief. He began to dab at his streaming cheek. Griselda's handkerchief was much too small.

"Are you going back to Kynaston?"

"I'm not going back to you."

"I see." He turned to Griselda. "And you? Where do you come in?"

It was difficult to know what to say. Lotus saved Griselda the trouble.

"Stop asking questions and leave the room, Barney." She took a short step towards him. It was like the school bully and her victim, Griselda thought.

"I'll kill myself."

"The best thing you can do."

His bloodstained face was now completely white.

"You don't believe me?"

"I don't care."

Hanging from the washbasin was a dirty towel, the property of a former tenant. It might have hung there for months. Lotus snatched it and flicked it with a loud report in Barney's face.

"Lotus." His voice was a voice from the tomb. "Lotus, I love you. I love you terribly, Lotus."

Before she had succeeded in driving him from the room, she must have been hurting him quite considerably.

When Barney was outside, Lotus locked the door and stuck the key into the top of her black corselette, which her exertions had exposed to view.

Griselda was alarmed. But Lotus only looked dreamily at her for several seconds, her large eyes full of lustre, her exquisite hands making small groping movements; then with a low cry fell upon the prostrate Kynaston, all beautiful compassion. Again she looked at Griselda.

"Do you know any first-aid?"

"A little." Griselda reflected. "Very little."

"Can you tell if he's alive?"

"I think I can."

Griselda held the mirror from her bag against the side of Kynaston's mouth pressed against the dust coloured carpet. A slightly yellow mist immediately clouded it.

"He's alive."

Lotus squatted back.

"I don't mind if you marry him so long as you let me go on seeing him. It's only his body I want really. I don't at all care about your having everything else."

"I quite understand. Hadn't we better try to bring him round?"

"So long as you understand. It'll be no different from any other marriage. Except, of course, that Geoffrey will never be able to keep you. Still I want him to be happy and might be able to help with that: always through you, of course. Geoffrey can't tell the difference between fourpence and ninepence."

"That's very kind of you."

"It's not only kindness. There's a close connection between a man's happiness and his vitality, you know. In many ways, men are exactly like animals. Perhaps you don't believe that?"

"Shall we chafe his extremities?"

"Why?"

"It's what we were taught."

"Then you'd better do it."

Griselda hesitated.

"Have you any brandy?" She thought that this might, among other things, get the door unlocked and Lotus out of the room.

"Of course."

"Do you think you could bring it?"

"I suppose so." Lotus rose to her feet, stretching the cramp from her leg muscles. "What a curse men are." She was looking for the key. "Wait." She had unlocked the door and was going upstairs. Indeed she had left the door open.

To her own surprise Griselda remained with the body.

When Lotus returned, she once more locked the door. "We don't want a crowd," she remarked. She bore a half-full bottle of excellent liqueur brandy; distinctly superior to what might be expected of Juvenal Court.

"Shall we force it down him?"

"I suppose so. I've never done it."

"I've never done it either. I always let other people deal with emergencies."

Tenderly Lotus rolled Kynaston on to his back.

"Give me that tooth-glass. I don't see why we shouldn't have some first. The whole thing's Geoffrey's own fault."

"It needs washing. There are two dead flies in it."

"All right. Wash it. But be quick."

Griselda emptied the flies to the floor and cleaned the glass to the best of her ability.

"I'll dry it." Somewhat to Griselda's distaste, Lotus dried the glass on the grimy towel. "Now then." She half-filled the glass with brandy. "Me first, if you don't mind." At once the glass was again empty. "Now you." Griselda's allowance was considerably smaller.

"Thank you." It was certainly wonderful stuff.

"How do you force drink between tightly clenched jaws?"

"Geoffrey's mouth is open."

"Oh yes. Still I don't want to waste it."

"Let me try." Griselda was beginning to worry lest Kynaston have concussion, whatever that might be.

"Careful."

Griselda poured about half a tablespoonful of brandy into the glass and released it drop by drop down Kynaston's throat.

"Careful."

When the glass was nearly empty, Kynaston seemed to have a violent spasm. He curled up instantaneously, like a caterpillar which has taken alarm. His mouth closed sharply and a curious rattle came from somewhere inside him. It frightened Griselda so much that she swallowed what remained in the glass.

"Of course," she said, "he's been having very little to eat."

Lotus stared at her dreamily; again half-filling the glass.

"Don't forget your promise," she said, drinking.

"What promise?"

"You may not think you'll marry Geoffrey. But he'll marry you. You won't be able to resist him: and he'll make marriage his price." She had unbuttoned Kynaston's shirt and was running her free hand over the upper part of his body. "Or part of his price."

"Shall we call a doctor?"

"How innocent you are, Griselda!"

Suddenly Lotus had cast the tumbler into a corner of the room, where it shattered with rather too much noise and into rather too many pieces; had thrown herself upon the half-naked Kynaston; and was frenziedly kissing his mouth. Instantly Kynaston sat up.

"Beloved," he said, clasping Lotus in his arms. Then, seeing Griselda, he gave a groan of shock and disgust, and was on his feet, buttoning his shirt.

Lotus lay on the floor. She appeared to be looking round for another glass. As with the locked door, she seemed to find difficulty, Griselda thought, in sustaining her romantic emphases.

"Come away at once," said Kynaston, apparently none the worse. "We shall have to live elsewhere." The knock-out seemed to have awakened in him a slightly hysterical dignity.

"No need at all," replied Lotus from the floor. "Griselda and I are on the best of terms. We are going to be great friends."

"I didn't know," said Kynaston. "Griselda needs some friends."

"We've made a bargain."

"What bargain?"

Lotus smiled her lovely smile. "Geoffrey," she said, "do organize a picnic for next Sunday."

"All right, Lotus."

"We'll all come. It'll be like old times."

"So long as no one crosses me about the arrangements."

"Who would?"

He smiled back at her.

"Griselda hasn't seen you at your wonderful best until she's been on one of your wonderful wonderful picnics."

Now Griselda smiled also.

Kynaston was at the door.

"It's locked."

All three were still smiling.

"Where's the key?"

Lotus knelt, sitting back upon her ankles, and, her hands clasped behind her, extended her plump black-corsetted bosom towards him.

"Reach for it."

The key being extracted, and the door opened, they left Lotus, the search for another glass abandoned, imbibing direct from the bottle.

"Marry-in-haste," she said between gulps.

"I never shall," said Griselda still smiling.

CHAPTER XXII

Through his door on the ground floor, Barney could be clearly heard grinding his teeth and his colours.

As Griselda and Kynaston passed into the summer night, the clock on the local Crematorium struck midnight, an intimation repeated a few minutes later by the doubtless more accurate clock at the Palace of Westminster.

"I should have told you about Lotus."

"She's no affair of mine."

"I never expected to see her again. It's Monica Paget-Barlow's fault. She misled me."

"I see."

"All the same she's rather splendid."

"Miss Paget-Barlow?"

"But I'm quite finished with her none the less. She lacks your glorious independence."

"I've lost the thread."

"You'll come on the picnic?"

"No. Thank you."

"Don't be jealous. It's absurd of you. Really it is."

"I'm not jealous. I have another engagement."

"What?"

Without particularly thinking, Griselda answered the truth. "I'm spending the day with my friend Peggy Potter."

"Where are you going?"

Regrettably, Peggy, with her passion for the provisional, always, when possible, refused to agree upon a plan in advance.

"Does that matter?"

"Bring her with you. There'll be a crowd. She'll pass unnoticed."

"No, thank you. She'd hate that."

They were walking southwards down Tottenham Court Road, as Griselda did not care to risk the passage of the back streets at midnight. Outside Goodge Street Station, Kynaston stopped, again took hold of Griselda's elbows, and said: "Griselda, I love you with all my heart." He seemed to mean it. But as he spoke a lift arrived, and they were pushed about by a load of tired revellers and resentful night workers.

Absurd though the declaration was, Griselda had too soft a heart to feel unmoved. "Where will you go tonight?" she asked sympathetically.

"I've made arrangements . . . Please marry me."

"No, Geoffrey. It's impossible . . . You'll be all right?"

"I'll be far from all right if you won't marry me. Besides I've got a slight headache."

"When do you take up your job?"

"On Liberation Day. Next Wednesday. It's a job for a D.Litt. There's very little money in it."

"Poor Geoffrey! I really must go. I shall miss the last tube." Griselda had previously intended to walk.

"You won't need an address for me as I shall look in the shop every day."

"No please, Geoffrey, I'm sure there'll be trouble with Mr. Tamburlane."

"Yes. I suppose there may."

"I wonder if Mr. Tamburlane's still alive? Poor Mr. Tamburlane."

"Promise to come on the picnic and we'll leave it at that for the moment. I've got a lot of things to do anyway before I'm tied by the leg on Liberation Day. Promise, Griselda."

"Certainly not."

"Ten o'clock next Sunday at Juvenal Court. Bring your own lunch. Tell your friend to bring enough for the two of you."

"Good night, Geoffrey."

"May I kiss you?"

"No."

He kissed her. Although it was Goodge Street Station and another lift had come up, Griselda realized that Kynaston really had feelings. It was most surprising.

Despite her efforts, he felt her respond.

"Griselda darling. . . ."

But Griselda had been swept away by a flood of sad ineluctable

memories and a posse of half-drunken suburbans on their way to
Hendon, Edgware, and Trinity Road, Tooting Bec.

The tide of grief because Louise had been lost was so overwhelming, and the prospect of Sunday spent alone with Peggy
so depressing (fond of Peggy though she was), that when she
arrived back at Greenwood Tree House, Griselda, though it was
late by Peggy's standards, knocked at her friend's door. With so
many weightier cares to keep her from sleep, Griselda knew that
she would lie awake all night unless she settled the matter of the
picnic before she retired.

"What is it?"

"It is I. Griselda. Please let me in." Peggy always locked her door.

There was a curious sound of shuffling and putting away,
which continued for an unexplained time. Then the key was
turned and Peggy stood in the doorway.

"Come in Griselda," she said quite pleasantly.

"You needn't have bothered to put on your dressing-gown."

Peggy said nothing.

"Do get into bed again. I can quite easily talk to you in bed."

"I'd rather not. Sit down."

They sat formally in the room's two chairs. Peggy must have
been putting away her clothes and underclothes, as none were
visible.

"Had you anything in mind for Sunday?"

"Need we settle so long beforehand? After all, it's not work.
Can't we leave it till the time comes?"

"We've both been asked on a picnic."

"Both?"

"I've been asked and asked to bring you."

"I see. Will the people like me? Seeing that they don't know me
or I them. I should hate to spoil your day."

"Of course you won't spoil my day, Peggy. I hardly know the
people myself. I shall be glad to have you for company."

"Are they a married couple?"

"There's to be quite a number of people, I believe. You'll be
able to pass unnoticed, if you wish."

"Not if they're my sort of person, I hope. And obviously not if they're *not* my sort of person," said Peggy, patiently smiling. "*Are* they my sort of person? You won't mind my asking."

"Not exactly," replied Griselda thoughtfully. "But I'm sure you'll like them. I do," she added without particular regard for truth.

"Could I let you know later?"

"No. I want to know now. Or I shan't sleep."

"All right, I'll come. Thank you for asking me."

"Thank you for coming."

"I suppose it must be important to you. There's someone expected? Someone in particular?"

"Nothing like that. Just a group of old friends. Very pleasant people," replied Griselda, seeing mental pictures of Lotus flagellating Barney with the towel and Barney trying to beat out Kynaston's brains.

CHAPTER XXIII

When Griselda arrived at the shop next morning, Mr. Tamburlane was taking down the shutters as usual.

"Since I had to hurry away last night, let me at once whisper in your hymeneal ear, Miss de Reptonville," he exclaimed as she approached.

"Are you quite safe, Mr. Tamburlane?"

"I glow. I bask. I kindle."

"Then that's all right." Griselda entered the dusky shop with its smell of scholarship.

"Advance the nuptials, Miss de Reptonville. It's the best thing you can possibly do. Afterwards you can throw the traces right over and—your tastes being what they are, of course—Society will do nothing but smile upon you."

"Please don't concern yourself."

"In my anachronistic way I feel called to advise you; both as your employer and also quasi-paternally."

"It shows thought, Mr. Tamburlane."

"But perchance the plough has entered the furrow without aid from me?"

At that point a young man came into the shop and saved the situation by calling, in an affected voice, for the Complete Incubology of St. Teresa of Avila, which had to be got up from the basement.

None the less, all day Mr. Tamburlane made himself quite a nuisance with his sympathetic but entire misunderstanding of Griselda's situation. Nor did the heat help.

Saturday was really hot.

"Need we go tomorrow?" enquired Peggy, as she lay beside Griselda in the Park, her head on an old copy of "Headway".

"It may not be so hot."

"Then it will be raining. It's August."

"Look at that duck."

"That's a widgeon."

"We don't have to go if you don't want to."

"I don't want to spoil it for you."

"I agreed to spend Sunday with *you*, Peggy. It's for you to say about the picnic."

"It's only the heat. I'd love to come otherwise."

"Surely it'll be hotter in Italy?"

Sunday was hotter.

Griselda had passed the night naked on top of her bed and had slept perfectly; but she feared that Peggy might not have slept at all.

"Are you awake, Peggy?"

"I'm making sandwiches. Come in."

Griselda entered. Peggy was fully dressed in a pale blue cotton frock covered with small sprigs of pale pink flowers; and was being exceedingly useful. Griselda was delighted by her energy and practicality. Kynaston's cynical suggestion was coming to pass. Peggy was preparing lunch for the two of them.

"I'll go away again and get some clothes on."

"Do you like mustard with tinned salmon?"

"Please. It adds a flavour."

Immediately Griselda thought that this might be interpreted as offensive. So she added. "They're beautiful sandwiches. So even."

"Got the knack at College," replied Peggy. "I made sandwich lunches for my group every day."

"Didn't the others ever take a turn?"

"Catch them," said Peggy with much meaning but no explanation.

Griselda put on a dark flame coloured silk shirt and her black linen skirt.

At five minutes to ten they were at Juvenal Court. Peggy had insisted on bringing her rucksack. It seemed to Griselda to go somewhat queerly with her cotton frock, but certainly came in useful as a repository for the little packets of food.

Seated on the steps were Barney, dressed precisely as before, and a young man in a tennis shirt, with fair hair and an open innocent face. Behind them on the step above, was a girl in a khaki shirt and grey flannel trousers. She had sharp but lively features, including a longish nose and almondish eyes; dark skin and black hair, drawn tightly back and tied with a length of wide khaki ribbon. She sat with her legs rather wide apart; but not sprawling: on the contrary, giving an impression of alertness and vigour.

Barney rose, followed by the innocent looking young man. The mark of Lotus's teeth was plain on Barney's cheek.

"How nice of you to be so punctual." It was as if nothing had happened; almost as if nothing had happened ever. Barney's tone was the pink of polite nothingness.

"We've walked," remarked Peggy. "From the other side of the Edgware Road." Griselda did not really understand Peggy. Possibly she profited from being brought out.

"How sensible of you to bring your rucksack."

"I like to keep my hands free."

"Naturally." Barney turned to Griselda. "Do introduce your friend."

"Peggy Potter. Barney Lazarus."

"The painter?"

"Himself. How do you do?"

"I know your work."

Barney was admiring Peggy's large bust.

"Better than knowing me."

"Stop fishing for compliments, Barney. She's only just set eyes on you." The girl on the step above was speaking. "I'm Lena Drelincourt."

"How do you do?" said Griselda. "I'm Griselda de Reptonville."

"Not patient Griselda?" cried the innocent looking young man in a public school voice and high glee.

"This is Freddy Fisher," said Barney, embarrassed because he had failed to introduce Griselda.

"I write," explained Lena Drelincourt.

"I work in a bookshop. Perhaps we stock you."

"I shouldn't think so."

"There are several more of us to come," said Barney, making conversation. "Guillaume and Florence. Your friend Geoffrey Kynaston. And, of course, Monica Paget-Barlow. And Lotus."

"And Lotus," said Lena Drelincourt, underlining.

"More women than men, I'm glad to say," resumed Barney.

"Twice as many," said Lena, "not counting Freddy, which you can't. It's an incitement to unnatural vice."

Freddy Fisher blushed all over his head and neck.

"So many of the younger generation of men like to stay in bed over the week-end," explained Barney.

"Where's Geoffrey?" asked Lena. "If he doesn't appear soon, I'm going to take charge."

"Why are the arrangements always left to Geoffrey?" asked Freddy Fisher.

"Because he makes a scene otherwise," answered Lena.

"He's not a child."

"No. He's a baby. He only feels grown up when other people do what he says."

A tired looking girl, obviously much younger than she seemed, with a small round head and a small round face, nondescript hair and nondescript clothes, came out of the house. Barney introduced her as Monica Paget-Barlow. She smiled quickly, said nothing, seated herself on the top step and began to knit.

She was immediately followed by Guillaume and Florence. Guillaume was an elderly-looking man (though he also was probably younger than he looked), with long sparse grey hair and an air of unsuccessfully applied learning. His other name was announced as Cook. He was exceedingly untidy.

Florence was a slender dark woman of about thirty with short brown hair and a Grecian nose. She gave an impression of quietness and docility, which, like her appearance, was far from unattractive. She wore a tight shirt of dark-blue jersey-silk, which emphasised her slenderness and lack of figure, and dark blue trousers. Consciously or otherwise, the costume was well chosen to present her to advantage. She was introduced as Florence Cook, but probably was not. Griselda liked her at sight, and wondered what she found in Guillaume, supposing that she found anything.

"We could hardly have a better day," said Guillaume in accents of deep anxiety. Before long Griselda perceived that it was his habitual tone. He spoke seldom and slowly and, though his words were commonplace, he appeared to worry very much over choosing them. Now he continued to stare at the sky, already almost colourless with heat.

"Have you all got your lunches?" enquired Barney.

Everyone had. Monica Paget-Barlow's was contained in a round bundle, somewhat resembling a pantomime Christmas Pudding.

"I could put some of the packets in my rucksack," suggested Peggy, who, though Griselda had sat on the step, still stood on the pavement.

"Splendid," said Lena. "Many thanks." She extended her packet.

"I don't think you should do that," said Freddy Fisher to Peggy. "Or let me carry the rucksack."

"I'm used to walking with a rucksack."

Florence was restraining Guillaume from offering their joint packet.

"There's Geoffrey," cried Freddy Fisher.

They watched him approach. He was entirely unencumbered. His dancer's gait was exhilarating.

"Hullo Griselda. Hullo everybody. Anyone got any lunch to spare?"

No one spoke.

"I expect there'll be things left over when the time comes. Where's Lotus?"

"Lotus!" shouted Lena Drelincourt without moving and at the top of her very clear voice.

There was an expectant pause. But nothing happened.

"Go and get her," said Lena.

Without either intending it, Barney and Kynaston looked at one another for half a second.

"Shall I go?" asked Freddy Fisher helpfully.

"You go," said Barney and Kynaston, each to the other; and Freddy Fisher went.

The expectancy became a strain.

"Where are we going?" enquired Florence.

"Epping Forest. Walk to the Dominion, Number Seven bus to Liverpool Street, train to Chingford," replied Kynaston. "There are Day Tickets."

"Tell us about the Forest," said Florence.

"There are parrots."

"Anything else?" enquired Lena.

"Epstein at work," said Barney.

"I know his work," said Peggy.

Suddenly Lotus appeared, followed by Freddy. It was as when the Conductor goes to fetch the Prima Donna. Everyone, moreover, stood up.

Lotus wore a black shirt buttoned to the neck, and a white linen coat and skirt, expensive, fashionable, and likely to remain clean for one day only, or for less. Alone among the women she wore silk stockings, and her shoes had the air of being specially made for her. By daylight, Griselda thought her lovelier than ever. Standing in the doorway with the dark passage behind her, she surveyed the party with her bright green eyes, looking through Barney, and over Peggy, until she saw Kynaston slightly concealed behind Guillaume.

"Geoffrey," she said, "let us lead the way together."

She looked like "Harper's Bazaar", but she walked like Boadicea. In fact, she could probably outwalk all of them, except Griselda, and (if the walk were far enough off the map) Peggy Potter.

On the Number Seven bus, Lotus sat with Kynaston in an empty front seat; Peggy with Barney; Monica with Guillaume;

Griselda with Florence; and Lena by herself, peeling a large pear with a larger clasp knife, which had been dangling from her belt. There was no seat for Freddy, who volunteered to stand inside; where, the others being all outside, he paid all the fares. Monica and Guillaume travelled in silence. At the bus stop Monica had brought her knitting from the discoloured circular reticule in which it travelled, and had resumed work, hardly ceasing even in order to climb the stairs of the vehicle. She was producing a small tightly knitted object, the colour of a brown-green lizard, more brown than green. Guillaume seemed lost in sad thoughts.

"He suffers a great deal," said Florence to Griselda, regarding with apparent fondness the blotchy back of his scalp. Her voice was sweet and quiet.

"Why?" asked Griselda.

Lena stopped peeling for a moment and cocked a faun-like ear.

"He is a disappointed man."

Lena resumed peeling.

"Why?"

"He is disappointed in the world. He is disappointed in himself."

"Can nothing be done?"

"I do what I can. But I sometimes think he's disappointed in me."

"That's absurd. I mean I'm sure he isn't."

"I am too small a thing really to enter into him."

"How long have you been together?"

Lena had finished peeling and begun eating, cutting the soft ripe flesh into precise sectors.

"Twelve years. Since I was nineteen. He has been my life."

"I know how you feel."

Lena glanced at Griselda sharply. Florence gazed at her for a moment, then said: "These picnics! Why do we go on them?"

"I don't really know," said Griselda. "It's my first."

"I wonder how many of us really enjoy them . . . I mean *really*. You know what I mean by enjoyment?" She looked solemn, and a little timorous.

"Yes," said Griselda. "I know what you mean by enjoyment."

In the front seat, Lotus, early in the day though it was, laid her beautiful golden-red head gently on Kynaston's shoulder; who squirmed slightly, then appeared to resign himself. The bus had only reached Holborn Viaduct. Barney and Peggy were talking about tactile values. Lena shut her big shining knife with a loud snap, and reattached the weapon to her person.

On the train they were unable to find a compartment to themselves and they had to pack in with a couple travelling from one side of London to the other, in order to spend the day with a married daughter. Even without Freddy, who was queueing for tickets, it was very congested on such a hot day. Monica's knitting needles became entangled from time to time in the male stranger's watch-chain.

"Yuman personality," said the male stranger to the female stranger. "It's sacred. You can't get past that."

"We're all as we're made," said the female stranger.

"No system of Government will change yuman personality."

"Either way it's the same."

"Yuman personality is sacred."

"It bloody well isn't," interjected Barney. "You try being a nigger in the deep south."

"Kindly refrain from using foul language in the presence of my wife," said the male stranger.

"Behave yourself, Barney," said Lotus. "Or you can go home."

"No offence," said the male stranger. "Not really."

"*I* am offended," said Lotus.

"I should think so too," said the female stranger. "Dirty Yid!"

Barney, so easy and self-possessed before Lotus had joined them, flushed slightly, but said nothing. Peggy threw Griselda a glance of unsatisfactory anticipations fulfilled.

Freddy only managed to race up the torrid platform and hurl himself amongst them just as the train started. There seemed nowhere for him to sit but the floor; with which, however, he professed himself quite content.

The embarrassment, discomfort, and tension were little relieved by Lena producing a thin pocket book from one of the breast pockets of her shirt and commencing to make some small drawings.

"Anti-semitism is so *unnecessary*, don't you think?" said Florence quietly to Griselda, as the train puffed up the incline to Bethnal Green. "I know it's one of the things *he* feels particularly. Though he doesn't say so, I know it."

"Is he a Jew?"

"Oh no. He feels with all who suffer. The people everywhere."

"Look at that," said the male stranger, savagely indicating Bethnal Green. "Shocking." He glowered accusation at the misjudged Barney.

"What does Lotus live on?" asked Griselda in an undertone.

"She's an heiress."

"Then what's she doing in Juvenal Court? I'm sure you know what I mean."

"She likes living with artists. Also she's in love with Geoffrey and he's not in love with her. It's her way of ever seeing him."

"Are you sure Geoffrey's not in love with her?" It was difficult to believe that any man could resist Lotus's beauty, passion, imperiousness, and riches. Moreover, she was holding Geoffrey's hand at that very moment.

"Quite sure. You can tell because he refuses to let her keep him. That's a sure sign with Geoffrey. Though he's weak of course, he refuses to be kept by anyone he's not in love with."

"Have you known Geoffrey for long?"

"He lived in Juvenal Court for two years; when he was teaching the recorder you know."

"Do you like him?"

"Everyone likes Geoffrey, He's weak, but sweet."

"Like that nauseating tea," said Lena quietly.

"Florence," said Guillaume across the compartment. "Look at the sunlight on the windows of that gasworks."

"Yes, darling. Beautiful."

"If only it could be made as sunny and glittering within." He seemed more troubled than ever.

"People like you and me don't know how the factory workers live," observed the male stranger, disentangling Monica's wool from the lower part of his braces.

"What the hell's the good of going somewhere as lovely as Epping Forest," soliloquized Lena in her clear voice, "without a man to ravish one?"

After that the strangers fell silent until the next station, at which they alighted.

At Chingford, under Kynaston's direction, they struck up the road to the Royal Forest Hotel, then descended to Connaught Water. Kynaston and Lotus still walked ahead, their easy efficient movements a pleasure to watch. Had she not known them, Griselda might have taken them for gods descended to Essex earth. The rest of them advanced en masse, two of the number knowing the others hardly at all, the rest knowing them perhaps too well. Peggy was conserving her energy, as if a range of mountains would have to be crossed before nightfall. Lena slouched with her hands in her pockets; but her slouch was somehow electric.

"Do you see how the water catches the reflection of the willows?" said Guillaume to Florence.

"Yes, darling. Beautiful."

Outside the Hotel were motor coach parties drinking. When they set eyes on Lotus, they whistled and catcalled because she was so beautiful: but Lotus strode past, like a Queen on her way to execution, not increasing her pace or diminishing her poise.

"Anyone know what that is?" asked Peggy, taking no notice and pointing to Queen Elizabeth's Hunting Lodge.

"It's one of the places where the upper classes get together to kill things," said Guillaume.

"Damn good sport," said Freddy Fisher. "Done any beagling?" he enquired of Griselda.

"No, never," replied Griselda.

"I beagled almost every day for a month last autumn. You can if you've got a fast car."

"What do you do with the rest of your time?"

"Learn to paint. Animals and birds, you know. I've got to for a living, more's the pity. Dad's lost his last halfpenny. Horses, you know."

"But you've still got a fast car?"

"Not any more."

"Oh dear."

"You're terribly pretty, Griselda. I should have liked to ask you home. Mum would have taken to you no end."

"Perhaps I shall meet her sometime," said Griselda politely.

"She's dead. Drugs. Dad was to blame."

"I am sorry. But I don't know that you should be so sure it was your Father's fault."

"Of course it was Dad's fault. He had to stop it all coming out at the inquest."

"Still it's often hard to be sure."

"Of course I'm sure. It's spoilt my whole life."

"Can we stop for a moment?" asked Monica. "There's a drawing-pin in my shoe."

When Connaught Water came in sight, covered with boats, Florence's sensitive face lighted up. "Oh I should like to go out in a boat."

Guillaume's brow became rigid with apprehension. "Hardly with so many other people, Florence. I am sure the boats must be dirty."

Florence smiled gently and said "It just passed through my mind, darling." Married or not, Florence was suffering from that cancer of the will which Griselda had observed so often to accompany matrimony. She and Lena exchanged glances.

At the lake they left the road and entered the trees. Within five minutes the clatter had become inaudible. They passed several times from thicket to clearing, the change in temperature being each time overwhelming, and soon were among the hornbeams.

"Everyone," cried Lotus over her shoulder, "must look for a parrot."

Kynaston caught Griselda's eye and looked deeply unhappy.

His distress of mind possibly accounted for the fact that within ten minutes from leaving the road, they were lost. Kynaston did not for some time admit this, but urged them on, with unnecessary expressions of confidence, along a rutty but diminishing track; they could make a right angle in any direction, but could not continue in their course.

"I wonder which of these would be the quicker?" soliloquized Kynaston. Clearly there should have been a path through the brambles which lay straight ahead.

"Don't be silly," said Lena, "they go in opposite directions. You'd better choose."

"I wish we had a map among us."

"We rely on you."

Kynaston looked wildly from left to right and back again while they waited for him to decide.

Guillaume broke the long silence. "Both ways look equally beautiful," he said helpfully.

"Does it matter?" cried Lotus. "Do we really have to get any-where?"

Peggy's expression changed from aloofness to horror.

"To travel is better than to arrive," said Guillaume.

"To travel *hopefully*," corrected Lena. "What hope have we?"

"Surely we should enjoy ourselves?" said Florence. "On such a lovely day?"

Monica had begun to knit. Freddy was brooding about his Father's wickedness. Barney had been filling his heart with tears ever since the train.

"The thing is, Griselda," said Kynaston desperately, "that I'm better at organizing picnics than walks."

"I remember," said Griselda, taking pity on him.

"Remember what?" enquired Lotus.

"I've been on a picnic with Geoffrey before. I enjoyed it."

"Shall we go back to the lake?" suggested Florence being con-structive.

"It's true that you're never actually lost so long as you can find the way back," observed Kynaston, hoping, like many greater men, to preserve his leadership by retreat.

"Surely we shouldn't admit defeat?" said Guillaume. He wished to keep Florence from the boats.

"Besides," enquired Lena, "can you find the way back?"

"Naturally, I can find the way *back*." The implication that he would rather they went forward contrasted so much with the attitude of his previous remark that it was obvious to Griselda that he could not find the way back, and had suddenly realized the fact. She wondered what he would do, thus totally trapped.

"For heaven's sake, let's go *somewhere*," cried Peggy. Her out-burst made Monica drop a stitch.

"Shall we toss for it?" suggested Florence, still patiently seek-ing to advance the general well-being. It struck Griselda that Florence would make a wonderful mother, though possibly her hips were too small for easy childbirth.

"Geoffrey!" said Lotus. "Tell us what to do and we'll do it. You *can* be so self-confident."

"This is the moment," said Lena.

Suddenly Kynaston resumed the leadership. "Let's have lunch. It's just the place."

Kynaston got very little. Peggy had at first said to Griselda that she had not walked far enough to acquire any appetite at all; but managed none the less to eat most of her share. Lotus, seated on a small mat, ate nothing but a little hothouse fruit (although it was summer) and some walnuts. Guillaume was on a diet which involved him in eating several times the normal amount of the few things he was permitted to eat at all. Barney almost surreptitiously unwrapped some unusual but not unappetising comestibles approved by his community. He insinuated himself alongside a tree which Peggy was occupying, somewhat in the background; and, glancing from time to time at Peggy's bust, began to cheer up.

At the end of the meal, the situation had once more to be faced.

After various desultory and generally unrealistic suggestions from the others, Lotus said "Why move from here? Are we not quite comfortable as we are?" She sank her left hand into Kynaston's hair as he lay on the ground beside her.

"Perfectly comfortable," said Guillaume, yawning as his diet disagreed with him.

Monica began to knit at a different angle. Perhaps she was turning the heel. But the rapidly increasing product of her labours seemed without any such precise points of reference.

"There's the difficulty that we don't know the way back," pointed out Florence.

"We'll be all right when the time comes." This was Barney.

"I," said Lena, "want a walk. Anyone join me?"

"I'll join you," said Griselda, rising. "What about you, Peggy?"

"It's too hot." To her surprise, Griselda, now that she was on her feet, could see that Peggy's ankles were tightly clasped in the crook of one of Barney's arms.

"Anyone else?" enquired Griselda. She had not expected to have to walk alone with Lena.

"I'd love to some other time," said Freddy regretfully. By this he meant that he would love to accompany Griselda, but he was frightened of Lena, whom he thought unsexed and a blue-stocking.

"Florence?"

Florence looked lovingly at Guillaume, who was beginning to fall asleep. "I don't think so, Griselda." There was something charmingly tender about her; something unusual and precious which Griselda felt was going to waste.

"Come on, Florence. I'd like you to."

Florence smiled and shook her head. Then she laid a hand-kerchief over Guillaume's brow, and settled down to watch over him.

Lena meanwhile was slouching up and down impatiently. Griselda walked across to her through the recumbent group.

"Which way?"

"Not again!"

"This way then." Griselda indicated the turn to the left.

"Thank God you know your own mind."

They set off along the track. Griselda's last recollection of the group was the look of agony in Kynaston's eyes as she vanished from his sight and a lock of Lotus's splendid red-gold hair touched his cheek.

CHAPTER XXIV

"Pity Florence wouldn't come."

"She's better where she is."

"Isn't Guillaume rather selfish?"

"That's why Florence loves him."

They walked some way in silence. It was almost too hot to talk. Also Griselda divined that Lena, although a little alarming, was one of the favoured people with whom silence is possible even on short acquaintance. Soon the track turned into a sunken glade.

THE LATE BREAKFASTERS 179

"What are your books called?"

" 'Inhumation' is the one I like."

"I should like to read it."

"It's not based on experience."

"I'm sure that doesn't matter."

"It matters to me. 'Inhumation' is based on frustration. I've never succeeded with men; although I've tried very hard from time to time. I'm too cerebral for the dear dolts. Not clinging and dependant. Florence is what they like. Or you."

"I'm not clinging and dependant."

"Aren't you? Sorry. I don't really know you, of course."

Again they walked for some time in silence. The glade was full of dragonflies, with their quaint air of impossibility.

"The only proposal I ever received," remarked Griselda after a while, "was on the grounds that I was *not* clinging and dependant. Proposal of marriage, that is to say."

"Geoffrey Kynaston is unlike the ordinary male. I should accept him. You'll be lost otherwise if you're the type you say you are. I'd take him myself if he'd have me."

Griselda had wondered why Lena had been so rude to Kynaston.

"How did you know?"

"Barney."

"Is Barney a good painter?"

"He's not a Rubens or George Goss. He can only paint Mothers. He has a fixation."

"I knew he painted Mothers."

"Udders, you know."

Griselda nodded.

After another silence, Lena said "Is love important to you, Griselda?"

"Yes, Lena," replied Griselda. "Love is very important to me."

"We're in a minority."

"I suppose so."

"I meant what I said in the train. I should like a man now."

"It's the main thing about beautiful places."

Suddenly they turned a corner and came to a high wrought-iron gate. It was surmounted by a painted though discoloured coat of arms, consisting simply of a mailed fist. It was apparent that the track had been constructed as a subsidiary drive to a house; and that the glade was an artificial excavation designed to keep the drive on a level.

"We can't go back," said Lena. "We shall rejoin the others, and I'm not ready for that yet."

"The gate's open," said Griselda.

Lena pushed it. It ground on its hinges, but opened wide at a touch. They passed through, and Griselda closed the gate behind them.

The drive stretched on among beeches which, though presumably in private ownership, were indistinguishable from the publicly owned beeches in the forest outside.

"Do you know who lives round here?" asked Griselda.

"I'm afraid not. I'm a stranger in these parts." Lena's tone had lost its previous habitual colouring of sarcasm. She had become entirely friendly. Griselda surmised that this might be a privilege, and that Lena might be a good friend to have.

"I suggest," continued Lena, "that we find our way out the other side of the Park, cast round in a circle, and rejoin the others from the opposite direction."

"Perhaps they will have gone?"

"Perhaps they will."

A few minutes later, Griselda said "I suppose we may be stopped?"

"You must use your charm, Griselda. It's there if you'll bring it out."

"What will you do?"

"I shall climb a tree."

"Are you good at that?"

"Watch."

She darted away from tree to tree.

"We must have a clean tree. I don't want to dirty my trousers. Wish I hadn't lent my blue ones to Florence." Even though she was quite close, the Forest had begun to echo her clear voice.

Suddenly she was ascending: with unbelievable speed and agility; like a small grey and buff monkey. In a minute or two she was out of sight among the dense green summer foliage.

"Be careful," called Griselda up the tree trunk.

"I'll be careful," cried Lena from the greenery; and the Forest shouted: "Careful, careful, careful."

"Look out below." Something was descending. It was a shoe. It was followed by another shoe. Then, a few yards away, at the perimeter of the tree, fell a pair of socks and Lena's shirt and trousers. Griselda looked up and saw Lena brown and naked at the very end of a thick branch. She was sitting on the branch with her legs drawn up; leaning back upon the left arm and hand, which rested on the bark behind her.

"How brown you are!"

"The sun was my stepfather." Now she was standing on the branch, her hands above her head and clinging to wisps of leafy twig hanging from the branch above. "I'm going to the top. Then down again. Wait for me, Griselda. I'll be very quick."

Griselda waved up to her and she had disappeared again among the leaves.

After a pause a fairly large whole branch crashed down from high above. It lay on the ground like the handiwork of a hooligan.

"Lena! Are you all right?"

There was no answer, but before Griselda felt alarm, Lena could be heard descending.

"Did you get to the top?"

Lena paused about twenty feet from the ground. In the hot streaks of sunshine she looked startlingly in keeping.

"We're nearer the house than we thought."

Griselda laughed. "Then you'd better dress quickly!"

"It's not that." Lena's manner had changed a second time. Now she seemed almost subdued. "There's something going on. There are tall trees near the house, but at the very top I could see over them. I think someone's dead."

"What did you see?"

"I'll dress and we'll go on. Then you can see for yourself."

She stood on the ground shaking bits of the tree from her brown body. In a minute and a half she was dressed, and combing her hair.

"What do you call those things you see in churches?"

"Cockroaches," said Griselda.

"Wooden things. To do with funerals."

"Coffins," said Griselda.

"You're wise to wear your hair short."

"Yours is too beautiful."

"I know. That's why I keep it. It's my sole physical asset."

"Not quite," said Griselda smiling.

"Much good has it done me." She was retying the khaki ribbon. "Now come and look." She slouched ahead, her hands once more in her pockets.

After two or three hundred yards, the track became paved with kidney stones, sunk far into the earth with neglect. After another two or three hundred yards, it gave upon a well-kept lawn, round which it curved to the door of a big late seventeenth-century house, in dark red brick, with large windows at long intervals, and heavy pre-Georgian details. The front door (from which the main drive stretched away in the opposite direction) was concealed by a bulky columned porte-cochère; high above which, rising on its own against the sky above the front wall of the house, was a massive relief representation in stone of the emblem which Griselda and Lena had noticed on the gate, the simple mailed fist. About the lawn were enormous isolated cedars of Lebanon.

Before they left the shelter of the Forest, Lena caught Griselda by the arm. "Look! that's a thing to see from the top of a tree."

In the sunshine before the porte-cochère, a strange figure sat upon the stones of the drive working. It appeared to be a dwarf. It had very long arms (like a cuttlefish, Griselda thought), very long black hair (somewhat like horsehair), and a completely yellow face. Its ears were pointed, with strands of stiff black hair rising from the top of them. It wore black clothes. Very industriously, despite the great heat, the figure was polishing a large black piece of wood.

"You were right," said Griselda, speaking unnecessarily softly; "that's a hatchment."

"Would that be the undertaker?"

"No. Undertakers must have charm."

"Dare we go past?"

"I think so. Unless you'd prefer to go back."

"Aren't we trespassing?"

"This is the twentieth century."

"Should we take advantage of that?"

"I'll apologize and ask the quickest way out."

They advanced from the safety of the trees. Instantly, against the ponderous grandeur of the house, they felt themselves misplaced and insignificant, wrongly dressed and intrusive.

The dwarf went on polishing until they were almost upon him, whereupon, without haste or appearance of surprise, he rose, bowed ceremonially, and extended his long left arm towards the door of the house.

"I'm afraid we've lost our way," said Griselda. "Will it be all right if we go on down the drive?"

The dwarf, who had completely black eyes, bowed again, and continued to point to the front door.

"Let's see for ourselves," said Lena after a second's silence. She tried to pass the dwarf on the other side, with a view to making for the drive.

The dwarf, still with his arm extended, stepped to the right and barred her way. Now by gestures with the right arm he seemed to reinforce the invitation already made with the left. Griselda saw that the big double front door stood wide open.

"Shall we go back?" said Lena.

The dwarf took a further step. He now stood facing the door and with the lawn behind him. Both his immense arms were fully extended, so that he looked like a queer tree. The hatchment lay face downward on the stones.

"What is there inside?" asked Griselda.

The dwarf bowed once more, this time stretching back his arms and upturning his hands. His hands were unusually large and white; and wiry black hair grew in the palms.

"Let's go," said Lena.

She looked about to run for it, but the dwarf, his arms still extended, leapt right off the ground like a goalkeeper, and descended in her course.

Griselda, anxious to prevent an unpleasant and undignified dodging contest, which, moreover, she feared the dwarf would, in at least one case, win, said "I think we'd better investigate. They may need help." Most of the blinds in the house were drawn.

"If you say so."

They entered the house, the dwarf one pace behind them.

When they were through the front door, he returned to his polishing in the sun.

The drawn blinds made the hall very dark, despite the strong light outside. At once, however, the two girls saw that a figure stood motionless at the bottom of the stairs which rose before them. It was an elderly woman, very tall, very upright, very grey, and wearing a grey dress reaching to the ground.

"So you've come. This way."

She began to lead the way upstairs, then stopped.

"Only one of you." She peered at them. "You." She indicated Griselda. "You," she said to Lena, "can go—or wait. Just as you choose. It won't take more than five or ten minutes now."

"There's some mistake," said Griselda. "We——"

"Hardly," interrupted the woman, smiling a slight, hard, weary smile through the gloom. "But you won't have to stay long. Your friend can wait if she chooses. Come upstairs, please."

"Why me?"

"I'm not sure your friend would serve. Please sit down," she said to Lena. "And wait."

"Why won't I serve?" enquired Lena.

"There is a condition which must be complied with. You'll be perfectly safe," she added somewhat contemptuously. "Both of you. Now," she said to Griselda, "follow me."

Griselda followed her up the wide staircase and into a gallery on the first floor, which seemed to run the length of the house and was filled with tapestries, there being apparently no other furniture of any kind except a carpet, though it was difficult to be sure in the dim light. Beyond the gallery were several large dark rooms filled with dust-sheets. Then there was a high double door.

The woman opened one of the doors very softly, disclosing artificial light within; and with an authoritative gesture from the wrist, indicated that Griselda should pass by and enter. The light in the room within enabled Griselda for the first time clearly to see her face. She looked imperious but sad; like one leading a dedicated life.

The room Griselda now entered was hung with black, which kept out all daylight. It was illumined by several hundred candles assembled on a frame such as Griselda had seen set before images in Catholic cathedrals; but larger, and formed of fantastically twisting golden limbs. The light fell upon a single enormous picture standing out against the black hangings: in an elaborate rococo frame, it depicted an Emperor or conqueror at his hour of triumph, borne by a white horse up a hill into a city, apotheosed alike by the paeans of his followers weighed down with loot, and by the plaints of the mangled, dying, and dispossessed. Opposite the picture was an immense four-poster bed, hung like a catafalque with black velvet curtains which descended from a golden mailed fist mounted in the centre of the canopy high up under the extravagantly painted ceiling. The carpet was of deep black silk. In the air was faint music.

The writhing candelabrum stood near one of the posts at the foot of the bed. While leaving all but the bed and the picture shadowy, it lighted up the room's occupant. Griselda at once recognized him. That look of a censorious Buddha, those clear yellow eyes, were, indeed, not to be forgotten. The man in the bed was Sir Travis Raunds. He looked older than ever, and horribly ill, but he was turning the pages of a black folio volume containing coats of arms exquisitely illuminated on vellum.

As Griselda entered, the sick man looked up from his escutcheons.

"Ah, my dear," he said in a high musical voice, "in a world as near its end almost as I am, you at least do not fall short. You are as lovely as any of the dear women who performed your office for my ancestors. Kneel; there, where there is light." He pointed to a patch of carpet, and Griselda knelt before his bed in the candlelight. Though the black curtains kept out the sun, the candles made the room very hot.

"Thank you. Now give me your hand." He made a slight, weak gesture. "You are perfectly safe. It will only be for a minute. Though time was——" But his remarks were tiring him, and he broke off with a Buddha-like smile.

Griselda extended her left hand. He took it in long thin white fingers, like those of a high-born skeleton, and lightly drew her towards him. She found that a stool stood beside the bed and seated herself upon it.

"How are you, Sir Travis?" she asked gently.

"Listen, my dear. Listen to your answer."

Griselda listened. The music was as of a very large orchestra very far off: too far off for any particular melody or instruments to be recognized.

"What is it?"

The dying man seemed to hear more than she did. "' 'Tis the god Hercules, whom Antony loved, now leaves him'." He was listening intently.

"Sir Travis," said Griselda, "tell me about life."

"Lord Beaconsfield told me that men are governed either by tradition or by force. I have since found it to be true."

"But," said Griselda, a little disappointed, "that's a rule for governing other people. What about yourself?" She noticed that the distant music was ebbing.

"You do not need to govern yourself, my dear, if you succeed in governing other people."

Suddenly Griselda thought of something: something that it was past belief she had not thought of before.

"Sir Travis," she said, eagerly; too eagerly for a sick-room.

He did not answer.

"Sir Travis!" She almost shook his hand and arm.

But Sir Travis's mind was elsewhere. "Tell Venetia," he said smiling wickedly, "that I'm leaving her for ever." And his high musical voice died away.

"Sir Travis!"

"One more thing only," said a voice from the shadows. "And then you will be free to go."

A young man in a dark suit stood before Griselda on the other side of the huge bed. He was small and looked French. He seemed to hold some small object clasped in each of his hands.

"I thought we were alone." Griselda looked over her shoulder. There was no sign of the tall woman, but the door through which she had entered, had disappeared behind the black hangings.

The young man smiled slightly; then stretching out his hands across the bed, opened the palms. In each lay a large gold piece, which glittered in the candlelight.

"You know what to do?" His alien mien was confirmed by a slight accent.

"Is he dead? How do you know?"

"I know."

Looking at the man in the bed, Griselda knew too.

"Poor Sir Travis!"

"Of course. It is very sad."

Griselda lifted the hand which had just held hers and laid it on the bed. She had never before touched a corpse. She almost expected the hand to be cold: it was much more shocking that it proved as warm as in life.

"You know what to do?" The young man still held out the gold pieces.

"I think so," said Griselda. "But why me?"

"It is all that remains. Then you can go."

Griselda took the pieces from his hand.

"They're five-pound pieces! And quite new!"

"Sir Travis made a special arrangement with the Mint."

"For this?" Griselda's voice sank in awe.

"For what else? Gold coins are no longer taken in shops. Only pieces of paper."

"They're beautiful."

But the young man indicated the slightest touch of impatience.

Very carefully and tenderly, Griselda laid the gold pieces on the dead man's eyelids.

"Thank you, mademoiselle," said the young man, indicating the slightest touch of relief. "Now if you will follow me."

Coming round the bed, he drew a section of the black hangings, and Griselda followed him back to the dim hall.

At the top of the stairs, the tall woman awaited them in the shadows.

"Is all in order, Vaisseau?"

"But naturally." His tone was as proud as hers.

"And she can go?"

"Immediately."

Lena stood below. "Is everything all right, Griselda?"

Griselda squeezed her hand. "There's nothing to keep us, Lena. Let us go."

The tall woman and the young man silently, and almost invisibly, watched them go back into the hot sun.

Outside was a strange disturbance. The hatchment had gone and the dwarf, it seemed, with it; but looking round for the origin of an unaccountable noise which filled the summer air, the two women saw him crouched on the paving stones in a corner behind the porch. He was not weeping, since there were no tears; he was crying like an animal, but like no known animal, for, as they now perceived, he had hitherto been dumb.

They looked up from the distressing sight and saw that high above them, beneath the immense mailed fist, hung the hatchment, polished and varnished and renewed, until in the afternoon sunshine it shone the very pennant of death triumphant.

CHAPTER XXV

Griselda was unable to imagine why she had never thought to look up Hugo Raunds's address in "Who's Who", or even in the Telephone Directory, and write to him for possible news of Louise's whereabouts.

Distracted by the omission, and full of resolve to repair it as soon as possible, she imparted to Lena, who seemed pleasingly without over-pressing curiosity, a somewhat slender account of her recent experiences.

"But is it a madhouse?"

"I *think* it's just a very old family."

They were walking down the drive towards the main entrance to the park. As the big elaborately wrought gates came into view, it appeared also that a small crowd was assembled outside. The first idea that they were faithful tenants come to enquire about the course of their protector's illness, or to mourn his passing, was dispelled by the way they stood packed together in the heat, by the fact that the lodge-keeper seemed to be remonstrating with them from behind the bars, and, most of all, by the noise they were making. In the end, Griselda saw that some of them carried placards, hideously lettered with slogans: "Aid To Abyssinia, Guatemala, Democratic Spain, And Chiang-Kai-Shek"; "Workers! The Intelligentsia Stands Behind You"; and, most immediate in its application, "Sir Travis Raunds Must Go". The inclusion of the title struck Griselda as a courteous detail, inconsistent with much else; but perhaps it served to spur David by making Goliath look fiercer.

"I wonder you 'aven't all something better to do on a nice day like this," the lodge-keeper was saying. Clearly he had allowed himself to be drawn into unwise disputation. He was a mild elderly man with lank hair and an habitual air of having recently been rescued from drowning.

His remark was greeted with catcalls.

"Why don't you join us in fighting the enemy of your class?" enquired a tall prematurely bald young man with spectacles. He carried a battered puppet dangling from a crude gallows, which he had looted, during a university rag, from a Punch and Judy stand. Two or three of his fellow demonstrators began to chant the Internationale.

"My tea's waiting for me, you know."

At this there was a burst of perceptibly forced laughter.

"I'll send for a policeman."

"Call out the Cossacks!"

Lena went up to the lodge-keeper and spoke in his ear. He stepped back. Lena raised her hand.

"Sir Travis Raunds is dead. He died this afternoon," she said in her clear voice. "So go home."

There were a few jeers, and a cry of "Why couldn't you say so?" but the group began to retreat, more or less content in the knowledge that they were alive and that the future was theirs. It seemed to occur to none of them to doubt Lena's statement.

"That was brave of you, Lena," said Griselda.

"So it was, miss," said the lodge-keeper. "But, of course, I 'ad old Cupid up my sleeve all the time."

"Would Cupid have helped?"

"Torn 'em apart, miss. Cupid only needed a word from me to tear 'em apart. Just one word. That's Cupid." He indicated a

vague black shape which looked too big for the white wooden
kennel placed in the lodge-keeper's miniature garden. "Sir Travis
named him after a gentleman he used to know when he was in
politics."

"Good old Cupid."

It seemed unnecessary to pat Cupid, as he was asleep. He wore
a collar with large spikes, like a drawing by Cruikshank; and his
muzzle was matted with some sticky substance. When Griselda
mentioned his name, he growled in his sleep.

"It's sad news about Sir Travis."

"Yes and no, miss. Times have changed since the Old Queen's
day. Not that either of you young ladies will care about that. But
up at the house it's just as if the Old Queen was still with us. Just
like Windsor Castle, it is."

"You don't say so?" said Griselda sympathetically.

"I expect you young ladies believe in being modern and up-to-
date?"

"You can tell at a glance," said Lena.

"It's the best thing. But Sir Travis, he never would see it."

Outside the park, they found their way without particular difficulty to where they had left the rest of the party.

"You're good at it," said Griselda. "You must have what is
known as a sense of direction."

"These little jaunts are symbolical," replied Lena. "Instead of
leaving the organization to me, who, as you rightly say, am good
at it, they will always leave it to Geoffrey, because they like him
and because he's no good at it at all, which saves them the anguish
of envying him. Not that I greatly care," she added. "I really only
come to watch."

"I'm not bad at finding the way myself, you know, Lena.
Women often are better at things than men, aren't they?"

"Men have uses, all the same."

Griselda said nothing; because at that moment the place
where they had lunched came into view.

There was no sign of the party. Instead, a troop of Boy Scouts
were learning about the Arctic.

"Was there anyone here when you arrived?" asked Griselda.
"Sitting on the grass?"

"No one at all," replied the scoutmaster. "Only rather a lot of litter, I regret to say."

A rustle went round the troop at Griselda's good looks and Lena's trousers.

"Come to the pictures, miss," cried out one of the more precocious scouts.

So Griselda and Lena had to find their way back to London unattended; which they did with much pleasure. The day ended with Lena accompanying Griselda back to Greenwood Tree House for coffee and anchovies. It was after midnight when Lena departed, but there was still no sign of Peggy.

CHAPTER XXVI

Hugo Raunds was not in the Telephone Directory, and even in "Who's Who" he figured solely as his father's heir, without even an address of his own. To Sir Travis were ascribed four different residences, one in each of the four kingdoms; but Griselda wrote to Sir Hugo at the one she knew. She asked simply if he had any knowledge of the possible whereabouts of a girl named Louise, whom she had met at Mrs. Hatch's house, Beams, had since lost touch with, and wished to meet again. "In the course of conversation she mentioned you several times; so I venture to trouble you."

One day in the shop a pleasant young man made a really determined attempt to engage Griselda's interest. Entering merely in order to enquire for a copy of "The Last Days of Pompeii", he had not departed before, in Mr. Tamburlane's temporary absence, he had persuaded her to accompany him that evening to the Piccadilly Hotel for drinks.

"We might dance somewhere afterwards."

"I don't dance."

"Then we'll go somewhere else and have some more drinks."

It proved all too true. By the time they had migrated from the Piccadilly Hotel to Oddenino's and from Oddenino's to the Criterion and from the Criterion to the Bodega, Griselda had begun to feel faint.

"Eat?" said the young man. "Of course. Come back to my place and my girl will run us something up. She's Italian, you know, or, more accurately, Sardinian."

He was out of the Bodega (Griselda had felt faint between drinks) and into a taxi with such dexterity that Griselda could not escape without an absurd and embarrassing scene before the cynical eye of the taxi-driver.

"By the way, my name's Dennis Hooper. You've probably heard of me? I should have told you before."

Griselda hadn't. She said nothing. The motion of the taxi was suddenly making her feel really ill; and also there seemed a case for reticence.

He didn't seem to mind that she hadn't heard of him.

"I bet your name's Anne?"

"How can you tell?"

"Every single girl I meet's called Anne these days. There's a positive Anne epidemic."

Griselda could for the moment do nothing but groan.

"What's your other name?"

Griselda clutched at a wisp of what she took to be worldly wisdom.

"Musselwhite."

"So you're Anne Musselwhite. One of the Brigade of Guards people?"

"No."

"I say, would you rather have gone to Scott's and had lobsters?"

"No."

"Not under the weather are you?"

"No."

"Shall we stop and have a drink? Might pull you round."

"No, thank you."

"We're there anyway. There'll be time for one or two quick ones before we eat. We might go somewhere afterwards and dance."

The taxi drew up at an exceedingly splendid block of flats. Hooper gave the driver a ten shilling note and waved away the thought of change.

They ascended by lift to the top floor. The flat had fashionable furniture, no pictures, and a view.

"Gioiosa! Do sit down."

Griselda seated herself upon a geometrical sofa, upholstered in a strident, headachy green, and applied herself to watching the rotating dome of the Coliseum through the long low windows.

The Sardinian girl entered. She was brown and luscious, and, bearing in mind the characteristics of her people, could not have been more than fourteen. She wore a black satin dress cut alarmingly low, and no stockings.

"We want to eat. What can you do for us?"

"A spiced omelette with sauerkraut? Some hot meat served in oil?"

"Anne Musselwhite. Which?"

"You haven't any fish?"

"Some potted squille only, signorina. Non troppo fresche."

"Could I just have a little bread and butter with some warm milk?"

Gioiosa looked at her employer.

"Anne Musselwhite, you've been deceiving me. You *are* under the weather. You must permit me to prescribe. All right," he said to Gioiosa, "anything you like."

"Anything you say, signore." She smiled bewitchingly and departed.

Hooper produced a bunch of keys and unlocked a vast antique cabinet bearing the Hat and blazon of some fourteenth or fifteenth century Prince-Bishop. He mixed a complicated drink, with ingredients derived from the interior.

"This'll make your blood run cold."

"No thank you. Could I just sit for a few minutes?"

"Of course. I'll leave it by you." He drew up a three-legged occasional table in cream aluminium.

"I'm sorry to be such a nuisance."

"I expect you've been overdoing it in the shop. We'll have to see about that." He poured himself a big round brandy-glass of neat whisky.

"If I could be quiet for a while, I'll be perfectly all right."

"I'll leave you by yourself." She smiled at him gratefully. Taking his whisky he opened a door into the next room. The door was decorated with scarlet zig-zags. In the doorway, Hooper looked back and said "Darling Anne Musselwhite." Then he withdrew, shutting the door. Instantly there was the sound of dance music. Hooper's gramophone was such a good model that it might have been in the room with Griselda.

Griselda removed her feet from the carpet (which was covered with representations of the Eiffel Tower in different colours) and placed them on the sofa. The dome of the Coliseum began to rotate faster and faster, and almost at once, despite the music, Griselda was asleep.

She first dreamed that she was climbing Mount Everest with Mrs. Hatch, who was dressed as a lama; then that Epping Forest was ablaze and Sir Travis Raunds's catafalque, four times life-size, reared itself incombustible in the midst; and lastly that she was dressed rather mistily in white and had just been married to Kynaston. Kynaston had insisted on removing her shoes in the Church Vestry; was embracing her and about to kiss her. It was, she felt, a perfectly agreeable prospect, because for some reason, not very clear, no responsibility attached to the transaction. But before the transaction was completed, Griselda awoke.

Hooper's arm was round her waist. With his free hand, he was unbuttoning her blouse. Moreover, he had already removed her shoes. Griselda felt it was a situation which Lotus (for example) would have managed better than she.

As she awoke, Hooper sat back a little.

"I do hope you are feeling cured."

"Yes, thank you." She was rebuttoning her blouse. "Well enough to go."

"But Gioiosa has prepared some food for us."

"Where are my shoes?"

"Please don't misunderstand me. I'm very fond of you, Anne Musselwhite."

"Where are my shoes?"

"Sit down and let's talk it over. I'll get you a drink."

Griselda crossed barefoot to the door.

"You can't very well go without your shoes."

"I'd rather not. I'll have to explain what happened in order to borrow a pair."

"Anne Musselwhite, you've got things all wrong." He was recharging his big brandy glass.

There was a knock at the door. Griselda opened it. It was Gioiosa.

"Ready to eat, signore."

Looking Griselda up and down, whom previously she had only seen seated, and discovering that she lacked shoes, Gioiosa went into extravagant foreign laughter.

"Grazie, signorina. Non conobbi."

She was about to go, but Griselda caught her by the arm.

"Lend me some shoes. Your feet are about the right size."

"*You* wear *my* shoes!" She was giggling like an imbecile.

It seemed hopeless. Griselda dropped her arm and made for the front door. In a moment she was running down the passage, shoeless like Cinderella at midnight. The carpet in the passage was thick and patterned like a tiger-skin. The walls bore large golden gulls in plastic relief. At the end, an under-porter had been working all day on a defective radiator, and the pieces lay scattered about until he could resume the next day. Some of them had already been kicked quite long distances by passing tenants and visitors.

As Griselda reached the corner where the stair-well began, there was a clatter behind her. She thought that Hooper was in pursuit; then realised that it was only a pair of shoes. She paused and looked back.

"I tell you, Anne Musselwhite, I think very little to you."

It occurred to Griselda that if she returned to pick up the shoes there might be further trouble.

"If you think it's fair," went on Hooper, "to take a man's drink and hospitality, and let him pay for you all round the place, and then give him nothing in return, I for one don't."

Griselda turned her back.

"Won't you think again? We might go dancing somewhere."

Griselda's back was negative.

"Oh, go to hell," said Hooper irritably and slammed the door.

All the same, thought Griselda, it was odd how after weeks and months of only Peggy, she should make so many new friends in so short a time.

Immediately she entered her room, Peggy knocked on her door.

"Come in Peggy. Sit down. Do you mind if I undress?"

"I have never thanked you for the picnic."

"No need to. I hope you enjoyed it?"

"I found them interesting to observe."

"Lena said something of the same kind."

"I thought Lena was more than a little affected, I'm afraid."

"Who did you *like*?"

"I haven't known them long enough to *like* any of them."

In view of Barney's attitude, and the lateness of Peggy's return from the jollification, Griselda thought that disappointing.

CHAPTER XXVII

Promptly, and on writing-paper which reminded her of Louise's, Griselda received her reply: —

Dear Miss de Reptonville,

Of course I know Louise. But I don't know where she is. I wish I did. I'm sorry.

Very sincerely yours,
Hugo Raunds.

Kynaston, installed as custodian of the Liberator's immortal memory, moved into an attic flat near his place of work. He had followed "Days of Delinquency" with "Nights of Negation", but his publishers took the view that the receipts from the former work did not justify further adventures; and he was in a state of melancholy mania.

"Why not try another publisher?"

"They all work in together."

Although it was obvious that he was still seeing Lotus (on one occasion he appeared with a strange scar on the side of his neck), or she him, he became really industrious in paying court to Griselda. He would not come to the shop, for fear of Mr. Tamburlane; but they would meet at the northern end of the Burlington Arcade, and Griselda would take him to Greenwood Tree House for a good meal and in order to listen to his difficulties and advise him.

"If I'm not a poet, Griselda, what am I? Am I any more than a current of hot air?"

Unlike Mrs. Hatch, Griselda herself did not care for Kynaston's poems. "You dance very well. Why don't you try to develop that?"

"I find it empty. As you dance so little yourself, it's hard to explain to you."

"I suppose so. Have some more stew?"

"Please."

"And more potato?"

"Please."

"And more seakale?"

"Please."

Griselda sat back. Fortunately Kynaston's attacks of self-doubt seldom upset his appetite.

"A piece of currant bread?"

"If you can spare it."

Later, when they were seated one on each side of the electric heater, and Kynaston had been describing the difficulties of his early manhood, and munching cream crackers, he said "This is what marriage would be like. I think it would be enchanting."

Griselda could not possibly go as far as that; but, after her recent loneliness and unhappiness, she admitted, though only to herself, that worse things might easily befall her. Kynaston was not very much of a man, but life, she felt, was not very much of a life.

So before he went she let him kiss her on the eyes, and even neck, as well as on the mouth. It was one thing about him that he had never attempted to seduce her. She was quite uncertain whether he cared for her too much or too little.

There were several fogs in November, a rare thing in London.

On the foggiest morning Mr. Tamburlane arrived late at the shop, wheezing slightly but jubilant. He wore a thick scarf in the colours (a little too vivid, Griselda thought) of the Booksellers Association, and a black Astrakhan hat.

"My waywardness has put you to the labour of taking down the shutters, Miss de Reptonville. I can but blame a higher power." He indicated the fog. "But your magnificent zeal is to be repaid a thousandfold. Yes, indeed." He sneezed.

"There's a new edition of the Apocrypha come in," replied Griselda demurely. "Shall I arrange some copies in the window?"

"Work," cried Mr. Tamburlane, sneezing again, "can wait. There are tidings of joy."

"What can they be? Shall I make you a warm drink?"

"A splendid and original device. Let us split a posset. There's nutmeg in a mustard tin behind the Collected Letters of Horatio Bottomley."

Griselda set to work in the back room, while Mr. Tamburlane sat complimenting her, his legs stretched out to the large gas fire in the shop. Soon the brew was prepared, and Griselda pouring it into large hand-thrown bowls, the colour of nearly cooked rhubarb.

"Miss Otter has news."

Griselda nearly scalded her uvula.

"Οτοτοτοῖ Τοτοῖ," exclaimed Mr. Tamburlane sympathetically. "Let us go further." He swept across Griselda's feet, and, unlocking a drawer, brought out a bottle. "We are warned against mixing our drinks, as the idiom is, but I think that on this occasion our common joy will absolve us. Here is finest coconut rum brought direct from the fever belt by one of my clients. It was all he had with which to meet his account, poor fellow. He described it as an antidote against cold feet."

"Thank you," said Griselda, taking the glass Mr. Tamburlane extended to her. "What is Miss Otter's news?"

"That," said Mr. Tamburlane swallowing his rum at a gulp, "I do not know. Miss Otter wrote to me that she will look in this morning to impart it in person. It must be something quite unconventional, because, as you know, this is not Miss Otter's day."

"And that's all you know?"

"Enough is as good as a feast, Miss de Reptonville. I counsel you to watch and pray. Although unswervingly antagonistic to an anthropomorphic theogony, I often find purgatation in the precepts of the primitives."

"Some more posset, Mr. Tamburlane?"

"Thank you, no. Warmth is already reanimating the various segments of my trunk. Nor, I conceive, should we continue imbibing stimulants until incapacity overtakes us. We should recollect that the hour for toil has but just now chimed; and summon forth our full self-mastery. Or do you differ?" He sat anxiously interrogative, with the bottle clasped motionless in the air between them.

"Far from it, Mr. Tamburlane. I agree entirely."

"What a reassurance that is to me. My inner demon has in it that which could so easily sweep all resistance away like chaff—which indeed on more than one occasion *has* swept it away like chaff—that I fear constantly the thickness of my own right arm." The bottle still hung in the air.

"I think we have a customer."

"Then let all be apple pie and shipshape."

Griselda drained her glass. She did not care for the coconut rum, because it tasted of coconut.

A young man had been standing outside the shop, looking in the window and hesitating. At first Griselda feared it might be Dennis Hooper, come with persuasive protestations of repentance; but it proved to be a young man looking for a chart of the Blackwater Estuary. From his demeanour outside and inside, it was clear that, like many of the customers, he seldom entered a bookshop.

"Charts, Mr. Tamburlane?"

Mr. Tamburlane ran both hands through his upstanding white hair. "Try in there, Miss de Reptonville." Griselda suspected that he had decided entirely by intuition.

"Nothing but almanacs," said Griselda rummaging.

"I always like to keep a stock of almanacs for past years," said Mr. Tamburlane to the customer in a spirit of affable salesmanship. "I am, I believe, the only London bookshop to do so."

The young man simply nodded. He was in a subdued frenzy for a chart of the Blackwater Estuary.

"It's ideas such as that, I always like to think, which set one apart from one's competitors."

"I want some idea where she dries out," said the young man anxiously. His eyes followed Griselda round the shop. It was clearly a matter of immense moment.

"I'm so sorry," said Griselda. "I'm afraid we've sold out that particular one just at the moment. Shall I order it for you?"

"My dear boy," said Mr. Tamburlane, laying his hands on the customer's arm. "For a sailor who has youth, there are always the stars."

Miss Otter failed to arrive.

Griselda, although she had never, except at the very beginning, dared to take that particular ridiculous business in the least seriously, found by midday that she was taking it seriously enough to feel sick.

She had nothing for lunch but bananas and cream, and a cup of black coffee. When she returned through the fog to the shop, she was even more alarmed to perceive that Mr. Tamburlane seemed really upset.

"Miss Otter is invariably the very figurehead of punctilio. You could, if I may employ a daring concept at such an anxious moment, use her as a regulator for a clock."

"Did Miss Otter not mention any time?"

"Tomorrow morning," said Mr. Tamburlane. "Yesterday, you understand."

"What about telephoning?"

"Out of the question. Miss Otter will have nothing electrical in the house."

"Perhaps she dislikes fog and has stayed at home."

Mr. Tamburlane's face lighted up. "Miss de Reptonville!" he cried. "I believe you have hit it."

At a quarter past four, when it was quite dark, a stranger entered the shop and asked to speak to Mr. Tamburlane. Griselda showed him into the back room and went on dealing with the arrears of orders sent by post.

About half an hour later, Mr. Tamburlane emerged, wearing his overcoat and scarf and looking altogether distraught. "All is over," he exclaimed. "Kindly put up the shutters immediately. Miss Otter has been run over by a postal van. I am informed that it was behind schedule owing to adverse weather."

"Then," cried Griselda, "shall I never know—?"

Mr. Tamburlane raised his hand. "Please say no more, Miss de Reptonville, lest it be taken down and used in evidence against me."

"Come along, please," said the visitor.

Griselda looked at his feet, which she had once read was the right thing to do; but could see nothing unusual. "What is the charge?" she asked.

"That has been under discussion with this gentleman for the last half-hour," said Mr. Tamburlane. "It appears that the authorities have visited Miss Otter's house and drawn their own conclusions. Entirely false ones, I am sure I need not add."

"Come along, please," said the visitor.

"Cut is the bough that might have grown full straight." Mr. Tamburlane extended both his hands.

"What can I do to help? Please tell me?"

Mr. Tamburlane suddenly became transfigured with an idea. "Officer," he said, "may I write a letter?"

"Time we was on our way."

"Only one line." Mr. Tamburlane looked exactly like half-a-crown.

"Make it short."

It was very short.

"Miss de Reptonville this is what you shall do. You shall not read this until five minutes after I am gone. Five minutes by any timepiece you choose." He had rolled the letter into a spill. Griselda took it. The visitor was looking vainly for his half-crown. "Promise."

"I promise."

"Get going," said the visitor sourly. "We don't go for your class of offence, you know."

A woman entered the shop. "I want a copy of 'Reader's Digest' for my little boy."

Mr. Tamburlane put on his astrakhan hat and cleared his throat. "Tell me," he said to his companion, "did you find time to visit Sing-sing this summer?"

When the five minutes were spent, Griselda uncurled the letter. Mr. Tamburlane had spoken the exact truth. Apart from his signature it consisted of a single line.

"I hereby give my shop and all its contents to Bearer."

CHAPTER XXIII

Griselda made diligent enquiries, partly in the forlornest possible hope that she might extract some news of Louise, partly out of gratitude to Mr. Tamburlane. But she found all channels blocked; largely, it seemed, at the particular direction of the accused. In the end she realized that in his own way Mr. Tamburlane had disappeared from her life as conclusively as Louise.

Often, however, as she served in the shop, her thoughts turned to him. She was advised in the particular circumstances to adopt another name for the business as soon as possible; and through much of a cold December week, the versatile Lena, clad in motorcycling costume, painted out "Tamburlane" and substituted "Drelincourt". This was because Griselda had invited Lena to go into partnership with her, and had no particular conviction that her own was a suitable name to place above a London shop. Already, after only a fortnight, Lena's knowledge of literature had proved as valuable as her capacity for odd but essential jobs. Griselda had insisted on placing in the window ten copies of 'Inhumation' (ordered without Lena's knowledge) on the very first day; and, oddly enough, by the end of the second day all were sold, and another ten had been ordered, to the conspicuous vindication of Griselda's commercial judgement and acquired experience of the trade.

The proposal of Kynaston's which Griselda accepted, was made one snowy night on the Central London Railway, between Oxford Circus and Marble Arch. Kynaston proposed immediately they entered the train, as indeed the shortness of the journey rendered necessary.

"I shall go to Canada, if you refuse," he concluded. "The Mounted Police are starting a ballet, and I've been asked to be régisseur."

There was a tired desperation about him which was very convincing.

"You don't mind that I love someone else?"

"Of course I mind. It's bloody for me."

"But you're willing to risk it?"

"I don't expect everything."

Griselda sank her head on his shoulder. But it was Bond Street Station, and she raised it again. It would be pleasant not to have to conduct so much of her emotional life on and near the Underground. She waited for the train to restart. Her heart felt quite dead; like a dry sponge, or a cauliflower run to seed.

"All right, Geoffrey, I'll marry you if you want it so much."

He said nothing at all and Griselda continued to stare before her.

"Let's make it soon," she said.

Kynaston still said nothing. From the corner of her eye, Griselda saw that he was quietly and motionlessly weeping. She laid her hand on his. He had attractive hands.

"Thank you, Griselda," he said at last. "Could you lend me your handkerchief?"

They had reached Marble Arch. Ascending on the escalator, Griselda reflected that there were said to be wonderful mysteries attendant on marriage. Long before the top, a freezing atmosphere enveloped her from the world outside.

In the Edgware Road it was as if all the air held particles of snow in suspension. None the less, before they reached Greenwood Tree House, they had decided to marry before Christmas. It would, Kynaston believed, require a special licence, which would involve extra expense; but now that Griselda had the shop, extra expense might be less of an obstacle.

At the outer door, Kynaston showed no particular inclination to accompany Griselda upstairs.

"My wretched shoes leak. I must buy some new ones before we marry. This snow could lead to chilblains."

But Griselda had no wish to be left with her thoughts.

"You can take them off in my room. It's just the sort of thing you've always wanted."

He did so. His socks were saturated with snow, and his feet were blue. They were, however, as male feet go, attractively shaped, Griselda was relieved to note.

"I can't lend you any socks because I don't wear trousers."

"I expect they'll dry." He hung them on the bars of a bedroom chair and pushed the chair in front of the electric heater. At once the socks began to steam profusely and also to fill the room with a faint but individual stench.

"I'll fetch Peggy. She'd better hear the news."

"Peggy frightens me, Griselda."

"I expect we shall both find it difficult with the other's friends, but Peggy's got a right to know."

If Kynaston had asked what right, Griselda would have found it hard to specify. But he merely said "I'd better put my shoes on."

Peggy, however, proved to be already in bed.

"Everyone at the Ministry has got a cold. I don't want to take an unnecessary risk."

"Peggy! I'm going to marry Geoffrey Kynaston." Griselda came very near to the tone in which such announcements are made.

"You said you weren't the marrying kind."

"I've changed."

"Not at all. I never believed you. Remember? I hope you'll be very happy, Griselda."

"Thank you, Peggy dear."

"I hope you'll find in him all you wish."

"Of course I shall. He's in my room now. I hoped you'd be able to join us."

Peggy smiled with irritating scepticism. "You can do without me. Just pass me down the bottle of Formamints before you go back to him, would you please, Griselda?"

"Is there anything else I can get you?"

"No thank you. I don't know how you're placed, but I could borrow my sister's wedding-dress if you'd like it. She was just about your size when she married and I know she's kept it for my nieces."

There was something about Peggy, fond though Griselda was of her, which tempted to the outrageous.

"Thank you. I doubt whether white would be appropriate."

But Peggy only smiled and said "That's for you to say."

CHAPTER XXIX

A special licence proved unnecessary, but there were difficulties of domicile, and it seemed that for the ceremony the only day convenient to all parties (but especially to the Registrar) would be Christmas Eve. Questioned as to his religion, Kynaston stated that he was loosely attached to the Baha'i Movement; and though Griselda belonged to the Church of England, she had small inclination for the chilliness of so many empty churches on a December morning. The Registry Office, though perhaps little warmer, offered a briefer ceremony, and one free from that undertone of morality still characteristic of so many churches.

As the day drew near, Griselda felt quite resigned. After Beams, her life had subsided into very nearly its former uneventfulness; so that for the present a change of any kind made an unconscious appeal. The only marked modification in her behaviour, however, was that she ceased to buy so many clothes. Also she spent two evenings a week trying to clean and decorate Kynaston's attic flat, which was to be her home until something more suitable could be both found and afforded. Lena assisted: clad in a dun coloured boiler suit, and after a busy day at the shop, she distempered the ceilings in pink and blue, and made water come out of the tap, before returning to Juvenal Court to resume work on her new novel, "Legacy Grass". Kynaston came to approve of her more and more until Griselda felt that she ought to feel jealous. Griselda, though good at walking, and good at the design part of interior decoration (she suggested they should try to instal some means of heating the water, even if obtained second-hand), was less good than Lena at implementing her suggestions. Kynaston had become radiantly happy, and restive about his terms of employment.

"After we're married, and now you two have got the shop,"

he said to Lena, who was laying a carpet which had been found rolled up behind some old stock in Mr. Tamburlane's former office, "I shall try again with my plastic poses. I often think they're the only thing I've gone in for which has community value. After marriage one must think of that."

Lena stopped hammering. "Think of what?"

"Community value. After marriage I mean to be less of a parasite."

"It's much more important for you to keep Griselda's body happy. Concentrate on that."

"Ça va sans dire."

"No man's quite a parasite who can do that for a woman. It's your only hope, Geoffrey."

"Hadn't we better change the subject? It's in poor taste in Griselda's own home."

"Griselda's opening a tin. Go and help her." Lena resumed hammering. The carpet was difficult to penetrate and smelt dreadfully of the East.

As a matter of fact, moreover, Lena was wrong for once. Griselda had heard every word.

She eyed Kynaston across the tin of pilchards. She supposed there might be some joy in the relationship which so many sought for and hoped for and worked for and suffered for. It certainly could not compensate for the loss of Louise, but it might be not wholly barren. Griselda shuddered slightly. It was attractive and Kynaston kissed her.

"Why pilchards, Geoffrey? Why not squille?"

"Because pilchards are cheap."

"They seem very oily."

"The fish themselves are quite dry."

There was no doubt he had a well-shaped body and much patient persistence in pursuit. It was necessary to hope.

On Christmas Eve it was foggier than on the day Miss Otter died and Griselda inherited the shop. Griselda and Peggy took forty minutes to find the Registry Office from Holborn Station; but fortunately (at Peggy's suggestion) they had started very early. Of the two Peggy looked much more like a bride: at extravagant expenditure she had acquired a magenta woollen dress with a salmon-coloured belt. The gesture testified all the more to her warmth of feeling, because, as she explained to Griselda in the Underground, it would be out of the question for her to wear the garment to the office.

The occasion had attracted an excellent attendance from among the friends of both bride and bridegroom (whose friends, as it happened, were largely held in common), and from the people of the surrounding district. Among the latter was even a barrister, on his way from Gray's Inn to Lincoln's Inn, whose large black hat and resonant professional diction enormously raised the tone and spirits of all present. When Griselda arrived, he was explaining that he had just been consulting his solicitor on a normal routine matter and had since been lost in the fog. The contingent from Juvenal Court had shared the cost of a taxi (which the barrister explained was a breach of statute) and stood grouped together protecting the bridegroom. They all wore sapphire coloured orchids paid for by Lotus, who, dressed in black chiffon and a Persian lamb coat, and pale to the lips and ears, was a centre of speculation among all who did not know her. Guillaume wore a fashionable suit hired from a reputable but humble competitor of Messrs. Moss Brothers; Florence a pale grey coat and skirt, home-made but none the less well made, and dark stockings sent as a Christmas present from Paris by an old admirer who had fled despairing her marmoreal devotion to another. Monica Paget-Barlow crotcheted away behind the Registry Office font. Freddy Fisher was interviewing the press, who took him for the bridegroom because he looked young and innocent and wore morning dress.

Kynaston entirely resembled Prince Charming in a midnight-blue suit he had salved from an unsuccessful production of a play by Maeterlinck.

As Griselda handed her raincoat to Peggy (she had followed Mrs. Hatch's precept and acquired a substantial one), Kynaston stepped forward from his ring of supporters, extended both his hands, and said "My love! This is our day. Let us not flinch."

"All right," said Griselda. "Shall we start?"

The Registrar's wife ceased her voluntary, and the Registrar himself loomed through the fog which filled the precincts. He was an impressive figure with a cold and wearing a frock coat, at which Griselda stared with interest. It was exactly like that worn by Joseph Chamberlain in Herkomer's portrait, a fine engraving of which hung above the sideboard in her Mother's dining room. Griselda supposed that her Mother might have forgiven her as it was her wedding-day. On the whole, she was glad that the chance did not offer.

The sacristan, a sleek young man in a pepper-and-salt suit reminiscent of Kempton Park, arranged the bride and bridegroom into a procession. At that moment, Griselda's eye fell upon Lena, for whom she had been searching. Lena, in a semi-polar outfit (she was much the most suitably dressed person present), sat in a corner of the Registry Office, obviously trying to comfort someone in distress, whose face was entirely concealed by Lena's handkerchief. The distressed one's clothes at once spoke for themselves, however. Before Griselda lighted up the entire half-forgotten panorama of society at Beams. Horror! It was Doris Ditton.

Now Griselda began herself to weep. The picture of Louise had projected itself with the rest in the so far greater intensity that memory offers than life.

Kynaston held out a twilight blue artificial silk handkerchief which went with the suit.

"Be strong, Griselda," he said. "Soon we shall be alone together, and *I* shall be needing *you.*" Lena waved to her slightly, affectionately. Kynaston had presumably not yet identified Doris. Or perhaps she was there by his invitation? Griselda could not see how else she had learned of the event; and had always understood that the bridegroom's guests at weddings consist predominantly of his past passions. Then she realized the answer: Lotus.

"Bride and bridegroom stand. All the rest sit," bawled the sacristan, his voice filled with the wind off Newmarket Heath.

Kynaston, in the hope of checking her tears, introduced Griselda to a small smooth man in a morning suit made splendid with orders and decorations.

"Colonel Costa-Rica, darling," he said. "The Orinocan Commercial Attaché."

Griselda transferred her handkerchief and extended the

appropriate hand. The Colonel fell upon it with his lips. His movement was like that of a closing knife. His cold eyes looked straight through Griselda's handkerchief and into her shivering soul.

"Enchanté mademoiselle. Et très bonne chance." When he spoke, his lips scarcely moved.

"English is the only European language the attaché doesn't speak," explained Kynaston.

"Excusez-moi?"

"Yes, certainly. Mais oui," replied Griselda in reasurrance. The Colonel sat down and began to brood upon the state of trade.

"All set," roared the sacristan. The bride and bridegroom were propelled forward to where the Registrar stood waiting, his book of runes in one hand, a small flask of eucalyptus in the other; there was a sound of military orders in the fog outside, and of rifle butts crashing on paving stones; and the greatest moment in Griselda's life had begun.

For one presumably experienced in his work, the Registrar seemed strangely dependant upon his little book. That being so, moreover, it was difficult to understand why he had never acquired a larger volume with better print. As it was, the limited natural visibility and archaic lighting (by gas produced from coal) clearly caused him much distress. He peered at the minute screed, varying its distance from his eyes, and every now and then looking upwards at the burner above his head with a demeanour which in another would have passed for distaste. Sometimes he stopped for several seconds in the middle of a passage or sentence. Punctuation, indeed seemed a complete stumbling-block. In consequence of all this, however, the literal dreadful meaning of the words merged happily into a synthesis properly evocative of a half-forgotten rite. Behind the Registrar the east wall of the building was crudely painted with admonitions headed 'Rules and Regulations Touching the State and Condition of Holy Matrimony,' varied by long closely printed notices signed on behalf of the Home Secretary. The stained glass window above the Registrar's head depicted a bygone Chairman of the London County Council kneeling before the goddess of fertility, represented traditionally. Doris's intermittent sobs offered an emotional continuo. Every now and then the heating system rumbled towards animation. The Registrar forged ahead, his mind on higher things. Regarding the grave mysterious figure, all goodness and wisdom, and his richly significant background, Griselda remembered that this was something she must never forget, even though she had great-grandchildren. Again she shuddered slightly. The congregation sympathetically attributed it to the weather.

Suddenly there was an interruption. The great pitch-pine doors parted and someone entered with firm, stamping tread. Griselda could not but look over her shoulder. It was a fine figure of a man in naval uniform. Before seating himself in the back row of chairs (next to Lotus), he caught Griselda's eye and waved breezily. Griselda stiffly inclined her head; then returned her attention to the service. Could this officer be responsible for the martial clatter outside? Possibly he was the next bridegroom, though he seemed elderly.

In the end the Registrar, with a final ejaculation of disgust, decided to abbreviate the liturgy; Kynaston produced the ring in excellent order (he had been wearing it on his forefinger); Griselda made a rash and foolish promise; and all was over. The ring was much too big for Griselda's particularly slender finger: it might have been made for a giantess, indeed probably had been.

"Sign please," said the sacristan producing a mouldering book from under the front row of chairs.

"Have your witnesses managed to get here?" enquired the Registrar.

"They're all our witnesses," exclaimed Kynaston full of the beauty of the ceremony and gesticulating expansively. Instantly he was deflated. "Dad!" he cried and looked quickly round him. The naval officer was thrusting forwards through the congratulatory crowd.

"Bravo, my boy," he cried. "I never thought you had it in you." His hand was extended. He was examining Griselda closely and added "Indeed I never thought it."

"Hullo, Dad," said Kynaston. In his blue suit, he looked quite green.

"Take your Father's hand and say no more. Remember I'm waiting to kiss the bride." He wrenched his son's hand.

"You must introduce me, Geoffrey," said Griselda hastily.

"My Father. Admiral Sir Collingwood Kynaston. This is Griselda, Dad."

"Delighted to meet my daughter." He kissed her overwhelmingly. "My boy and I have fought like tigers ever since he was born, but that's all over and you mustn't believe a thing he says about me."

Griselda thought it might be discourteous to say that Kynaston had never mentioned him (as was the case); and all the witnesses were waiting to sign.

"A good hard cudgelling on both sides hurts neither," affirmed the Admiral, scrawling his name ahead of the rest. "And the old man's made full amends. Wait for them. Just wait."

Freddy Fisher took the opportunity to ask for the Admiral's autograph. "I only collect leaders of the services," he said.

"Lucky to find one who can write," replied the Admiral jovially. "Is that one of your bridesmaids, my dear?" he enquired of Griselda, indicating Lotus.

In the end everyone had signed and the Registrar had come forward with his account.

"Leave it me," said the Admiral. "It's only once in a man's life that his boy gets himself spliced and he must expect to pay the piper. Though that reminds me," he continued, while the Registrar stood respectfully in the background, "what about you, my dear? Are you an orphan?"

"My Father died of Spanish influenza," replied Griselda. "I never knew him. From my Mother I have long been estranged."

"Lone wolf, eh? See yourself in the same galley with Geoffrey. Never mind. You'll grow. Being a widower I'm always persuasive with women of my own generation." He made a handsome settlement on the Registrar, who became profuse with improbable felicitations before retiring into his vestry.

"Now then," said the Admiral. "Just you see."

The sacristan threw back the big shining doors and Griselda saw. Outside, drawn up in the fog, were two lines of bluejackets. As the doors opened, an order rang out, and they crossed carbines.

"I really must protest," said Guillaume, his face grey with inner conflict, "at the use of force. Surely the occasion is sacramental?"

The Admiral only beamed at him. Then he glared at Kynaston.

"Well, my boy, get on with it. Give her your arm, like a man. If you don't, I shall."

The reconciliation between father and son seemed already strained.

Kynaston was white to the finger-nails. For a moment there was silence, broken by one of the bluejackets uttering.

"No, Dad," cried Kynaston. "I refuse." He gathered strength. "Come on Griselda. Let's find another way out of this place."

"Oh, well done," said Guillaume under his breath. Florence drew closer to him.

The admiral seemed unexpectedly taken aback. "You can't refuse," he cried in a shrill voice. "I've ordered luncheon for everyone at the Carlton."

"Sorry, Father," replied Kynaston. "Griselda and I have another engagement."

Peggy had drawn back some time ago, embarrassed by the Admiral's display of emotion, and had somehow got into what seemed mutually satisfying intercourse with Doris, who was regarding Kynaston's heroism with soft wondering tear-soaked eyes. By this time all the strangers had withdrawn to form a crowd outside.

The Admiral looked with some anxiety at the guard of honour. Clearly he felt that the situation could not be much longer continued without becoming legendary on both lower and upper decks for years to come.

He glared at his son. "Boy," he said sotto voce, "I have only one thing to say. Be a man."

"That's just it, Father. I am a man."

"Oh I say," interposed Freddy Fisher, who had lost sympathy with Kynaston. "Surely you can compromise?"

Outside, the Petty Officer cleared his throat. The men were tiring under the strain of the crossed carbines.

The admiral wheeled. "Dismiss your men." Then amid the necessary bellowing and stamping, he cried to the party "Those who wish for luncheon may follow me. There are cars outside;" and, ignoring the newly married couple, he left the building.

There was another pause.

"Go on," said Kynaston. "Have lunch. Griselda and I will see you later." Lena's eyes were moving round the group. The sacristan was waiting to lock up.

"I would rather beg my bread on the Victoria Embankment," said Guillaume. He was in a passion of indignation. The guard of honour could be heard marching away. Soon the fog hushed them.

"Please go and enjoy yourselves," said Griselda.

A motor-horn blared commandingly. Florence looked out into the murk. "That lawyer's got in," she reported.

Among the rest of them Guillaume's opinion seemed to prevail. Even Freddy Fisher, though horribly disappointed by the turn of events, abided by an unconscious loyalty, to none could clearly say what.

After another minute or two the cars drove off; the Admiral in the first of them, with his only guest; the remainder empty.

Griselda felt still further cut off from the world which had been hers until she visited Beams; a feeling enhanced by Peggy coming up to her, thanking her for the wedding, wishing her happiness, and then departing, her new dress hardly displayed, clearly much upset. Doris, after quietly congratulating the bridal couple, departed with her.

CHAPTER XXX

They lunched at the Old Bell Restaurant, recommended by Barney, who now appeared. He had been delayed by the completion of a commission, his work being much in demand about Christmas time.

"You can depend on a Trust House for a sound middle of the road meal," he said. "Besides there's a dome of many coloured glass: the finest thing of its kind in London."

In the Ladies' Room, two things happened. Griselda found that she had already lost her overlarge ring (and Kynaston, of course, had been unable to afford an engagement ring: indeed there seemed, in retrospect, to have been no very clear period during which Griselda had been engaged). Then Lotus pinned her in a corner and said "Remember." It was just like the ghost of Hamlet's father. Griselda wondered what would come out of it all.

At luncheon (where Monica would eat nothing but salad) Barney enquired after Peggy; Lena, ostensibly for Barney's information, told the story of the Admiral's intervention; Kynaston kept feeling for Griselda's hand; and Freddy Fisher became drunk with extraordinary rapidity. Lotus seemed increasingly out of it. Griselda wondered whether she was contemplating a final disappearance to a wealthier milieu; then supposed that she could not be, in view of her reminder in the Ladies' Room. Lotus's beauty and passion and sense of dress would make her rather a forlorn figure in any modern environment that Griselda could conceive. After a while, Lena, who, unlike Freddy, was drinking heavily, removed her polar outfit, and emerged in her usual shirt and trousers. As well as drinking, she was talking continuously, and without adapting her talk to the particular listener. Griselda looked at her a little doubtfully. Lena often seemed highly strung for a business partner.

Luncheon ended with Carlsbad plums in honey, halva, black coffee, and (at Lotus's expense) Green Chartreuses all round. There was some disputation, more or less affable, as they allocated among themselves liability for their respective parts of the bill; during which one of the business men who constituted the main element among the customers, approached Griselda and insisted on presenting her with a large bunch, almost bouquet, of Christmas roses.

"You look so happy," he said, "that I should like you to have it." Since the beginning of their meal, he had spent his luncheon hour searching the cold streets and stuffy shops. Instantaneously and for an instant it almost made Griselda feel as happy as she looked.

Then Barney was making a speech, and all the waiters and some of the bar and kitchen staff, had entered the room to listen to it. Lotus sat sneering slightly, which only made her more seductive than ever; and indeed it was not the best speech which even Griselda had ever heard. The business men listened like professionals, and at suitable moments led the applause. The speech ended by Barney announcing that now they would leave the happy couple alone together; at which, despite the hour, there was a pleasant round of cheers. Barney then spoke to a waiter, who flashed away. In a moment he was back and speaking in Barney's ear.

"I have ordered," said Barney, "a taxi; and what is more, paid for it. It is yours to go anywhere not more than ten minutes away, or a mile and a half, whichever is the less."

Everybody leaned from the windows of the Old Bell and cheered as the happy pair entered the taxi, which, having been decorated with white streamers at lightning speed by the driver, was already surrounded by a cluster of strange women, haggard as witches with Christmas shopping.

"Best of luck," screamed Freddy Fisher and threw a toy bomb which he had acquired next door at Gamage's for the purpose. Considering its cost, it was surprisingly efficacious.

"Where to?" enquired the driver.

There seemed nowhere to suggest but back to the attic flat.

CHAPTER XXXI

Griselda wondered when the mysteries would begin.

It seemed not immediately. In the taxi, Kynaston concentrated upon his achievement in routing and evading his father (which had, indeed, impressed Griselda considerably); and in the flat, having changed his suit, he continued alluding to the same subject. He described the wretchedness of his childhood for more than an hour and a quarter, a topic with which Griselda was fairly sympathetic; then unexpectedly said "I think we'd better go to the pictures. I feel we should celebrate, and all the cinemas will be shut tomorrow."

Griselda quickly made tea (neither were especially hungry after their plateful of venison at luncheon) and they found their way through the fog to a double-feature programme which did not come round again until past nine o'clock. Most of the time Griselda sat with Kynaston's arm round her. She found it pleasant, but detrimental to concentration upon the films. However,

it being the programme immediately before Christmas, the films
were undemanding.

"Let's go to Lyons," said Kynaston. "You'll have plenty of
opportunity for home cooking in the years ahead." He smiled at
her affectionately. Griselda smiled back, though suddenly she had
wondered what the food was like at the Carlton.

At Lyons, however, the big new Corner House at St. Giles's
Circus, the food was, as usual, unlike the food anywhere else,
though the ornate building was full of fog, through which the
alien waiters called to one another in little-known tongues above
the tumult of the orchestra. Griselda and Kynaston ate Con-
sommé Lenglen, turkey and Christmas pudding, followed by
portions of walnuts; so that it was nearly eleven before they left.

When they emerged, their heads spinning with Viennese
music, the fog was so thick that the busmen had gone on strike,
leaving their vehicles standing about the streets and blocking
most of the other traffic. In some of the buses passengers bearing
holly and rocking-horses, were defining and proclaiming their
rights; in some, mistletoe was being hoisted; and in some, tramps
were beginning to bed down for the holiday. Every now and then
a bus became dark, as its battery failed or miscarried. Over all
could already be felt the spirit of Christmas.

"Let's look for the tube."

But when they found it, the Underground had ceased to run.
Across the entry was a strong iron gate, bearing the notice "Spe-
cial Christmas Service", surrounded by little figures of Santa
Claus.

"Let's walk. Do you mind, Griselda?"

"Of course not, Geoffrey."

"Fortunately I'm good at finding the way."

"I can't see my feet."

Allowing for errors of direction, and the further time consumed in retracing their steps, the walk took until a quarter to
one. By the time she reached their attic flat, Griselda's legs were
cold, her respiration clogged, and her spirits chastened.

Kynaston left her alone in their bedroom (where his single
divan bed had been supplemented by its double) to undress.
Almost at once she was in bed. Rather charmingly, Kynaston then

appeared with a glass of hot milk and some bread and treacle.

"Would you like a hot water bottle?"

"It's lovely of you, Geoffrey, to work so hard, but I don't use them."

"I do."

"That's all right."

Kynaston disappeared again and was gone some time. After the hot milk, Griselda felt not anticipatory but comatose. Ultimately Kynaston returned. He wore pyjamas. He must have changed in the sitting room.

He crossed to Griselda's bed, where she lay with her eyes shut.

"You look tired, darling. I suggest we just sleep. There's all day tomorrow."

Griselda opened her eyes. "Yes, darling, let's just sleep." He kissed her lips fondly.

All the same it was disappointing. Griselda could not resolve how disappointing.

Kynaston put out the light.

"I think we'd better keep to our own beds. For tonight. Else we might spoil things. Because I'm sure you must be cold and tired."

"I agree." But Griselda was now perfectly warm and, for some reason, much less tired.

She rolled round and round in her bed several times.

Then without warning in the darkness Kynaston said "Are you a virgin?"

And when Griselda had explained the position, he said "I expect we'll be able to manage;" then sighed and began to snore.

On Christmas Day Griselda became quite fond of Kynaston. He performed unending small services, and seemed to be filled with happiness every time she smiled. He spent the morning writing a sonnet, while Griselda made a steak-and-kidney pudding. In the afternoon he attempted to codify some new plastic poses, while Griselda mended his clothes. At about the time of the King's broadcast, however, Griselda became aware of an undefined, unacknowledged strain. At dinner it seemed to have affected Kynaston's appetite: a very unusual circumstance. Griselda herself continued more cheerful than she had expected. Kynaston's slight nerviness seemed to make him more attentive than ever, almost anxiously so; and the immediate future aroused interest and curiosity.

After dinner, Kynaston began to read "The Faery Queen" aloud. Fortunately he did this very well. Every now and then he broke off while Griselda made some more coffee in a laboratorial vessel of glass and chromium which Lotus had given them as a wedding present. On one of these occasions Griselda noticed that Kynaston's hand shook so much that he spilled the coffee into the saucer.

"Is anything wrong, darling? You're shaking like a leaf."

"I'm not used to so much happiness."

"Does happiness make you tremble?"

"Of course. Now I'll go on reading."

His explanation was convincing but unsatisfying. Griselda felt that happiness precluded while it lasted the thought of its own fleetingness. Kynaston, moreover, every now and then between stanzas, flashed a look at her which was positively panic-stricken.

After several hours of reading, and several rounds of coffee in the pretty shepherdess cups which had been Peggy's wedding present, Kynaston reached the lines:

> "'Or rather would, O! would it be so chanced,
> That you, most noble sir, had present been
> When that lewd ribald, with vile lust advanced,
> Laid first his filthy hands on virgin clean,
> To spoil her dainty corps, so fair and sheen
> As on the earth, great mother of us all,
> With living eye more fair was never seen
> Of chastity and honour virginal:
> Witness, ye heavens, whom she in vain to help did call!'"

At this Kynaston broke off, thought for a moment, while Griselda continued mending a sock, then, with glassy eyes said "Darling. Would you care to take off your sweater and skirt?"

"Of course, darling. If you wish." Griselda laid aside the sock and complied with Kynaston's suggestion.

He looked at her doubtfully, his eyes still glassy. "You won't be cold?"

"That depends."

"You mean on how much longer we go on reading?"

This seemed not to require an answer, so Griselda simply smiled.

"I'll finish the canto."

Griselda sank to the floor and sat close to the heater. Lena had given her a quantity (much greater than Lena could afford) of attractive underclothes as a wedding present, and she felt that she looked appealing as long as she could keep warm. Kynaston resumed:—

> " ' "How may it be," said then the knight half wroth,
> "The knight should knighthood ever so have spent?"
> "None but that saw," quoth he, "would ween for troth,
> How shamefully that maid he did torment:
> Her looser golden locks he rudely rent,
> And drew her on the ground; and his sharp sword
> Against her snowy breast he fiercely bent,
> And threatened death with many a bloody word;
> Tongue hates to tell the rest that eyes to see abhorred." ' "

At the end of the canto, Kynaston looked at the floor and said: "Magical, isn't it? And so modern."

"How much more is there?" asked Griselda. She liked "The Faery Queen", but was increasingly troubled by the draught along the floor.

"We're less than a third through. There are six books. Spenser actually hoped to write twelve. Each is concerned with a different moral virtue. We've only just begun Book Two. On Temperance."

"I remember," said Griselda. "What's Book Three about?"

"Chastity."

Griselda's bare arms were beginning to make goose-flesh.

"Shall we go to bed, darling? It's past midnight."

Kynaston nodded. Griselda put away her pile of socks. Kynaston crossed the room like a man heavily preoccupied, and replaced "The Faery Queen" on her shelf. Then, pulling himself together, he said "Shall I bring you some hot milk? To make you sleep?"

"I don't know, darling. Should you?"

Kynaston turned, if possible, a little paler.

"Or should we both have a stiff drink?"

"Would that be a good thing?"

"I'd like you to have what you want."

"I want bed. I'm frozen."

"I'm terribly sorry. Really I am."

"I didn't mean that at all."

The sudden turning on of the light emphasized the quantity of fog which had entered the little bedroom. Griselda realized that it was the only day for many months on which she had taken no exercise. With shaking hand, she cleaned her teeth, and fell into bed exactly as she was. She lay in the foggy freezing room (for the heater had not yet begun to take effect) with the light on, waiting for Kynaston.

He took much longer to appear than on the previous night. When he entered his face was set in a way which recalled to Griselda his repudiation of Lotus and his defiance of his father. Without a word he turned off the light and the heater, and climbed into his bed. He had not even bidden Griselda good night, or kissed her.

In the foggy darkness there was silence for a while. Then Kynaston said "Shall I turn on the heater again? We might leave it on."

"We can't afford it, darling."

"Of course I'd rather not get up, but I don't want you to be cold in bed, darling."

"I don't want to be either."

This time there was a really long silence. Griselda, who was positively rigid with wakefulness, wondered if Kynaston had fallen asleep. Then she recalled that when asleep, he snored. Suddenly he spoke. "Griselda."

"What is it darling? I was thinking about 'The Faery Queen'."

"On the subject of any physical relationship between us."

"Living together as man and wife?" Griselda elucidated helpfully.

"I imagine all that's of secondary importance to you."

"Why?"

"Because you have always said you don't love me."

It was odd, Griselda reflected, how few people seemed to know the condition of being to which she would refer that word. She supposed she knew, and would always know, something that few knew, or would ever know. She felt to Kynaston as she had once felt to Mrs. Hatch: very superior. Though she had lost, she had loved. All the same it was difficult to explain to Kynaston that lack of love as she understood the word, did not necessarily imply precisely proportionate lack of love as Kynaston understood it.

"I married you."

"Yes." He sounded as if it was a case of forebodings being fulfilled.

"I knew what I was doing, Geoffrey darling."

"Of course, darling . . . I'd better go on with what I was saying."

"I'm sorry not to be more helpful."

"No, it's I who am sorry. You're utterly in control."

"Go on, darling. What do you want to say?"

He gulped; and sucked at the bedclothes. "First, it's marriage. At least I think it is. You know how it is with men?"

"Not very well, darling, I'm afraid."

"A man sees marriage in terms of affection, domesticity, and inspiration."

"I understand that."

"With me it's particularly true. I need a woman—a woman of character, like you, Griselda—to mould my life."

"I remember your saying so."

"You've seen Lotus. You understand that there's been something between us?"

"I guessed there had."

"You don't mind?" It was as if he hoped she did.

"You say you love me."

"Passion's possible with Lotus, great drowning seas of it, but none of the other things."

"Whereas with me——" A hard shell was beginning to enclose Griselda's entire body; beginning with her still cold feet.

"With you the situation is further complicated by what you said last night. Whatever Lotus is like in other ways, she is good at making things easy. I hope you'll let me put it clearly. Because I love you so much."

"Do you mean, darling, that you married me just because I *don't* love you?"

"Of course not, darling. I'm utterly determined to *make* you love me. I don't think it would help for us to begin with a physical misunderstanding."

That, however, was what they did begin with. Griselda, her new shell hardening and tightening all the time, had supposed that now for certain she would be spending the night alone, and an uncertain number of future nights, until (she surmised) she broke down in health or espoused a good cause. But, instead, Kynaston almost immediately entered her bed and gave her ample and unnecessary proof that his hints of unease and inadequacy to the circumstances were firmly grounded. Things were not made better by a continuous undertow of implication that it was all to please Griselda. At the end, there was very little mystery left, and less wonder.

After similar experiences at irregular and unpredictable intervals on twenty-eight occasions, Griselda, when a twenty-ninth occasion offered, felt positively but indefinably unwell. It would be deplorable, she spent much of the time reflecting, if, moreover, nature, despite counter-measures, took her course. She began to wonder more than ever whether she was truly suited to marriage.

Energy, thwarted of satisfactory direct outlet, expended itself obliquely, as is the way in marriage. Griselda began to apply herself more steadily and more forethoughtfully at the shop; and also to see that Kynaston applied himself as efficiently as his temperament and his job permitted. Soon the shop became the subject of a note in "The Bookseller", and Colonel Costa-Rica was holding before Kynaston the possibility of a position, at higher pay, in the Orinocan Intelligence Service. Not only did they become richer, their increase in income being coupled with a diminished desire to expend; but they began to scent the first faint sunrising of social approbation renewed.

Before long Kynaston was losing interest in both poetry and

his plastic poses, in favour of a projected Anthology of Curator-
ship, for which he hoped to obtain a Foreword from the Editor
of "Country Life". Sometimes they found themselves invited
to visit homes of repute and to mingle on equal terms with the
enbosomed families. More and more the shop stocked books
which might sell, instead of minority books. Lena, over whom,
of course, hymeneal happiness had yet to hover, regarded this
last tendency disapprovingly; though the proceeds conveniently
augmented the slight returns from her own new book. A climax
was reached when Kynaston received an invitation to stand in
the Labour interest at the Parish Council Elections. He declined,
because he deemed politics to obstruct full self-realisation; but he
declined politely, conscious that, far more than any other party,
the Labour party gives careful heed to the morals and probity of
all it permits to join its pilgrimage.

When she had been married nearly a year, Griselda one morning realized with surprise that Lena, to judge by some remarks
she made, regarded her state with envy.

"But, Lena, you don't have to marry a man in order to enjoy
him."

Lena leaned back against the counter, her hands in her pockets.
"There are times, Griselda, when your superficiality is equalled
only by your smugness."

She had never before spoken so to Griselda, though given to
the style when speaking to certain other people. Griselda had
observed, however, that Lena's censoriousness, though seldom
judicious, was seldom wholly undeserved.

"Am I becoming smug, Lena?"

"I apologize for what I said. I'm a bitch."

"But am I becoming smug?"

"As a matter of fact, you are."

"What should I do about it?"

"I wish I knew."

Before the matter could be taken further, they were interrupted by the arrival of a thousand copies of a book describing
the atrociousness of the new German government.

Not the least remarkable change in Kynaston was his sus-
tained firmness in dealing with the problem of Lotus. Quite soon

Lotus was reduced to supplicating Griselda: a procedure which Griselda considered superfluous and irrelevant, though, with a perverseness new to her nature, she did not say so to Lotus.

"You gave me your word," cried Lotus, her beauty rising from her tears, like Venus from the flood.

And instead of simply pointing out that she had in no way broken it, Griselda replied reflectively "Things are never quite the same after marriage as they were before it," and offered Lotus another glass of lemon tea.

After weeks of apparent rebuff and equivocation Lotus tumultuously capitulated at the end of February.

"You've won him and I've lost him," she said to Griselda over morning coffee. "You've been stamping out my body like wine beneath your little feet. I need renewal. I always find it in the same place."

"Where's that?"

"Sfax."

In due course, a picture postcard of a grinning Arab under a palm tree laden with dates, confirmed Lotus's decision; but Griselda wondered what in Kynaston's life had replaced the satisfactions, however limited, which, even by his own account, Lotus had given him. She looked at the sky of Sfax, almost unnaturally ultramarine, at the camels on the horizon, at the Wagons-Lits official in the foreground; and supposed that Kynaston must at last have found a purpose in life. Really it was most unlike him.

About a week after Lena's outburst in the shop, Griselda received a visit from Guillaume. It was a Saturday afternoon; and Griselda was lying on her back, gazing at the ceiling, and eating Pascall's crèmes-de-menthe. She and Kynaston had not yet found a better place to live; indeed lately the search itself had flagged.

"Sorry Geoffrey's out. How's Florence?"

Guillaume was wandering about the small sitting-room collecting cushions.

"Losing weight just a little, I'm afraid. She strains you know. I try to open her eyes to the wonder of life, but I doubt if the brightness of it all is ever wholly clear to her."

He filled an armchair with his accumulation and sank his large body slowly into the midst of it.

There followed a long silence. Guillaume looked like a dingy Mother Goose.

He restarted the momentum of intercourse. "I thought I'd take a chance of finding you in."

"Have a crème-de-menthe?"

"May I take a handful?" He nearly emptied the small green tin. "I'm engaged on research at Soane's. The work of years. Probably my very last chance. The final brief passage before the volume closes."

"Surely not?"

"I'm a disappointed man, you know, Mrs. Kynaston." He smiled like the last sunset of autumn. He had difficulty in extracting the sweets entirely from their papers, so that every now and then he ejected a tiny moist scrap which had accidentally entered his mouth.

"Florence told me."

He seemed disturbed. "That she had no right to do. Even a failure has his pride."

"I shouldn't have mentioned it. Where is it that you've failed?"

"Can you look at the world around you and ask me that?" he replied. "On the one hand the dream. On the other the reality. And I started with such hopes." He was feeling for his pocket handkerchief. Griselda feared that he was about to weep, but he only sought to remove some of the stickiness which his large moist hands had retained from the sweets.

"Take only one case," he continued. "Take the state of affairs in denominational schools. Little children exposed naked to the blast of bigotry. Take the mines. Do you know that the faces of miners are black all the time they work? Men born as white as you or I. Take the so-called catering industry. Have you ever worked for twenty-four hours on end in an underground kitchen? Do you know that the world's supply of phosphorus is being consumed at ten or twenty times the rate it's being replaced? Look at the cruelty and waste involved in the so-called sport of polo alone! If you live in Wallsend, you have to walk ten miles to see a blade of grass. Is anything being done to harness the energy in the

planets? Even though there's enough to extirpate work everywhere. Think of the millions deceived by so-called free insurance
schemes, paid for out of profits!"

"I see what you mean," said Griselda.

"And in other countries things are worse. What have you to
say about the Japanese? Or the Andaman Islanders, who pass
their entire lives in a prison camp? Or the so-called freed slaves in
Liberia?"

"Perhaps we'd better stick to England. At least to start with."

"There's a great danger in parochialism. The aboriginal Tas-
manians discovered that."

"How?"

"Very simply. They were trapped, killed, and eaten by men of
more progressive outlook."

"I think there is a lot in what Lord Beaconsfield said."

"Of course there is," said Guillaume unexpectedly. "But did he
put it into practice?"

Griselda was far from sure. But almost certainly Guillaume
was thinking of some other remark of the sage's. In any case, he
resumed speaking immediately.

"Though who am I to throw the first stone?" he enquired.
"William Cook, the failure. You didn't even know that my real
name was William?"

"It would never have occurred to me. I suppose you disliked
being called Bill? I know I should."

"In those days no one would have ventured. I was a man of
spirit then. I knew Hubert Bland quite well: and Hyndman too.
No. I changed my name, Mrs. Kynaston, solely in order to appear
to advantage with women."

"I'm sure you did impress them."

"Not one. I might have saved myself the cost. Never has one
woman truly opened her heart to me, although my heart finds
room for the whole human race." He looked into Griselda's eyes
and coughed back into his mouth a crème-de-menthe which had
involved itself with the lump in his throat.

"You have Florence. She's devoted to you."

"A mere Ahaviel. A simple handmaiden," he replied irritably.
"If I could have made my own, utterly my own, a woman of

spiritual power, comparable with mine, mountains would have moved."

For some reason this remark annoyed Griselda. "I think Florence is one of the nicest people I've ever met."

"Nice is the just word," he replied bitterly. "But you speak to a prophet. My responsibility is wide. I seek the divine flame, not soapsuds."

"I won't have this," said Griselda quietly and putting on her shoes. "I am fond of Florence. You're lucky to have her."

"Florence is Florence. Naturally no one estimates her more justly than I do."

"She is beautiful and intelligent and devoted and faithful and kind. Kind people are rare. As a prophet you ought to know that."

Guillaume eyed her through the gathering October dusk. "I understand why you set store by at least one of those qualities."

"I set store by all of them." Griselda suspected another attempted seduction.

"We need not pretend. Your business partner still lives at Juvenal Court, you know. Florence has known Lena for years."

Griselda thought quickly and clearly before deciding what to say next. Then she decided.

"I'm sorry I can't offer you tea. I've arranged to join Geoffrey."

"Like everybody else, you under-estimate me. Had you been taking tea with Kynaston, I should not have chosen today to visit you."

Griselda had not expected that either. But for reasons she had not yet had time to determine, Guillaume's surprising remarks had the effect of clearing rather than unsettling her mind.

"I'm afraid I must ask you to go. Please give my love to Florence."

"I am quite used to eviction and condemnation, as to many other unpleasant things. I should be a poor creature if by now I had not my philosophy, strong as iron." Laboriously he rose from his cache of cushions, like the nook of an animal about to hibernate. Still sucking and spitting, he crawled across to the window and stared into the encroaching night. Griselda stood by the open door, waiting.

"I was absorbing the peace of the lamplighter at work," said

Guillaume after a while, "like a glowworm. Or, perhaps more nearly, a firefly."

"I often watch him," said Griselda, who had never previously noticed him.

" 'Like a good deed in a naughty world.' You are sensitive to the beauty of words?"

"Of course. I own a bookshop."

"It would be pleasant to live so high up." Guillaume sighed and looked about in the twilight for his hat.

"Here." Griselda extended the object. It was a close replica of that worn by Mazzini when in disguise.

"Good-bye," said Guillaume, assimilating and retaining her hand. "I grieve for you."

"Quite unnecessary," replied Griselda, struggling slightly.

"You mustn't deny me that single luxury." He kissed her heavily and adhesively upon the brow and went away, reeking of charity and peppermint.

Griselda drew the curtains, turned on the lights, and prepared for herself a satisfying, solitary tea, including cucumber sandwiches, and custard creams, new and crisp. For the first time since before Christmas, she felt able to regard herself and find all her faculties present and functioning. Before long she wondered whether it was not even more than that: whether she was not in process of restoration against the consequences of losing Louise. It might be that her marriage to Kynaston had been required to achieve that.

The only awful thought was that Guillaume's hints, bearing in mind Guillaume's nature, might have been untrue.

CHAPTER XXXII

Griselda thereafter took particular trouble to be kind and understanding to Lena, despite provocations which steadily increased.

One morning, as the anniversary of her wedding drew near, Griselda sat in the little office after the shop had closed. She was writing and addressing Christmas Cards, designed by herself. Lena had been supposed to be keeping an appointment of some kind, but at the last moment had decided not to go. She was wandering about the shop examining the stock with dissatisfaction.

Just as Griselda decided that she was not called upon to send a specially designed Christmas Card to Mrs. Hatch, Lena called out "Griselda. May I talk to you? Or do I interrupt?" She was seated on top of one of the shop ladders.

"Of course you don't interrupt. I've hardly spoken to you alone for weeks."

"I think our books are frightful. There's an entire shelf of Warwick Deeping."

"It's right up under the ceiling. No one can see it."

"And under it Jeffrey Farnol."

"That's just old stock."

"And under that J. B. Priestley."

"We've got to live."

"I'd rather live honestly."

"Come down and talk about it."

Lena descended and entered the office. She had taken to wearing dresses; which did not suit her personality. Griselda reflected with interest upon the deterioration in her own clothes since marriage.

"I want to hand back my partnership. With thanks, of course, Griselda."

"I can't do without you."

Lena upturned the wastepaper basket, and sat upon it. The floor was now covered with the transactions of the day.

"I'm going to live abroad."

"Where?"

"Somewhere warm."

"North Africa?"

"Possibly."

"Dear Lena. Of course, it's a man?"

"The feeling when you haven't got one is exceeded only by the quite different feeling when you have. But you don't know about that."

"You don't like it?"

"Not this particular example of it."

"Then why leave the shop?"

"I told you. I don't like the books we stock. The books we have to stock. I admit that. I still don't like them."

"Is it that he still chases you?"

"Mind your own business, Griselda." Then she added "You'll be much better without me." Griselda had never seen or even imagined her so distressed. She spoke very gently.

"It's Geoffrey, I think."

Lena shook her head.

"I recognized him from your description."

"It's over, Griselda. At least for me. I'm not sure about *him*, I'm afraid. I feel a pig, pig, pig."

"You needn't. I believe I'm grateful to you. Anyway I know very much how you feel. I feel some of it myself. Please don't feel it any more. It's quite unnecessary. I do know."

"You're good to me Griselda." She looked at the pile of Christmas cards. "Shall I stick on stamps?"

Griselda smiled and nodded. Soon Lena's tongue was inflexible with mucilage.

"May I stay in the shop?"

"I can't do without you."

CHAPTER XXXIII

Griselda felt more than ever that marriage did not suit her. She supposed that she should have a plan to extricate herself; since resignation, the other possibility, had never suited her either. The trouble was that Kynaston was clearly coming to depend upon her more and more. Worse still, his marriage had enabled him to acquire and develop a variety of social and professional responsibilities and entanglements, which he would be wholly unable to sustain unaided. Griselda found difficulty in deciding how far these were expressions of Kynaston's personality, previously kept latent by restricted conditions, and how far mere substitute outlets for energy diverted by marriage from true and individual aims. Things were not made easier by Lena's normal defence mechanism of aggression turning against herself, and manifesting as acute guilty embarrassment, whenever she came into contact with Kynaston. This led to Lena absenting herself from the shop whenever she thought Kynaston might appear; and to Kynaston making sour remarks about Lena whenever opportunity offered. In the end he suggested that he himself might take Lena's place.

"I could begin by organizing a display of ballet books. Give the entire shop over to it, I mean."

"It wouldn't be fair on Lena, darling. After all she's done nothing wrong."

One day in November Griselda received a letter from Lotus. It was on a large sheet of paper in a large envelope, possibly because Lotus's handwriting was so large; but the contents were brief. It simply invited Griselda to luncheon at Prunier's the same day. It was the first she had heard of Lotus since the postcard view of Sfax. Apparently she was now staying at the Grosvenor Hotel.

Lotus was very brown, a little plumper, and even better dressed than usual. But her big green eyes were deep rock pools.

She lightly touched Griselda's hand, swiftly looked her over, and led the way without speaking to a reserved table.

"Is it true?" Her voice seemed to Griselda softer and more stirring than before she left England.

"Which particular thing?"

"That Geoffrey loves Lena, of course."

"In a way."

"The only way?"

The waiter brought Lotus a large menu. Lotus, without consulting Griselda, ordered at length for both of them in rapid convincing French. The waiter, who was a Swede, departed much impressed.

"Saves misunderstanding," said Lotus. "But you haven't answered me."

"Is it necessary? You seem to know."

"Of course I know. Of course it's not necessary. Things like that are always true. I knew it inside me. But I wanted to hear you say it. I needed to touch bottom." Two very large small drinks arrived.

"All the same how *did* you know? Does Geoffrey write to you?"

"Write to me! He never even thinks of me! Never once since I went away."

"Have you been in Sfax all this time?"

"Sfax failed me."

"Where else have you been?"

"Twice round the world."

Mussels arrived.

"I wish I had been once round."

"The world's become very crowded." She was consuming mussels with enviable grace and firmness. "I've been in Johannesburg for the last six weeks. Buying clothes and buying men. Then throwing them away again. I couldn't go back to Sfax while the hot weather lasted."

"I thought Sfax was always hot."

"It's still hotter during the hot weather. After what you've told me I leave again tonight. I'm living on Victoria Station, you know. I sit all day at my window watching the boat trains and wishing myself beneath their wheels."

"You mean you still love Geoffrey?"

"He is my god. I know that now."

"Take him with you Lotus."

"Please don't laugh at me."

"He's yours. I don't want him and nor does Lena. Take him."

"You offer to sacrifice your whole life to my great love? You are pure, Griselda. You will go to heaven."

Coquilles arrived. Two each.

"Of course, I'm not sure that he'll go. He's become a little set in his ways."

"What am *I* now? Tell me, Griselda, where should we go, he and I? If I accept your sacrifice, that is. I feel you know both our hearts. Tell us where we should be happy."

"I don't think Geoffrey's good at being happy. Men aren't, do you think?" The shells were rattling about on Griselda's plate, making a noise like dead human hopes.

"Then we'll be splendidly, radiantly miserable. But where?"

Griselda considered the maps of the continents in her school atlas. Australia, of course, was out of the question.

"I suggest the Isle of Wight. I've never been there, of course; but I believe it's full of picturesquely wicked people."

"An island!" cried Lotus. "Like George Sand. And Geoffrey

likes Chopin. He could play mazurkas to me. We could throw away our clothes and dance. And aren't there coloured cliffs?"

"And a Pier. It's nearly a mile long."

"And great birds flying into the sun."

"And palm trees."

"There were palm trees at Sfax."

Before the arrival of the bouillabaisse it was settled.

"Where is Geoffrey?" asked Lotus. "I must find him immediately. The Grosvenor's gone and let my room to a party of nuns."

"I'll take you. He's still with the Orinocans. There's a reception this afternoon. The President's in England."

Lotus's eyes were misty and mysterious. "No formality, Griselda," she said, clutching Griselda's hand across the table. "Geoffrey and I will creep away like children; hand in hand into the dusk." Griselda was fascinated by the solid banks of emeralds in her bracelet. They were so nearly the colour of her eyes.

The Liberator's birth-place was en fête. All the windows were shut and fastened, and the lower ones additionally protected by closed iron shutters. There were swags and clusters of artificial flowers in the national colours; and a huge entirely new flag swirling in the November breeze which set the teeth of the spectators on edge with the chill foreboding of even worse weather inescapably ahead. Up the steps to the door was a red carpet showing even yet, and despite hard scrubbing, marks left by the blood of an earlier notability. Above the line of the cornice could be detected the glint and reassurance of steel helmets. The shivering crowd was laced with detectives, chilled to the bone and waiting for trouble. One or two common constables stood grumbling about their pay and working conditions. They were conscious of being outnumbered and outclassed. Preliminary entertainment was provided by a small brass band which was accompanying His Excellency on his travels. As a compliment to England, they played the same tune again and again, being the only English tune they knew except only "The Holy City", which they had learnt instead of "God Save the King." It was "Poor Wandering One"; and, what is more, no royalty was being paid to Mr. D'Oyly Carte.

Lotus and Griselda arrived by taxi four and a half minutes before the climactic moment. Lotus ordered the taxi to wait, despite dissent from a section of the crowd which had been there since dawn and now found its view obstructed. Fortunately, however, the taxi-driver was very old and queer, and fell into a deep sleep every time his vehicle became inanimate. Lotus was shaking all over with nerves. Her face was so thickly veiled as to be quite invisible in the dim taxi; but her sable coat scented the stale cold air with wealth and the anticipation of desire fulfilled. The taximeter was defective and appeared to be running downwards instead of upwards. Every now and then there was a little crisis, when a spring seemed to go; but each time the invincible machine recovered itself and recorded a sum smaller than ever. The watchers on the pavement went on complaining unpleasantly, but took no further action. Griselda found it impossible to withhold admiration for Lotus's Johannesburg hat. Griselda herself wore a large black velvet beret, à La Bohème.

"Where is he?" asked Lotus in a low voice, further muffled by layers of expensive veiling. "When shall I see him?"

"I expect he's inside. They may have lighted a fire as the President's coming."

"When he comes out, what do you advise me to do, Griselda? I trust you absolutely."

"Wait until the end of the ceremony. Geoffrey usually makes himself some toast before he leaves. You can help him with the sardines."

"Will it be long?" Lotus's lovely voice was throbbing.

"We'll see. Here's the procession."

The common constables had been active and were thrusting people back behind invisible lines. Soon Lotus's taxi was isolated. Griselda found it rather exciting. She supposed that Lotus and she must be taken for persons of privilege. Doubtless Lotus's veil was responsible. She resolved to acquire a veil herself as soon as Geoffrey was off her hands. The watchers on the pavement could be heard expressing further resentment as they were lined up behind a huge pantechnicon which, having missed the diversion notices, was waiting for the crowd to clear, while the driver looked for a public house. The constables were quipping and appealing obliquely to the crowd's common humanity in order to reconcile them.

Then from the other direction a scout from New Scotland Yard roared into being on his splendid motor bicycle; and some way behind him came a funeral Daimler, bearing a tiny silk pennant. Without a sound the Daimler ceased to move; the footman opened the door; and, as the crowd cheered half-heartedly, eight men alighted, in various different kinds of overcoat. Simultaneously the front door of the house opened with a deep clanking, as of heavy chains falling on to a deck; and Colonel Costa-Rica in a pale blue uniform and a feather at least two feet tall, descended the steps to greet the First Citizen of his homeland. After a moment's confusion, the band rushed into "Sheep may safely graze" which had been adopted as the Orinocan national anthem. Their performance would have been better if they had not been so unaccustomed to prolonged damp cold.

Then Lotus gave a suppressed cry. Behind the Colonel, Kynaston had appeared. He wore a frock coat, which Griselda supposed must be retained by the Embassy for such occasions; a discreet rose in his buttonhole; and pale grey spats. He carried a silk hat almost as tall as the Colonel's feather; but could have done with a suitable overcoat. Griselda was surprised she had not before noticed that he was gathering weight. He looked anxious but determined, as at other turning points in his career at which she had been present. Lotus clung to Griselda's hand. Rapture made her speechless.

Among the men getting out of the car Griselda recognized the Under Secretary for Foreign Affairs, a raw youth whom she had met at the All Party Dance. She remembered him as suffering from a conclusive impediment in his speech. Now he was followed by a tottering figure from his Department, and by the Orinocan Ambassador, who looked as pleased and as unchallengeable as if he had just captured the national meat-packing contract (as was quite possibly the case). The Ambassador was accompanied by a Chargé d'Affaires, indistinguishable from Mr. Jack Buchanan, and by the Military Attaché, who, though a small man, based his style on Field-Marshal Göring, thus being entrusted with as many personal confidences as professional. Behind this brilliant figure, appeared the chef de cabinet and the President's aide-de-camp, the former somewhat younger than the latter, which was opportune as the two looked so South American as to make distinction between them otherwise difficult. Griselda would have expected the President to appear first, but, in fact, he appeared last; possibly in consequence of having been the first to enter the well filled vehicle. He was a commonplace stocky man, in movement staccato from years of watchfulness, and with a head like a small round cannon-ball. His sharp nasal voice could be clearly heard, carried on the chill moist air as he addressed his entourage. He seemed dissatisfied with something. Griselda knew from Kynaston that he was of Irish extraction, a fact which he concealed under the name of Cassido.

Despite the autumnal weather, Griselda enjoyed looking on from the sanctuary of the cab. Indeed she found many of the conditions perfect for witnessing a spectacle of the kind. It was almost cosy. Lotus, however, had begun to pant slightly, filling the enclosed space with delicate vapour filtered by her veil. Quickly, as Colonel Costa-Rica was saluting, she lowered the window of the cab and, putting out half her body, ecstatically waved her handkerchief, executed for her by Worth's South African branch. The draught in the cab was really appalling; and Griselda, moreover, was reduced to looking out through the unsatisfactory little panel at the rear.

The cab being, like most of its kind, old and almost in pieces, the sudden frenzied lowering of one of its windows was audible above "Sheep may safely graze" and the fury of the President. The distinguished visitor still stood with his back to the saluting Colonel, so that Kynaston, waiting to be presented, permitted his attention to be drawn by the obtrusive clatter. Through her tiny window Griselda saw him go very white and drop his silk hat.

Lotus uttered a cooing cry of reunion. The President, his round Irish face black with passion, had begun to wave both arms above his head and to jump up and down on the pavement. Then there was a shot. The Military Attaché, secure in his diplomatic immunity, was effecting a coup d'état.

Griselda saw the President jump higher than ever. Clearly as yet he was little, if any, the worse. Kynaston was stooping for his hat, which had rolled down the red carpet. Then there was a second shot and Kynaston disappeared. By this time one of the common constables, who a second before had seemed to be standing a long way off, had covered the ground and, disregarding international law, thrown his arms round the Attaché's middle. Colonel Costa-Rica, supposing all to be over with the Father of his People, continued at the salute. Then, looking much mortified, he lowered his arm as unobtrusively as possible. The President was intact, though in a worse mood than ever.

History, or such of it as was under proper direction, related that a young foreigner privileged to work at the shrine of the Liberator, had had the honour of offering his life to save the life of President Cassido. Even a gringo, indicated history, was thus exalted after only a single meeting with the Liberator's great successor.

Occasionally Griselda wondered, not without remorse and self-questioning, whether Kynaston had not preferred death to Lotus; but on the whole she was convinced that his end had been sadly but entirely accidental.

To Colonel Costa-Rica it is to be feared that the incident presented itself mainly in the light of another contest with an obstructive charwoman upon the subject of once more cleaning up that unlucky carpet.

PART THREE

CHAPTER XXXIV

One day between Christmas and Near Year Griselda and Lena were dusting some of the stock. The shop had just opened. They worked along the upper shelves taking out the books one at a time, dusting their top edges, and replacing them. Every now and then there was a long pause while one or other of them investigated a volume entirely new to her.

The door opened and a tall man entered in a Gibus hat and a black cloak covered with snow.

"Good morning," said Griselda from the top of her ladder. She had just been dipping into Pears' Cyclopedia.

"Please don't come down," said the visitor. "I'll look round, if I may." He removed his hat. He had curling black hair, parted down the middle.

"Certainly," said Griselda. "Won't you take off your cloak?"

"Thank you." He looked up at her. He was very pale; with large but well-shaped bones, and black eyes.

"There's a stand in the corner. Under the bust of Menander."

"I didn't know there was a bust of Menander."

"It's conjectural."

"Like so much else." Griselda thought he almost smiled.

He removed his cloak. He was wearing evening dress with a white waistcoat; and across his breast ran the bright silk ribbon of a foreign order.

He hung up his coat and hat, and began to examine the books. He went along the shelves steadily and methodically, noting every title and frequently extracting a book for similarly exact scrutiny of its contents. Some of the books he bore away to Griselda's desk, where he had soon built a substantial cairn. Griselda and Lena descended alternately to serve other customers. Many of them seemed surprised by the distinction of the stranger's appearance.

Before his circuit of the shop was three-quarters completed, he came to rest by the desk. "Alas, I must go. You see: I am awaited." He extended his hand towards the wintry morning outside the shop window. The snow clouds were so heavy that it hardly seemed day; but as Griselda followed his gesture, she saw that the dim and dirty light was further diminished by some large obstruction.

"I'll make out a bill and then pack up the books in parcels."

"Please don't trouble. My coachman and footman will load them into the carriage."

He went to the door and spoke briefly to someone outside.

A man of about thirty, with very long side whiskers, entered, and began to bear away armfuls of books. He wore a beaver hat, a long dark green topcoat with a cape, and high boots. Clearly he had been sitting on his box in the snow while his master shopped.

"Don't take them before Miss de Reptonville has accounted for them."

Griselda put some shillings in the pounds column and Lena slightly damaged the dust-jacket of "The Light of Asia"; but both took care to display no surprise.

"Ask Staggers to help you, if you wish."

"No necessity, sir. One more trip and I'll finish. Staggers needs to hold the umbrella between the door and the carriage."

"Of course. Most proper."

Griselda, being unproficient at arithmetic, could only hope that the grand total could be substantiated. It was certainly the grandest total since she had entered the shop.

The customer produced an unusually large cheque book from a pocket inside his cloak and wrote out the cheque in black ink. Griselda saw that the cheque, which was on a small private Bank previously unknown to her, bore the drawer's coat of arms and crest. One glance at this last and she had no need to look at the signature.

The customer was regarding her. "I received your Christmas Card. Thank you."

"I was grateful for your letter."

"Nothing would have pleased me more than to have been able to help you." He spoke with much sincerity.

An invisible hand lightly squeezed at Griselda's throat.

"I must give you a receipt."

She was unable even to stick on the stamp symmetrically.

"Please introduce me to your friend."

"Of course. Please forgive me. Both of you. Lena Drelincourt. Sir Hugo Raunds."

Lena descended. She looked a little startled. Their visitor removed a white kid glove, more than slightly discoloured with his recent work, and put out an elegant and well kept hand.

"I like your shop. I used to know Mr. Tamburlane quite well. I shall hope to visit you again. May I?" It was if he were a caller rather than a customer.

"As soon as possible," said Lena.

"Lena writes."

"Of course. Her three books are by my bed, and I admire them more at every reading."

Lena went slightly pink and looked charming.

"Good-bye then, Miss de Reptonville."

Griselda took his hand. It was firm and dry and cool.

She looked him in the eyes. "There's no news?"

"No news." He still held her hand. "I hope I need not say I should have told you?"

"No . . . I couldn't help asking."

He said nothing for a moment; then silently released her hand. All the while he was returning her gaze. Lena was looking on flushed and fascinated.

"All packed up, sir," said the footman from the exactly right distance between the group of them and the shop door.

"I'm coming. You can tell Staggers to get back on his box."

"Very good, sir."

Their visitor put on his cloak. He had reached a decision. "I propose," he said, "to ask you to come and stay with me. Both of you." He seemed to speak with hesitation. "But naturally only if you wish to do so. Please say nothing now. There will be a formal invitation; which if you wish to decline or ignore I shall entirely understand."

At this moment Griselda recalled old Zec's curious behaviour at the All Party Ball when Hugo Raunds was mentioned.

"We'd love to come," said Lena casually.

He made no reply, but bowing slightly and saying "Your servant, ladies," departed into the London snow.

Griselda and Lena followed him to the door. His carriage was an immense affair, with the familiar crest upon the door and at the base of the massive brightly polished lamps. Drawn by two proportionately immense black horses, with wild eyes, nostrils steaming like volcanoes, waving manes, and long undocked tails, it was governed by an immense coachman, so rugged and round and red as to overawe all possible comment. His red hair stuck out horizontally from beneath his huge tilted beaver. His red beard was snowy as Father Christmas's. His red ear was curiously round, like the top of a red toadstool.

As the equipage drove away into the thickly drifting snow, Griselda and Lena perceived that on the opposite pavement, previously obscured from them by the bulk of the carriage itself, had accumulated, even in the teeth of the weather, a small cluster of passing Londoners. Rage and contempt were in every face and posture. Griselda had seldom seen any gathering of people so much under the influence of their emotions.

CHAPTER XXXV

Griselda had told Lena about Louise and said that she had mentioned the family which dwelt in the house they had entered on the day of Kynaston's final picnic. Now she told her about Zec and his wife, whom for a long time she had forgotten; and of Louise's words "Hugo is a very *secret* man."

"You mean," said Lena, "that after Mr. Tamburlane you've had enough of secret men?"

"Not altogether that. I don't think Hugo Raunds is like Mr. Tamburlane, do you, Lena?"

"Not altogether, I should say."

"I just thought that if we're going to stay with him—are we, by the way?"

"It'll mean coffins for beds and tooth mugs in gold plate."

"If we *are* going to stay, perhaps we could find out just why people don't seem to like him."

"I don't know that that's any great mystery," said Lena. "If you think what people are like. Still I agree we might dig about."

But it was hard to know which piece of ground to turn first; so that by the time the invitation arrived, they had discovered nothing more about their host whatever.

They were invited to visit a house which seemed to be in the Welsh Marches; and no term was set to their stay. The brief letter ended with the words "Come and see for yourselves. Then please yourselves."

"Hell of a journey in February," remarked Lena, "and, I should say, doubtfully worth the expense seeing that we can't both leave the shop for more than a day or two. Still, better than that mausoleum in Essex doubtless. I suppose I shall have to freeze in a skirt all the time as it's a country family?"

"Louise said that Hugo Raunds lived entirely for clothes."

"I can imagine what that means. Brittle women in models."

"Surely not in Montgomeryshire?"

"Unlike us they travel wrapped in mink in centrally heated Rolls-Royces."

"Shall we not go?"

Lena thought for a moment. Then she said gently "You go, Griselda. They'd only eye me."

"I won't go without you."

"It's much the best thing. You could do with a holiday, and I could look after the shop. Stay a long time if you find you like it. As long as you want to. You're beautiful and it's a kind of thing you need. One kind of thing. Sometimes, anyway. So, please."

"You need a holiday too."

"Less than you."

Griselda put her arm round Lena's shoulders.

"You're good to me, Lena, I'm grateful."

"You gave me half a shop. *I'm* grateful. I'll look you up a train to Montgomeryshire."

Of course Griselda had to change at Shrewsbury, but she had

never expected to have to change at Welshpool as well.

Darkness had descended long before she arrived. The minute but not inelegant Welsh station seemed high among the mountains. A small but bitter wind crept murderously along the single platform. There was one oil lamp, and otherwise not a light to be seen anywhere. Griselda was the only passenger, but two figures awaited her on the platform.

One was clearly the station factotum, though his aspect, demeanour, and even uniform seemed of an antique type. He came forward, touched his cap, and, though able to speak little but Welsh, bade Griselda Good evening, and took her bag. After a wait of only some seconds, the engine whistled, and the train drew out as if glad to be away.

The second figure was a woman. She was closely muffled in a hood and wore some long garment reaching to the ground. Her perfume hung on the cold air. She extended her gloved hand and, having confirmed Griselda's identity, said "My name is Esemplarita. I look after things at the Castle. Hugo asked me to apologize for being unable to meet you himself. He turned his ankle yesterday fencing." When Griselda had greeted her and expressed her regret about her host's misadventure, the woman continued "We have to go down a narrow path to the lane, where the carriage is waiting. But Abersoch will go first with the lamp."

Abersoch lifted the single lamp from its bracket and led the way.

"You go next," said Esemplarita to Griselda.

They descended a cinder way which zig-zagged down a high bank to a tiny sunken lane below. At the bottom of the path Abersoch's lamp fell upon a small black cabriolet with a gleaming horse.

"Good evening, miss," said another Welsh voice from the box.

Abersoch opened the door and handed up Griselda's luggage, which the coachman placed in a high-sided cage on the roof.

"Your ticket if you please, miss."

Griselda had to grope by the light of Abersoch's lamp, but in the end she found it and delivered it up.

"Not all of it, miss," said Abersoch. He bisected the ticket and gave her half of it. "You may be wanting to go back."

"Thank you," said Griselda smiling. "So I shall."

"It's entirely up to you, miss."

Griselda stepped into the carriage. The interior was pitch black and filled with Esemplarita's scent. Esemplarita followed her in. There was scarcely room for two on the seat. Abersoch shut the door and again touched his cap, the light falling on his face as in an old-fashioned coloured drawing. The carriage began to move.

"I'm afraid the road is atrocious almost all the way."

To Griselda this seemed to be true.

After a considerable period of compressed jolting silence, while Griselda tried to think of something to say, Esemplarita took up the conversation. "I believe you don't know Hugo very well?"

"No. He's really a friend of a friend of mine."

"I know. Your friend gave Hugo a good account of you."

"When?" Griselda's heart was beating among the beating of the horse's hooves.

"Some time ago. As you know, we're not in touch with her at the moment. But I wanted to speak of something else. You have heard, of course, that Hugo's life—and the lives of all of us—differ from the lives people lead nowadays?"

"I was told a little—by the friend we have in common. A very little. I have noticed—some small differences. I know almost nothing."

"The Castle is, so to speak, enchanted. Your friend gave Hugo to understand that you might like to know about it; to see for yourself."

"She was kind."

"The opportunity is mutual. We want suitable people to visit us."

"I see."

"There are very few suitable people."

"Can you define?"

The carriage had plunged across what Griselda took to be a series of deep diagonal ruts frozen to the unyieldingness of stone, before her companion answered "It cannot truly be defined. You will soon begin to see. There is only one thing."

"Yes?"

"Your friend commended you for your acceptance of what life can offer. Your lack of surprise. You understand that?"

"Yes."

"Lack of surprise is taken for granted at the Castle. That is what I wanted to say."

"I see . . . I love your scent."

"Thank you." Then she added kindly "That is the sort of thing not to be surprised about."

For some time they compared tastes in books and music. Then the carriage stopped.

"The Castle gates," said Esemplarita.

Griselda could hear the clanking and grinding as the lodge-keeper opened them. Remarks were exchanged in Brythonic between him and the driver. Then the carriage proceeded on a much better surface. Griselda could hear the gates closing behind her.

The distance up the drive seemed very long. Griselda and her companion turned to the subject of edible fungi: how to find and prepare them, and which of them to eschew. Esemplarita explained that she had known nothing of these matters until she came to live at the Castle, but that now they had fungi with almost every meal.

In the end Griselda felt the carriage following a huge arc, as if going round the edge of an immense circus ring. Then it stopped again and the driver was opening the door.

Griselda realized that the Castle was not, as she had supposed, mediaeval, but Gothic revival at the earliest. The long front before her was decked with three tiers of lighted windows. Clearly Sir Hugo was entertaining largely.

When the coachman had rung the ornate bell, the door was opened by a footman. Griselda entered, followed by Esemplarita. The coachman was getting down Griselda's bag to give to the footman.

The big Gothic revival hall was hung with paintings, and lighted with hundreds, possibly thousands, of candles, in complex candelabra descending from the ceiling, and storied brackets climbing the walls. There was an immense carpet, predominantly dark green; and involved painted furniture. At one end of the hall was a fire which really filled the huge grate and soaked all the air with warmth. Round the fire was a group of men and women. They sat or lay on painted chairs and couches and on the predominantly dark green floor. Griselda thought at first that they were in fancy dress. Then she turned and saw that Esemplarita was dressed like them. She remembered that she must not be surprised.

Instead she smiled. She felt as one returned to life. She was relieved of care and accessible to joy.

Esemplarita went round introducing her. Several of the names were known to Griselda. If she was not surprised, neither, it was clear, were they.

Then she heard herself greeted. She stood with her back to the the blaze, a huge portrait of Jeanne de Naples above her head, and saw her host standing at the foot of the wide staircase. He wore a dressing gown in mulberry silk and leaned on the baluster. Behind him stood a figure Griselda recognized. It was Vaisseau.

"Are you pleased?"

"It is beautiful."

"It is doomed of course."

"Of course."

"You are smiling."

"I am happy."

The men and women round the fire had kept quite silent during this colloquy. Now a tall woman came to her and said "Would you like to change? There's no need if you'd rather not. But if you'd like to, I could help."

"Thank you," replied Griselda. "I'd like to."

ENVOI

Before many days Griselda found that happiness unfitted her for the modern world; and, though the master of the Castle, as she knew, often travelled, as on occasion did most of the others, decided to give her half of the shop to Lena, who, despite the warmest of invitations, persisted in her attitude that Wales was a waste of oracles and oratorios.

Griselda was happy, though cognizant that sooner or later the spell would be broken by public opinion and Order in Council; but whenever there was mention of Hero and Leander, about whom one of the others was writing a poetic drama, and indeed whenever her thoughts were idle, she knew that if only Louise were there, then indeed would she be whole.

MY POOR FRIEND

I was at the time employed by an organization which had been formed to advocate the use of small rivers, and even streams, for the generation of local electricity. Like many such bodies, the Society had been started by an enthusiast but had soon come to rely for the main part of its income upon business combines which stood to benefit, sometimes rather mysteriously, from any successes it might achieve. The inaugurator, a corpulent, middle-aged agricultural engineer with sparse red hair, named Wycliff Bessemer, had become convinced that the future of Britain depended upon the reinstatement of comparatively small, comparatively self-sufficient rural communities. He was bitterly aware of the irony of having to depend for a fighting fund largely upon impersonal cartels of electrical manufacturers and bellicose public works contractors.

Nor was this the only irony which came to weigh upon the basically prophetic but rather slow-thinking Bessemer, as time went on. It was difficult not to notice, for example, that nearly all the private members of the Society were markedly urban in background. I myself further noticed that most of them were far more interested in discussing endlessly the technical minutiae of electrical generation than in saving the nation. Bessemer may have missed that point because he was very much a man for electrical detail himself. In the end, I began to wonder whether, indeed, the genesis of the whole thing had not been an inflation by Bessemer of a personal hobby into a means of general redemption.

I became involved myself when I left ICI. That made the third such episode: I had already disagreed with Shell-Mex and even with the John Lewis Partnership. My then wife, Virginia, suggested that I might be happier in a much smaller enterprise: a bigger duck in a narrower pond, as she put it. After a few weeks of pretty desperate correspondence and going for interviews, I saw Bessemer's advertisement, inserted anonymously, with only a box number, in the *Daily Telegraph*. According to the advertisement, a charitable organization with wide national aims sought what it called an administrative secretary.

Bessemer told me later that he had received more than six hundred answers, and I still do not really know why he offered the job to me. I suspect, from my later knowledge of him, that it was mainly laziness. The pay offered was only slightly more than half what I had received from ICI, and there was no welfare, but Virginia said I should seize the chance to escape from the commercial rut. As she would be involved in considerable sacrifice herself, to say nothing of the twins, it seemed to me likely that she really had an insight into my true needs. I daresay she had. It proved to be odd and frustrating work, but I have not come upon anything else which has suited me better.

The administrative secretary was the universal factotum: he had to do virtually everything. The only other staff which could be afforded was a part-time typist: either a married woman with all the edges rubbed from her wits, or a very young girl, at once precocious and useless, seldom even a sexual temptation. I should say that during my time there were as many as fifteen or sixteen replacements.

Bessemer himself had his agricultural work to do, and his temperament by no means afforded a surplus of general energy. Weeks on end would pass without my hearing from him at all. Then I would receive five or six quarto pages of the Society's paper closely typed by Mrs. Bessemer on both sides in single spacing. It was usually a mixture of three ingredients: complaints and very impracticable suggestions which had been made to Bessemer by members of the Society who were personal friends of his, and had therefore gone behind my back, or at least disregarded me; instructions to do this or that which even Bessemer could not have asked for if he had been as much in touch with the day-to-day situation as was the general office; and long paragraphs of what Bessemer frequently referred to as his philosophy, but was seldom more than grumbling and rambling. The general office, needless to say, was an upper room off Grays Inn Road. I used to think that, if it hadn't been for the limitations of the typist, I could have done something more lucrative there between whiles, such as run a correspondence course in dinghy sailing or in How to Succeed.

I did think that, and it was inevitable, but I must not give the impression that I was sceptical about the Society's aims. I was not, nor am I now. Virginia was quite right in thinking that I needed an outlet for idealism, and Bessemer's ideal was well argued, well informed, well founded. Britain would indeed, in my opinion, be a better place if she would carry out Bessemer's program. She would be mistaken if she entrusted the direction of it to Bessemer, but pioneers seldom qualify as executives. I soon came to see why. What really did make me sceptical, what in the end almost broke me up, was contact with Parliament, or rather, with the House of Commons, the filter of all public action, of all idealism, all personality, all hope.

Who cares what I think on such a subject? I used to bind on to Virginia about it for hours at a time, for months on end, but what one says to one's wife cuts no ice outside the home, almost by definition. I am compelled to say a little about it now, because only so can I indicate what seemed to me to mark off Walter Enright from the run of M.P.s—apart from the fact that, for one reason and another, he was the only M.P. I could ever have called a friend, a private and personal friend, that is, as distinct from a public friend. Nor am I implying that all M.P.s are queuing up even to be one's public friend. Far from it.

I entered into the Society's employ at the time when the executive council was set upon establishing a "parliamentary committee," which might press the cause at Westminster. When I arrived, I supposed that the executive council, though probably seldom to be seen, must be composed, or largely composed, of persons whose names were known to the public. This last, I soon realized, was not the case: apart from one Liberal ex-mayor of a town in the Home Counties, and one fairly distinguished but very senior naturalist, it contained no one whom the public was likely ever to have heard of. I was right, however, about the executive council's invisibility. Nearly a year passed before my first council meeting, and when it took place, only about a third of the people appeared who were entitled to attend. Bessemer did almost all the talking, except on the subject of the parliamentary committee. That was something which everyone thought very important, and I made quite a mark for myself by saying that a committee was nearly in being. Most of the work had been done, in reality, by my predecessor before he had left for South Africa, but it is often more difficult to follow in another man's tracks than to engrave one's own, so I did not think the praise I got excessive.

I saw much of the parliamentary committee before I myself left, and indeed of Parliament, because I was the only one who attended all the committee's meetings—or rather, all of those to which a representative of the Society was admitted. The Parliamentary Committee for Local Electricity, as it termed itself, continued long after my time and indeed until Bessemer's accident brought the Society to an end.

Parliament, then.

Everybody nowadays thinks it is a bad joke that the Member of Parliament can almost never decide how he will vote, but is compelled, nonetheless to spend most of his parliamentary life attending "debates" based fundamentally upon the premise that he can so decide and is, therefore, accessible to argument. A smaller, better informed number thinks it a bad joke that the "debates" are, in the event, for the most part hardly attended at all, though almost all M.P.s in default of special personal arrangements have to hang about while they are going on, in order to pass through the division lobbies whenever required, which is often unexpectedly: day after day, week after week, month after month. A still smaller number thinks it a bad joke that we have abandoned the hope, and to some extent the practice, of government by those who are born and trained to power, in favor of government by those who have to struggle, fight, defame, blarney, manipulate, bribe, and conspire to get power, and then to go on struggling, fighting, defaming, blarneying, manipulating, bribing, and conspiring in order to keep it: men and women of one particular kind, in fact, or at least with one particular, not obviously desirable, thing in common. Government, one may say all government, must at the best be exceedingly imperfect (so that the less there is of it quantitatively, the better); but the earlier ideal would still seem to hold more promise than the later.

Generalizations such as these are common talk. What upset me was how it works in practice.

Government has been carried on less and less visibly for a long time; but the critical thing in Britain has been the swift development of official public relations. Every public authority that knows its business now has what may be termed a paddock for its critics and opponents, not excluding those inside Parliament. Quite rapidly it has become almost impossible to be a rebel. Today the rebels are put in a paddock and then built into the structure. They are patiently listened to when they have made themselves assertive enough. They are pressed to deliver their ideas in writing. They are invited to serve on joint committees. It is implied to them that if they keep their criticisms "constructive," they may even become O.B.E.s. "Look at our splendid collection of rebels. It proves how strong, important, and on the right lines we are." The Speaker's Corner technique, one may call it: intensely British, brilliantly adaptable, utterly null. Faced with it, Bessemer emerged, quite unawares, as a mere nineteenth-century evangelist; not only incapable of planting his petards deep enough, but incapable of even seeing that he was paddocked, that his ostensibly critical notions were being applied, judo-wise, to the actual strengthening of his opponents. It is sadly true that only the power to inflict actual damage of some kind holds any hope of surmounting the official techniques.

Members of Parliament, already persons willing to put up with the conditions I have referred to—fighters, above all, pushers, wheedlers, conspirers—appear today in the hour of their supposed success merely as front figures for an impersonal power machine. The inner conflict, added to the odious daily life, added to the "constituency surgery," whereat the supposed legislator of peace or war is reduced to the procurer of a supplementary pension and/or surgical appliance for every elector; all this is too much for any man or woman, any mere human. Degeneration is inevitable, even if it has not largely taken place before adoption as a candidate. The professional politician's characteristic rejoinder is to multiply his salary and demand that sessions last all day, instead of beginning in the afternoon, so that the shop would be closed in favor of his special—not obviously desirable—type.

Yes, of course I speak with some bitterness, but anyone who doesn't is in the paddock with Bessemer. Also I speak with some knowledge . . . No matter. I introduce Enright; Enright the exception.

He was exceptional—for me—from the start in the way I met him. It was not among the Palace of Westminster phantoms but at one of Mrs. Havengore's parties. Mrs. Havengore was a disinterested, indeed maniacal, enthusiast for local electricity. She was a middle-aged lady with large bones, who lived in a shapeless house in Leicestershire and spent the rest of her time hunting. She would invite to "drinks" large and miscellaneously influential groups of people who could not care less about local electricity (indeed, she knew many of them through the hunting field), and compel me to attend in order to address the company for ten or twelve minutes. Mrs. Havengore's cheeks would grow pinker and pinker, her eyes more and more challenging as I held forth, but she was the only one. The attitude of the others blended tepid spitefulness with the implication of knowledge far greater than mine. I observed these responses at the very first of the parties (as on so many other occasions), and it cannot have strengthened my discourse on subsequent visits, though the effect of my words on Mrs. Havengore herself was always identical. At the end of the party, I had to catch the last, slow train back to London from Melton Mowbray, traveling third, which was all the organization could pay for.

Walter Enright had apparently attended the previous weekend meet, and there he was, all by himself, caught by Mrs. Havengore even though his constituency was far from Leicestershire. It was during a parliamentary recess, but Mrs. Havengore would probably have captured him in any case because she knew how to make real rudeness the only alternative, even a real quarrel. This is a useful gift for the public campaigner.

Enright sat on a faded chintz-covered stool at the back of the room. He had carved-out, very clear-shaven features, and startlingly fair hair. It was noticeable, however, that he was smoking an unusual type of cigarette; also that he had narrow, bright blue eyes. He wore a tight gray suit.

He manifested no obvious interest in my lame little talk but seemed, indeed, conspicuously preoccupied with some problem of his own. I observed that he warded off approaches from the rest of the company without even much politeness. Soon he was standing about near the door, still essentially isolated, and twitching slightly.

Mrs. Havengore hauled me away from a circle of tormentors and pushed me toward the guest of honor.

"Here's the man who can *really* do something about it," she said. "Didn't you think Mr. Grover-Stacey's lecture was quite wonderful?"

"Very good talk," said Enright, looking at the floor. "I congratulate you."

"Thank you," I said.

"*Won't* you make Parliament listen to him?" besought Mrs. Havengore.

"I'll try." Enright's manner was dry and distant, but not malicious, as was that of the other guests.

"Couldn't you get him an introduction to the prime minister?"

"It's more the concern of the minister of fuel and power."

"*I* always believe in going straight to the top," said Mrs. Havengore.

"We'll have to wait for the next session in any case."

"I'll leave you together to talk. I know *you* can make it happen if you really believe in it."

Mrs. Havengore passed on to bore others. There is nothing people hate more than a cause which is practical but disinterested.

Enright glanced at me for the first time, then looked back at the floor.

"I've been very undecided," he said, "whether or not to stand again at the next election."

"I hope you decide in favor," I replied with imitation urgency. After all, I was Mrs. Havengore's guest, and it seemed necessary to emulate her attitude.

"I have," said Enright. "Indeed, I had little real alternative." He got out an unfashionable elaborate gold case and extracted another long cigarette.

"Forgive my not offering you one. They're a special blend, and not everyone likes them."

"I don't smoke," I said.

"I only smoke these." From his tight waistcoat, he produced a small, cylindrical, gold lighter from which a tiny green flame erupted upon silent pressure at the base. When he put the cigarette in his mouth, it was as if it had been put between the lips of a wooden figure. Moreover, the cigarette, glowing more yellow than red, apparently gave off no smoke. It was, no doubt, a parliamentary cigarette. Enright's blue eyes seemed to become more limpid as he smoked it.

"So," said Enright, without further explanation, "I need something new to take my mind off things. It strikes me that this idea of yours might do quite well."

"It was very good of you to come all this way in order to listen to me."

"Members of Parliament have to do things like that sometimes."

"I suppose so."

"I might set up a committee."

"We've got one already."

"Are they any good?"

"That's perhaps not for me to say."

"How often do they meet?"

"I haven't heard of them actually meeting for some time."

Enright showed added interest, insofar as he showed anything. "In that case, believe me, they're probably dead. Parliament is rather like a university. All kinds of causes are always being taken up and make quite a stir for a time, but unless the government adopts them, or unless there's a big publicity interest in them, they soon die, and people turn to something else. Who is or was the chairman?"

"Mr. Biggles."

"I don't know him, but I'll have a word with him and see what can be done. If I'm to go on, I need some line to take up and be associated with. I'm not in the running for office, and I must have something."

"Thank you." I was beginning to notice the fumes of Enright's special cigarette in the crowded room, stuffy with platitudes.

"Of course I shall need to learn more about it. Come and

see me after the recess. I can't make it sooner because I'm compelled to go abroad. Give me a ring when I get back. I mean
it."

"I will," I said. "I really am most grateful."

"All this is confidential, of course. You won't forget that?"

"Of course," I said. "I'll remember."

"You might thank Mrs. Havengore. Someone's waiting for
me."

"Certainly."

He disappeared swiftly and quietly, and I could see no reason
why I myself need stay much longer.

Enright had not given me a telephone number, nor could I find
him in the directory, nor did his entry in *Vacker's Parliamentary
Guide* include a private address. As ringing up a Member at the
Houses of Parliament is a short route to insanity, and as I had had
no assistant whatever at that time for some weeks, I might well, I
fear, have done nothing except possibly send a letter to Enright at
some future time when the pressure upon me had become less.
About a week before the commencement of the new session,
however, Enright telephoned me. He began by inquiring why he
had not heard from me but then invited me round that evening to
his flat behind Victoria Street. I was to arrive at six.

It was a big red block of about 1905, when flats were comparatively new to Britain. Enright admitted me himself. It struck me
that he looked pale and also that he was wearing the same tight
suit that he had worn at Mrs. Havengore's party.

"I won't offer you a cigarette," he said, "because I have a special kind which doesn't suit everyone."

"I remember."

"But do have a drink." Without further consultation, he poured
me a weak whisky from an Edwardian decanter and depressed the
lever of a heavily wired gasogene. It yielded a little soda water and
then glugged out.

"Damn," said Enright. He extended the half-filled tumbler
toward me. "Do you mind?"

"Not at all. It's all I want in any case."

"My mother, who looks after me now, always forgets to put in a new cartridge. Or refuses. Years ago, she broke a finger on one of these things, and it's a case of once bitten, twice shy. I myself am not drinking just now."

"It's perfectly all right."

"Do sit down."

The quite large but rather dully proportioned room was in remarkable disorder. Drifts of parliamentary papers lay on the furniture and floor, mingled with children's toys. I had looked up *Who's Who* before I left and learned that Enright had a wife and two sons. I pushed aside some papers on the huge gray sofa and sat on it near the middle.

Enright was walking up and down, paddling through paper.

"This thing of yours. I read a book about it when I was abroad. I had to go, you know, and I thought I might as well do something while I was there. Book by a man called Thesiger. Do you know it?"

"Bessemer, perhaps. He's my immediate employer; he started the Society."

"What do you think of it?"

"The Society?"

"The book."

"I think it makes a very good case. I hope you thought the same."

"How do you think it would go in Parliament?"

"Surely you must be able to judge that better than I can."

"I've seen Biggles."

This statement greatly surprised me. I wasn't accustomed to Members of Parliament really doing such things, or even remembering names. All of them are expected to keep in mind such an enormous quantity of stuff.

"What did he say?"

"It's just what I thought. Between ourselves, Biggles isn't what he was. Not that I knew him before. I didn't. But what's quite obvious now is that he's on the bottle."

This didn't surprise me at all. Many others had said the same to me.

"Poor chap," said Enright.

"It does seem a pity. A bad thing for local electricity. I should very much appreciate your advice, and so, I am sure, would Mr. Bessemer."

"Don't worry," said Enright. "Don't give it a thought. I'm going to move in myself. I've made up my mind to it. I simply must find something, and, after all, why not?"

"Mr. Bessemer will be delighted. He was asking me only last month what had happened to the parliamentary committee."

Enright stopped his abstracted pacing up and down. He stared at me looking slightly wild.

"Are you all right?"

"Perfectly."

"Have another drink?"

"Thank you very much. No."

"Have some without soda?"

"No, thank you."

Enright started walking up and down once more.

"Since we're going into this thing together, I'd better mention the question of my wife. It'll have to be mentioned sooner or later, and we may as well make it now."

I suppose I must at once have looked as though I found the subject more interesting than local electricity.

"My wife's left me. But it's only temporary, you understand. And it's not in the least her fault. I'm an impossible brute to be married to, and then there were the two children, one after the other. One was bad enough, but two! It was enough to drive any woman clean out of her mind, let alone being married to me as well. Look at that."

Enright picked off the floor a crude wooden railway engine, painted red. With his other hand, he was showing me some marks in the frame, or, more accurately, small circular holes. There was a line of them, in the shape of a crescent.

"And at that."

Enright turned over the engine and showed me several similarly shaped groups of holes, but this time at the front end of the circular wooden boiler itself.

"Teeth," said Enright, dropping the toy on the floor. "Just teeth."

It was, as you can see, difficult to think of anything to say.

"You mean there's something unusual about the children?"

"They're not human at all. They ought not to live. But my wife naturally doesn't see it like that."

"Perhaps it might be better for both of you if they could be brought up in some special place?"

"No special place could take them in. It simply would not be possible."

I did not inquire where the children then were, but merely said how very sorry I was.

"My wife says I've failed her by becoming a Member of Parliament."

"I can't really believe it."

"You'd believe it if ever you were to meet her."

"Why not a Member of Parliament?"

Enright gave one of the toys a sudden kick. It flew across the room and cracked the lower part of a glass-fronted bookcase containing thick, bound volumes of *Proceedings*.

"Never at home. Never loving. Never even living. And it's all so bloody true. Nothing real at all. Not one bloody thing."

"I remember you saying you had thought of giving up Parliament."

"Well, of course," cried Enright. "But you can't. At least you can't when your people don't want you to. You haven't one hope in hell."

"I didn't know the party machine was quite as strong as that."

"They like to get something on you. Most business is like that nowadays, as well as politics. In my case, they had no difficulty."

"I suppose most of us are vulnerable somewhere if only people knew."

"No doubt," said Enright. "But in my case it was my wife. She simply went to them and told them."

"It's hardly my business, but in that case it would seem to be a good thing she's left."

"On the contrary, my dear fellow," said Enright, suddenly sitting down beside me. "On the contrary, I am simply not alive without her. Now do let me get you another drink, and we'll talk about something more interesting."

I agreed, accepting a whisky neat, though only a small one.

Enright now seemed easier in his mind. We talked of local electricity. I was once more impressed by his approach to the subject.
He entirely avoided the usual procedure of talking about how
to do it before knowing whether or not it was to be done at all.
He spent no time, as most of them did, on trying to impress me
with how important it was to do things parliamentary in exactly
the right way, treading on no toes, rolling the pitch, and so forth.
After half an hour, and a third small whisky, I began to think that
soon he would be speaking of such down-to-earth techniques as
bribery and battery.

"You *will* stay and have something to eat?" asked Enright
abruptly, breaking off a list we were making of Members of Parliament whom he considered to be in his debt for past favors of
one kind or another.

"Would that really be all right?"

"Of course it would. I'll dig out my mother and introduce you.
Help yourself to some more whisky."

Whisky is not a favorite drink of mine, but I thought I had
better show willing.

In a moment, Enright came charging through the door.

"Curse it. I've got to go and vote. I didn't realize it was so late.
But I'll be back soon, and then we'll eat. Here's Mother." He
dashed away.

Mrs. Enright was a thin, gray lady: her hair, her eyes, her expression, her face, even the dressing gown she was wearing were gray.

"How do you do, Mr. Grover-Stacey," she said in a gray voice.
"Please forgive my dressing gown. I always spend the evening
lying down before preparing Walter's supper. He usually comes
in for it after the ten o'clock division, you know, and late hours
make me so tired."

"In that case, Mrs. Enright, I am sure I should go. I shall be
perfectly all right and I really must not trespass on your kindness.
My wife will run me up something."

"Not at all, Mr. Grover-Stacey. I am certain that Walter would
never forgive me. So few people come here nowadays, and then
only constituents. Such terrible creatures. You are more fortunate than Walter in having a wife. Do please sit down and tell me
about her."

"Really there's nothing much to tell."

I subsided reluctantly and swilled off the remains of the fourth whisky.

"My poor son's domestic life has brought him nothing but sadness. Such sadness." Her voice was shaking like pampas grass.

"I can't pretend I don't know something about it," I replied, "because your son has just been telling me."

"Everyone knows about it by now," said Mrs. Enright. "She was nothing but a common harlot."

It was obviously embarrassing, but it would have been inhuman not to be curious.

"From what your son was saying, it seems particularly terrible about the children."

"It is beyond even the forgiveness of God," said Mrs. Enright in her tired, gray voice.

"Surely these cases are not matters for forgiveness exactly?"

"I just said that forgiveness was impossible. Unthinkable."

Of course it was not what I meant. But there was one thing I particularly wanted to know.

"Tell me, if you think you should, where *are* the children? Where are they now?"

Mrs. Enright said nothing but merely jabbed sideways with her gray thumb toward the wall behind where I sat. It seemed an unusually large, bony thumb, but that was probably because the whole visit was beginning to get on my nerves.

"You mean they're in the next room?"

Mrs. Enright nodded with careful gravity. The way in which she did it slightly irritated me.

"I can't hear anything," I said.

"They have to be put to sleep for most of the time. My son couldn't possibly do his duty as a Member of Parliament if they weren't. Have you children of your own, Mr. Grover-Stacey?"

"Yes, I have. Twin girls."

"How old are they?"

"Seven last month."

"Don't you find them destructive, Mr. Grover-Stacey?"

"No more than other children."

"Very likely not. Most children are the same. It is often difficult to distinguish. But Walter's children are *really* different. When you go into the bathroom to wash your hands, you will see. And it's the same in many other places. It is going to be difficult if ever we have to leave the flat."

I think I can only have stared at her because she spoke again.

"Go and look for yourself."

The room we were in was entered by a door at the end of a longish passage, as often in flats of that period; the front door being opposite it at the passage's other end. Leading off one side of the passage were a number of other doors. Mrs. Enright got up and, opening the door of the sitting room, stood pointing to one of the green doors along the passage. I went to look.

It was too absurd, especially as the room really was the bathroom. I opened the door with considerable caution, expecting some frightful chaos, but really there was little unusual to be seen. At first, indeed, when I had switched on the light, I thought there was nothing, and the idea was passing through my mind that both Enright and his mother were a little queer, when I saw some odd marks round the window. It was a single square sheet of glass, hinged at the top, and opening onto a well. Round the edge were scratches in the paint work. As I have said, they were not very noticeable, but, when examined, they proved to be surprisingly deep. They crisscrossed one another irregularly, as if made with perhaps a sharply pointed file. They were possibly a quarter of an inch wide, and the most remarkable thing, it suddenly struck me, was that they went all round the window. It was as if some small, flying, clawed thing had been scratching to get out. I am sure that many other explanations were possible, but that one was so real to me that I could almost hear the thing buzzing as it came and went, battering and scraping. Or even, possibly, things.

"Now you believe it."

Mrs. Enright stood in the doorway behind me. I realized that the window was quite high in the wall, and that I had been standing on the edge of the bath in order to examine it closely enough. I descended without dignity.

"It hardly amounts to wrecking the flat," I said soberly.

"They did that in under a minute. Under two minutes, anyway."

We seemed to be returning to the untidy sitting room.

"How did it happen?"

"She let them out in order to upset my son. We had to use all kinds of things to get them back in again: the bag in which my son's special post arrives, old army blankets, worn-out mackintoshes, things like that. We had the most frightful time, and she just stood there screaming with laughter and scarcely half-dressed."

At this point I should perhaps mention that I wrote down the main heads of this conversation that same evening. I happen always to keep a fairly careful diary. In fact, that night, I wrote it up not very long after the time I have now reached.

I was then deciding that I could not stand the Enright flat much longer.

"Tell me, Mrs. Enright," I said, "why are you saying all these things to me?"

We were standing opposite one another, somehow unable to resume our seats. She looked away.

"I am not sure that I know, Mr. Grover-Stacey. Please forgive me if I am embarrassing you."

"If I can't help in any way, I'm sure I had better go. Your son may be a long time coming back."

"He seems to have to stay later and later. All night quite often."

"Yes, I read about it in the papers, and sometimes hear about it too, from other Members of Parliament"

"Then you know some *other* Members of Parliament?"

"Lots of them."

"I believe they used to come here often, many of them, when *she* was here. I fear it seems not to have been my son they came to see, because none of them come now. Though, of course, a Member of Parliament who is the subject of a scandal, as my son is, however undeserved, becomes a leper, an untouchable."

We were still on our feet, but I found it difficult quite to conclude the conversation.

"Oh, surely not as bad as that. Indeed, your son was telling me that he had thought of resigning but had actually been stopped by his friends."

Mrs. Enright smiled; a gray smile, needless to say.

"They think it better to keep their claws in him than let him get away scot-free."

Circumstances made her metaphor peculiarly unpleasant.

"I am going," I said with conviction. "I suppose it would only be ironical to say that I hope things turn out better than you and your son may think. I am so sorry."

"Of course," said Mrs. Enright, delaying me, "of course she *was* beautiful."

"I imagine she must have been."

"One of the papers said she was the most beautiful of all the Members of Parliament's wives."

I in my turn smiled. Not that there are not one or two M.P.s who have beautiful wives.

"It became quite the accepted idea."

"Forgive me. I haven't even told them at home that I should be so late back."

"Look." Mrs. Enright went over to the mantel above the electric heater and began to fish about behind the invitation cards to embassies, business promotions, and voluntary societies that descend continuously upon all Members of Parliament. "Just look."

In her hands was a thick tress of very fair hair. She held it, short of the two ends, between the thumb and first finger of her hands; then moved the hands outwards, until the tress was fully extended. It was about two feet long but seemed as fat as the cable of a liner.

"People said they were like two angels when they were married. Owing to them both having such fair hair and blue eyes. They were married in the Crypt, of course. You can see the sheen now."

As a matter of fact, I thought I could, even in the artificial light. It was as if the all but silver hair were phosphorescent. It gleamed like a nimbus.

"Hold it in your hands."

It surely was fascinating. I took the hair and held it as Mrs. Enright had held it. I then looked at the two ends, just for something to do with it, while Mrs. Enright watched me. At one end of the tress, the separate hairs passed away into infinity, as hairs do. At the other end, I could not but notice some very unpleasant brown marks. It would be a great exaggeration to speak of matting with blood, but blood I was sure it was and quite a bit of it.

I laid down the tress on the huge gray sofa. The hair was so heavy that even now it seemed to cling or stick together just as it had been last cut and, I think the word is, set.

I said a firm and final farewell to Mrs. Enright and fled.

I must admit that when I got home, Virginia did not believe a word of all this. I do not mean that she was vulgarly suspicious of where I had been. She knew quite well that I was incapable of deceiving her in that sort of way. I mean that she accepted my sincerity but was sceptical herself.

"Do I gather," she asked, plunging a tablespoon into the remaining sector of sponge, "that the young woman is now to be regarded as alive or dead?" Virginia picked up that way of speech at a university, where she did much better than I could ever have done.

"Alive, surely," I replied, dissociating a sultana from the general alluvium. "Enright said that the separation was only temporary. He could hardly have been more emphatic in the way he spoke. I can well believe that it's not true, but it does seem to mean that she's still alive." But the brown sultana spot in the yellow trifle made one wonder all the same.

"It would be interesting to hear her side of the story," said Virginia, kissing the lobe of my left ear.

A few minutes later, she went off to bed with a thick paperback, and I wrote it all down in my diary, as I have described.

Enright did telephone me the next morning in order to apologize for depriving me of my supper, as he put it ("You should have insisted," he said), but the next weeks of my association with him were entirely parliamentary. Biggles was, none too constitutionally, propelled out of the committee chairmanship, and Enright installed. Most of the other committee members, as usually happens, had just faded away without specifically withdrawing. Enright found replacements, who seemed much keener, brisker, and neater than their predecessors—at least for the first month or two. He also found a new committee secretary: a young furniture dealer from the suburbs, whose first Parliament this was. His name was Barker. He was incredibly clean-limbed at all hours, and he had learned to stumble and stutter fashionably as he spoke. His gusto for local electricity seemed to be almost unsurpassable. Bessemer, however, did not take to him. I think he found him too optimistic.

At the peak of our effort (in this phase), we got down four Questions in the Commons and six in the Lords. My diary contains the pasted-in Hansard records of all of them and of what happened to them. I was so keen at this time that I bought Hansard for myself on the days in question to supplement the copy supplied on annual subscription to the general office, and there put to store in the dark basement, by arrangement with the anti-wrestling group which leased the ground floor.

At the very climax, Enright got us an adjournment debate, which I attended. It came on at just after 1 a.m., which was considered quite early for such nongovernment business, and it continued for more than forty minutes. There were eleven people in the public gallery besides myself, more or less equally divided between representatives of interests liable to be damaged by local electricity and the usual pathetic figures with nowhere else to go. On the floor of the House, there were as many as nine M.P.s who were not actually compelled to be there. To the infrequent attender at Westminster, this may seem a small number, but it is above average for such an occasion and proved that Enright had done quite well for us. Enright spoke first and was truly eloquent, describing in broad terms what local electricity could do for England's future and not omitting reference to his own constituency. Barker followed him but was compelled by the conventions of the rules (I forget which) to speak for so short a time that he could not be expected to contribute anything very definite. Most of the debate was occupied, as often, by the parliamentary secretary, who applied much of his speech to reading extracts from the previous official utterance on our subject, made before the war, and expanding widely on the theme of how times had changed so much since then that comparisons were difficult and almost certainly dangerous. The debate was concluded unexpectedly (and yet not, when one has gathered experience of these occasions) by an interloper: a radiantly bald honorable and gallant who informed the house in some detail of the experiments in the generation of electricity which he and his friends, all, alas, killed in one or other of the wars, had started in the early 1900s. The experiments had never been brought to a conclusion. Might not this be the moment? Rather, of course, than a lot of airy-fairy stuff (though the honorable and gallant did not wish to be offensive) about streams and ditches. They had used streams and ditches for something else when he was a boy. Laughter—though one rather wondered at what.

We all know how it goes when one really cares about anything, and I must agree that neither the outburst of parliamentary questions nor the adjournment debate suggest anything in Enright that was exceptional. At this point, however, he began to change. I noticed it first in the central lobby.

The central lobby, as it is called, of the Houses of Parliament is about the last place in London really to recall Hogarth. Sights of such astonishment are to be seen, and so many of them, that one might almost be said to learn more by just sitting there solitary, looking and listening, than from supposedly more intimate converse with the residential owls and badgers. In my time, there was still that peeress, since consumed by fire in a foreign casino, who was taken to be in quest of justice but who was really in quest of girls, simply girls; and that all but daily, in and around the central lobby. There was Old R. (everyone called him Old) who came in ever-new disguises to hand out pamphlets demanding the impeachment of the income tax and who had been thrown out by the police more often than anyone else, and always by a whole posse, as he knew how to thrash about. There were the vendors of parfaits and macaroons—almost all war veterans, limping, torn, half-mad. There were the bishops in the white lawn of God, bowed down by six-pound crucifixes. There was the daily Speaker's procession with chaplain and headsman, for which bells toll, and all, upon police order, fall motionless and silent. There were the call girls, often working in the typing pool or the snack bar. There were the fashionables in hats, angling for tea on the terrace, for that at least, and often displaying their charms, as it is called, more abundantly than in any other place I for one have ever got to. Traditionally, they have causes to advance, though I found it hard to believe that they or anyone else made much progress with anything serious. No matter: they are the flowers of Parliament, and the compost makes them bloom more red.

And, of course, there are the divine victims themselves. When I was there, Attlee still stole around, distinguishable from Lenin only by the lesser efflorescence of whisker; you could see Cripps, rigidified into near-sainthood by psychosomatic illness; Shawcross, handsome as the morning. There were the philanderers on the right, the homosexuals on the left (Parliamentary privilege came in here, to judge by the things one saw), and the alcoholics everywhere (and no wonder). There were also the incorruptibles, bearing each his or her thumbscrew and rack; and the nobles, electorally free men, turning to the south from the central lobby, where the conscripts turn to the north.

On that particular afternoon, I had not seen Enright for a week or so. That is a quite long gap when a private parliamentary campaign is at its height. Moreover, he turned up twenty or thirty minutes late. That is customary: one reason why the even comparatively regular visitor to Parliament sees so much of the central lobby, and one reason why those he sees there are there so much, is that the life of a Member of Parliament makes private punctuality totally impossible. On that afternoon then, I sat thinking with some despair about local electricity and half-watching an organized party of middle-aged ladies from East Grinstead curtsy every time a Conservative privy councillor crossed the arena.

Suddenly Enright materialized. He clutched my arm without greeting and said: "I'm not satisfied about this thing, I'm not satisfied at all."

"You mean the minister's answer?"

"I do. Blast the little runt is what I say. I've been thinking, Grover-Stacey, and I've made up my mind. I'm really going into it. Up to the neck." For some reason, we had never become Walter and Jocelyn to one another, as nowadays happens so quickly at Westminster because the Members fear, above all, to be accused of snobbery. I daresay it is one more proof that a friendship between us there really was.

"Come with me," continued Enright. "I want to have a word with you by ourselves."

He led me out of the mêlée, up stairs, down long passages, and up more stairs. In the end, he pushed open a door marked "Pipe Office." A uniformed man inside touched his cap and vanished. Clearly there had been prearrangement, but it was of a kind to which I had become accustomed.

"Sit down," said Enright. "Now I want to say right away that if you reveal a word of all this, you'll be skinned. I don't mean by me, of course, but skinned you'll be."

"I quite understand," I replied.

So, obviously, I cannot impart exactly what he did say. The critical point, and this I feel I can disclose, was that he felt we had been so slighted that he was resolved to embark upon special methods. They included putting in jeopardy his receipt of the party whip, which for a modern M.P. is not only professional suicide but social ruin also; and they included certain other proposals which would never have so much as entered the minds of any other Member of Parliament I have met. Not that there was anything wild or revolutionary about these proposals. What they called for in the main was simply a degree of refusal to compromise, a willingness to risk a certain unpopularity . . .

"It's perfectly splendid of you," I said, "and all of us should be eternally grateful. But there is one thing."

"What's that?" Enright's left foot, tightly shod, was on one of the Gothic chairs. His forearm, supporting his sharp, woodcut head, rested on his angular knee.

"Speaking entirely for myself, I think I ought to say that I am not sure whether local electricity, important though it is, justifies these risks. I am not sure that it is big enough." The shaggy baggy shape of Bessemer was in my mind's eye.

Enright concentrated his gaze upon me even more intently.

"Maybe it isn't. Indeed, it certainly isn't. But I've got to start somewhere." He removed his foot from the chair and stood erect. His cast of face and his pale gray suit against the colored glass in the cusped window, through which a little sunlight straggled, made him look like an Arthurian knight in armor. "You don't know what it means to be a Member of Parliament and still have feelings, thoughts of your own, even ideals, conceivably even something really creative in you."

"I can imagine," I said.

"I have an idea that *you* perhaps can—up to a point. But you I regard as a friend—pretty well my only one just now. Do you mind my saying that?"

"Of course not. It's very nice of you."

"Not all that nice. I'm a ruined man and dangerous to be associated with. That's why I'm going to have a real go at things. Because not even you can have any idea of the utter futility and frustration. No, those are weak words. It is something worse than either of those things. Something that most people have ceased even to feel. Ever. You have to be *me* and you have to be *here*— here always, I mean, tied here—to know. Still, thank you, my dear chap, it's extremely good of you to bother."

I wasn't altogether sure what he was thanking me for, but I replied by saying how sure I was now that local electricity would really go places.

It was on the very next day, as so often happens in life, that the renewed faith which Enright had given me was specifically diminished.

Among all the Members of Parliament who had at one time or another offered their support, even though in most cases only on condition that we compromised almost totally, a single one had actually paid a subscription and joined us: an M.P. named Chalkman. It would be absurd to complain that the number was not larger: Members of Parliament cannot sensibly be expected to subscribe financially to every cause they take up, and it would often not be in the best interest of the cause itself for them to do so. This general philosophy, moreover, received strong support from the actual case of Chalkman. Having paid up, he did nothing more for us and rather ostentatiously left the merely parliamentary battle to others. What Chalkman did was to visit our general office at unproclaimed though frequent intervals and to stay a long time. This he happened to do on the day after Enright's rededication.

Chalkman, a fat, wheezing, formless figure in very old clothes that smelled faintly and never varied, used to potter round lifting everything up and looking underneath it, and reading all the carbon copies and memoranda and letters from other Members that he could put his hands on.

"Take no notice of me," he would say. "Don't let me stop you working."

Needless to say, he never showed the slightest grasp either of what the Society was really aiming at or the current condition of the campaign in Parliament or elsewhere. Every time he asked for both things to be explained to him. The explanation, and answering his questions, always took at least an hour. At the end of it, Chalkman regularly summed up: "I have said it before and I shall always say it. The thing to do is to trust the people." He then shambled out—well, ten or fifteen minutes later—none the wiser and with no excessive expression of gratitude or even courtesy.

Hardly a man to be swayed by, you would think, and yet one felt that where Chalkman trusted the people, they probably trusted him, so that he was likely to be a man of the kind with whom ultimate power lay. For richer for poorer, in sickness and in health. Even for the future of local electricity.

"Who looks after you now down at the gasworks?" Chalkman asked on this occasion.

"Mr. Enright, mainly," I replied. "You may remember that he followed Mr. Biggles as chairman of the Local Electricity Committee. The new secretary is Mr. Barker."

"Barker is fairly sound," said Chalkman, "but however did you get hold of Enright?"

The two things that Chalkman knew about Parliament were the rules of procedure and the daily standing of every individual Member, whom to latch on to, whom to shun.

"Mr. Enright has been helping us for some time now."

"Yes, but who found him? Where did you meet him?"

"As a matter of fact, I met him myself at a party given by our member, Mrs. Havengore, of Leicestershire. He was a friend of hers."

"I have said it before and I shall say it again. Never accept offers from Members of Parliament met only socially."

Chalkman was always right about things like that, and I began at once to feel disproportionately depressed.

"Some people say the exact opposite," I replied ineffectively.

"No doubt they do. It takes a long time to learn about Parliament even when you're a Member of it. If you're not, it's impossible to learn. I've been a Member for thirty-four years and five months, and I'm still learning every day. Well, you'll do no good with Enright."

My heart sank a little lower.

"He seems to me to have already done more for us than any other M.P. has ever done."

"No doubt he has."

"What's the objection to him?"

"He's out of the running for office and therefore he carries no weight. He thinks he can override or get round the customs and traditions of Parliament, which is the greatest mistake an M.P. can possibly make. He tries to rely on what he considers to be personality, whereas in Parliament soundness is the only thing that counts in the long run. And with the electorate too, I may add."

Chalkman then put his large handkerchief to his nose and tumultuously expelled what must have been several ounces of mucus, whooping it up again and again.

I was still further lowered. It was quite obvious that what Chalkman had said was true, and he had not even mentioned Enright's private affairs. I found it impossible to go through the motions of argument.

"I advise you to make a change," said Chalkman, gasping for air.

"You don't mean that Mr. Enright is likely to lose his seat?"

"No, I don't mean that. He's not popular with the voters, as I've said, but we shall see that he doesn't go because we don't want him turned loose on the world."

"Why not?" I asked as naïvely as I could. It was a thing I had never understood.

Chalkman smiled like the wise old man he was.

"You know the saying that if you can't beat them, you join them?" I nodded. "In the same way, if you distrust them, you hold on to them. That's Parliament."

"I see."

"Now," said Chalkman, his eyes glazing, "tell me. I'm not sure that I've ever completely understood. Tell me what this Society of yours is really up to."

You know how it is: doubts lead, even unconsciously, to one's avoiding the person doubted. Also the whole tone of Enright's discourse to me in the Pipe Room seemed to leave the next step to him. It appeared hardly in key for me to ring him up and read him a communication I had just received from the town clerk of Romsey, as I otherwise should have done. Finally, it seemed possible that Enright was wishful at the moment, and having explained himself to me, to go it strictly alone.

Anyway, the next time I found myself in the central lobby it was to see a different M.P. His name was Jupon. If this had been today, so to speak, you would have heard of him; but nowadays Members of Parliament, other than Members like Chalkman, come and go and are fundamentally anonymous, so that Jupon had been forgotten. At that time he was ascending and was gen-erally regarded as an opportunist, especially as he was the king-pin of a small trade union that clamorously excluded itself from the TUC. Indeed, I was doubtful, after Chalkman's monitions, whether he was the right kind of M.P. for me to see at all. But he had written to me very politely, saying that the ideal of local elec-tricity had appealed to him since his primary school days, that he thought offbeat causes of any kind had a value of their own, and that he would like to talk to me if I could spare the time. And here I was.

Jupon was not merely late, but very late. I was seriously think-ing of departing and writing to him saying, with dignified regret, how busy I was, when I noticed a woman in a black dress on a bench opposite me. She was beautiful enough to make me think again, for the moment, about going.

I began, as one does, to stare furtively at her. She was a very pale blonde, and her face was almost as white as her dress was black. She sat very tensely, as if waiting for news of life or death. Of course that is a common sight in the central lobby.

I suppose that another ten minutes passed before Jupon at last appeared. I had not spoken to him until then. He went into full detail of why he was late, taking perhaps a further ten minutes. I realized throughout that first encounter with me that words never failed him, and as I think back about him, words are almost all I can recall, wave upon wave of self-sufficient, overwhelming words. One struggled at least to remain within one's depth, but the waves rose higher and higher, denser and denser, greener and darker, so that in the end one could escape only by waking up. Anyway, even Jupon's first apology for being late so enveloped me that I failed to notice the departure of the woman in the black dress. As we trailed off to the snackbar (the young Harold Wilson was there, carting his famous fish and chips round on a little tray), I simply observed that she was gone and noticed also that the entire green bench on which she had sat was empty, although all the other green benches were packed tight.

I don't know when exactly it first occurred to me that this woman in the black dress might be Enright's wife. Really the only evidence was the locale and the hair; but the former clue came to appear more weighty as I began to see the woman again and again. I saw her more than once in the Distinguished Strangers Gallery, which suggested that she must have influence, and listening to the dullest of debates, insofar as comparisons in that respect are meaningful. Perhaps she wasn't exactly listening. I saw her several times more in the central lobby, always seated on a bench alone, though never once did I chance to notice her either come or go. I saw her occasionally in the passages, but always when there was a crowd, and always the back of her only. But, now I come to remember, there was a third clue, and the biggest: the woman always wore the same black dress. This it was which more than anything convinced me that there was something rum about her. There was also the fact that whenever I saw her, she was by herself. Her general appearance made this unlikely, though it is true that she continued to look stricken.

These varied glimpses of the woman were spread over three or four weeks, during which I was visiting Parliament constantly. I look back upon it otherwise as the period of my Jupon servitude. I think that Jupon, rising man though he was, found it difficult to keep himself in listeners; who had to be unflagging, not hopelessly unintelligent, and reasonably in his power, certainly not rivals or competitors of any kind. I am sure that at monthly or six-weekly intervals he had to endure the loss of even those who, like me, had passed the original test. Some of the others may well have had to take a costly cure at this point, but I had been spared from having to attend to Jupon's actual words by my increasingly acute preoccupation with the appearing and disappearing woman. I had found a quite new interest in Parliament, it struck me one morning.

Jupon, as may be gathered, belonged to the opposite side of the House from Enright's side, but Enright continued silent and invisible, while Jupon, during one's weeks with him, consumed all the time and energy which a single person could be expected to allot to Parliament, and much more. I did, however, one morning receive a letter from Enright: "Dear Grover-Stacey, Don't think I'm falling down on the job. I'm trying something new which I can't tell even you about. When I surface again, we must meet. Keep your pecker up, we'll knock them yet. Always yours, W.E. PS. Remember me to your wife." Enright had never met Virginia, but he often spoke of her warmly.

Immediately I had opened my post, I had to dash off to meet Jupon. It was the hour for the committees which consider the different bills, taking evidence upstairs for days at a time in a slow mumble. Parliament was almost cloistral. It is extraordinary, as all agree, how beautiful the Palace of Westminster can be at such times, when one can hear one's steps echo in Speaker's Court, when William Rufus's great hall is for treason and tragedy, not trippers, when the sirens of the river tugs boom and shriek through the empty corridors and spinning traceries, making the whole vast fabric seem translucent and insubstantial. To the contemplative visitor, the Palace at such times seems to be made of crumbling crystal or of falling water. The charivari of the central lobby has become a saraband.

I sat there that morning watching the host of cleaners stacking up the garbage and heaving it into rubber-tired handcarts with large crowns painted on the sides. It appeared that Jupon was late. I sat thinking, as always, of local electricity, but also, more dreamily, of Parliament, the great Mother of us all, so ancient, so moving when one is not doing actual business with her, even so beautiful with, around me, those towering symbolizations of the four constituent kingdoms in statuary and colored glass. Apart from the cleaners, who at Westminster are but as the technically invisible stagehands in an Eastern play, I was alone. It was the first time I had ever been alone in the central lobby. When the great clock struck, the whole building shook, and all the cleaners looked at their watches. Outside it was pelting. The rain smashed against the ornate windows high above me, far, far up.

It seemed as if a bird had got in. I was sure that something was flying round under the vaulting of the distant stone ceiling. I could not see the bird because until the ornate brass lights are turned on, the central lobby is dark at the best of times and that day was heavily overcast. Still I could hear the thing quite clearly. It flew with a dry, rustling, even rattling sound, making a very quick stroke with its wings: it occurred to me that it ought logically to be a rather heavy bird with slightly insufficient flying capacity. One sometimes thinks the same of a fat old bluebottle. I then began to think, with the same logic, that it might suddenly fall on me, and that is a thought which no one likes. I could hear the sound of flight first in one place, quite distinctly, then, with equal distinctness, in another. The flying object, though still invisible to me, seemed to make a remarkably local disturbance of the upper air.

I considered the cleaners. They gave no sign of noticing anything, not even me. Doubtless they were not paid to extrude strange flying things. They were, however, almost finished and about to trundle away the trucks packed high and hard with yesterday's rubbish. The cleaners seemed committed without reservation to this task. The Palace has methods for securing to itself only the best of everything such as cleaners.

As they were rumbling slowly off (the loaded carts seemed to be really heavy), I looked upwards again. I could now have sworn that there were two birds. The central lobby is big, and there were quite clearly two separate areas of disturbance and twice the noise. At the best, there is always something upsetting about a flying creature which is trying to get out. It is a phenomenon at once frightening and humiliating. I have to admit that all I did was to sit there paralyzed, and that the paralysis simply grew more leaden. I felt disgust and fear creep out from my stomach and spine and soak through my body. I can remember feeling the same in infancy and in war. The things above me were becoming more and more noisy. The dry, clacking sound was growing sharper. Unable to escape through the painted, devotional glass of the windows, they were descending, nearing the floor, whirling round me, cutting me off.

It was darker still as the storm cloud rolled on down the river on the southwesterly gale, but I then saw the figure of the woman in the black dress. She was dimly standing beneath the center of the tall Gothic arch opposite the St. Stephen's Hall arch which leads to the public exit and entrance. In the thin light, she looked paler and more ravaged than ever. Beyond doubt, she was aware of me, even looking at me, but certainly not smiling. Smiles are for daylight and the common earth, for girls, for provincial marriages, for the Royal Assent to legislation; not for a rendezvous of this kind. Because a rendezvous it seemed to be. In the dim light, the woman moved her head, as who should say Follow; and I followed.

I followed her out of the central lobby; past the rectangular stonework of the Civil Service Monument, grim and hideous, with the inscription by Sir Henry Taylor; and up more and more stairs. As I stumbled through the murk, I heard behind me the rustle and clatter of the birds, keeping their distance, but plainly following. We traversed long passages, passing committee rooms with light shining out beneath the doors, the only sound a low unbroken moan. We brushed against relegated statues of greater men than the relegators. We climbed still further stairs. It seemed incredible that even our legislators, those who struggle, fight, defame, blarney, manipulate, bribe, and conspire to get power over us and to keep it when got, should demand a still huger building, as demand they constantly do. Soon, surely, we should have reached the eaves.

But then the woman stopped. She was several paces ahead of me and was standing at a door in one of the endless corridors of proof and of power. It was unexpected, and I stopped also. A second time the woman seemed to incline her head and seemed then to pass through the door to the room within. I came on after her, but not before I had noticed that there was now no sound of the birds, or of anything else but the driving rain against the Gothic windows. In the Palace of Westminster I had come upon a patch of silence.

Believe it or not, the door was not only shut but locked. I joggled on the medieval handle but could hardly move it at all. There are rooms in the Palace of Westminster which have not been entered during the last fifty years, a number of them, and some said to be quite large; and that whatever may be asserted by the M.P.s who complain of cramp. Even in the bad light, I could see the rust and grime on my hands; but the real question, of course, was what had become of the pale-haired, pale-faced woman in black.

It was still silent in the corridor. Not only was no one about, but it was hard to believe that any man or woman currently passed that way often. Disregarding the filth, I tried the door handle again, with vigor, perhaps violence. Suddenly something frightening happened. I became aware that another hand was on the other end of the handle, and a strong one. The door burst open, screaming along the stone floor, and standing inside was the individual who had opened it. It was Walter Enright.

The light was so bad that it was difficult to be sure of details, but he seemed to be wearing very old clothes and to be covered in sweat. Nonetheless, his jacket was buttoned up in nineteenth-century style, so that no shirt could be seen, and his trousers were tucked into huge, old-fashioned boots. About one thing there could be no mistake: in his left hand was a small saw—a child's toy saw, I should imagine.

We stared at one another, perhaps each the more astonished. Then Enright made an effort and deposited the saw on a huge dirty table, of which I could see only a corner.

"Grover-Stacey," he said, gulping, "my dear old chap. Don't say I've forgotten an appointment?"

"No," I replied, managing somehow to find the same key. "But possibly it's time there was one."

"I'm damned well sure it is." He was dabbing at his brow, while trying not to draw attention to the fact. "The thing is that we M.P.s have so many different jobs on our hands." And Enright actually looked at his hands, though only for a second.

"Perhaps you would be able to give me a ring so that I could pass on the latest news?"

A remarkable expression of gratitude lit up Enright's carved-wooden features. It was as if thankfulness had overpowered him, do what he could to suppress it.

"I'll do just that," he said. "Thank you, Grover-Stacey, for reminding me. I've been working," he added lamely.

He felt for his cigarettes and produced the unfashionably elaborate gold case from the side pocket of his pea jacket. Though his hand was shaking, he began to extend the open case to me. "No, of course not." As he remembered, he seemed to fall into a trance. He just stood there, silent and rigid with the unlighted cigarette in his hands. Then he uttered a sort of groan, dropped the cigarette, and pressed both his hands against his face. Down the passage came the whistle and the clatter of dry wings.

"Get out, Grover-Stacey," cried Enright, with a degree of urgency that I should never have thought possible and that I shall never forget. "For God's sake go away!"

He fell to his knees and seemed to be trying to make himself as small as possible against the stone floor. It was obvious that he was under attack, but I could see nothing but his own crouching, cringing contracting mass.

"Go," he cried in a high voice. "That's all I ask. Go. Go."

There were curious new sounds—tapping, shuffling, scraping, might be words for them—but it was difficult to see that Enright was taking any harm, except, so to speak, emotionally. I could see nothing but his grotesque figure, shrinking and shrinking.

I admit that I just stood there, staring no doubt, and listening, but basically just stupefied. I could not even surmise how I or anyone could help.

In the end, quite soon no doubt in reality, I became aware that the odd sounds had stopped. Once more there was nothing to be heard but the rain beating on the tiny medieval panes.

The figure on the stone floor began to swell again toward its normal bulk, and in a moment Enright was on his feet. His face was very white, and his narrow blue eyes were bitterly hostile.

"Next time you might do what I ask," he said, and without saying more, re-entered the room behind him and shut the door. I felt as if I had stared inexcusably while a friend endured a fit or a convulsion. At least that was *among* the things I felt.

I wove my way down by way of the endless passages and staircases, but it was now the busy coffee period, and I doubt whether anyone paid me particular attention. This may have been just as well because I probably looked very queer. I slipped out through the central lobby and St. Stephen's Hall without a single interrogation, even though I suspect that in the end I was almost running.

I simply could not go back to the office, though there were many things to be done, and I knew that if I went home, Virginia would be out at work and unable to telephone the girl to explain my absence. I dealt with this situation by just doing nothing. That is to say, I did go home but simply lay down on the daybed.

I dealt with various other elements of the case in much the same way. In particular, I told no one what had happened, or any part of it, not even Virginia.

When Virginia returned, I explained that a horror of Parliament had been steadily rising in me, over the past few months at least. She knew this already and was completely understanding (as she always was until the day she left me—and, as a matter of fact, after that as well). I told her that, quite suddenly, I could stand no more of it and should have to change my job once again. At the time, she seemed nothing but sympathetic.

I don't know at what hour Jupon ultimately rolled up, only to miss me in turn of course.

I give the impression of having kept my head, of having behaved sensibly, in the degree that is incredible. It would indeed have been incredible. I have set forth the surface of events but must now say a few words, very few, about what was really happening.

It could hardly have been more obvious that sooner or later, even in an obscure attic of the mastodon Palace of Westminster, evidence might be found. The long fear set in, which did not diminish as time passed but grew. Fear, left to itself, feeds on itself. I could not even decide what was likely to happen to me; the possibilities seemed to range from a serious misunderstanding with Virginia, coupled probably with general social ostracism, to an actual charge of complicity together with who knew what of posthumous retribution. I dreaded, and my spirit shrank and shrank, all without a word to anyone, for at least two years. Believe me, it was incomparably the worst part of the whole experience.

After about two years, I became more or less inured. Samuel Butler suggests that one of the defects in the theory of hell is that, if left there for eternity, the damned would get used to the torments. I must not, however, set my own poor case quite on that level. I admit that in the end I began to wonder whether at least some parts of my experience (which surely had been a terrible one?) might not have been, I will not say a dream, but an hallucination, perhaps originating in too much contact with Parliament by someone unsuited to it temperamentally.

To set against that comparatively comforting notion, I have to consider what happened to my poor friend Enright. Many will, indeed, remember what happened to him, or more or less. I myself never saw or heard from him again after that fantastic morning. Enright was taken ill, as the saying goes, while walking home across Smith Square, only eight or nine days later. It was raining heavily at the time, but three different people who had been crossing the square said at the inquest that Enright, though all of them saw this at some distance, was waving his arms above his head, seeming to beat something off. One of them, an elderly woman, went to help him but found him already dead. The medical evidence was to the effect that his face, and the whole upper part of his body, had been almost torn to shreds, but the coroner thought, as coroners will, that Enright might somehow have done this himself. Coroners are often whimsical in their insights.

Dreadful in itself, Enright's end was also personally disappointing because it had early occurred to me that I might that morning have done something to save Enright, though possibly at no small cost to myself. That would have been something to show for it all. Now I fear for what may happen to me too in the end for having become involved in these events (even though I no longer worry much about an official hue and cry), and I lack even the satisfaction of having helped my friend. The inevitable depression resulting from these thoughts may have played its part in losing me Virginia. My only hope is that somehow I may have handled in the right way at least the original situation with the woman in the black dress. Time alone can show; but I remain extremely anxious.

I have heard nothing of anyone entering that upstairs room since Enright himself last went there, but of course it is not the sort of thing the authorities would put in the paper, especially now that the authority concerned with the conduct of the palace is the parliamentary membership itself and no longer a court official responsible to a higher quarter.

I myself have never set foot in the place again; but, in fairness, I suppose I should quote an observation I have lately come upon as attributed to Winston Churchill: "Democracy seems impossible, until you examine the other system." Maybe it really is just part of the fall of man and irredeemable without special grace.

THE VISITING STAR

The first time that Colvin, who had never been a frequent theatre-goer, ever heard of the great actress Arabella Rokeby was when he was walking past the Hippodrome one night and Malnik, the Manager of the Tabard Players, invited him into his office.

Had Colvin not been awarded a grant, remarkably insufficient for present prices, upon which to compose, collate, and generally scratch together a book upon the once thriving British industries of lead and plumbago mining, he would probably never have set eyes upon this bleak town. Tea was over (today it had been pilchard salad and chips); and Colvin had set out from the Emancipation Hotel, where he boarded, upon his regular evening walk. In fifteen or twenty minutes he would be beyond the gas-lights, the granite setts, the nimbus of the pits. (Lead and plumbago mining had long been replaced by coal as the town's main industry.) There had been no one else for tea and Mrs. Royd had made it clear that the trouble he was causing had not passed unnoticed.

Outside it was blowing as well as raining, so that Palmerston Street was almost deserted. The Hippodrome (called, when built, the Grand Opera House) stood at the corner of Palmerston Street and Aberdeen Place. Vast, ornate, the product of an unfulfilled aspiration that the town would increase in size and devotion to the Muses, it had been for years unused and forgotten. About it like rags, when Colvin first beheld it, had hung scraps of posters: "Harem Nights. Gay! Bright!! Alluring!!!" But a few weeks ago the Hippodrome had reopened to admit the Tabard Players ("In Association with the Arts Council"); and, it was hoped, their audiences. The Tabard Players offered soberer joys: a new and respectable play each week, usually a light comedy or West End crook drama; but, on one occasion, *Everyman*. Malnik, their Manager, a youngish bald man, was an authority on the British Drama of the Nineteenth Century, upon which he had written an immense book, bursting with carefully verified detail. Colvin had met him one night in the Saloon Bar of the Emancipation Hotel; and, though neither knew anything of the other's subject, they had exchanged cultural life-belts in the ocean of apathy and incomprehensible interests which surrounded them. Malnik was lodging with the sad-faced Rector, who let rooms.

Tonight, having seen the curtain up on Act I, Malnik had come outside for a breath of the wind. There was something he wanted to impart; and, as he regarded the drizzling and indifferent town, Colvin obligingly came into sight. In a moment, he was inside Malnik's roomy but crumbling office.

"Look," said Malnik.

He shuffled a heap of papers on his desk and handed Colvin a photograph. It was yellow, and torn at the edges. The subject was a wild-eyed young man with much dark curly hair and a blobby face. He was wearing a high stiff collar, and a bow like Chopin's.

"John Nethers," said Malnik. Then, when no light of rapture flashed from Colvin's face, he said "Author of *Cornelia*."

"Sorry," said Colvin, shaking his head.

"John Nethers was the son of a chemist in this town. Some books say a miner, but that's wrong. A chemist. He killed himself at twenty-two. But before that I've traced that he'd written at least six plays. *Cornelia,* which is the best of them, is one of the great plays of the nineteenth century."

"Why did he kill himself?"

"It's in his eyes. You can see it. *Cornelia* was produced in London with Arabella Rokeby. But never here. Never in the author's own town. I've been into the whole thing closely. Now we're going to do *Cornelia* for Christmas."

"Won't you lose money?" asked Colvin.

"We're losing money all the time, old man. Of course we are. We may as well do something we shall be remembered by."

Colvin nodded. He was beginning to see that Malnik's life was a single-minded struggle for the British Drama of the Nineteenth Century and all that went with it.

"Besides I'm going to do *As You Like It* also. As a fill-up." Malnik stooped and spoke close to Colvin's ear as he sat in a bursting

leather armchair, the size of a Judge's seat. "You see, Arabella
Rokeby's *coming*."

"But how long is it since—"

"Better not be too specific about that. They say it doesn't
matter with Arabella Rokeby. She can get away with it. Probably
in fact she can't. Not altogether. But all the same, think of it. Arabella Rokeby in *Cornelia*. In *my* theatre."

Colvin thought of it.

"Have you ever seen her?"

"No, I haven't. Of course she doesn't play regularly nowadays.
Only special engagements. But in this business one has to take a
chance sometimes. And golly what a chance!"

"And she's willing to come? I mean at Christmas," Colvin
added, not wishing to seem rude.

Malnik did seem slightly unsure. "I have a contract," he said.
Then he added: "She'll love it when she gets here. After all: *Cornelia*! And she must know that the nineteenth-century theatre is
my subject." He had seemed to be reassuring himself, but now he
was glowing.

"But As *You Like It*?" said Colvin, who had played Touchstone
at his preparatory school. "Surely she can't manage Rosalind?"

"It was her great part. Happily you can play Rosalind at any
age. Wish I could get old Ludlow to play Jaques. But he won't."
Ludlow was the company's veteran.

"Why not?"

"He played with Rokeby in the old days. I believe he's afraid
she'll see he isn't the Grand Old Man he should be. He's a good
chap, but proud. Of course he may have other reasons. You never
know with Ludlow."

The curtain was down on Act I.

Colvin took his leave and resumed his walk.

Shortly thereafter Colvin read about the Nethers Gala in the
local evening paper ("this forgotten poet", as the writer helpfully
phrased it), and found confirmation that Miss Rokeby was indeed
to grace it ("the former London star"). In the same issue of the
paper appeared an editorial to the effect that wide-spread disap-
pointment would be caused by the news that the Hippodrome

would not be offering a pantomime at Christmas in accordance with the custom of the town and district.

"She can't 'ardly stop 'ere, Mr. Colvin," said Mrs. Royd, when Colvin, thinking to provide forewarning, showed her the news, as she lent a hand behind the saloon bar. "This isn't the Cumberland. She'd get across the staff."

"I believe she's quite elderly," said Colvin soothingly.

"If she's elderly, she'll want special attention, and that's often just as bad."

"After all, where she goes is mainly a problem for her, and perhaps Mr. Malnik."

"Well, there's nowhere else in town for her to stop, is there?" retorted Mrs. Royd with fire. "Not nowadays. She'll just 'ave to make do. We did for theatricals in the old days. Midgets once. Whole troupe of 'em."

"I'm sure you'll make her very comfortable."

"Can't see what she wants to come at all for, really. Not at Christmas."

"Miss Rokeby needs no *reason* for her actions. What she does is sufficient in itself. You'll understand that, dear lady, when you meet her." The speaker was a very small man, apparently of advanced years, white-haired, and with a brown sharp face, like a Levantine. The bar was full, and Colvin had not previously noticed him, although he was conspicuous enough, as he wore an overcoat with a fur collar and a scarf with a large black pin in the centre. "I wonder if *I* could beg a room for a few nights," he went on. "I assure you I'm no trouble at all."

"There's only Number Twelve A. It's not very comfortable," replied Mrs. Royd sharply.

"Of course you must leave room for Miss Rokeby."

"Nine's for her. Though I haven't had a word from her."

"I think she'll need two rooms. She has a companion."

"I can clear out Greta's old room upstairs. If she's a friend of yours, you might ask her to let me know when she's coming."

"Not a friend," said the old man, smiling. "But I follow her career."

Mrs. Royd brought a big red book from under the bar.

"What name, please?"

"Mr. Superbus," said the little old man. He had yellow, expressionless eyes.

"Will you register?"

Mr. Superbus produced a gold pen, long and fat. His writing was so curvilinear that it seemed purely decorative, like a design for ornamental ironwork. Colvin noticed that he paused slightly at the "Permanent Address" column, and then simply wrote (although it was difficult to be sure) what appeared to be "North Africa".

"Will you come this way?" said Mrs. Royd, staring suspiciously at the newcomer's scrollwork in the visitor's book. Then, even more suspiciously, she added: "What about luggage?"

Mr. Superbus nodded gravely. "I placed two bags outside."

"Let's hope they're still there. They're rough in this town, you know."

"I'm sure they're still there," said Mr. Superbus.

As he spoke the door opened suddenly and a customer almost fell into the bar. "Sorry, Mrs. Royd," he said with a mildness which in the circumstances belied Mrs. Royd's words. "There's something on the step."

"My fault, I'm afraid," said Mr. Superbus. "I wonder—have you a porter?"

"The porter works evenings at the Hippodrome nowadays. Scene-shifting and that."

"Perhaps I could help?" said Colvin.

On the step outside were what appeared to be two very large suitcases. When he tried to lift one of them, he understood what Mr. Superbus had meant. It was remarkably heavy. He held back the bar door, letting in a cloud of cold air. "Give me a hand, someone," he said.

The customer who had almost fallen volunteered, and a short procession, led by Mrs. Royd, set off along the little dark passage to Number Twelve A. Colvin was disconcerted when he realized that Twelve A was the room at the end of the passage, which had no number on its door and had never, he thought, been occupied since his arrival; the room, in fact, next to his.

"Better leave these on the floor," said Colvin, dismissing the rickety luggage-stand.

"Thank you," said Mr. Superbus, transferring a coin to the man who had almost fallen. He did it like a conjuror unpalming something.

"I'll send Greta to make up the bed," said Mrs. Royd. "Tea's at six."

"At six?" said Mr. Superbus, gently raising an eyebrow. "Tea?" Then, when Mrs. Royd and the man had gone, he clutched Colvin very hard on the upper part of his left arm. "Tell me," enquired Mr. Superbus, "are you in love with Miss Rokeby? I overheard you defending her against the impertinence of our hostess."

Colvin considered for a moment.

"Why not admit it?" said Mr. Superbus, gently raising the other eyebrow. He was still clutching Colvin's arm much too hard.

"I've never set eyes on Miss Rokeby."

Mr. Superbus let go. "Young people nowadays have no imagination," he said with a whinny, like a wild goat.

Colvin was not surprised when Mr. Superbus did not appear for tea (pressed beef and chips that evening).

After tea Colvin, instead of going for a walk, wrote to his mother. But there was little to tell her, so that at the end of the letter he mentioned the arrival of Mr. Superbus. "There's a sort of sweet blossomy smell about him like a meadow," he ended. "I think he must use scent."

When the letter was finished, Colvin started trying to construct tables of output from the lead and plumbago mines a century ago. The partitions between the bedrooms were thin, and he began to wonder about Mr. Superbus's nocturnal habits.

He wondered from time to time until the time came for sleep; and wondered a bit also as he dressed the next morning and went to the bathroom to shave. For during the whole of this time no sound whatever had been heard from Number Twelve A, despite the thinness of the plywood partition; a circumstance which Colvin already thought curious when, during breakfast, he overheard Greta talking to Mrs. Royd in the kitchen. "I'm ever so sorry, Mrs. Royd. I forgot about it with the crowd in the bar." To which Mrs. Royd simply replied: "I wonder what 'e done about it. 'E could 'ardly do without sheets or blankets, and this December.

Why didn't 'e *ask*?" And when Greta said, "I suppose nothing ain't happened to him?" Colvin put down his porridge spoon and unobtrusively joined the party which went out to find out.

Mrs. Royd knocked several times upon the door of Number Twelve A, but there was no answer. When they opened the door, the bed was bare as Colvin had seen it the evening before, and there was no sign at all of Mr. Superbus except that his two big cases lay on the floor, one beside the other.

"What's he want to leave the window open like that for?" enquired Mrs. Royd. She shut it with a crash. "Someone will fall over those cases in the middle of the floor."

Colvin bent down to slide the heavy cases under the bed. But the pair of them now moved at a touch.

Colvin picked one case up and shook it slightly. It emitted a muffled flapping sound, like a bat in a box. Colvin nearly spoke, but stopped himself, and stowed the cases, end on, under the unmade bed in silence.

"Make up the room, Greta," said Mrs. Royd. "It's no use just standing about." Colvin gathered that it was not altogether unknown for visitors to the Emancipation Hotel to be missing from their rooms all night.

But there was a further little mystery. Later that day in the bar, Colvin was accosted by the man who had helped to carry Mr. Superbus's luggage.

"Look at that." He displayed, rather furtively, something which lay in his hand.

It was a sovereign.

"He gave it me last night."

"Can I see it?" It had been struck in Queen Victoria's reign, but gleamed like new.

"What d'you make of that?" asked the man.

"Not much," replied Colvin, returning the pretty piece. "But now I come to think of it, *you* can make about forty-five shillings."

When this incident took place, Colvin was on his way to spend three or four nights in another town where lead and plumbago mining had formerly been carried on, and where he needed to consult an invaluable collection of old records which had been presented to the Public Library at the time the principal mining company went bankrupt.

On his return, he walked up the hill from the station through a thick mist, laden with coal dust and sticky smoke, and apparently in no way diminished by a bitter little wind, which chilled while hardly troubling to blow. There had been snow, and little archipelagos of slush remained on the pavements, through which the immense boots of the miners crashed noisily. The male population wore heavy mufflers and were unusually silent. Many of the women wore shawls over their heads in the manner of their grandmothers.

Mrs. Royd was not in the bar, and Colvin hurried through it to his old room, where he put on a thick sweater before descending to tea. The only company consisted in two commercial travellers, sitting at the same table and eating through a heap of bread and margarine but saying nothing. Colvin wondered what had happened to Mr. Superbus.

Greta entered as usual with a pot of strong tea and a plate of bread and margarine.

"Good evening, Mr. Colvin. Enjoy your trip?"

"Yes, thank you, Greta. What's for tea?"

"Haddock and chips." She drew a deep breath. "Miss Rokeby's come ... I don't think she'll care for haddock and chips do you, Mr. Colvin?" Colvin looked up in surprise. He saw that Greta was trembling. Then he noticed that she was wearing a thin black dress, instead of her customary casual attire.

Colvin smiled up at her. "I think you'd better put on something warm. It's getting colder every minute."

But at that moment the door opened and Miss Rokeby entered.

Greta stood quite still, shivering all over, and simply staring at her. Everything about Greta made it clear that this was Miss Rokeby. Otherwise the situation was of a kind which brought to Colvin's mind the cliché about there being some mistake.

The woman who had come in was very small and slight. She had a triangular gazelle-like face, with very large dark eyes, and a mouth which went right across the lower tip of the triangle, making of her chin another, smaller triangle. She was dressed entirely in black, with a high-necked black silk sweater, and wore long black earrings. Her short dark hair was dressed like that of a faun; and her thin white hands hung straight by her side in a posture resembling some Indian statuettes which Colvin recalled but could not place.

Greta walked towards her, and drew back a chair. She placed Miss Rokeby with her back to Colvin.

"Thank you. What can I eat?" Colvin was undecided whether Miss Rokeby's voice was high or low: it was like a bell beneath the ocean.

Greta was blushing. She stood, not looking at Miss Rokeby, but at the other side of the room, shivering and reddening. Then tears began to pour down her cheeks in a cataract. She dragged at a chair, made an unintelligible sound, and ran into the kitchen.

Miss Rokeby half turned in her seat, and stared after Greta. Colvin thought she looked quite as upset as Greta. Certainly she was very white. She might almost have been eighteen . . .

"Please don't mind. It's nerves, I think." Colvin realized that his own voice was far from steady, and that he was beginning to blush also, he hoped only slightly.

Miss Rokeby had risen to her feet and was holding on to the back of her chair.

"I didn't say anything which could frighten her."

It was necessary to come to the point, Colvin thought.

"Greta thinks the menu unworthy of the distinguished company."

"What?" She turned and looked at Colvin. Then she smiled. "Is that it?" She sat down again. "What is it? Fish and chips?"

"Haddock. Yes." Colvin smiled back, now full of confidence.

"Well. There it is." Miss Rokeby made the prospect of haddock sound charming and gay. One of the commercial travellers offered to pour the other a fourth cup of tea. The odd little crisis was over.

But when Greta returned, her face seemed set and a trifle hostile. She had put on an ugly custard-coloured cardigan.

"It's haddock and chips."

Miss Rokeby merely inclined her head, still smiling charmingly.

Before Colvin had finished, Miss Rokeby, with whom further conversation had been made difficult by the fact that she had been seated with her back to him, and by the torpid watchfulness of the commercial travellers, rose, bade him, "Good evening", and left.

Colvin had not meant to go out again that evening, but curiosity continued to rise in him, and in the end he decided to clear his thoughts by a short walk, taking in the Hippodrome. Outside it had become even colder; the fog was thicker, the streets emptier.

Colvin found that the entrance to the Hippodrome had been transformed. From frieze to floor, the walls were covered with large photographs. The photographs were not framed, but merely mounted on big sheets of pasteboard. They seemed to be all the same size. Colvin saw at once that they were all portraits of Miss Rokeby.

The entrance hall was filled with fog, but the lighting within had been greatly reinforced since Colvin's last visit. Tonight the effect was mistily dazzling. Colvin began to examine the photographs. They depicted Miss Rokeby in the widest variety of costumes and make-up, although in no case was the name given of the play or character. In some Colvin could not see how he recognized her at all. In all she was alone. The number of the photographs, their uniformity of presentation, the bright swimming lights, the emptiness of the place (for the Box Office had shut) combined to make Colvin feel that he was dreaming. He put his hands before his eyes, inflamed by the glare and the fog. When he looked again, it was as if all the Miss Rokebys had been so placed that their gaze converged upon the spot where he stood. He closed his eyes tightly and began to feel his way to the door and the dimness of the street outside. Then there was a flutter of applause behind him; the evening's audience began to straggle out, grumbling at the weather; and Malnik was saying "Hullo, old man. Nice to see you."

Colvin gesticulated uncertainly. "Did she bring them all with her?"

"Not a bit of it, old man. Millie found them when she opened up."

"Where did she find them?"

"Just lying on the floor. In two whacking great parcels. Rokeby's agent, I suppose, though she appeared not to have one. Blest if I know, really. I myself could hardly shift one of the parcels, let alone two."

Colvin felt rather frightened for a moment; but he only said: "How do you like her?"

"Tell you when she arrives."

"She's arrived."

Malnik stared.

"Come back with me and see for yourself."

Malnik seized Colvin's elbow. "What's she look like?"

"Might be any age."

All the time Malnik was bidding good night to patrons, trying to appease their indignation at being brought out on such a night.

Suddenly the lights went, leaving only a pilot. It illumined a photograph of Miss Rokeby holding a skull.

"Let's go," said Malnik. "Lock up, Frank, will you?"

"You'll need a coat," said Colvin.

"Lend me your coat, Frank."

On the short cold walk to the Emancipation Hotel, Malnik said little. Colvin supposed that he was planning the encounter before him. Colvin did ask him whether he had ever heard of a Mr. Superbus, but he hadn't.

Mrs. Royd was, it seemed, in a thoroughly bad temper. To Colvin it appeared that she had been drinking; and that she was one whom drink soured rather than mellowed. "I've got no one to send," she snapped. "You can go up yourself, if you like. Mr. Colvin knows the way." There was a roaring fire in the bar, which after the cold outside seemed very overheated.

Outside Number Nine, Colvin paused before knocking. Immediately he was glad he had done so, because inside were voices speaking very softly. All the evening he had been remembering Mr. Superbus's reference to a "companion".

In dumb-show he tried to convey the situation to Malnik, who peered at his efforts with a professional's dismissal of the amateur. Then Malnik produced a pocket-book, wrote in it, and tore out the page, which he thrust under Miss Rokeby's door. Having done this, he prepared to return with Colvin to the bar, and await a reply. Before they had taken three steps, however, the door was open, and Miss Rokeby was inviting them in.

To Colvin she said, "We've met already", though without enquiring his name.

Colvin felt gratified; and at least equally pleased when he saw that the fourth person in the room was a tall, frail-looking girl with long fair hair drawn back into a tight bun. It was not the sort of companion he had surmised.

"This is Myrrha. We're never apart."

Myrrha smiled slightly, said nothing, and sat down again. Colvin thought she looked positively wasted. Doubtless by reason of the cold, she wore heavy tweeds, which went oddly with her air of fragility.

"How well do you know the play?" asked Malnik at the earliest possible moment.

"Well enough not to play in it." Colvin saw Malnik turn grey. "Since you've got me here, I'll play Rosalind. The rest was lies. Do you know," she went on, addressing Colvin, "that this man tried to trick me? You're not in the theatre, are you?"

Colvin, feeling embarrassed, smiled and shook his head.

"*Cornelia* is a masterpiece," said Malnik furiously. "Nethers was a genius."

Miss Rokeby simply said "Was" very softly, and seated herself on the arms of Myrrha's armchair, the only one in the room. It was set before the old-fashioned gas-fire.

"It's announced. Everyone's waiting for it. People are coming from London. They're even coming from Cambridge." Myrrha turned away her head from Malnik's wrath.

"I was told—Another English Classic. Not an out-pouring by little Jack Nethers. I won't do it."

"*As You Like It* is only a fill-up. What more is it ever? *Cornelia* is the whole point of the Gala. Nethers was *born* in this town. Don't you understand?"

Malnik was so much in earnest that Colvin felt sorry for him. But even Colvin doubted whether Malnik's was the best way to deal with Miss Rokeby.

"Please play for me. Please."

"Rosalind only." Miss Rokeby was swinging her legs. They were young and lovely. There was more than one thing about this interview which Colvin did not care for.

"We'll talk it over in my office tomorrow." Colvin identified this as a customary admission of defeat.

"This is a horrid place, isn't it?" said Miss Rokeby conversationally to Colvin.

"I'm used to it," said Colvin, smiling. "Mrs. Royd has her softer side."

"She's put poor Myrrha in a cupboard."

Colvin remembered about Greta's old room upstairs.

"Perhaps she'd like to change rooms with me? I've been away and haven't even unpacked. It would be easy."

"How kind you are! To that silly little girl! To me! And now to Myrrha! May I see?"

"Of course."

Colvin took her into the passage. It seemed obvious that Myrrha would come also, but she did not. Apparently she left it to Miss Rokeby to dispose of her. Malnik sulked behind also.

Colvin opened the door of his room and switched on the light. Lying on his bed and looking very foolish was his copy of Bull's *Graphite and Its Uses*. He glanced round for Miss Rokeby. Then for the second time that evening, he felt frightened.

Miss Rokeby was standing in the ill-lit passage, just outside his doorway. It was unpleasantly apparent that she was terrified. Formerly pale, she was now quite white. Her hands were clenched, and she was breathing unnaturally deeply. Her big eyes were half shut, and to Colvin it seemed that it was something she *smelt* which was frightening her. This impression was so strong that he sniffed the chilly air himself once or twice, unavailingly. Then he stepped forward, and his arms were around Miss Rokeby, who was palpably about to faint. Immediately Miss Rokeby was in his arms, such emotion swept through him as he had never before known. For what seemed a long moment, he was lost in the wonder of it. Then he was recalled by something which frightened him more than anything else, though for less reason. There was a sharp sound from Number Twelve A. Mr. Superbus must have returned.

Colvin supported Miss Rokeby back to Number Nine. Upon catching sight of her, Myrrha gave a small but jarring cry, and helped her on to the bed.

"It's my heart," said Miss Rokeby. "My absurd heart."

Malnik now looked more black than grey. "Shall we send for a doctor?" he enquired, hardly troubling to mask the sarcasm.

Miss Rokeby shook her head once. It was the sibling gesture to her nod.

"Please don't trouble about moving," she said to Colvin.

Colvin, full of confusion, looked at Myrrha, who was being resourceful with smelling-salts.

"Good night," said Miss Rokeby, softly but firmly. And as Colvin followed Malnik out of the room, she touched his hand.

Colvin passed the night almost without sleep, which was another new experience for him. A conflict of feelings about Miss Rokeby, all of them strong, was one reason for insomnia: another was the sequence of sounds from Number Twelve A. Mr. Superbus seemed to spend the night in moving things about and talking to himself. At first it sounded as if he were rearranging all the furniture in his room. Then there was a period, which seemed to Colvin timeless, during which the only noise was of low and unintelligible mutterings, by no means continuous, but broken by periods of silence and then resumed as before just as Colvin was beginning to hope that all was over. Colvin wondered whether Mr. Superbus was saying his prayers. Ultimately the banging about recommenced. Presumably Mr. Superbus was still dissatisfied with the arrangement of the furniture; or perhaps was returning it to its original dispositions. Then Colvin heard the sash-window thrown sharply open. He remembered the sound from the occasion when Mrs. Royd had sharply shut it. After that silence continued. In the end Colvin turned on the light and looked at his watch. It had stopped.

At breakfast, Colvin asked when Mr. Superbus was expected down. "He doesn't come down," replied Greta. "They say he has all his meals out."

Colvin understood that rehearsals began that day, but Malnik had always demurred at outsiders being present. Now, moreover,

he felt that Colvin had seen him at an unfavourable moment, so
that his cordiality was much abated. The next two weeks, in fact,
were to Colvin heavy with anti-climax. He saw Miss Rokeby only
at the evening meal, which, however, she was undeniably in process of converting from tea to dinner, by expending charm, will-
power, and cash. Colvin participated in this improvement, as did
even such few of the endless commercial travellers as wished to
do so; and from time to time Miss Rokeby exchanged a few pleasant generalities with him, though she did not ask him to sit at
her table, nor did he, being a shy man, dare to invite her. Myrrha
never appeared at all; and when on one occasion Colvin referred
to her interrogatively, Miss Rokeby simply said, "She pines, poor
lamb," and plainly wished to say nothing more. Colvin remembered Myrrha's wasted appearance, and concluded that she must
be an invalid. He wondered if he should again offer to change
rooms. After that single disturbed night, he had heard no more
of Mr. Superbus. But from Mrs. Royd he had gathered that Mr.
Superbus had settled for several weeks in advance. Indeed, for
the first time in years the Emancipation Hotel was doing good
business.

It continued as cold as ever during all the time Miss Rokeby
remained in the town, with repeated little snow storms every
time the streets began to clear. The miners would stamp as they
entered the bar until they seemed likely to go through to the cellar
beneath; and all the commercial travellers caught colds. The two
local papers, morning and evening, continued their efforts to set
people against Malnik's now diminished Gala. When *Cornelia*
was no longer offered, the two editors pointed out (erroneously,
Colvin felt) that even now it was not too late for a pantomime:
but Malnik seemed to have succeeded in persuading Miss Rokeby
to reinforce As *You Like It* with a piece entitled A *Scrap of Paper*
which Colvin had never heard of, but which an elderly local citizen whom the papers always consulted upon matters theatrical
described as "very old-fashioned". Malnik caused further comment by proposing to open on Christmas Eve, when the unfailing
tradition had been Boxing Night.

The final week of rehearsal was marred by an exceedingly
distressing incident. It happened on the Tuesday. Coming in

that morning from a cold visit to the Technical Institute Library,
Colvin found in the stuffy little saloon bar a number of the Tabard
Players. The Players usually patronized an establishment nearer
to the Hippodrome; and the fact that the present occasion was out
of the ordinary was emphasized by the demeanour of the group,
who were clustered together and talking in low, serious voices.
Colvin knew none of the players at all well, but the group looked
so distraught that, partly from curiosity and partly from compassion, he ventured to enquire of one of them, a middle-aged actor
named Shillitoe to whom Malnik had introduced him, what was
the matter. After a short silence, the group seemed collectively
to decide upon accepting Colvin among them, and all began to
enlighten him in short strained bursts of over-eloquence. Some
of the references were not wholly clear to Colvin, but the substance of the story was simple.

Colvin gathered that when the Tabard Players took possession
of the Hippodrome, Malnik had been warned that the "grid"
above the stage was undependable, and that scenery should not
be "flown" from it. This restriction had caused grumbling, but
had been complied with until, during a rehearsal of A *Scrap of
Paper*, the producer had rebelled and asked Malnik for authority
to use the grid. Malnik had agreed; and two stage-hands began
gingerly to pull on some of the dusty lines which disappeared
into the almost complete darkness far above. Before long one of
them had cried out that there was "something up there already".
At these words, Colvin was told, everyone in the theatre fell
silent. The stage-hand went on paying out line, but the stage was
so ample and the grid so high that an appreciable time passed
before the object came slowly into view.

The narrators stopped, and there was a silence which Colvin
felt must have been like the silence in the theatre. Then Shillitoe
resumed: "It was poor old Ludlow's body. He'd hanged himself
right up under the grid. Eighty feet above the floor of the stage.
Some time ago, too. He wasn't in the Christmas plays, you know.
Or in this week's play. We all thought he'd gone home."

Colvin learnt that the producer had fainted right away; and,
upon tactful enquiry, that Miss Rokeby had fortunately not been
called for that particular rehearsal.

On the first two Sundays after her arrival, Miss Rokeby had been no more in evidence than on any other day; but on the morning of the third Sunday Colvin was taking one of his resolute lonely walks across the windy fells which surrounded the town when he saw her walking ahead of him through the snow. The snow lay only an inch or two deep upon the hillside ledge along which the path ran; and Colvin had been wondering for some time about the small footsteps which preceded him. It was the first time he had seen Miss Rokeby outside the Emancipation Hotel, but he had no doubt that it was she he saw, and his heart turned over at the sight. He hesitated; then walked faster, and soon had over-taken her. As he drew near, she stopped, turned, and faced him. Then, when she saw who it was, she seemed unsurprised. She wore a fur coat with a collar which reached almost to the tip of her nose; a fur hat; and elegant boots which laced to the knee.

"I'm glad to have a companion," she said gravely, sending Colvin's thought to her other odd companion, "I suppose you know all these paths well?"

"I come up here often to look for lead-workings. I'm writing a dull book on lead and plumbago mining."

"I don't see any mines up here." She looked around with an air of grave bewilderment.

"Lead mines aren't like coal mines. They're simply passages in hillsides."

"What do you do when you find them?"

"I mark them on a large-scale map. Sometimes I go down them."

"Don't the miners object?"

"There are no miners."

A shadow crossed her face.

"I mean, not any longer. We don't mine lead any more."

"Don't we? Why not?"

"That's a complicated story."

She nodded. "Will you take me down a mine?"

"I don't think you'd like it. The passages are usually both narrow and low. One of the reasons why the industry's come to an end is that people would no longer work in them. Besides, now the mines are disused, they're often dangerous."

She laughed. It was the first time he had ever heard her do so. "Come on." She took hold of his arm. "Or aren't there any mines on this particular hillside?" She looked as concerned as a child.

"There's one about a hundred feet above our heads. But there's nothing to see. Only darkness."

"Only *darkness*," cried Miss Rokeby. She implied that no reasonable person could want more. "But you don't go down all these passages only to see darkness?"

"I take a flashlight."

"Have you got it now?"

"Yes." Colvin never went to the fells without it.

"Then that will look after you. Where's the mine? Conduct me."

They began to scramble together up the steep snow-covered slope. Colvin knew all the workings round here; and soon they were in the entry.

"You see," said Colvin. "There's not even room to stand, and a fat person couldn't get in at all. You'll ruin your coat."

"I'm not a fat person." There was a small excited patch in each of her cheeks. "But you'd better go first."

Colvin knew that this particular working consisted simply in a long passage, following the vein of lead. He had been to the end of it more than once. He turned on his flashlight. "I assure you, there's nothing to see," he said. And in he went.

Colvin perceived that Miss Rokeby seemed indeed to pass along the adit without even stooping or damaging her fur hat. She insisted on going as far as possible, although near the end Colvin made a quite strenuous effort to persuade her to let them return.

"What's that?" enquired Miss Rokeby when they had none the less reached the extremity of the passage.

"It's a big fault in the limestone. A sort of cave. The miners chucked their débris down it."

"Is it deep?"

"Some of these faults are supposed to be bottomless."

She took the light from his hand, and, squatting down on the brink of the hole, flashed it round the depths below.

"Careful," cried Colvin. "You're on loose shale. It could easily slip." He tried to drag her back. The only result was that she dropped the flashlight, which went tumbling down the great hole like a meteor, until after many seconds they heard a faint crash. They were in complete darkness.

"I'm sorry," said Miss Rokeby's voice. "But you did push me."

Trying not to fall down the hole, Colvin began to grope his way back. Suddenly he had thought of Malnik, and the irresponsibility of the proceedings upon which he was engaged appalled him. He begged Miss Rokeby to go slowly, test every step, and mind her head; but her unconcern seemed complete. Colvin tripped and toiled along for an endless period of time, with Miss Rokeby always close behind him, calm, sure of foot, and unflagging. As far into the earth as this, it was both warm and stuffy. Colvin began to fear that bad air might overcome them, forced as they were to creep so laboriously and interminably. He broke out in heavy perspiration.

Suddenly he knew that he would have to stop. He could not even pretend that it was out of consideration for Miss Rokeby. He subsided upon the floor of the passage and she seated herself near him, oblivious of her costly clothes. The blackness was still complete.

"Don't feel unworthy," said Miss Rokeby softly. "And don't feel frightened. There's no need. We shall get out."

Curiously enough, the more she said, the worse Colvin felt. The strange antecedents to this misadventure were with him; and, even more so, Miss Rokeby's whole fantastic background. He had to force his spine against the stone wall of the passage if he were not to give way to panic utterly and leap up screaming. Normal speech was impossible.

"Is it me you are frightened of?" asked Miss Rokeby, with dreadful percipience.

Colvin was less than ever able to speak.

"Would you like to know more about me?"

Colvin was shaking his head in the dark.

"If you'll promise not to tell anyone else."

But, in fact, she was like a child, unable to contain her secret.

"I'm sure you won't tell anyone else . . . It's my helper. He's the queer one. Not me."

Now that the truth was spoken Colvin felt a little better. "Yes," he said in a low, shaken voice, "I know."

"Oh, you know ... I don't see him or—" she paused—"or encounter him, often for years at a time. Years."

"But you encountered him the other night?"

He could feel her shudder. "Yes ... You've seen him?"

"Very briefly ... How did you ... encounter him first?"

"It was years ago. Have you any idea how many years?"

"I think so."

Then she said something which Colvin never really understood; not even later, in his dreams of her. "You know I'm not here at all, really. Myrrha's me. That's why she's called Myrrha. That's how I act."

"How?" said Colvin. There was little else to say.

"My helper took my own personality out of me. Like taking a nerve out of a tooth. Myrrha's my personality."

"Do you mean your soul?" asked Colvin.

"Artists don't have souls," said Miss Rokeby. "Personality's the word ... I'm anybody's personality. Or everybody's. And when I lost my personality, I stopped growing older. Of course I have to look after Myrrha, because if anything happened to Myrrha— well, you do see," she continued.

"But Myrrha looks as young as you do."

"That's what she *looks*."

Colvin remembered Myrrha's wasted face.

"But how can you live without a personality? Besides," added Colvin, "you seem to me to have a very strong personality."

"I have a mask for every occasion."

It was only the utter blackness, Colvin felt, which made this impossible conversation possible.

"What do you do in exchange? I suppose you must repay your helper in some way?"

"I suppose I must ... I've never found out what way it is."

"What else does your helper do for you?"

"He smooths my path. Rids me of people who want to hurt me. He rid me of little Jack Nethers. Jack was mad, you know. You can see it even in his photograph."

"Did he rid you of this wretched man Ludlow?"

"I don't know. You see, I can't remember Ludlow. I think he often rids me of people that I don't know want to hurt me."

Colvin considered.

"Can you be rid of him?"

"I've never really tried."

"Don't you want to be rid of him?"

"I don't know. He frightens me terribly whenever I come near him, but otherwise . . . I don't know . . . But for him I should never have been down a lead mine."

"How many people know all this?" asked Colvin after a pause.

"Not many. I only told you because I wanted you to stop being frightened."

As she spoke the passage was filled with a strange sound. Then they were illumined with icy December sunshine. Colvin perceived that they were almost at the entry to the working, and supposed that the portal must have been temporarily blocked by a miniature avalanche of melting snow. Even now there was, in fact, only a comparatively small hole, through which they would have to scramble.

"I told you we'd get out," said Miss Rokeby. "Other people haven't believed a word I said. But now *you'll* believe me."

Not the least strange thing was the matter-of-fact manner in which, all the way back, Miss Rokeby questioned Colvin about his researches into lead and plumbago mining, with occasionally, on the perimeter of their talk, flattering enquiries about himself; although equally strange, Colvin considered, was the matter-of-fact manner in which he answered her. Before they were back in the town he was wondering how much of what she had said in the darkness of the mine had been meant only figuratively; and after that he wondered whether Miss Rokeby had not used the circumstances to initiate an imaginative and ingenious boutade. After all, he reflected, she was an actress. Colvin's hypothesis was, if anything, confirmed when at their parting she held his hand for a moment and said: "Remember! *No one.*"

But he resolved to question Mrs. Royd in a business-like way about Mr. Superbus. An opportunity arose when he encountered her after luncheon (at which Miss Rokeby had not made an

appearance), reading *The People* before the fire in the saloon bar.
The bar had just closed, and it was, Mrs. Royd explained, the only
warm spot in the house. In fact it was, as usual, hot as a kiln.

"Couldn't say, I'm sure," replied Mrs. Royd to Colvin's firm
enquiry, and implying that it was neither her business nor his.
"Anyway, 'e's gone. Went last Tuesday. Didn't you notice, with
'im sleeping next to you?"

After the death of poor Ludlow (the almost inevitable verdict was
suicide while of unsound mind), it was as if the papers felt embarrassed about continuing to carp at Malnik's plans; and by the
opening night the editors seemed ready to extend the Christmas
spirit even to Shakespeare. Colvin had planned to spend Christmas with his mother; but when he learned that Malnik's first
night was to be on Christmas Eve, had been unable to resist defer-
ring his departure until after it, despite the perils of a long and
intricate railway journey on Christmas Day. With Miss Rokeby,
however, he now felt entirely unsure of himself.

On Christmas Eve the town seemed full of merriment. Colvin
was surprised at the frankness of the general rejoicing. The
shops, as is usual in industrial districts, had long been off-setting
the general drabness with drifts of Christmas cards and whirl-
pools of tinsel. Now every home seemed to be decorated and
all the shops to be proclaiming bonus distributions and bumper
share-outs. Even the queues, which were a prominent feature of
these celebrations, looked more sanguine, Colvin noticed, when
he stood in one of them for about half an hour in order to send
Miss Rokeby some flowers, as he felt the occasion demanded. By
the time he set out for the Hippodrome, the more domestically-
minded citizens were everywhere quietly toiling at preparations
for the morrow's revels; but a wilder minority, rebellious or
homeless, were inaugurating such a carouse at the Emancipation
Hotel as really to startle the comparatively retiring Colvin. He
suspected that some of the bibbers must be Irish.

Sleet was slowly descending as Colvin stepped out of the swel-
tering bar in order to walk to the Hippodrome. A spot of it sailed
gently into the back of his neck, chilling him in a moment. But
notwithstanding the weather, notwithstanding the claims of the

season and the former attitude of the Press, there was a crowd outside the Hippodrome such as Colvin had never previously seen there. To his great surprise, some of the audience were in evening dress; many of them had expensive cars, and one party, it appeared, had come in a closed carriage with two flashing black horses. There was such a concourse at the doors that Colvin had to stand a long time in the slowly falling sleet before he was able to join the throng which forced its way, like icing on to a cake, between the countless glittering photographs of beautiful Miss Rokeby. The average age of the audience, Colvin observed, seemed very advanced, and especially of that section of it which was in evening dress. Elderly white-haired men with large noses and carnations in their buttonholes spoke in elegant Edwardian voices to the witch-like ladies on their arms, most of whom wore hot-house gardenias.

Inside, however, the huge and golden Hippodrome looked as it was intended to look when it was still named the Grand Opera House. From his gangway seat in the stalls Colvin looked backwards and upwards at the gilded satyrs and bacchantes who wantoned on the dress-circle balustrade; and at the venerable and orchidaceous figures who peered above them. The small orchestra was frenziedly playing selections from *L'Étoile du Nord*. In the gallery distant figures, unable to find seats, were standing watchfully. Even the many boxes, little used and dusty, were filling up. Colvin could only speculate how this gratifying assembly had been collected. But then he was on his feet for the National Anthem, and the faded crimson and gold curtain, made deceivingly splendid by the footlights, was about to rise.

The play began, and then: "Dear Celia, I show more mirth than I am mistress of, and would you yet I were merrier? Unless you could teach me to forget a banished father, you must not learn me how to remember any extraordinary pleasure."

Colvin realized that in his heart he had expected Miss Rokeby to be good, to be moving, to be lovely; but the revelation he now had was something he could never have expected because he could never have imagined it; and before the conclusion of Rosalind's first scene in boy's attire in the Forest, he was wholly and terribly bewitched.

No one coughed, no one rustled, no one moved. To Colvin, it seemed as if Miss Rokeby's magic had strangely enchanted the normally journeyman Tabard Players into miracles of judgment. Plainly her spell was on the audience also; so that when the lights came up for the interval, Colvin found that his eyes were streaming, and felt not chagrin, but pride.

The interval was an uproar. Even the bells of fire-engines pounding through the wintry night outside could hardly be heard above the din. People spoke freely to unknown neighbours, groping to express forgotten emotions. "What a prelude to Christmas!" everyone said. Malnik was proved right in one thing.

During the second half, Colvin, failing of interest in Sir Oliver Martext's scene, let his eyes wander round the auditorium. He noticed that the nearest dress-circle box, previously unoccupied, appeared to be unoccupied no longer. A hand, which, being only just above him, he could see was gnarled and hirsute, was tightly gripping the box's red velvet curtain. Later in the scene between Silvius and Phebe (Miss Rokeby having come and gone meanwhile), the hand was still there, and still gripping tightly; as it was (after Rosalind's big scene with Orlando) during the Forester's song. At the beginning of Act V, there was a rush of feet down the gangway, and someone was crouching by Colvin's seat. It was Greta. "Mr. Colvin! There's been a fire. Miss Rokeby's friend jumped out of the window. She's terribly hurt. Will you tell Miss Rokeby?"

"The play's nearly over," said Colvin. "Wait for me at the back." Greta withdrew, whimpering.

After Rosalind's Epilogue the tumult was millennial. Miss Rokeby, in Rosalind's white dress, stood for many seconds not bowing but quite still and unsmiling, with her hands by her sides as Colvin had first seen her. Then as the curtain rose and revealed the rest of the company, she began slowly to walk backwards upstage. Door-keepers and even stage-hands, spruced up for the purpose, began to bring armfuls upon armfuls of flowers, until there was a heap, a mountain of them in the centre of the stage, so high that it concealed Miss Rokeby's figure from the audience. Suddenly a bouquet flew through the air from the dress-circle box. It landed at the very front of the heap. It was a hideous dusty laurel wreath, adorned with an immense and somewhat tasteless purple bow. The audience were yelling for Miss Rokeby like Dionysians; and the company, flagging from unaccustomed emotional expenditure, and plainly much scared, were looking for her; but in the end the stage-manager had to lower the Safety Curtain and give orders that the house be cleared.

Back at the Emancipation Hotel, Colvin, although he had little title, asked to see the body.

"You wouldn't ever recognize her," said Mrs. Royd. Colvin did not pursue the matter.

The snow, falling ever more thickly, had now hearsed the town in silence.

"She didn't 'ave to do it," wailed on Mrs. Royd. "The brigade had the flames under control. And tomorrow Christmas Day!"

LARGER THAN ONESELF

Upon the death of his father, Vincent Coner got out of mine owning, which had always been the family business, and invested heavily in popular journalism with himself as editor in chief. It is hard to believe that in any other place or time, past or future, his publications would have found many readers; but as it was, the thing most needed by his generation seemed to be the recipe he offered: the sweet things in life (the more obvious of them) smeared and contaminated with envious guilt.

A typical man of his time, Coner throve exceedingly. While at Cambridge, he edited a symposium of modern philosophy, which attracted considerable attention; and he soon became known for his advocacy of a synthesis between the best of this world and the best of the next. Already he was giving parties: his thin figure, precociously bald, wove in and out pouring gin while others talked. Occasionally he would bring the uproar back to the point as he conceived it. He developed an exceptional eye for the view which would prevail.

With increasing popular success, easily acquired, Coner's main business in life became more and more an almost paranoiac pursuit of self-integration. He read Berdyaev, Maritain, and C. S. Lewis, and even the first thirty pages of Ouspensky. Almost he believed what he read. Kierkegaard and Leopardi, rebound by a refugee craftsman, always attended his bedside (he had married a nightclub singer named Eileen); and Pascal he constantly redis-covered with new understanding, gorging on the insane root as he passed class-conscious photographs for the press. At the time Mrs. Iblis entered his life, he was greatly interested in several of the newer spiritual movements competing to offer a deadbeat world metaphysical immunization against its own shadow. He had decided to ask the different leaders to Bunhill for the week-end in order that they might have the chance to exchange views on neutral ground. A symposium for *Roundabout* might emerge, a real chance to give a lead.

Mrs. Iblis entered Coner's life in the usual way through the front door. While waiting for the bell to be answered, she was joined on the large white step by two other visitors, who introduced themselves as David Stillman and Ruth. Ruth was not Mr. Stillman's daughter, but Mrs. Iblis was unable to catch her other name, nor did she ever learn it. Mr. Stillman appeared to be a prosperous businessman. He arrived in a large car, which, when he had alighted, immediately drove away. He was well preserved and had excellent manners, but Mrs. Iblis had had little contact with Jews. Ruth was a highly strung voluble creature, little more than a girl in appearance, small and thin, with tousled hair, a round face, and restless hands. She wore red corduroy trousers, a shapeless jumper, and sandals. Mrs. Iblis had been speaking to Mr. Stillman when she appeared, presumably from the dense bushes which closely lined the drive, but carrying a bulging reticule with two handles. Mrs. Iblis had a suitcase; Mr. Stillman a dressing case of a type which Mrs. Iblis had thought obsolete.

Presumably the din inside the house made it difficult for the servant to hear the bell, so, at Mr. Stillman's suggestion, Mrs. Iblis rang again. Ruth maintained an intermittent flow of observations about the difficulty of reaching Bunhill (or indeed anywhere) by train and her own trials with the timetable.

"I do hope you've not been kept waiting." The door had been opened by Mrs. Coner, wearing a long tight dress of bluebottle green and smoking a cigarette from which the ash needed removing. "My husband's sent all the servants to a Domestic Science Congress at Littlehampton, and we're entirely in the hands of the caterers this weekend. Do come in."

Immediately inside stood a large figure in evening dress, with drink written all over him.

"Your names, please." He prepared to tick them off on a list with an indelible pencil.

"Mrs. Iblis."

He crawled slowly through the list, stopping at each name with the pencil. Three raw youths in dinner jackets had seized the visitors' luggage and were standing at the ready.

"Could you spell it?"

"I—B—L—I—S."

He repeated the search, then turned with irritation to Mrs. Coner.

In the meantime, the masterful figure of Coner had appeared from the crowd within. "Ruth, my darling. How lovely to see you." He kissed her mouth violently but dispassionately. "Did we ask you this weekend, or have you just dropped from heaven?"

"Surely you asked me, Vincent."

"It's wonderful to see you anyhow. Do come and join in right away. It will be really valuable to have the orthodox point of view."

"Could I have a sandwich first?"

"Have everything there is. Haven't you lunched?"

"I left London at half past ten."

"If we'd known, we'd have sent a car. It only takes half an hour by road. But come on and eat." Gripping her round the waist, he dragged her towards the hubbub.

"Vincent." His wife had clutched him by the other sleeve of his beautifully made gray suit. He stopped.

"What is it, Eileen?"

"Why do we have to have that damned list?"

"I've told you more than once. The people we've asked this weekend have all been carefully picked by me for the contribution they can make. As I've hardly met any of them before, we must have a list and keep to it. What's gone wrong?"

"Two people have arrived. They are not on the list. They both say they were told to arrive at three. I can hardly send them away."

"All the people this weekend were told to arrive for breakfast if they could. Who are they?"

"Mrs. Iblis and Mr. Stillman. They don't seem like the others." The suspect guests could be seen in the still open door miserably awaiting their fate.

"Mavis!" Coner bawled at the top of his voice. "Forgive me a moment, Ruth." With a violent squeeze, he released her.

A tall, bony, off-blonde, ageless woman strode forward. Coner succinctly outlined the crisis.

"I'll have a look in the invitations book, Mr. Coner." She departed.

Coner addressed his wife. "I leave it to you, my dear. But whoever they are, we don't want them unless they harmonize. Come on, Ruth." Resuming his python hold round Ruth's narrow waist, he propelled her forward.

Mavis returned with a huge folio volume of the minute book type. It must have contained five hundred pages. It was ruled into dates and packed with thousands of names in Mavis's small clear writing.

Almost at once Mavis had the answer. "They're left over from the lot we asked before Mr. Coner decided on the Forum. Haven't they had their postponement letters?"

"I'd better let them in. They'll have to share rooms with someone."

"Everyone's doing that this weekend, Mrs. Coner."

"Can you take over, Mavis?"

Explaining the situation about the rooms in a few courteous but emotionless words, Mavis was simultaneously scanning the hired butler's list of guests and their accommodation. "So I do hope you don't mind sharing," she concluded. "This weekend is rather a special occasion."

Mr. Stillman smiled acquiescence, though he did not look too happy. Mrs. Iblis said: "Please do not go to any trouble about me."

"No trouble at all." Then Mavis decided. "Mr. Stillman can have the Louise Room. I doubt Rabbi Morocco will come at all now. And perhaps Mrs. Iblis won't mind sleeping with Sister Nuper? Our House Sister, you know."

"Is part of the house used as a hospital?"

"Oh no. It's just in case of sudden or serious illness. And Sister Nuper advises us on our diet and on questions of personal hygiene as well. You'll find her a delightful person. Really, you couldn't find anyone better to room with."

The youth who had seized Ruth's piece of luggage had long ago departed with it, presumably to her room. Now the other two youths constituted themselves escorts to Mr. Stillman and Mrs. Iblis.

"The lift's through 'ere." They held back heavy, dark brown velvet curtains.

The lift, a Waywood-Otis installation capacious enough for

twelve at a hoist, was descending. When it reached the ground floor, there emerged two apparently identical Negroes in clerical dress. Small, compact, and beautifully polished, they looked like marionettes. They smiled and bowed in unison to the new arrivals, then walked off in step, conversing enthusiastically in some African tongue.

At the first-floor landing (Mrs. Iblis felt that it would have been quicker to have walked it), Mr. Stillman was at once shown into an enormous room which even through the door Mrs. Iblis could see contained at least two canopied beds. Mrs. Iblis was led away down a long passage, not too well proportioned, decorated in goose gray and lined with modern religious paintings, ascending on occasion as high in the scale as Vanessa Bell, and even Rouault. (Mrs. Iblis could not be sure, however, that they were not merely good reproductions.) From the opposite direction advanced an extremely good-looking woman of bold proportions; she was wearing a heavy black brassière, black-and-white striped knickers, and huge furry slippers. She made no acknowledgment of Mrs. Iblis's presence, still less of the luggage carrier's, and in the end, having passed the lift, vanished round the corner beyond the Louise Room, as Mrs. Iblis was unable to resist turning to see.

Sister Nuper's room was beautifully light and filled with built-in cupboards. There was a large, double divan-bed with silk sheets. Above the bed was a ghastly and lurid cartoon of the Crucifixion by Edward Burra. Mrs. Iblis was unable to make up her mind whether the artist was in favor of religion or against it. A satinwood bookcase, which had been scraped and painted white like the other furniture, proved to contain mainly volumes of the more popular nursing and home medical journals (bound by Coner's refugee craftsman). A French window and small balcony overlooked a garden of about an acre, from which rose a smell of intensive composting. A figure in a boiler suit could be seen at the dark work now.

Mrs. Iblis peered into one of the built-in cupboards. It was stuffed with evening dresses, depending from a thick chromium-plated rail and each in a transparent envelope made of plastic.

Not caring to unpack without consulting Sister Nuper, Mrs. Iblis nonetheless changed into the other dress she had brought.

Looking for an ashtray, she noticed the Sister's bedside book: entitled *Bowel Discipline*, it was a lesser work by a well-known member of the Labor party. A realistic colored drawing on the jacket depicted the alimentary system surrounded by a luminous radiation.

For some time after Mrs. Iblis had descended (by the stairs) into the mêlée below, no one took any notice of her. The Forum, about fifty strong, were surging and wheeling between the drawing room, the dining room, and the large hall. Most of them, of course, were shouting at the tops of their voices, or reasoning at the full stretch of their intellects; but some, Mrs. Iblis noticed, sat or even stood perfectly silent and ignored. She had read an article in the *Evening News* of the previous night upon the value in a bustling noisy life of regular periods of meditation, and gazed at these mute figures with interest and awe. Press photographers moved about the throng. In the end Mrs. Iblis's eye lighted upon Ruth eating a strawberry ice cream. This being the only person present to whom she had ever spoken (there was no sign of Mr. Stillman), Mrs. Iblis advanced.

"Hullo. I'm afraid I know no one else here but you. Can you tell me who some of these people are?"

"Don't know. I'm strictly orthodox."

"How interesting! In what way?"

"Full Anglican. I accept the Thirty-Nine Articles. Unconditionally." Ruth looked round for somewhere to deposit the ice cream glass.

"Well, so do I, I suppose."

"What's Article Thirty-three?"

"I can hardly recall the exact words."

"Then you're not an Anglican, are you?" Ruth was reduced to laying the receptacle in much jeopardy on the floor.

"Can *you* recite Article Thirty-three?" This feeble rejoinder was the best Mrs. Iblis could muster. It was so long since one had been at school.

"That person which by open denunciation of the Church is rightly cut off from the unity of the Church and excommunicated ought to be taken of the whole multitude of the faithful as a Heathen and Publican until he be openly reconciled by penance and received into the Church by a Judge that hath authority thereunto."

"Not a very Christian sentiment surely?" Mrs. Iblis inquired almost involuntarily.

"Why not?"

"More like the Church of Rome. Excommunication and penance, you know."

"I do penance daily." Ruth's voice was dreamy, her eyes blank.

"You can hardly be as wicked as that!" But Mrs. Iblis's mind recalled the alarming figure she had seen upstairs in the passage, and was instantly less sure.

"Not wicked. Sinful."

"Is there any difference?"

"Sin is a sense of something larger than oneself."

"Ah, now I understand you." Mrs. Iblis began to glance about for some sign of tea, surely overdue. "I think that is something we all feel."

But Ruth ignored her. "To merge," she cried in her soft, light voice. "To break through the barrier and become One. For a single infinitely small person to meet the infinitely vast. The end of every pilgrimage must be orthodoxy." Her eye lighted upon a fellow guest the other side of the room. "You see that man to the left of the big 'Annunciation'?"

"The red-haired one in tweeds?"

"He's a Lewisite. He's misplaced, like me."

"I thought lewisite was a kind of explosive."

Ruth merely said in the most casual way, "Have you read *Arrival and Departure*?"

"No."

"I'm going to look for another ice."

Before she had disappeared, Mrs. Iblis had time to ask: "Do you know what time we get tea?"

Ruth replied: "Any time you like. Ask at the buffet in the billiard room." And she was gone before Mrs. Iblis had completed the horrifying realization that at Bunhill there were no regular meals.

The better to face the situation, Mrs. Iblis opened her handbag and produced a compact. Peering into the little mirror, she failed to notice that two strange men now stood before her.

"Permit me to introduce my friend, Professor Dr. Borgia, principal of the Demokratischereligion Gesellschaft of Zürich." The speaker was a rotund young man of highly educated accent and masterful demeanor.

"How do you do? I suppose you must be used to people asking whether you are really one of the Borgias?"

"But *natürlich* I am one of the Borgias." The professor had the strongest of Teutonic accents. He was a slight, worn, Semitic-looking figure, with large fanatical eyes. "The Borgias were a great *aristocratische* family of old Spain. My family."

The rotund young man said: "I am sure you will both have much to say. Will you excuse me if I seek a word with Dr. Spade?" He was gone.

Professor Borgia rolled his eyes. "Have you found spiritual proficiency, *gnädige Frau*? You see I come straight from the point."

Mrs. Iblis considered carefully. "Well, actually, not yet, I think."

"Mine is the shortest way to truth." His diction had much of the charm of the German classical actor, the aptitude for making the most commonplace words profound and stirring. "I am in a sense a commercial traveler for God." This was uttered in a tone which recalled Manfred confronting the abyss. "You have first to sign your name only." He was holding out a quite fat booklet closely printed in a way which reminded Mrs. Iblis of Dutch seed catalogues.

"Thank you very much. I shall look forward to reading it."

"Reading alone will not avail. Words reach only the mind. It is the spirit, the *Geist*, we grope for, *nicht wahr*?"

"I suppose so." Mrs. Iblis was beginning to feel cowed and upset, unequal to life.

"Do you come much to Switzerland?" He pronounced the English name so elaborately that Mrs. Iblis had difficulty in following him.

"Only for the winter sports, I'm afraid. And that not for some years now."

"*Ach, so*? But no matter. We are starting an *Enfiedelei* in London this very winter. There will be your rebirth."

At this point it dawned on Mrs. Iblis that quite possibly the rotund young man had merely intended to unload upon her a bigger than ordinary bore, a person recognized to be such even in this company.

Excusing herself, she began firmly to look for the billiard room. The professor stood quite still, smiling after her retreating figure.

En route she passed a particularly frenzied group, at the center of which a man was saying, "Now can't we reduce our differences to a few simple points which we could talk over?" This, though Mrs. Iblis did not know it, was her host.

"What is the use of words if the spirit is wrong?" screamed out a woman whose style of looks Mrs. Iblis considered obsolete, and who wore a complex, black tea gown. For people who set so little store by words, they seemed to Mrs. Iblis remarkably dependent on them.

There were only ten or eleven people at the buffet, eating and drinking not being primary interests of the present gathering (unlike some at Bunhill). The billiard room also contained two tables, on one of which a couple of young waiters were playing half-hearted snooker. Above the dark brown mantelpiece was a huge vague-colored drawing of a Universal City designed by Patrick Geddes. A new strip-lighting system had been installed; but something had gone wrong with it and instead of giving better than daylight, it emitted a depressing yellow red glare as dusk descended outside.

As Mrs. Iblis stood drinking Indian tea and nibbling a maid of honor, a massive figure approached her, wearing enormous highly polished shoes.

"And what do *you* make of it all?" The accent was transatlantic.

"I'm afraid I know very little about it. I'm not really a member of the Forum."

"Nor I, ma'am. I just dropped in to see that Coner's on the right lines."

"And is he?" There seemed nothing else to say.

"Well now, I'm a Canadian. I'm also a businessman and editor, like Coner. But that doesn't mean I'm impervious to spiritual values. Quite the contrary. The one thing the whole world needs, the one thing every man's heart is sighing for—and every woman's—is a big spiritual revival. And what I say is, it's up to us servants of the public to get things rolling."

"I always think the press could be such an influence for good," said Mrs. Iblis, selecting an éclair. "After all, it's foolish not to take things as we find them."

"Sure, sure. Those are wise words, ma'am. I swear to you that not a copy goes out of a single journal in my group without it contains both a passage from the good book and some words of cheer by one of a panel of leading ministers."

"That must be very nice for your readers." Mrs. Iblis wished she had a larger handkerchief on which to deposit some of the sticky chocolate now coating her fingers. Nonetheless, she took a second éclair.

"You should see the thankful letters. Never less than sixty a day and often above the century. I tell you they make me a humble man. But I'm not a narrow man either, and I tell you something more is needed."

"Yes?" said Mrs. Iblis.

"After all, what are sects? What are denominations, creeds, dogmas, rituals? Aren't we all the same where it really matters— in our hearts? What are the little orthodoxies besides the great universal need, man's eternal quest for something larger than his puny self? That's what I'm doing here this very afternoon. Watching Coner pull the old country's socks up." His somewhat inflexible features almost beamed upon Mrs. Iblis.

"You think all this will really lead to something useful?" She turned to the buffet. The waiter was at the other end, and Mrs. Iblis raised her voice: "Could I have another cup of tea, please?"

"Sure, sure. There's just nothing that can't be had if you'll give your soul for it." Mrs. Iblis turned back to him with some surprise; but now he had seized the sleeve of a cadaverous, academic-looking young man with an enormous Wellingtonian nose. "And you, sir. What do you think?"

The young man merely snatched away his sleeve without a word or even a glance. He was like a preoccupied child. In ardent tones, he addressed his friend: "You know, Neville, I've found that much of the best modern thought, the really deep stuff, now comes from inside the Salvation Army."

"I still remain faithful to the dear old Hibbert Journal. That and my Karma Research Group. Let's have a cup of char, then I'll

tell you about a new technique we're working on to accelerate
the ecstasy." His voice had hushed almost to inaudibility. They
glanced at one another, conscious of secrets shared.

The Canadian was now conversing with an enormously fat
woman in a cassock. About her neck, on the end of a brass chain,
hung an object which Mrs. Iblis fancied was called an *anhh*. Or
was it a *crux ansata*?

At this point an exceedingly attractive woman entered the
billiard room accompanied by a positive throng of unusually
handsome young men. She wore a gray nurse's uniform made of
silk, like the nurse's uniforms worn by film stars in the early silent
days, and a high white collar. Mrs. Iblis had been about to leave
the billiard room but, supposing that this might be Sister Nuper,
remained for a moment.

The posse advanced upon the buffet, laughing and calling
loudly for refreshments, which seemed to be brought to them
with more alacrity than had attended the service of the other
guests. They stood in a group exchanging merry commonplaces,
carefree, exuberant. They were totally unlike the rest of the
Forum, but no one other than Mrs. Iblis and the waiter seemed
to be taking any particular notice of them. To Mrs. Iblis, however, they seemed in the end even to be engaged in parodying the
transactions around them.

"And what faith are you, my pretty maid?" cried out an Apollo-
like young man.

And Sister Nuper (if she it was) instantly replied in a cooing,
but perfectly clear, voice: "I worship St. Nicholas, sir," she said.

At this all the young men laughed very loudly. The group made
Mrs. Iblis feel a wild girl again. But the billiard room was emptying
and the waiter beginning to assemble supper dishes and bottles of
beer. Mrs. Iblis felt she could not stay longer without becoming
conspicuous, possibly a butt, not for any sort of unkindness (the
group did not seem unkind), but simply for witty remarks calling
for witty answers which she had never been able to provide, even
long after the need. Before she left, she noticed through the line
of long windows that the lurid light in the billiard room seemed
to have its counterpart in a livid autumnal glare outside. Was it
something to do with the equinox, she wondered.

"Shall I find you a chair?" The speaker was a shaggy, elderly, paternal figure.

"That would be very kind of you. Such tiring weather."

He guided her gently forward by the arm. They reached a small sofa. He seated himself beside her. This was not exactly what she wanted.

"Permit me to introduce myself. O'Rorke: founder of the New Vision Movement, small for the present, it is true, but a veritable seed of mustard, if I may quote from an anachronistic scripture."

"How do you do? My name is Iblis. Mrs. Iblis."

"Ah yes." He seemed abstracted. "I think I have convinced Mr. Coner. I think I have moved his heart to see that a new world demands a new faith and will not be put off." The speaker appeared to be at least seventy-five.

"There have indeed been many changes."

"But still we worship the old false gods! Still we prostrate ourselves before the concepts of medieval anthropomorphism." He looked exactly like a cathedral figure of St. Peter.

"Life is not easy," said Mrs. Iblis.

"But need we therefore rend ourselves like vultures? Can we not seek the truth each in his own way? Or, of course, hers? After all, in every heart is an unimaginable arcana: must we sell out to the money changers of the temple? Evil is, after all, so very small."

Mrs. Iblis looked up. "Is it?"

"Indeed it is. In how many mythologies the Devil is represented as a little fellow, as Mannikin or Peterkin, and how rightly! It is only the sophisticated theologians who make him vast and roaring and terrible: in order that we may be afraid of him and in their power. But pluck up your heart, Mrs.—er—" He stumbled for the name. "Only God is vast and great: that is to say, Good; for they are one and the same."

"How convincingly you put it!" Mrs. Iblis said this without the slightest irony. It was merely that the lowering weather was giving her a headache. Even as she passed her hand across her brow, there was a distant roll of thunder, too faint to be generally heard above the many voices, the diversities of business.

"It is God who speaks through me," said the patriarch modestly. "Or rather Good, the life spirit of the universe, to which it is within all of us to hearken."

Mrs. Iblis wondered whether Sister Nuper could produce some aspirin. Somehow it seemed improbable. It also seemed almost impossible to ask her.

Suddenly, however, the chic but world-worn figure of Mrs. Coner leaned over the back of the sofa and spoke in Mrs. Iblis's ear.

"Mavis tells me that you are unfortunately not feeling too good." Mrs. Iblis had not consciously set eyes on Mavis since her arrival.

"I *have* a slight headache, I'm afraid. It is foolish of me. The weather, I think."

"Take my advice and have a rest on your bed. Mavis is mixing you a draught."

With relief, Mrs. Iblis rose to her feet. "You are very kind." She addressed the patriarch: "Please excuse me. I'm not feeling very well, I'm afraid. I am going to rest for a little. I expect we shall meet again later."

He grasped her hand and held it. "Hold on to the spirit, Mrs.—er—I shall confidently await your return—purged and splendid." It was not quite what was usually said in such circumstances.

Mrs. Coner came with her upstairs. As they passed the door to the Louise Room, Mrs. Coner said: "We've been having some trouble there, I'm afraid. Mavis thought that Rabbi Morocco and your friend Mr. Stillman would have a lot in common. Anyway, she didn't expect Rabbi Morocco to turn up at all. But he has. And he and Mr. Stillman seem to be somehow different *kinds* of Jews. I don't really get it. They always seem to cause some sort of trouble, don't they?" She and Mrs. Iblis exchanged glances.

Lying on Sister Nuper's double bed was a girl in her underclothes and black silk stockings. Her thick black hair was drawn into a ballet dancer's bun, and she was reading a tome by Karl Barth.

"Sorry, Mrs. Coner. I thought Sister Nuper wouldn't mind." She sat up, staring at Mrs. Iblis.

"I am sure she won't, Patacake. But haven't we given you a room?"

"Can't stop. Have to get back to the Shelter."

"Oh." Mrs. Coner didn't seem to like her very much. But she did her duty as hostess. "This is Mrs. Iblis. Lady Cecilia Capulet."

"How do you do?" said Mrs. Iblis. "Please don't move." But her head was splitting, and she very much hoped that Lady Cecilia would move.

"I must go anyway." With great elegance she crossed to the window and looked out between the bright Gordon Russel curtains. "Oh God, it's raining."

Mavis appeared, bearing a large graduated glass filled to the brim with a blue green liquor, seething and opaque.

"Vincent's special," said Mrs. Coner. "Drink it down."

"You're really very kind," said Mrs. Iblis weakly. She sipped. Mavis, she noticed, had changed her dress and now wore a flame-colored model, very out of key with her apparent general temperament. Lady Cecilia was washing her hands and forearms with great thoroughness.

"It's almost pure peptomycin," said Mavis encouragingly.

The beverage tasted of liquid candle-grease gone flat with the years.

"Down the hatch," said Mrs. Coner, displaying for the first time the slightest hint of impatience.

There was a terrific crash of thunder. The four women looked at one another momentarily. Mrs. Iblis felt quite frightened.

"Christ!" ejaculated Lady Cecilia. "Can you lend me a mack, Mavis?"

"Of course, Patacake—if you'll give me five minutes." Mavis collected the now empty glass (a sticky bright yellow sediment occupied the last inch of it), said "Thank you" to Mrs. Iblis, and departed. It was now thundering briskly.

"Well now," said Mrs. Coner, once more sensibly sympathetic. "Lie down with your feet up so that the vapors can rise, and get some sleep. When you're better, come down again. The Forum will carry on most of the night, I expect, so you needn't rush things." She dragged out the bolster from the head of the bed and put it under Mrs. Iblis's feet. Mrs. Iblis had cast off her shoes but did not care to remove her dress, being conscious that her underclothes compared unfavorably with Lady Cecilia's. Lady

Cecilia was now carefully rubbing under her arms with (presumably) Sister Nuper's Arrid.

"Bye-bye," said Mrs. Coner in the idiom of her former avocation. She went, shutting the door which Mavis had left open.

"These clothes do make one stink." Lady Cecilia was putting on a plain navy blue skirt. Mrs. Iblis only wished she would go. Then Lady Cecilia put on a matching tunic, and Mrs. Iblis realized.

"I've never actually met a Salvation Army lassie before."

"It gives one a standing," said Lady Cecilia. "At places like this and times like the present. Major Barbara was on to something." She had buttoned the tunic to the neck. "It's a damned fetching outfit, you know." She extended one black silk leg. "The number it fetches might surprise you."

"Are you making it your career?"

"Until they chuck me out." There was a tap on the door. It was Mavis with an emerald-colored silk mackintosh. "How frightfully sweet of you! I'll be back immediately the Shelter shuts."

"Hurry. The Forum will give out if you don't keep their glands working."

"Your book!" cried Mrs. Iblis. It had obviously been forgotten.

"You read it," said Lady Cecilia. "*Auf Wiedersehen.*"

Mrs. Iblis had hoped to see Patacake put on her bonnet; but she was gone with no sign of the object.

"Shall I lock you in?" inquired Mavis. "It might be quieter for you, and there's a bell."

"Thank you very much," said Mrs. Iblis. "But no."

When Mrs. Iblis awoke, she felt extremely hungry. Used to four reasonable meals a day, she had had nothing of the kind since an early and rushed luncheon at the London railway terminus. She had turned out the light but could see by the illuminated dial of her wrist-watch that it was half past eleven. Despite Mrs. Coner's words, surely the party below might be over? Panic seized Mrs. Iblis, confronted with a foodless night. Switching on the bedside light, she rose, tried to smooth her dress, and put on her shoes. If the party were over, then Sister Nuper would have been with her by now. The thunder and rain seemed to have stopped, though Mrs. Iblis did not give the time to making sure. She felt once more in vigorous health, considering the hour. Mrs. Iblis did what she could with her hair and hastened downstairs.

There was still a great crowd, but the atmosphere had changed. There was very little light (Bunhill was supplied by two separate circuits, one of which had been affected by the thunderstorm) and astonishingly little noise. People were sitting about in small groups, often on the floor: and the general conversational level rose little above a mutter. Mrs. Iblis recalled a number of the faces, but none in the hall (to her relief) belonged to anyone with whom she had spoken.

To reach the billiard room, it was necessary to pass through the drawing room and take a passage leading off between the drawing room and the dining room. In the murky drawing room (decorated with neutral-colored abstractions screwed in pale frames to the walls) Mrs. Iblis noticed the unmistakable figure of Ruth. She was lying on the antique-shop chaise longue, with an entirely blank expression on her round face and clasped frankly and ruthlessly in the arms of a man whose back was turned to Mrs. Iblis, but who was wearing a black suit. Ruth's moplike hair was in worse disarray than ever. Mrs. Iblis could not help wondering if Ruth were happy.

From off the passage led an apartment known as the music room, which Mrs. Iblis had not so far entered. The door of this room was open, and from it came a loud and cheerful noise, contrasting with the subdued, almost dead tone which ruled elsewhere. When Mrs. Iblis reached the door, she could not but look in. Seated on top of a vast black concert grand was the woman she had supposed to be Sister Nuper, in her silken nurse's dress and tall stiff collar. She appeared to be administering some kind of light-hearted "quiz" to her group of young men, now apparently increased in number, who were gathered round her on the floor. They had mostly placed themselves very close to her. The prevailing attitude among them was far from one of relaxation; on the contrary, most of them were kneeling and leaning eagerly forward. Though the distance from the door was not great, Mrs. Iblis was unable to hear the question asked in Sister Nuper's soft cooing voice; but a number of the young men appeared to answer in unison. Sister Nuper's position, dangling her beautifully shaped legs in gray silk stockings from the piano, enabled Mrs. Iblis to see that, unlike most tenders of the sick, she was wearing shoes with enormously high heels. In the back row of the cluster of men, one figure, Mrs. Iblis noticed, seemed almost hysterically eager to answer the question or to answer it first. As Sister Nuper asked another question, Mrs. Iblis passed on. She was far from sure that she agreed with Mavis's view that no better person than Sister Nuper could be found with whom to share her bedroom.

The billiard room, still illuminated from the defective strip, looked exactly as before, except that there was now only one surviving waiter, the toiler behind the buffet, the other two having cut the cloth to bits and then gone back to London together, leaving the damaged table littered with colored balls and cubes of chalk. As before, there were about a dozen guests eating and drinking. The tone of their hushed conversations suggested that they were complaining of one another to confidential friends.

Mrs. Iblis asked what there was to eat. Little seemed visible on the buffet but débris.

"There's only lobster salad." The waiter had had enough.

It was not at all what Mrs. Iblis wanted. "That will be delicious." She recognized that it was late.

The waiter shoved up from under the buffet a plateful assembled many hours earlier.

"Cider? No beer."

"I'd love a glass of cider."

It was drawn from a plywood cask and was a product of a local industries group which Coner fostered. The smell and flavor were unusual, but Mrs. Iblis almost at once recognized that the brew was potent.

She was so hungry that the lobster salad was soon gone, though normally she avoided tinned shellfish.

"There's some cake."

"Thank you. I'd love some cake." Again, however, she felt that there were at the moment more desirable foods.

The waiter gave her two large pieces, as the buffet was soon to close. The plate was too small for its load, but the cake was cake, not good, not bad, not indifferent.

This time no one came near Mrs. Iblis, or enforced conversation. This time she would almost have been glad for someone to do so (though not, for choice, any single one of the day's previous new acquaintances).

"Could I possibly have some coffee if there's any left?" She had not yet finished the cider.

The waiter glared at her, then went to the other end of the buffet, produced a full cup from under it, and returned to her without a word. He had slopped much of the contents into the saucer. The coffee was far from hot and contained insufficient sugar. When it was finished, Mrs. Iblis was unsure what to do next. She stood sipping the remains of the peculiar amateur cider. To the waiter she might not have existed. To her fellow guests, as they finished their scraps of food and drink, she might have been a hostile object.

In the end she was almost alone and contemplating a return to bed, when Coner entered. Mrs. Iblis identified him at once as the overanxious figure in the back row round Sister Nuper. He advanced upon the buffet. His face was strained and his gait slightly shambling.

"Got any Scotch?"

"Only cider left, Mr. Coner."

Encountering her host thus for the first time, Mrs. Iblis wondered whether good manners enjoined that she should speak to him. On the whole, she thought it would be simpler to do nothing. Coner, however, took the initiative. Glancing round the room before departing to unlock his spirit store, his eye lighted upon her isolated figure, still holding the glass. He stared at her for several moments, then advanced.

"Who are *you*?"

"I'm Mrs. Iblis. I've no business here, really. My invitation was postponed on account of the Forum. But your wife asked me to stay as I didn't get the letter of postponement."

"I'm glad she did." Coner was still staring hard. The flesh on his face was like a loose mask covering another face beneath. "I hope they're looking after you properly."

"Perfectly, thank you. I'm having a lovely time."

"What d'you think of the Forum? We've got pretty well every-one who carries weight, don't you think?"

"I'm afraid some of it's rather above my head."

Though continuing to stare at her in a way which Mrs. Iblis was beginning to find odd, Coner seemed hardly to be attending.

"No real synthesis has emerged," he said. "Nothing beyond the separate individual arguments and experiences." He spoke like a defeated general referring to reinforcements. "Pity about Rabbi Morocco having to go home. He could have helped a lot."

"How?" Mrs. Iblis wanted to enter into the spirit of it.

"The A. G. S. is making headway all the time, you know."

"I'm sure I've no business not to know, but what is the A. G. S.?"

"The Avant Garde Synagogue. Something entirely new. It's a great mistake to ignore what the Jews are doing."

"I am told that the Salvation Army are doing a lot too," said Mrs. Iblis, greatly venturing.

"Of course Patacake's utterly irreplaceable. One just wouldn't try." His eyes were now wandering up and down her body in a way to which she was unaccustomed; but he sank into silence.

"Will you be writing about the Forum in your papers?" inquired Mrs. Iblis, in order to say something.

"The whole of the next issue in each case except for a slaugh-terhouse feature in *Roundabout*. But I doubt whether we really reach them." He seemed in the last stages of gloom.

"Oh, I'm sure you do," said Mrs. Iblis comfortingly. "All those millions of copies. Power like that over people's minds must be a rather terrible thing." She was conscious that the very strong cider had reached her very weak head from her very empty stomach.

The pupils of Coner's eyes seemed to perform a complete half-circle. Then he said: "You should wear nothing but black. Cut rather low. The sort of style young girls can't manage." He had placed his hand firmly on Mrs. Iblis's thorax to indicate precisely how low. Mrs. Iblis withdrew slightly with a distinct shudder.

"Thank you for the advice."

He stepped toward her again. "I find something quite remark-ably charming about you. Even in pale blue."

Without the cider, Mrs. Iblis would probably have blushed and felt flattered. As it was, she answered: "Nonsense, Mr. Coner. I'm not quite so silly as that."

The waiter had just drawn a greasy overcoat from the hidden recess which had earlier evicted lobster salad. He departed, worming his way into the garment.

"Shall I leave the lights, Mr. Coner?"

"Yes. I'll put them out."

The last guests having also withdrawn, Mrs. Iblis was alone in the billiard room with her host and a dish filled with sliced cake.

"What's your name?"

"Iblis. I—B—L—I—S."

"How much do you know about me?"

"Very little more than I've read in the papers and so forth. Only what everyone knows."

"Shall we sit down?"

Mrs. Iblis wanted few things less. However, they sat in the depressing yellow glare on blue basketwork chairs brought in for use by frequenters of the buffet. It was not even very warm.

"It's close." Coner passed his handkerchief round the inside of his collar. "But never mind that. Now where shall I begin?" This question was for answer by the speaker himself. Clearly he was about to tell his life story.

"I expect you'll soon have to join your other guests, so I mustn't keep you too long."

"Oh God," said Coner, "the world's weight! The terror of one's own littleness." He was even whiter and had begun to weep profusely. His head dropped onto his hands, so that they covered his face. A cataract of tears fell through his fingers onto his gray trousers, which became as if spattered with ink.

Mrs. Iblis, who had never seen a man behave like this before (and hardly even a woman), was completely at a loss. After all the events of that day, Coner's demonstration was too much for her. Her body was insufficiently nourished, her mind awash in homemade cider. She too began gaspingly to weep. The scene in the billiard room was as if the two of them had just forsaken the last childhood's illusions.

Coner seemed quite lost to the world. Tears flooded his cloth-
ing. His body shook. His mind might have ceased to function.

Mrs. Iblis was less collapsed. The tears raced down her face,
but she scrabbled through her handbag for a handkerchief and
after a few minutes had somewhat pulled herself together.

"Please forgive me, Mr. Coner," she said. "Is there anything I
can do to help?"

Coner went on sobbing and shivering like a man whose heart
was long since broken and for whom such episodes as this were
regular occurrences.

"Please, Mr. Coner." She extended her own rather unsteady
hand and touched his shoulder. "What can I do?" Afraid, like
most women, to go too far in sympathy lest the sympathy be
misinterpreted, she had never in her life gone further than this.

Coner began to babble distressingly of his littleness and inadequacy; his responsibilities; his uncertainties; his health troubles.
"The human mind is such a minnow," he spluttered out. "If only
one could find some all-embracing pattern to guide one."

"The human mind is a whale." The speaker was Mr. Stillman,
who had entered the large murky room unnoticed. It was the
first time Mrs. Iblis had seen him since her arrival. He looked
businesslike and prosperous in his well-cut dark suit. He carried a
copy of the *Jewish Monthly*.

"The human mind is a whale," said Mr. Stillman again. "It's all
there inside you, enormous unknown things, difficult to reach.
And woe betide the man who looks outside himself for what he
can only find inside. That is surely one thing which modern psy-
chology has made clearer than ever. The subconscious mind, you
know. So much larger than the conscious. The subliminal self." He
paused. His eye was traveling along the buffet. "Ah, cake. There
are hungry people in the house. Do you mind if I take the cake?"

Coner was staring at him, his face like an idiot's.

Mrs. Iblis replied: "I am sure that will be all right."

"Thank you," said Mr. Stillman, picked up the large white dish
in his free hand, and left.

Coner now partially came to. "That's what we're all trying to
do," he said. "To find ourselves."

"I gather not," rejoined Mrs. Iblis, with what might almost

have been acerbity. "You're all trying to find something larger than yourselves."

She rose and left the billiard room, leaving Coner recumbent like a drenched tea cloth.

Everybody was eating cake and seemed more cheerful. It was like the miracle of the loaves, until Mrs. Iblis realized that volunteers had scoured the house for food and had stumbled upon a cache in the little pantry allotted to the caterers for their supplies. Also in the pantry were traces of proteinous foodstuffs which the hired staff had withheld and taken home to sell. The discovery had diverted much of the conversation to questions of supply and then rapidly to politics. Altogether, though disagreeing with many of the views expressed, Mrs. Iblis had never felt so much at home at Bunhill as now. Even Professor Borgia made comparatively agreeable company when discoursing upon the complexities of Swiss dietetics. Mrs. Iblis took another piece of cake herself, though it was long past her hour. After the last crumb went down, Sister Nuper emerged from the music room at the head of her young men. Idly curious, Mrs. Iblis counted them. They numbered no less than twelve, each as radiantly good-looking as the rest. Would Sister Nuper, her pleasant evening over, now proceed to bed? Apparently not: Sister Nuper went directly to the front door, opened it, and led the way out into the chilly night, closely attended as ever by her faithful followers. The door banged loudly behind the last of them, shaking the house.

Mrs. Iblis now dared to ask questions. "Where are they going at this hour?"

Her neighbor, a metaphysical daredevil who had recently been the youngest Ph.D. of his year, became suddenly reserved, almost aggressive. "They've gone for a walk," he replied rudely, as if it were no business of hers.

Mrs. Iblis did not care to invite another snub from these strange people by pursuing the matter further. Despite the welcome loosening up of the talk, she had the irritating feeling that she alone (or almost alone) was excluded from a general and advantageous secret. Of course, she reflected, she had not been really intended to be present that weekend.

Nonetheless, she felt piqued. She decided to go to bed and

went. One or two of her fellow guests to whom she said good night (there was no sign of Coner or Mrs. Coner, or even Mr. Stillman) seemed surprised, but only faintly.

Mrs. Iblis turned out the light and drew back the curtains, glad to stand for a moment in the cool darkness. Though the storm was long since over, the sky was not clear. There appeared, on the contrary, to be a dense ceiling of low cloud obscuring the stars but tinged with a radiance towards the east, which Mrs. Iblis supposed to come from the moon.

In the comfortable bed Mrs. Iblis soon fell asleep once more, despite the uncertainties relating to Sister Nuper's movements. After a dreamless span of uncertain length, she was awakened by a knocking on the door, at once purposeful and agitated.

"Come in, come in," said Mrs. Iblis rather peevishly. She switched on the bedside light.

She supposed it to be Sister Nuper (in who knows what condition?); but, in fact, it was Mavis. She wore saffron silk pajamas and no dressing gown. Her face was covered with unpleasing traces of what Mrs. Iblis presumed to be a "pack."

"I'm sorry, but there's something wrong. I'm frightened." Mavis was shivering noticeably.

Mrs. Iblis felt none too helpful. "You should have put something on."

"Yes. I suppose I should." Mavis vaguely clasped her pajamas about her.

"Have my dressing gown?"

"Thank you." Rather halfheartedly, she donned it. "Forgive my coming to you. Mrs. Coner's right out."

"Out?"

"Stuff she takes to make her sleep. She's never *compos mentis* till midday."

"What about the other guests? Not that I don't want to help," Mrs. Iblis added. Still, she did feel that this was the last straw.

"That's just it. They're not in their rooms. I'm frightened," repeated Mavis. "It's bloody awful."

Mrs. Iblis was now sitting up in bed and herself feeling none too warm. "Tell me exactly what's the matter."

"There's a queer light." Mavis crossed to the window and slightly drew back one of the curtains. "Look!"

"It's the moon."

"There's no moon."

"How do you know?"

"We compost the garden. You need to know for that. It's left to me, like most other things. I do know."

"Do you think it's a fire?"

"No." Mavis further withdrew the curtain. "Do you?"

A white radiance filled the air.

"It was beginning when I went to bed. I thought it was the moon. Are you quite sure?"

"Quite sure. It comes from the other side of the house."

"Searchlights?"

"It's not in beams. It's everywhere."

Mrs. Iblis felt no particular eagerness to leave her bed and investigate further.

"Have you *looked* on the other side of the house?"

"No. I wanted some moral support. Things go on here, you know." Mavis looked around the room so as to seem in part to localize her reference in a way which Mrs. Iblis found rather unpleasant. "I went to Ruth's room and it was empty. Then I went to several other rooms. They are all empty."

"So then you thought of Sister Nuper?"

"No. I thought of you. Will you come down with me?"

"Yes, of course, if you wish it." Mrs. Iblis got out of bed. "But why do we have to go down? Is that the first thing?"

"They're all in the hall. I can hear them."

Mrs. Iblis was reduced to putting on her overcoat. "Well now, let's see."

In what was precisely a half-light, the house did seem to Mrs. Iblis somewhat eerie. A life-sized figure of Buddha stood on the half landing, serenely menacing.

Through the thick brown curtains below and up the stairwell ascended a wavering hubbub. Then, just as Mrs. Iblis and her companion reached the bottom, a woman screamed sharply. She controlled herself almost at once.

The scene in the hall was certainly the strangest Mrs. Iblis had yet seen. The entire Forum (or so it seemed) were packed in, like refugees from some catastrophe. All appeared to be in their nightclothes, and there were the usual contrasts, comic and revealing. Professor Borgia's friend, the rotund young man, Mrs. Iblis noticed, was wearing a rich Oriental dressing gown. The leader of the New Vision Movement was wearing a nightshirt. Mrs. Iblis looked at once for Coner but could not see him.

In the poor light the throng appeared all to be gazing at the front door. They were now quite silent. Ruth, in the loose sweater and trousers she had worn by day, was elbowing her way forward, her face like that of St. Joan en route to the stake. Mrs. Iblis realized that she was going to open the door and deduced that someone had screamed when Ruth had made clear this intention.

All their faces were wrung in a conflict between a dreadful curiosity and the instinct to flee. A grim figure of the Kingsley Martin type collapsed upon his knees and, sinking his tortured face in his hands, began to pray. The rotund young man glanced at him and smiled faintly. A tall woman in an ulsterlike garment began to emit crooning sounds. Her face was stony with dread. Mrs. Iblis suspected that it had been she who had screamed.

Ruth had now struggled through to the door. With a final self-dedicatory gesture she lugged it open.

The strange luminosity fell upon her martyr's face. The doorway was filled with light. Behind could be seen a huge luminous shape. The light filled this shape and seemed to go towering upwards. The shape recalled in Mrs. Iblis's mind some common quotation: something about the feet of the gods on the mountains.

The Forum began to creep out into the garden, silently like snails under the moon.

"Come away," said a voice quietly to Mrs. Iblis. "Come upstairs." Mr. Stillman, in white silk pajamas and a black dressing gown, had gently touched her arm. He still carried a copy of the *Jewish Monthly*, his finger between the pages. Round his neck was a scarf with the colors of some good club.

Mrs. Iblis glanced at Mavis.

"You come too," said Mr. Stillman.

"I wonder what's become of Mr. Coner?"

"He's in good hands," said Mr. Stillman; and Mavis seemed willing to leave it at that.

The trio ascended to the first floor. There Mrs. Iblis had expected them to stop. But Mr. Stillman said: "We're going on the roof."

They went up two more stories; then by a Slingsby ladder to the roof, which Coner had laid out for sunbathing and deck games. Inflatable rubber objects lay about, once bright and crude, now discolored. Every now and then one stumbled over a quoit. The house was L-shaped, so that, by looking over the rail, Mrs. Iblis could see the Forum still issuing slowly from the front door. The light kept burning all night in Mrs. Coner's bedroom could also be seen.

Once outside, members of the Forum seemed to lose initiative and to accumulate in a mass against the wall of the house. The entire atmosphere was filled with the strange light, but Mrs. Iblis began to realize that the light nonetheless had a distinct source, a source independent of the general air. It was like the concentration and narrowing of the perceptions which often follow emergence from an anesthetic. The cause of the confusion was simply the vastness of the source. Up here it looked as if the air was alight: but in fact it was a vast shining figure which filled the entire visible earth and sky. As each member of the Forum realized this fact, he or she drew back into the company of the other members against the wall.

Although the members of the Forum might have been frightened, Mrs. Iblis found the scale of the occurrence simply too large for fright. She quite consciously rehearsed this fact over to herself in her mind. Mavis, however, was shaking more than ever and looked about to faint. Mrs. Iblis drew forward a striped deck chair and seated Mavis upon it, whispering some comforting words to her. She noticed that the strange light drew all the strong color from Mavis's pajamas. Mr. Stillman was looking on at these particular workings of the universe with apparently complete equipoise. The paper in his hand might have been a program of events.

The light suddenly increased around and upon the Forum

huddled against the wall to the left of the front door. It was as if an immense spotlight picked out a group of the opposition about to be laid low with machine-gun fire. But in fact it was that the vast figure was looking downwards from the empyrean.

Mr. Stillman had placed his forearms on the railing round the roof. Mavis had sunk her head between her knees. It was only Mrs. Iblis who looked upwards, and what she saw nearly finished her.

When Mrs. Iblis came round, the radiance in the air was much diminished. Mavis and Mr. Stillman had lifted her into Mavis's deck chair. It was cold.

Mrs. Iblis peered through the railings. There was no one in sight. Only the light in Mrs. Coner's bedroom burned reddish through the glimmer.

"Where are they?"

"They have merged," said Mr. Stillman. "They are at one." He was rubbing her left wrist. Mavis, now apparently much recovered, was rubbing her right.

"Where have they gone to?"

Mavis made a slight gesture away from the house. "We shan't see *them* any more."

Mrs. Iblis hardly dared to follow with her eyes. Then she saw that the radiance had entirely faded. It was a starry, moonless night without a cloud in the sky.

"I no longer feel frightened."

"Nor I," said Mavis. "Only cold. Why don't we?"

"Why should you?" said Mr. Stillman. "They've got what they wanted. As everyone does." He retied the cord of his dressing gown. "Shall we go down?" He led the way.

"I must look for Mr. Coner," said Mavis as they descended. Mrs. Iblis realized that she had not noticed her host among the group in the garden.

They found him sitting in the empty hall. He was drunk and still drinking. The key of his private spirit store was gripped tightly in his hand. The hall looked as if recently swept by a cyclone.

Mr. Stillman shut the open front door.

"Please God," said Coner in weak and sozzled accents, "please God give me something larger than myself."

He dropped into stupor, knocking a full glass to the floor. The disordered room began to reek of whiskey.

"Let me give you a hand," said Mr. Stillman to Mavis. They began to ease Coner toward the lift. "I think *you'd* better get some sleep," said Mr. Stillman to Mrs. Iblis. "Good night. See you in the morning." Mavis merely smiled at her.

Just as the cortège had passed through the brown curtains, the front door burst open once more. It was Sister Nuper and her friends. Their clothes seemed much damaged and covered with mud. It was as if they had been riding to hounds. But they all seemed as cheerful and gay as ever.

Mrs. Iblis had withdrawn into the shadows. She rather gathered that the revelers were contemplating final drinks.

Sister Nuper, graceful even in fatigue, dropped into the armchair just vacated by her employer. The bad light fell upon her beautiful features. Her face was glistening in a way Mrs. Iblis did not like. Her eyes were filled with such happiness that Mrs. Iblis was thoroughly scared all over again.

Unnoticed by the group of companions, Mrs. Iblis slipped away. Rather than pass what was left of the night with such a happy woman, she hastened to that room with the painted Crucifixion in it, she stuffed her possessions into her suitcase, and she left the house by a window at the back which had been carelessly left open by the hired staff.

A ROMAN QUESTION

It was that cursed and special boredom of middle married life that made us go to the so-called conference at all. In the early period, you spend most of your time desperately struggling (working, a serious-minded friend of mine calls it) to accommodate to one another—if you are both people of goodwill, that is, which Marguerite and I most certainly were, and are. In the final period, you are both too sunk for anything really to matter, except trivialities like food, drink, and shelter. It is in the long middle years that the feeling of all-round frustration is consciously dominant. Anything that either of you really wants to do seems spoilt even to think about by the fact that the other has to do it with you; and by the fact that the other cannot possibly be held to blame, except at moments of really complete unreason. You sink together, yet apart, into tighter and tighter quicksands, while your faces grow blanker and blanker, and your children either struggle to get away (ours were at boarding-school), or make no attempt to get away at all. But I find that I never like the middle period of anything. I start things rather too easily, and find that I grow quite cheerful when the end comes into sight. Middles are dead nothings.

The so-called conference was one of the things I entered upon too easily, dragging Marguerite with me. Our circle included a woman artist named Neptuna Adams. She drove forward along the borderline between commercial art and real art, and therefore did quite well financially, especially as, throughout the world, the two regions came more and more to overlap. She was a square, flat woman, who had had three separate husbands, none of whom ever married again, and all of whom dropped in to see Neptuna at frequent intervals, sometimes, by chance, two at a time. She was not the kind of artist non-specialists would hear of, but, as I say, she did pretty well for herself, and she also had a kind and open heart, quite open enough to know people like Marguerite and me, who could neither talk constructively about

Jackson Pollock, nor bring forward friends who might commission decorating jobs in branches of banks.

Neptuna was a committee member of a society of business
artists. One evening, after dinner in her studio (always a good
square meal), she pressed us very strongly to come with her to
the society's forthcoming conference in Birmingham. It was the
first such event, she explained, though the society had now been
in existence for almost seven years, so that she was under a considerable obligation to contribute to its success. She would drive
us up in her car (a huge, thirty-year-old Daimler), and arrange for
our accommodation. It would cost only a few pounds for each
of us, as there was substantial aid both from the rates and from
the Ministry of Education, Rawley, her second husband, would
be coming too, as her assistant; and perhaps one or two others. I
cannot say that I was really eager to go. Possibly I was more eager
just to please. Marguerite, when we discussed it that night, said
she was sure I should not like it; implying that, therefore, she
would not like it either. It was true enough, as a segment of the
total problem, but on that basis we should never have done anything; so away we went.

We were greatly delayed on the journey by a wheel coming
off the car as we descended the hill between Banbury and Warwick on the A41. Neither Rawley nor I were very quick at repairs,
and the third man, whom Neptuna had dragged in at the last
moment, never seriously offered to help at all, but sat hugging his
girl-friend in a corner of the back seat while we worked.

It would be absurd to say that the time thus lost really mattered, as the conference was hardly a conference at all. Half the
total number of advertised speakers (three out of six) failed to
appear, though two of them did send eloquent apologies: these
three were to have been the spokesmen for business and industry.
The three spokesmen for the arts who did appear, were in two
cases so short of material that they petered out long before their
announced times (and without apology), and in the third case so
humourless and axe-grinding as to be unendurable, at least by
Marguerite and me. "Debates" followed, which could have been
of interest, we thought, only to close friends of the contributors.
The general inarticulacy came to a climax on the first evening, at

the reception by the Lord Mayor, where no one seemed able to say anything. At the two conference lunches, Marguerite and I had as neighbours people (different people at each) who took no interest in us, and could hardly have been expected to. Over all lay a pervasive uncertainty as to what was going to happen next, a recurrent, ever-unsatisfied call for improvisation. And so I could continue. But I do not want merely to be catty about Neptuna's conference. Doubtless it was simply not adapted to outsiders. Neptuna herself did apologize to us several times. "These things are always like this," she said, "but people insist on having them, and one has to play ball or lose face." We absolutely understood. It was we who had been weak.

That was the background for something quite different.

It will be remembered that Neptuna had said she would arrange for our accommodation. The plan was that committee members and speakers should be housed in the Queen's Hotel; other attenders in private houses. The Queen's Hotel group was, of course, paid for by the society; and I take it that the feeling, perhaps in some way the experience, was that most of the others would balk at modern hotel prices. A local group had accordingly made an appeal of some kind to householders. I am not sure that the operation had been handled much more skilfully than the other aspects of the conference. At least, Neptuna confided to us during the void left by the absence of the first afternoon's speaker that, owing to a muddle, three of us had been housed together: Marguerite and I, and the last-minute man's girl-friend, but not the last-minute man himself. The last-minute man was so furious, said Neptuna, that he had sulked right off, gone home by British Rail. It was not the kind of thing that was easy to adjust, added Neptuna, unless you knew the people.

"Do you mean we're all going to be together in one room?" asked Marguerite, who had already enjoyed the conference even less than she had expected.

"Who's to say? Do you mind?"

Of course Marguerite minded, and I was none too keen myself. The kind of thing that might once have been a mild adventure was nowadays a mere perturbation and nuisance.

We should really have looked at the place in the morning, the conference having been timed to start at midday in order to make this easier. As it was, the three of us set off that evening in Neptuna's huge car, with me at the wheel, Neptuna being unable to get away. It was about six o'clock: an official break, or "Delegates' Free Time", between the afternoon paper, one which had miscarried, and the municipal reception in the evening. Marguerite sat beside me, the other girl in the back. Her name was apparently Deirdre. She was small, silent, dark, and not very well dressed.

Fortunately, I have known Birmingham quite well for a number of years, as, never the simplest place to find one's way about, it has been made almost impossible by the new regulations. Before leaving the Matthew Boulton Hall, where the conference was based, I had looked up the address we had been given on the street plan I had brought with me. Now Marguerite had the plan and gave me directions. She was, and is, good at this. Any kind of firm, practical enterprise brings out the best in both of us. It would have been alarming to have had to seek directions from people in the street, because, even without that, a cluster of children tended to gather and jeer at the antique car every time we stopped for the lights. We were bound for some street out behind Alum Rock. Marguerite never missed a trick and brought us there beautifully. Peevers, we had been told, was the name of the people. Major and Mrs. Peevers.

It had struck me in advance as not necessarily a fertile area for field rank, but it proved to be rather different from what one had expected.

No. 47 was indeed semi-detached, but the entire locality seemed to have been cleared at some time, probably just after the First World War, and tidily redeveloped by a charitable trust or public authority. Indeed, there really was something military about the uniform houses in dark red brick: quite large, solidly built, sparsely adorned, blackened by Birmingham; some distinct suggestion of married quarters. The straight road was quite empty both of vehicles and people, unlike all the others we had come through. The front garden of No. 47 offered no flowers, but only dark green bushes, small and tight; with patchy grass, indifferently trimmed. The path from the very heavy gate in ornamental wrought iron was paved with square slabs of concrete, every one badly chipped at the corners and all sooted. The house next door, the other semi-detached, was obviously empty; really quite dilapidated. It was late September and getting dark.

The Major himself opened the door.

"Peevers," he cried in self-introduction, holding out his hand. "Wakefield, I presume?"

He was a lean, bony man of less than middle height, with spare white hair at the back of his cassowary-like skull, and protruding grey eyes. He wore a black suit and a black tie.

I introduced Marguerite and the silent Deirdre.

"Better put the car somewhere safe," said Major Peevers. "There is a good place over the top of the hill and turn right. Not more than half a mile."

"Oh, surely," I demurred, looking up and down the empty street.

"It's all right now," said the Major, "but it's later the trouble starts."

"We've got to leave again in a couple of hours," I protested.

"It's not our car," Marguerite reminded me. So I expelled the small pieces of luggage, and drove off. I saw that the Major had picked up all three objects and stuck them about his person, like a continental railway porter.

Needless to say, the garage proved to be full right up, and at the next one I found the Black Country dialect impossible to penetrate. The third garage was one of a large chain, and could find room even for Neptuna's dinosaur, though rather at a price, I thought; but unfortunately it was now quite a walk back to the Major's abode. In fact, it was almost dark when I arrived.

Once more it was the Major who let me in. "Hell, isn't it, with no street lights?" he said. "We've all been going at the Trustees for years, but nothing happens." Inside they were having tea. The room, papered in pale watered green, contained a dry, yellow plant in a darker green earthenware pot on a wooden stand, a wall-case of medals, and opposite the fireplace a big pastel of a youth in private's uniform; amateurish but eye-catching. The seats seemed to be of the adjustable variety: wide armchairs and chaises-longues with straight, sloping backs upheld by crossbars fitting into grooves; all in scratched dark wood, almost as much of it as in an early loom, with faded green slabs of upholstery, tolled out hard and thin by use.

"Meet my wife," said Major Peevers. "She won't get up. Trouble with the muscles."

I bowed. Mrs. Peevers was also dressed entirely in black, though in many different bits and pieces of it. She looked patched up, and likely to fall to pieces if the patches were removed. Nonetheless, she was holding forth as we entered, and had obviously been doing so for some time.

"Please don't let me interrupt," I said.

"Have some food," said the Major.

There was nothing on view but the usual Birmingham pile of dry sandwiches, and some sliced Scribona.

"Thank you, but I mustn't eat too much. We've got the Lord Mayor's reception just ahead."

"You won't get much there," cried the Major. "I advise you to tuck in before you go."

I helped myself to one of the sandwiches.

"Elsie, give Wakefield a fresh cup of tea. He can't listen when he's dried right out."

Mrs. Peevers, in fact, passed me a cup that had been already standing there full. Her arms seemed as weak as her legs, and I had to leap forward and snatch it.

"I've been telling them about Harry," said Mrs. Peevers, regarding me very seriously. "Harry is our son." She indicated the big pastel.

"A good-looking young man," I said, chewing flavourless near-ham. "Got his father's eyes, I see." The tea was duly quite cold.

"For us it's the most beautiful picture in the world," said Mrs. Peevers.

"Who painted it?" I said; merely, of course, because I had to say something.

"It was painted by a dear friend of our son. His name was Jim Tale. They were like brothers: right back in the old days at Erdington, and all the way on."

What lay behind was more or less obvious, but it was Marguerite who put it into words.

"Mrs. Peevers's son was unfortunately missing in the war," she said.

"I am sorry to hear that. Where did it happen?" I became aware that the Major had come up behind me, and was standing silently with a hand on each side of the high, adjustable back of my chair.

"Your wife didn't say Harry was *dead*," replied Mrs. Peevers sharply. "Missing, not dead."

"Yes," I said, "but he must have been missed on some particular occasion. Surely they always tell you that?" As a matter of fact, I was far from certain.

"Not always, it seems," said Mrs. Peevers.

I put down my cup on the floor. The tea was not only cold, but Birmingham-strong. On the instant, the Major darted down and picked it up.

"More tea, Wakefield?"

"No, thank you. It's very welcome, but one cup's enough."

"Really?" said the Major, a little ambiguously. "Then go on, Elsie." He returned to the back of my chair.

"I'd better start again right at the beginning," said Mrs. Peevers, speaking as if the trouble, though now indispensable, could quite easily have been avoided by a little more thought on the part of others.

"I'd be most interested to hear all about it, but I am sure I can pick up from where you've got to. My wife can fill in for me later."

I noticed that the girl Deirdre seemed to be sitting there quite listlessly. No one could say that she appeared to be paying any particular attention, but on the other hand, she wasn't perceptibly doing anything else—thinking, remembering, knitting.

"Well," said Mrs. Peevers, "I suppose you have to go to this reception or whatever it is, so I'll simply carry on. Where had I got to?"

"Harry was just going to his first school," said Marguerite.

"His *first* school? In Erdington? Not the Grammar School?"

"His first school, I *think*," said Marguerite.

"It was Mr. and Mrs. Meatyard's," said Mrs. Peevers. "Perhaps you know it?"

"Unfortunately not," I replied.

"They take all ages of boys, from toddlers to university

leaving, and they have a splendid record, in terms of character-building as well as tuition. There's no one of good class right through the Midlands who doesn't know and respect Hugh and Letty Meatyard."

"Private schools must have a much harder time of it nowadays," I remarked; again because one had to seem interested.

"The Meatyards don't worry about *that*. They know *they'll* win through somehow, even if no one else does."

I did wish, among other things, that the Major would go and sit down. Instead, he went on standing at my back, listening raptly to his wife as if he had never heard any of it before.

"It was there that Harry first met Jim Tate," continued Mrs. Peevers. "Right down among the three- and four-year-olds."

"I suppose there were girls too at that level," I said, continuing to appear alert.

"Not at all. Hugh Meatyard says that boys should be only with boys right from the very start. He lays great stress on it. And Letty Meatyard always agrees. In any case, I can't imagine our Harry looking at a mere girl when he had Jim Tate." In fact, Mrs. Peevers was almost smiling even at the thought of it.

Marguerite looked distinctly irritated, and it was, of course, an odd thing to say, especially nowadays.

"But later," said Marguerite, "Harry went on to a grammar school?" A perhaps odder thing was that whereas before my arrival Mrs. Peevers appeared to have been discoursing fluently, now she was halting and in need of being helped forward. Probably she was accustomed, in Midlands style, to talking seriously only when alone with her husband or with women,

"To the fine new one at Farmer's Bridge," said Mrs. Peevers. "Hugh Meatyard thought he'd be better for a change. Harry had always been a very sensitive child—in his own way, of course. He passed the Entrance with all colours flying," she added proudly.

And so we went on. With Marguerite patiently prompting and leading, though it was obvious to me, who knew her, that she can have been interested in none of it, with the girl Deirdre reclined like a slender gipsy on the wide, slope-backed chair, with even me putting a word in from time to time, we wended our way through the hopes and fears, scholastic and athletic, they had held for Harry, his actual successes and failures, his and their feelings about the different masters, his long expeditions with Jim Tate, who had continued with the Meatyards and therefore could be met only after school hours and in the holidays, the prizes he had won, and those Jim Tate had won. Major Peevers actually left his place to go to a cupboard and bring out a presentation volume in brown and gold.

"Take it in your hands," said Mrs. Peevers.

It was entitled *Early Man in the Western Midlands,* and appeared to be illustrated abundantly with conjectural reconstructions. It had been awarded, as a fanciful bookplate confirmed, for "All Round Excellence". "The Headmaster's special prize," said Mrs. Peevers, "given to the boy of his personal choice." It was by now a little less than pristine. "They ask first what subject the winner would like the book to be about. Harry replied 'Anthropology.'" The word alone seemed to imply what a deep chap Harry already had been.

" 'The proper study of mankind is man,' " said the Major, staring at me.

"A very interesting subject. Did Harry become an anthropologist himself?"

"Certainly not, nothing like that," replied Mrs. Peevers. "It was just a hobby. Hobbies can be very important to a sensitive boy."

"Was painting Jim Tate's hobby?"

"Certainly not. Jim Tate became a proper pukka painter. There is a portrait of Alderman Concannon by Jim Tate in the Municipal Offices. It's not on view to the public, but they might show it you at the reception if you ask them. He was only twenty-two when he did it, but Alderman Concannon had made quite a favourite of him. He was Chairman of the Parks and Gardens at the time."

"We've a school of art here," said the Major, still watching me. "Equal to anything abroad. Much better, some say."

Marguerite surfaced again. "What did Harry do next?"

"When he left school, you mean?"

"Yes, Mrs. Peevers, when he left school."

It was the Major who replied. "He knocked around; got to know the world, you know; became a man."

"I see," said Marguerite.

"Jim Tate gave him all the time he could," added Mrs. Peevers defensively. "They were like David and Jonathan."

"You know how it is, Wakefield," said the Major, beginning to move up and down. "I was in business myself at the time. Sort of. But Harry just didn't want it. I didn't blame him, either. I still don't. The war was the best time in *my* life, and I don't care who hears me say so. The first war, I mean, of course. We were men then, and England was England. I don't care what they say. It was just as well about Harry, too. In 1938 the business popped right off. We'd have all starved if I hadn't been able to wangle us in on the estate. Best job of work I did since the war ended for me. The first war, I mean. A real home for heroes, and I should think so too. They even give us a small allowance, you know, Wakefield, to supplement our pensions. God knows the pension's small enough. The allowance pays for our luxuries."

"I'm glad," I said.

"It paid Harry's fines too," said the Major with a sudden laugh which made his eyes protrude still further. "Kept him out of jug. Except once when he went *too* far. You know what I mean?"

He seemed to expect an answer, but Mrs. Peevers released me. "Harry is a *good* boy," she said. "Harry has never been anything but a *good* boy—in himself, I mean."

"Well, we're very sorry about it all," said Marguerite, saving me in turn.

She even got us out of the room and upstairs "to change", though it was still too soon, and the spare bedroom was both chilly and ill-lit.

"Where's Deirdre been put?" I asked Marguerite, who had plainly been upstairs before.

"I don't know at all," said Marguerite.

Deirdre had, for some reason, not come up with us.

"Anyway, she's not in here."

There was only a double bed, an arrangement which neither of us liked. The bed was made of the same wood slats as the furniture below, and looked far from strong.

"No," said Marguerite.

"Just as well."

Marguerite did not feel like changing into anything much lighter (while I merely changed into something a little darker), and the girl Deirdre, who proved to be awaiting us below, could not change at all because she had nothing to change into. They said, therefore, that they were willing to walk up the road with me and over the top of the hill to the chain garage. Marguerite and I had already got through some waste time trying to read our papers by the bad bedroom light.

In the course of this stroll, Deirdre made her first remark which I found noticeable.

"I feel so sorry for the Peeverses," she said,

"Yes, they do seem to have had a rough passage," said Marguerite, fitting in.

"I should like to help them," said Deirdre, in the nowadays familiar tone of young people about to join the Peace Corps or start an anti-apartheid riot.

"I'm not sure it would be too easy," said Marguerite. "Older people get set in their ways, especially when they have very little money."

"I think I may be able to help," repeated Deirdre, "and I want to."

I was quite surprised by her.

The Lord Mayor's reception was, as I have already implied, dreadfully tedious. The Lord Mayor himself could not think of anything much to say about the importance of the occasion and it was embarrassingly plain that the people nominated to speak for Business Art were quite inexperienced in addressing civic dignitaries. Nor were the subsequent less formal sociabilities more successful: the two contingents present seemed totally unable to achieve intercourse. The only exception that I saw was a professor-like man who succeeded in driving the Lord Mayor himself into a corner and there holding him down for perhaps as much as ten minutes, after which the Beadle, or whatever the functionary is called, came to remind the Lord Mayor that he had two more receptions that night. Marguerite and I rather obviously belonged to neither contingent, so could not even join one of the alternative groups which were discussing respectively the plan for a new swimming stadium and the difficulty artists experience in holding their clients to agreed payments. There remained the magnificent civic architecture of Birmingham, with Hansom's splendid Town Hall just outside the windows, and floodlit: it was simply, as so often, the people who were the trouble.

Neptuna dug us out and explained that for a group there was to be a party afterwards at the Queen's. She thought that we could probably be fitted in, and indeed pressed us to come, but she said that Deirdre couldn't be asked, as two more would have to be the limit. No doubt the society's funds were involved, but I felt that Neptuna was annoyed because Deirdre's young man, in whom she was probably more interested than in Deirdre, had gone back to London. The question arose, of course, of getting Deirdre back to No. 47.

"There are plenty of taxis," said Neptuna.

"That really wouldn't be fair," said Marguerite, She meant that Deirdre almost certainly lacked the money, but I doubt whether Marguerite really wanted to go to the party herself.

"She must learn to look after herself," said Neptuna.

This time it was for me to rescue Marguerite. "It's quite a long way and rather a rough area," I said.

"I think we should take Deirdre back if you can spare your car until tomorrow morning,"

"Take her back then, and afterwards come on to the Queen's."

"Could we possibly leave that open and see how things go? We'd love to come, if we can."

"It's in what they call the Guy of Warwick Room. Do come. Laurie's promised to do his strip-tease."

"Do you want to go to the party?" asked Marguerite, as we looked for Deirdre, who at the reception had been invisible as well as silent.

"Not if you don't," I replied.

Most of the people at the reception had gone somewhere else before we found Deirdre. We really had quite a search, with

Neptuna irrupting at intervals as she accumulated her party, and
bidding us give it up and come on.

Deirdre proved to be sitting by herself on the parapet of the
big Chamberlain Fountain in the square outside. She had apparently spent most of the time there, even missing the speeches.
The Birmingham youths were jeering at her when we found
her, but, for some reason, they remained on the other side of the
fountain, and she did not seem to have come to any harm.

"Aren't you cold?" asked Marguerite.

Deirdre just shook her head.

"Would you like to go now?" I asked.

Deirdre nodded: not, I thought, with emphasis, or even with
much interest. We walked off to the huge municipal car park on
the site of the former canal basin. The night appeared to be cold
enough to make Neptuna's car difficult to start, but Birmingham
stands high, and is often windy.

Just as we neared No. 47, there was an incident which, though
apparently irrelevant, seemed to upset Marguerite at the time
very much.

"Look out," she cried after we had all been silent for a longish
spell.

The estate, as will be remembered, had no street lighting, and
most, possibly all, of the houses were in darkness as well, so that
it took Marguerite's vision, much better than mine, to see what
was really no more than a shapeless heap on our side of the road.
The object must have been a little blacker than the night, or even
Marguerite could not have seen it.

I swerved out to the right much too impulsively, though fortunately it was a road with little traffic. I even stopped dead, in
the middle of the road, with the black heap over on our left. The
ancient engine stopped as we did: a habit it had. I realized that I
was probably not in the middle of the road, but far over on the
right of it.

"Whatever is it?" asked Marguerite. There was a cold thread
of fear in her voice, which made her sound like someone else. It
quite frightened me. I thought that she might have seen or gathered more than I had. Deirdre, of course, was quiet and dark in
the cavernous back of the car.

We all got out through the two doors on the offside of the car; almost on to the right-hand pavement. The pavement was composed of the same cracked slabs as the pathways up to the houses; and the road itself of naked, dirty concrete.

"It's a horse," cried Marguerite, "a huge black horse."

We stood around looking at it. It spread from almost the centre of the road to the gutter, and overlapped on to the other pavement. Some little time passed.

"I'll get Neptuna's torch out of the car," I said.

"No, don't." It was Deirdre.

Marguerite spoke. "But the horse might still be alive. We might be able to do something."

"The horse is dead." Deirdre sounded very strung up, but one felt she was strung up precisely because somehow she knew the truth of what she had said.

"I must say I think so too," said Marguerite.

"If there's nothing to be done, we'd better go on," I said.

"Yes," said Deirdre. "Let's go."

But she didn't come at once. As she spoke, Marguerite and I went round to the other side of the car and climbed back into the front seat, quite a business for Marguerite, who had to dodge round the wheel and the levers.

"Where's Deirdre?" Marguerite asked, when we were settled.

There was a further quite definite passage of time as we sat there in the dark, then Deirdre appeared and got into the back of the car without a word. I was slightly relieved: it had occurred to me that she might have lost her head in some way, or even fainted.

The engine re-started at once, which it by no means always did; and we completed the short remainder of the journey. Another thing about which I felt slightly relieved was that we appeared not to have awakened the neighbours: a colloquy about the horse in Black Country dialect would have been formidable indeed. As a matter of fact, No. 47 was only a few hundred yards down the same road. The estate descended from the Alum Rock region, and then rose again to the main road just beyond the ridge, where the garages were.

Marguerite had seemed so shaken, and Deirdre also, that I

thought I had better take them inside before disposing of the car.
The unpleasant episode of the horse had, among other things,
possibly confirmed the Major's suggestion of a threat to Neptuna's machine: and the idea of Marguerite and me going to the
party at the Queen's seemed more unlikely than ever.

Marguerite however, would not hear of it. "We're perfectly all
right now," she said. "If you once come in, you'll never get out
again, and the garage will shut."

So I wasn't there to hear the matter of the horse raised in its
first freshness, with the Peeverses. When I returned from the
garage, where a special late arrival charge had been levied upon
me, although it was only a little after ten, what I found was Marguerite and Deirdre seated on either side of Mrs. Peevers, who
was showing them an album of snapshots, while the Major sat
opposite and watched their reactions.

"I don't know whether my wife has told you," I said, "but there
seems to be a dead horse in the road."

"Probably a stray," said the Major. "We were just looking at a
few photographs."

"Shouldn't something be done about it?"

"What?"

"We might telephone the police."

"The nearest telephone is up the hill, near where you've left
the car. We don't need a telephone ourselves."

Naturally, I gave it up.

"I'll make some more tea," said the Major. "We've got some
special Darjeeling from Brooke Bond."

"Have you any lump sugar?" asked Deirdre. It was a simple
enough question, but, coming from Deirdre, unexpected.

"Why, certainly we have, Deirdre," replied Mrs. Peevers, using
a Christian name for the first time in my hearing. "It's still done
up in a parcel, but Gregory shall open it, if you would like it very
much." It was true that at tea-time there had been only a little
granulated.

"If you can give me some lump sugar," said Deirdre, "I will
try to bring Harry back. But I shall need quite a lot; and everyone
must join in. I learnt how to do it when I was working at the hospital. Of course I can't promise anything."

"My boy Harry is not something to make game of," said Mrs. Peevers.

"No, indeed," confirmed the Major, blowing hard.

"It's not a game. More like an experiment. It's called Absent Friends. We often did it at the hospital. It helped to pass the evenings. We got lots of people back."

"Deirdre," said Marguerite, "you mustn't upset Mrs. Peevers."

"I'm not in the least upset," said Mrs. Peevers sharply. "I think it is a very nice thought of Deirdre's. If she learnt about it at the hospital, it's sure to be all right, and we must all do it."

"I'll go and get the sugar," said the Major, rather astonishingly, and stumped off.

"We'd do *anything* to bring Harry back," announced Mrs. Peevers, with defiance.

"How far away were the people you brought back to the hospital?" I asked Deirdre.

"All kinds of distances."

"Do you mean they were sick people?" asked Marguerite.

"Not all of them."

"Isn't this sorcery?" persisted Marguerite. "Like the witch of Endor?"

We could hear the Major tearing at the packing in the back regions.

"Not quite. Harry's not *dead*. Is he, Mrs. Peevers?" It was an acute rejoinder, in its way.

"Of course Harry's not dead. Missing, not dead."

"You don't understand, Mrs. Wakefield." The Major had returned with the sugar. "When we say that Harry's missing, we mean that he's missing. Harry had his reasons for being missing, if you follow me."

"I see," said Marguerite. "But this still seems to me like witchcraft. If we're really expected to take it seriously, that is."

I noticed, and Marguerite must have noticed too, that a considerable flush of rage passed over Deirdre's somewhat nondescript face. It came and went in a moment, but, while it was there, it was murderous.

"You can call it what you like, Mrs. Wakefield," was all she said, and quite quietly. "Or me. The question is simply do we want to help Major and Mrs. Peevers, or don't we?"

"I very much hope you will," said the Major breezily. "What do I do with the sugar? Do we all suck it?"

"We really want a bigger table," said Deirdre.

"We could go in the dining-room if you'll all give me a hand with Mrs. Peevers."

"No, the picture of Harry will help to bring him back. We should work in the same room with it. The coffee-table will do if we sit close together."

In the end, and after moving almost every piece of furniture in the room except Mrs. Peevers's chair, we disposed the coffee-table in such a way that Mrs. Peevers required only to be turned slightly on her own axis, and was seated between her husband on her left and Marguerite on her right. Deirdre, placed beneath Harry's portrait, came next to the Major, with me on her other hand. The big blue bag of sugar stood in the middle. We were assuredly very close to one another, the table being small and Mrs. Peevers large.

"You do really need all of us?" asked Marguerite.

"Even sceptics, if we can't do any better," replied Deirdre, and I was almost certain that she pressed my knee slightly. "There are not really enough of us, as it is. If Harry is a long way away, we may not make enough power."

"How do you make power, dear?" asked Mrs. Peevers.

"There are lots of different ways of making power, Mrs. Peevers, some of them not polite, but tonight we are going to make it out of sugar." Deirdre did seem quite changed.

"That's right," said the Major. "Sugar's pure energy. The purest there is. We used to suck lumps of it when we went over the top." He drew several lumps from the bag and put them in his mouth. "God, it takes you back."

"What do we do now?" asked Marguerite.

"Just what I tell you," replied Deirdre. "We first make what is called the General Disposition. The General Disposition we're going to make tonight is called The Straits. The men and the women do different things. The women make the ocean and the men make the ship."

"Bless my soul," said the Major. "I forgot about the tea. Would you all like some?"

"There must be nothing on the table but the sugar."

"Then we'll have some tea later."

"The women take thirty lumps of sugar each, and set them out in two parallel straight lines, a little way apart but not too much, with three lumps on each side curving outwards at the end nearest you."

"And what do the men do?" asked the Major, his eyes popping.

"The men take thirty-one lumps of sugar each, and they lay out two columns, close together, with the odd lump coming first, also at the end nearest you; the sharp prow of the ship."

Inevitably, she had to say most of it again, but all of us started doing it.

"It would be so much simpler if you would *show* us, dear," said Mrs. Peevers, when each of us had counted out the appropriate quota. "Instead of just describing."

"I'm not allowed to show you," said Deirdre. "It's forbidden. You have to work it out for yourselves from what I have told you. I do something quite different."

"What do you do?" asked the Major.

"I have to work on my own. I draw the power from what you are doing."

In the end, we had laid out the two longboats and the two channels. Owing to the smallness of the table, they had become rather jumbled up,

"Not bad," said Deirdre, who had done nothing. "But Mrs. Peevers's lines are too far apart, and Mr. Wakefield's ship is too far from its course."

We tried to adjust.

"Now," said Deirdre, "listen carefully. What you have to do is this. The man steers his ship through the straits. He does it by moving two lumps of sugar at a time from the bottom end of the ship, up to the top end, just under the prow. Each time he does it, he pushes the prow that much forward. In this way he enters the straits at the bottom end, goes through to the top, and then comes out the other side. At the same time the woman moves one side of the strait over to the other, one lump of sugar at a time, taken from each side alternately. She begins by moving the end lump from the left-hand curve to the top of the right-hand column, and sets about making a similar curve there. Then the end lump from the right-hand curve goes to the top of the left-hand column and does the same thing. When the woman has completely inter-changed the two sides, and moved the two curves to the other end, so that the ship comes out between them, the work is done. I shall explain it all over again in a moment, but there are two more things."

"I shall *never* remember," squeaked Mrs. Peevers.

"You'll find it easier than you think when you come to do it. But the first thing is this. You all take it in turns to move, and every time you move a lump of sugar, every single time, you must say 'Harry, come down'; each one of you, every time. If one of you misses even once, Harry can't come. So it's very important. You see, the General Disposition can be used for other things than bringing people back, and you wouldn't want one of them to happen."

It suddenly struck me that in just such soothing but steely accents must Deirdre have talked at the hospital.

"What's the second thing?" I asked.

This time I was absolutely certain about the pressure on my knee. In fact, I could feel it all up my leg.

"The second thing—and you mustn't let this frighten you, Mrs. Peevers—is that you have to do it all in the dark; or rather by special light only, which you will find rather faint. I've got this special light with me in my handbag, but I mustn't tell you any-thing about it."

Just so: doctors, surgeons, nurses, cleaners, and all the legion of supplementary easers in and out; so spake they, all minutely and fractionally charged with power of life and death.

And just as they do, so Deirdre explained again.

"Every time the man moves two lumps of sugar, and every time the woman moves one lump, he or she says 'Harry, come down'. Speaking right out boldly. Do you understand, Mrs. Wakefield?"

"I understand perfectly," said Marguerite. "If someone fails, even once, anything may happen." No doubt she was being sar-castic, but she sounded quite peaceful.

"That's how it is," said Deirdre. "And the point is that I cannot remind you when the time comes. So don't forget. Because we can't just stop, either. Now give me the sugar bag. It has to stand in front of me, and now I'll explain what *I* do."

"What do *you* do?" asked the Major.

"Every time one of you moves, I take a new lump out of the bag."

"Suppose we hadn't had all this sugar?" I asked.

"Then we'd have had that much less power."

"And suppose there'd been more sugar?"

"That wouldn't have mattered. You can't make more than a certain amount of power without more people. It's the people who make the power, not the sugar."

"Like the Romans looking into the entrails of animals to see the future."

"What've animals got to do with it?" asked Mrs. Peevers.

"Simply that it was something in the soothsayers which did the foretelling. The animal's inside was merely an instrument, like a crystal, or like tea-leaves."

"A medium, in fact," said Marguerite.

"Those old soothsayers were a lot of cock and bull," said the Major. "At least for the most part."

"Animals are quite serious," said Deirdre. "Hospitals use them the whole time."

"What do you do with *your* lumps of sugar," I asked.

"I pile them up. They draw in the power from the rest of you, or they should. At the end, I do something to them, which I can't tell you about. Then we just wait. My sugar ought to go into a silk bag, but I don't expect you've got one, Mrs. Peevers."

"A silk bag. I don't think I have, Deirdre."

"An unused stocking will do. Have you got that, Mrs. Peevers, because I know I haven't? Not here."

"I don't think I've got that either, not just now."

"An unused stocking *I* can contribute," put in Marguerite neatly. "Shall I get it now?"

"It'll do quite well at the end, Mrs. Wakefield. Shall we start, then? Major Peevers, will you make it dark?"

During the fuss caused by the Major's stumbling return through the murk, Deirdre produced her "special light". Suddenly it was on the table in the midst of us, glowing pale blue.

"What *is* that?" asked Marguerite through the murk.

"Ask no questions and you'll be told no lies," replied Deirdre, pressing against my leg again. "Now: through the straits. You start, Major Peevers. Harry's your son."

And away we all went: everyone word and motion perfect, as far as I could tell. It was the first time I had ever attended such a session in my whole life, and I must acknowledge there was soon a certain excitement. I should be surprised if all of us did not feel it. Marguerite actually admitted to it later. At first, the incantations of "Harry, come down" sounded self-conscious and half-hearted, but they quickly became almost agitating. At least that was my experience. One really *wanted* to say it. One could hardly wait for one's turn. It was apparent, too, that the Peeverses particularly were becoming more and more emotional in their calling; which, in the near darkness, probably infected Marguerite and me. The faint blue glow; the simple, ordered movements, however ridiculous; the crying and shouting; the unaccustomed sensation of involvement, even though only with Marguerite and the two elderly Peeverses: all built up to an atmosphere which made me feel pleasantly irresponsible, much as if under the influence, I thought, of some light drug.

Deirdre kept putting her free hand on my thigh, and even about that there was something odd. At first, naturally, I found it embarrassing and squalid, as most people, I imagine, usually do find such things. It had certainly never occurred to me that there was anything attractive about Deirdre as an individual, and this was hardly the way to make me feel otherwise. But before the session ended, there was a moment, more than just one moment, when I felt that Deirdre was totally and wonderfully different from what I had supposed. It was as if I saw into, or had even momentarily entered into, her soul. I also recalled that a man had gone back alone by railway to London solely because he had not been allowed to share a room with her. For a spell, then, Deirdre's pawings and pressings, Deirdre herself, seemed transfigured. It was soon over, needless to say, and I never felt anything like it again; but then the session itself was soon over—far *too* soon, as I was surprised to find my self thinking.

"It is for the women to say when the work is done," cried out Deirdre, speaking for the first time since the Major had switched off the light.

"I have finished what you said," replied Marguerite. "Is that all there is?"

"And the ship has come out the other side?" Deirdre was stacking her own heap of sugar with both hands.

"Pretty well. Anyhow, I've played my part."

"Then you must stop," said Deirdre. "What about you, Mrs. Peevers?"

There was no answer.

"Come on, old girl," said the Major. "What about it?"

"I've finished too," said Mrs. Peevers in a very low voice.

"Speak up," said the Major.

"And the ship has come out the other side?"

Again Mrs. Peevers did not speak.

"You bet it has," said the Major, after a tiny pause.

"Everyone scramble the sugar," cried Deirdre. "All of it. Carefully."

We conscientiously scrambled. Deirdre, I am sure, watched to see that we did it properly.

"Major Peevers," said Deirdre in her hospital voice, "will you please turn on the light?"

The Major's left leg had gone to sleep, but he managed it. There we all were: somehow quite different people. Mrs. Peevers was as red and strangled as if she had been crying. The Major was bending and straightening his leg. Marguerite's hair, always conspicuously neat, was wispy and straggly. I discovered, to my humiliation, that I was shaking all over, even shuddering. I could not stop it for several minutes at least, though I tried hard. Deirdre just sat there, looking calmer than any of us, with her two hands flat on her own heap of sugar.

"Mrs. Wakefield," she said. "Could you bring me that unused stocking? It really is unused?"

"Quite unused," said Marguerite, putting her hand to her hair. "I'll get it." She seemed glad to go.

"There is one more thing to be done," said Deirdre, "but I do it in private."

"I'll get the tea," said the Major, walking like a war hero of old. "I'm sure we'd all like some."

"That's very good of you," I replied.

"Sorry I can't offer you something stronger, Wakefield."

"Don't think of it."

Mrs. Peevers had become even redder. The Major seemed not to notice it, for he departed and began to clatter.

Immediately he had gone, Mrs. Peevers stood up. It was the first time we had seen her on her feet.

"Well?" she asked in the low, suppressed voice in which she had spoken before. "Where's Harry?"

"It doesn't work as quickly as *that*, Mrs. Peevers. We found at the hospital that it often took days, weeks sometimes. Besides, I haven't finished yet, as I told you."

"It's all a fraud," said Mrs. Peevers in her low voice, and taking two steps towards Deirdre. "A tale."

Deirdre moved not at all.

"Oh no, not necessarily," said Marguerite, returned with a dark stocking in her hand and her hair instantaneously restored. "We must give it more of a chance than that, I am sure."

"Thank you, Mrs. Wakefield," said Deirdre. "For the stocking, I mean."

"I suppose I don't get it back? I was going to wear it at the dance tomorrow night."

How far away all that seemed!

"Yes, you can have it back," said Deirdre. "I'll wash it for you."

"Will that be necessary? Of course we don't know what you're going to do with it."

"I think you'd prefer it," said Deirdre. She was putting her heap of sugar into the stocking, holding it at the more coarsely woven top and letting each lump drop to the pendant toe.

"You two might help with putting your own sugar back into the bag. Unless Mrs. Peevers would rather you didn't put it back?"

Marguerite and I looked at Mrs. Peevers.

She walked across to the dry, yellow plant in the corner of the room, lifted up the dark green earthenware pot, which must really have been quite heavy, and began to shake and agitate it. Dry, yellow leaves fell in a shower to the carpet.

"I'd like the sugar thrown away. All of it, including what's still in the bag."

"Oh, surely not, Mrs. Peevers," said Marguerite. "No harm's been done."

"I should say not," shouted the Major, off. "I overheard that one. You people should know that it's jolly well all the sugar we've got. All the real sugar, I mean. The old woman's not herself." He reappeared, much agitated.

"Elsie," bawled the Major. "You'll fall."

Mrs. Peevers stopped shaking the plant, and put it back on its stand. "I don't think so, Gregory. I'm quite firm."

"Excuse me," said Deirdre, disappearing with Marguerite's stocking.

"My wife hasn't walked without support for three and a half years," explained the Major,

Mrs. Peevers strode back, quite steadily, to her seat. "Well, where's the tea, Gregory?" She was speaking more normally again.

The Major brought it, and in a moment we were all lapping it up.

"Not *that* sugar," said Mrs. Peevers. "I said so. Throw it away."

"She must think we've come into money," said the Major. But he departed and returned with the dreary granulated.

Not long after, Deirdre came back, "I'll let you have your stocking in the morning. It'll be almost as good as new."

"Thank you very much," said Marguerite.

Soon it was the end of the evening, and we went to bed.

"What do you make of all that?" I asked Marguerite as she took off her dress.

"It certainly gave Deirdre a chance to come out of her shell."

"Odd thing about Mrs. Peevers's legs."

"Psychosomatic. "

"So they always say. But, nonetheless, it happened, it worked."

"What worked?"

"Deirdre's miracle. Perhaps Harry will come back in the same way?"

"I shouldn't think so. It's obvious that Harry knows when he's well off. Anyway, would *you* come back?"

She was seated in her underclothes, manicuring her toes in the bad light.

"Perhaps little Deirdre leaves one no choice."

That, needless to say, is more or less how people talk in middle married life. Not unintelligent, simply *familiar*. Not hostile; but not loving. With full mutual understanding; but little mutual interest. Never radical, or perhaps always radical. Not really bad at all; but not at all good. Not antagonistic, except for tiny runs of frustration; merely hopeless. There was shapely Marguerite sitting there in her pretty pants, and I could not even weep.

"Deirdre," said Marguerite, "is simply the medium. Like the sugar."

"What do you suppose she did to the sugar? The sugar she took away, I mean."

"I'll ask her."

"Not that it really matters."

Marguerite looked up from her toes and smiled. "It would be amusing to know," she said.

I got into bed first, and when Marguerite ultimately joined me, I realized that it was quite late, especially for such a household as the Peeverses. We fell untidily asleep.

During the night, I was awakened by Marguerite hitting at me.

"Sorry to wake you up," she said very quietly, "but there's a funny noise." Everything that had occurred that evening came back to me, as happens at such times. But I could hear no particular noise.

"It sounded just like someone on the roof," said Marguerite. "Above our heads."

I now realized that the first grey light was filtering through the protective lace curtains.

"I can't hear anything."

"Listen a little longer. I heard it several times."

We waited.

"I'm sorry," said Marguerite, "to have woken you up. I was frightened."

"That's all right," I said. "I'll get up and have a look."

I suppose I intended it simply as a gesture of willingness to take action on her behalf. It was hard to imagine what anyone could possibly expect to see. But as soon as I parted the lace curtains on the creepy autumn dawn, there *was* something to see; of a kind.

The window looked on to the depressing concrete road, with its line of identical semi-detacheds on the other side, dark-red by nature, but black in the early light. Up the road to the left was a big vehicle, grey as the dawn, and bearing on its side the words BIRMINGHAM CORPORATION DISPOSALS and a coat of arms; and on to it a group of men, black shadows like the houses, were elevating the great black horse.

"They're taking away the dead horse," I cried. "Come and look."

"Must I?"

"Yes, you should."

Marguerite came and stood beside me in her nightdress.

"That's a nice thing to see at four o'clock in the morning, or whatever it is," she said.

"It explains the noises you heard."

"I don't think so. The noise I heard was quite different, and much nearer. It sounded like someone in the house, or, as I said, on it."

"It must have been something to do with the horse. It's only logical. You think you hear noises, and then something as odd as this proves to be going on. It's obvious that there's a connection."

"If you say so," said Marguerite. "Anyway, I'm going back to bed."

I stayed to look a little longer at the silent heavings and lurchings up the road. It seemed likely, I thought, that some kind of crane would have helped. But in the end the cold became impossible, and I too returned to bed.

There had still been no odd noises that were audible to me. I found Marguerite lying on her front, with her face sunk hard into the big pillow with its wide edge of trimming.

"I don't suppose there'll be anything more," I said rather vaguely, but trying to reassure her.

She made no reply, but went on lying there. I pulled up the bedclothes over her back, and over myself too.

"It was quite a frightening evening in its way," I went on, putting on display the obvious explanation.

She still made no move. It struck me that very possibly there had never been any noises, not serious noises anyway, so to speak, and that Marguerite had really wanted something quite different. Possibly she was upset by the evening, as she had been at least momentarily when we first saw the horse.

If so, it was difficult, as the trouble with me was Deirdre, and what she and I had been doing together during a brief period earlier; and this despite the fact that I did not care in the least about Deirdre, not in any way, as I knew perfectly well. Of course one commonly encounters such fleeting paradoxes in the difficult matter of sex.

Maybe, however, I was still wrong about Marguerite. The odd evening could cause later disturbances of more than one kind. I tried again to rally her, but the warmth of the bed crept back over me, and I fell compulsively back into sleep. I did not even consciously hear the Disposals vehicle drive away.

"Clean as a baby's bottom," said Deirdre the next morning, half throwing the dark stocking back at Marguerite. She was wearing the same dull dress. I thought that Marguerite was very tolerant of her continuous near-rudeness.

The second day of the so-called conference was even flatter than the first. After another tiresome lunch, I went so far as to suggest to Marguerite that we cut the afternoon session and go to Dudley Zoo instead. She replied that she thought we had better not, meaning socially, but I divined from her look that the horse was in her mind, and that I had tactlessly proposed the very least suitable thing. I suppose, indeed, that it was the horse which had been on my mind too, and had unconsciously led to my suggestion, though all I had remembered had been visits to Dudley with my uncle and cousins when a child. The matter was settled by Neptuna coming up and strongly confirming that we had better not. She actually asked us, in so many words, not to abandon the conference. "I know it's awful, but I very much hope you'll see me through." She seemed genuinely dependent on us in some way. Perhaps we really were more to be depended upon than the

professional rivals who otherwise surrounded her, largely commercial artists at that. And, of course, we were her guests.

"We hope to rig something up for this afternoon, as Lord
Boothroyd apparently can't come."

It seemed incredible that any human enterprise could be run
quite like that, for so long, and by university graduates, as many
of these people were, but in fact, of course, it is quite common,
and I daresay the casualness, which Marguerite and I found so
irritating, really serves a useful purpose of some kind, possibly
quite as useful as any other kind of administrative attitude.

So we endured, we remained, we actually went to the conference dance, which was not even to be dressed up for, though
Marguerite wore her famous unused stockings. We slapped
and hopped around as best we could. We ate *cipolate,* drank
Sauternes and gin, sucked at ice-cream bricks. Deirdre seemed
to have returned to her original quiet unobtrusiveness, but she
did come back with us to the dance, still in the same dress. I must
say also that I was very tired of being unable to leave Neptuna's
car outside the house, even while we changed. No real reason for
this ever emerged, except that, as Marguerite pointed out, the
car was Neptuna's. That constant walking up or down the hill
seemed an additionally unreasonable nuisance, to say nothing
of the increasing familiarity at the chain garage, but old Peevers
remained adamant, and Marguerite was pursuing a determined
policy of fitting in with everyone.

There I was doing it for the last time but one, after we had
returned from the dance; and there were Marguerite and Deirdre
going inside to first pull on the Major's tea. It was remarkably
cold too, as I descended the hill: with frost very obviously closing in, and also the beginnings of that freezing haze which is a
Birmingham speciality, and which can chill one right through
almost before one is aware that it is there. I wished I had included
an overcoat in my luggage, even a heavy one. As usual, there was
no one about and no lights in the houses: Peevers had explained
to me that most of the people liked to save the money. The cold
Birmingham mist seems always to carry sounds rather than to
muffle them, improbable sounds too sometimes; so that now I
clearly heard the big clock of the distant Town Hall strike mid-

night. The grimy road and pavement stood out as almost white, and it was just as well. There were distant stars, but no moon; and the faster I walked, the colder I grew. I must say I looked forward to the tea.

But that night there was no tea.

The atmosphere inside was little warmer than outside. Marguerite and the two Peeverses were just standing about waiting for me.

"Ah, there you are, Wakefield. I gather you didn't enjoy the dance. Don't blame you, either. I've just been explaining to Mrs. Wakefield that I've grown too old to take two late nights running. So do you mind if we all go to bed? Sorry I can't offer you something strong."

"Bed would be just the thing."

"You know the way."

They bade us firm good nights and up we went.

"She's still walking," I said to Marguerite.

"So it seems."

"You'd think they'd show more gratitude."

"Gratitude's difficult. It would probably send her off again. Look at us. Are we grateful to Neptuna?"

It was literally cold in the house, as well as figuratively. I could almost hear my teeth chattering.

"What happened to Deirdre?"

"She took the hint when we came in and disappeared. Why?"

"I was just thinking of Mrs. Peevers's legs. You know, I'm going to bed in my dressing-gown."

"There are plenty of blankets." Marguerite was completely refined at almost all times. It was second nature to her, if not first.

"All right, then I won't."

"Please yourself; of course. It's a pity there's no hot-water bottle."

"Or even a heater of some kind."

"Or thicker roof and walls."

"I should say they *are* quite thick. For a house of this type, of course."

Marguerite was climbing into bed, having left several things undone that she usually did. She began attending to her hair, which more often came at an earlier stage. She wore her hair tighter at night than by day, so that it should not lose its daytime shape. This motive was absolutely reasonable, and one had only to look at Marguerite to see it, but I should have found her tight night hair positively attractive, if only her motive for making it tight had been entirely different. Such is the familiar complexity of sex-appeal. "The roof didn't sound very thick last night," said Marguerite.

"I'm sure that what you heard was something to do with the horse," I replied, shivering into my pyjama legs. "It stands to reason."

"You might hear it yourself tonight if you will keep awake and listen."

"I'm not very likely to do that if I can help it."

"Quite right," said Marguerite, making her hair tighter and tighter. "It's a terrifying sound. Probably the most awful sound I ever heard. Well, since I was a child."

Cold though I was, I stopped and looked at her. "As bad as *that*?"

"Quite as bad. I kept trying to tell you."

"I'm sorry. I didn't realize."

I wanted to comfort her, as I had failed to do the night before. I went to her and put my arm round her shoulders. But it was little good. It is always extraordinarily difficult to be affectionate in that kind of way with a person to whom one is bound for life; and now I was both too late and too frozen, she too preoccupied with her hair.

"Come to bed," she said, neutrally but nicely. "I shall be finished in a few minutes."

"I'll wait until I can put out the light," I said; the only switch being, of course, by the door.

"Sorry, I'll be as quick as I can."

"Perhaps it was the cold coming on that made the noises. Timbers contracting, brickwork settling, and all that."

She said nothing.

"Besides there's the empty house next door. Noises might easily come from there."

"Yes," said Marguerite. "People could wait there—hide there —until it was night."

"That's absurd," I said. "Going *too* far."

"It happens everywhere nowadays. Harry, for example, might have waited in there for years without anyone knowing whom he didn't want to know."

"But why should he hide himself away from his own parents?"

"Why does anybody?"

"Marguerite," I said, "this is what is called letting your imagination run away with you."

She simply replied "Of course it is," and I didn't at all know what to make of it.

Then she said "I'm finished now." Her head was as trim as a newly opened horse-chestnut. I killed the dim light and joined her.

I lay there sleepless. It was the cold. It was the tension of middle marriage. But it was also fear. I slept from time to time, and one usually much exaggerates the duration of unwanted wakefulness, but certainly I had long enough to work myself into a horrible state of nerves. My hearing grew sharper and sharper, until every creak of the furniture made me jump. Every time I woke after dozing off I felt a shock of terror run quite slowly through my whole body, almost making me sick; and sometimes a second shock, as I confirmed to myself that indeed I was not dreaming. Sensibly, there was no sufficient reason for such alarm: I suppose it was the familiar stress of my relationship with Marguerite enhanced by something in or about the house and by what had happened there.

Anyhow, when I first heard the scratchings and slippings of someone trying to climb the wall outside, I was absolutely wide awake. Oddly enough, Marguerite was snoozing rather breathily. The sounds were far from loud, because we had not opened the bedroom window, but I had no doubt of what they implied. Someone was down there in the garden (if one could call it a garden) and coming up, or trying to come up.

And again, it was faint dawn; the faintest and earliest Birmingham dawn, hardly discernible at all, especially through the lace. Snatch and scramble; rise, fall, and try again: so it went, against the dark brickwork and, as it sounded, below our own window.

Marguerite was now breathing unevenly, nearly inaudible for two or three minutes, and then almost sobbing and gurgling. There was, in fact, every evidence that her sleep was very shallow and that she would wake at any moment. I stopped myself from positively rousing her. I was not sure whether or not I wanted her awake.

So I was alone when I heard the climber at long last reach the sill; faintly discolour the faint dawn through the lace curtains; stand for a moment on the ledge, no doubt recapturing his breath and recouping his strength; then go on up.

I was alone when he reached the roof and began to move about up there, stumbling and crawling from point to point. He seemed to lumber around for at least ten or fifteen minutes, sometimes noisier as he passed immediately overhead, sometimes quieter as he moved over to other areas, but always audible, though sometimes so indistinctly as to be confusable with other sounds of the night. Once I even thought I heard him talking.

It went on and on, coming and going, so that in the end I woke Marguerite as gently as I could, then put my hand on her mouth.

"We're going," I said. "Now. When I put on the light, dress quickly, while I do the same, and we'll get out."

Immediately there was a light, the noises seemed to stop entirely. I am not sure that Marguerite heard them at all this second morning. She always said she didn't.

She did what I said without a word. We were always at our joint best when in a tight spot. She was packed and ready to dash even before I was.

"Do you think we should leave a note?" she asked, quite calmly.

"No," I replied. "We'll write to them when we get home."

"What about the car?"

"It's an all-night garage."

So we crept down the narrow staircase, leaving our bedroom light on.

And at once in the room below we saw that the light was on also.

It was Deirdre; standing there alone, dressed and packed, in so far as one could apply the words.

"I want to go too. Will you please take me?"

I looked at Marguerite, but she said nothing.

"Come on, then."

We turned out the light in the room with the faded green paper and the dropping yellow plant, and we quietly shut the front door. We set off up the cracked, concrete road in the first light of morning; shivering and silent.

It was impossible to speak of anything but practicalities. I suggested that we drive Neptuna's car to London, as we had all had enough of Birmingham, and that I try to persuade one of Neptuna's husbands to drive it back and collect her. None of the husbands had regular work, and it would be easily possible for the car to be back in Birmingham once more by mid-day. This plan was briefly accepted, and we fell silent again. I was required, however, to pay a still larger special charge for taking the car from the chain garage at that peculiar and suspect hour. A policeman who was gossiping there even asked to see my licence.

It was in the absurd context of a coffee on the motorway that some of our real thoughts found expression, and it was Marguerite who put forth certain of the words.

"At No. 47," she began to Deirdre. "The night before last. What was that light you used! I wondered very much. Could you tell us? Now that it's all over."

"It was a horse's eye," said Deirdre, looking at the floor and away from the transport roughs who were staring at her. "I thought you knew."

"I assure you I never thought of it," said Marguerite. "And what did you do to the sugar?"

"That's my business."

"And the horse? How did it come to be there at all? So conveniently, I mean?"

"I expect it just felt tired and died, Mrs. Wakefield," said Deirdre, distinctly in her former manner. Some tag came to me about opportunities varying widely in their incidence, but the important thing being the capacity to seize them, when offered.

"I expect so," I said. "But tell us something else. What made *you* want to leave this morning? Surely everything was going to plan from your point of view?"

Deirdre looked at the floor again. "There were two of them," she said. "Two of them came back. Didn't you hear them talking? Harry brought someone back with him. I thought it might be that Jim Tate."

"Well?" I said. "Harry's mother told us they were inseparable. You might almost expect them to be still together."

"She told *me* that Jim Tate was killed in the war. Harry wasn't, but Jim Tate was."

Deirdre had never at any time seemed to have much real imagination (at least at any normal time), and even now she appeared more embarrassed and uneasy than scared or upset. But Marguerite, who hitherto had been so good, had turned dangerously white. I tried to get her a brandy at the counter, but, of course, it was illegal. They suggested instead some chemical from the first-aid box, and I had difficulty in warding off a trained volunteer.

"I'm sorry to have upset Mrs. Wakefield," said Deirdre, when I returned. "You did ask me."

"There is no evidence at all that it was Jim Tate," I said.

"Not what you'd call evidence," said Deirdre. "But I don't take chances on funny business. I just don't like it, if you'll excuse me. I only wanted to help those poor Peeverses."

"If there were two of them, something must have gone wrong, according to your own account. We only called for Harry."

"If something went wrong, it wasn't my fault."

It would have been difficult to miss the implication that it was ours; but it is never any use arguing with young people when they are set to do good.

All went well about returning the car to Birmingham.

I reminded Marguerite to write and thank the Peeverses, and she did so almost at once. Naturally, we had not expected any reply, but we received one. Mrs. Peevers explained that she and the Major were only able to offer hospitality to people attending conferences in Birmingham on the understanding that a small payment would be made. The rate which most of the married couples among her guests found acceptable was thirty shillings per night; much less, Mrs. Peevers pointed out, than a hotel. I sent off a cheque for three pounds. I can't remember whether or not we ever wrote to thank Neptuna.

In the end, Marguerite and I calmed down about the whole incident; and sooner rather than later, as one usually does. Even the
capacity for shock is among the things that steadily diminish as
life goes on. We came to making an occasional joke about it: "It's
surprising," I might say, "what one can do with a horse's eye and
a little human—" well, I won't finish that sentence, because one
says these silly things in married life, which are not worth repeating to the wide world.

As will be gathered, we never learned whether Harry really
had returned: our sole communication from No. 47 was entirely
a matter of business.

But then one evening, two or three years later, we told the
story, or some of it, to a man who came with his wife to dinner
with us, and who, like Harry, had an interest in anthropology,
though, again as with Harry, it was not his real business.

"That's one of Plutarch's Roman questions," the man said
when we had finished. "It's not uncommon, I believe. Even in
Plutarch's time it seems to have been quite old hat. Not that I
mean any offence, of course."

And when the man's wife wrote to thank us she enclosed a slip
of paper with the following, which she had typed out in double
spacing:—

"Question No. 5. Why are they who have been falsely reported
dead in a strange country, although they return home alive, not
received nor suffered to enter directly at the doors, but forced to
climb up to the tiles of the house, and so to get down into the
house from the roof?"

It had been Marguerite, of course, who had opened the letter
of thanks. But I had picked up the typed slip as it fluttered out,
and I read it aloud to her.

"But—" said Marguerite, struck by a phantom thought and
chasing it.

"Yes?" I said.

"But if we believe that, it might mean that only one of them
could have come back, and that the one was Jim Tate. He was
the one who was reported dead, and Harry wasn't. It could quite
easily mean that when you think about it."

"I thought I heard voices myself. I've told you."

"Or a voice. So you said."

"He would hardly be talking to himself; one would suppose. Not all alone up on the roof. But I haven't finished." I went on reading. "In his book, *The Temple and the House*, Lord Raglan, President of the Royal Anthropological Institute, writes of Plutarch's Question No. 5: 'A satisfactory explanation seems not to have been suggested.' "

"Perhaps Deirdre could suggest one?"

But after we deposited her early that morning between Chalk Farm and Camden Town, we never saw or heard of Deirdre again.

MARK INGESTRE: THE CUSTOMER'S TALE

I met an old man at the Elephant Theatre, and, though it was not in a pub that we met, we soon found ourselves in one, not in the eponymous establishment, but in a nice, quiet little place down a side turn, which he seemed to know well, but of which, naturally, I knew nothing, since I was only in that district on business, and indeed had been in the great metropolis itself only for a matter of weeks. I may perhaps at the end tell you what the business was. It had some slight bearing upon the old man's tale.

"The Customer's Tale" I call it, because the Geoffrey Chaucer implication may not be far from the truth: a total taradiddle of legend and first-hand experience. As we grow older we frequently become even hazier about the exact chronology of history, and about the boundaries of what is deemed to be historical fact: the king genuinely and sincerely believing that he took part in the Battle of Waterloo; Clement Attlee, after he was made an earl, never doubting that he had the wisdom of Walpole. Was Jowett Ramsey's Lord Chancellor of Clem's? Which one of us can rightly remember that? Well: the old man was a very old man, very old indeed; odd-looking and hairy; conflating one whole century with another whole century, and then sticking his own person in the center of it all, possibly before he was even born.

That first evening, there was, in the nature of things, only a short time before the pubs closed. But we met in the same place again by appointment; and again; and possibly a fourth time, too. That is something I myself cannot exactly recollect; but after that last time, I never saw or heard of him again. I wonder whether anyone did.

I wrote down the old man's tale in my beautiful new short-hand, lately acquired at the college. He was only equal to short installments, but I noticed that, old though he was, he seemed to have no difficulty in picking up each time more or less where he left off. I wrote it all down almost exactly as he spoke it, though of course when I typed it out, I had to punctuate it myself, and no

doubt I tidied it up a trifle. For what anyone cares to make of it,
here it is.

Fleet Street! If you've only seen it as it is now, you've no idea
of what it used to be. I refer to the time when Temple Bar was
still there. Fleet Street was never the same after Temple Bar went.
Temple Bar was something they simply couldn't replace. Men I
knew, and knew well, said that taking it away wrecked not only
Fleet Street but the whole City. Perhaps it was the end of England
itself. God knows what else was.

It wasn't just the press in those days. All that Canadian news-
print, and those seedy reporters. I don't say you're seedy yet, but
you will be. Just give it time. Even a rich journalist has to be seedy.
Then there were butchers' shops, and poultry and game shops,
and wine merchants passing from father to son, and little places
on corners where you could get your watch mended or your old
pens sharpened, and proper bookshops too, with everything
from *The Complete John Milton* to *The Condemned Man's Last Tes-
timony*. Of course the "Newgate Calendar" was still going at that
time, though one wasn't supposed to care for it. There were a
dozen or more pawnbrokers, and all the churches had bread-and-
blanket charities. Fancy Fleet Street with only one pawnbroker
and all the charity money gone God knows where and better not
ask! The only thing left is that little girl dressed as a boy out of
Byron's poem. Little Medora. We used to show her to all the new
arrivals. People even *lived* in Fleet Street in those days. Thousands
of people. Tens of thousands. Some between soft sheets, some
on the hard stones. Fancy that! There was room for all, prince and
pauper; and women and to spare for almost the lot of them.

Normally, I went round the back, but I remember the first time
I walked down Fleet Street itself. It was not a thing you would
forget, as I am about to tell you. There were great wagons stuck
in the mud, at least I take it to have been mud; and lawyers all over
the pavement, some clean, some not. Of course, the lawyers stow
themselves away more now. Charles Dickens had something to
do with that. And then there were the women I've spoken of;
some of them blowsy and brassy, but some soft and appealing,
even when they had nothing to deck themselves with but shawls

and rags. I took no stock in women at that time. You know why
as well as I do. There are a few things that never change. Never.
I prided myself upon living clean. Well, I did until that same day.
When that day came, I had no choice.

How did I get into the barbershop? I wish I could tell you. I've
wondered every time I've thought about the story, and that's
been often enough. All I know is that it wasn't to get my hair cut,
or to be shaved, and not to be bled either, which was still going on
in those days, the accepted thing when you thought that something was the matter with you or were told so, though you didn't
set about it in a barbershop if you could afford something better.
They took far too much at the barber's. "Bled white" meant
something in places of that kind. You can take my word about
that.

It's perfectly true that I have always liked my hair cut close,
and I was completely clean-shaven as well until I suffered a gash
from an assegai when fighting for Queen and Country. You may
not believe that, but it's true. I first let this beard grow only to save
her Majesty embarrassment, and it's been growing and growing
ever since.

As a matter of fact, it was my mother that cut my hair in those
days. She knew how *I* liked it and how *she* liked it. She was as
thorough as you can imagine, but all the while kissing and joking
too. That went on until the episode I am telling you about. Never
again afterward.

Often she had been shaving me too; using my dead father's old
razors, of which there were dozens and dozens. I never knew my
father. I never even saw a likeness of him. I think my mother had
destroyed them all, or hidden them away. If ever I asked her about
him, she always spoke in the same way. "I prefer you, Paul," she
said. "You are the better man. I have nothing to add." Always the
same words, or nearly the same. Then she would kiss me very
solemnly on the lips, so that there was nothing I could do but
change the subject.

How, then, could I possibly have entered that shop? I have an
idea that the man was standing outside and simply caught hold
of me. That often happened, so that you had to take trouble in
looking after yourself. But, as I have told you, I truly do not know.

I suspect that things happen from time to time to everyone that they don't understand, and there's simply nothing we can do about them.

I was in the chair immediately, and the man seemed to be clipping at my locks and lathering my face, both at the same time. I daresay he had applied a whiff of chloroform, which, at that period, was something quite new. People always spoke about a whiff of it, as if it been a Ramón Allones or a Larraniaga.

There were three chairs in the shop, but the man had firmly directed me to a particular one, the one to my left, because that was the one where the light was, or so I supposed was the reason. The man had an assistant, it seemed, in case the shop might suddenly be packed out. The assistant struck me as being pretty well all black, after the style of a Negro, but that might have been only because the whole shop was so dark and smoky. In any case, he could only have been about four feet two inches high, or even less. I wondered how he managed at the chairs. Probably, when at work, he had a box to stand on. All he did now was lean back against the announcements in the far-right-hand corner; waiting until he was needed. The master was as tall as the assistant was short; lean and agile as a daddy longlegs. Also, he was completely clean-shaven and white. One could not help wondering whether anything grew at all, or ever had. Even his hair could well have been some kind of wig. I am sure that it was. It was black and slightly curly and horribly neat. I didn't have my eyes on the pair of them for very long, but I can see them both at this very moment, though, in the case of the assistant, without much definition. Sometimes we can see more without definition than with it. On the marble slab in front of me was a small lighted oil lamp and a single burning candle; smoking heavily, and submerging the other smells. This in the very middle of an ordinary weekday morning. Probably, of course, it was only imitation marble. Probably everything in the shop was an imitation of some kind.

Having your hair cut at that time cost only a few pence, though there was a penny or two more for the tip; and being shaved was often a matter of "Leave it to you, sir." But I knew nothing of that, because, as I have said, I had never had either thing done to me for money in a shop. I began to count up in my head how much I might have in my pocket. I had already begun to support my mother, and, in the nature of things, it can't have been a large sum. Frightening ideas ran about my mind as to how much might be demanded of me. It seemed almost as if I were being treated to everything that the shop had to offer. I tried *not* to think of what might happen were I unable to pay in full.

At one time, the man was holding a bright silvery razor in either hand; which I suppose had its own logic from a commercial point of view. The razors seemed far shinier than those at home. Reflections from the two of them flashed across the ceiling and walls. The razors also seemed far sharper than ours, as was only to be expected. I felt that if an ear were to be streaked off, I should be aware of it because I should see the blood; but that my whole head could go in a second, without my knowing how small my head was, and how long and thin my neck. In the mirror I could see something of what was in hand, but not very much, because the mirror was caked and blackened, quite unlike the flickering razors. I doubted whether blood could have been made out in it, even a quite strong flow. I might well see the blood itself, long before the reflection of it.

But the worst thing came suddenly from behind me. Having no knowledge of what went on in these shops, I had never heard about the practice, then taken for granted, of "singeing." The customers regularly used to have the ends of their hair burnt off with a lighted taper. I don't suppose you've even heard of it happening, but it went on until fairly recently, and only stopped because the shops couldn't get the trained assistant. It was said to "seal" the hairs, as if they had been letters. All that may sound like a good joke, but the thing itself was not at all like a joke.

It was of course the dusky assistant who was doing it— though it suddenly struck me that it might be a disease he had, rather than his natural colouring, perhaps something linked with his being so short. All I know is, and this I can swear to you, that he did not light the taper he held, at either the candle or the lamp. At one moment the bright light behind me was not there, or the assistant there, either. At the next moment the light was so strong and concentrated that, even in the dirty mirror, the reflection was dazzling me.

I think that really it was hypnotizing me. Hypnotism was something else that was fairly new at the time. It wasn't even necessary for the two in the shop to set about it deliberately. The idea of being hypnotized was in the air and fashionable, as different things are at different times. People suddenly went off who would have felt nothing at all a few years earlier.

I felt that my whole body was going round and round like a Catherine wheel, feet against head. I felt that my head itself was going round and round in the other dimension, horizontally, so to speak, but faster. At that age, hypnotism had never actually come my way, even though it was being joked about everywhere. As well as all this, there was a sound like a great engine turning over. I think that really I lost myself for a short spell. Fainting was much commoner in those times than it is now, and not only with young girls. What it felt like was a sudden quick fall, with all my blood rushing upward. There were effects on the stage of that kind: clowns with baubles going down through trapdoors and coming up again as demons with pitchforks. They don't show it on the stage anymore, or not so often.

When I came round I was somewhere quite different. Don't ask me exactly how it had come about. Or exactly where I was, for that matter. I can only tell you what happened.

The first thing I knew was a strong smell of cooking.

Baking was what it really smelt like. Everyone at that time knew what baking smelt like, and I more than most, because my mother baked everything—bread, puddings, pies, the lot, even the cat food. I supposed I was down in the cellar of the building. Anyway, I was in *some* cellar. Of course, the kitchen quarters were always in what was called the basement, when the house was good enough to *have* a basement. So the smell was perfectly natural and acceptable.

The only thing was that the place seemed so terribly hot. I thought at first that it might be me, rather than the room, but that became hard to believe.

I was sprawled on a thick mattress. It seemed just as well, and kind of someone, because the floor as a whole was made of stone, not even smooth stone, not smooth at all, but rough. There was enough light for me to see that much. My mattress was considerably fatter than the ones given to the felons in Newgate or to the poorer debtors, and it was most welcome, as I say, but the stuff inside was peeping out everywhere through rents, and the color of the thing was no longer very definite, except that there were marks on it which were almost certainly blood.

I put my hand to my head, but I didn't seem to be actually bleeding through the hair, though it was hard to be sure, as I was sweating so heavily. Then I gave a gulp, like a schoolboy. I suppose I *was* still more or less a schoolboy. Anyway, I nearly fainted all over again.

At the other end of the cellar, if that is what the place was, a huge woman was sitting on a big painted chair, like a throne. The light in the place came from a small lamp on a kind of desk at her side. She had heavy dark hair falling over one shoulder, and a swarthy face, as if she had been a Spanish woman. She wore a dark dress, open all the way down the front to the waist, as if she had just put it on, or could not bear to fasten it owing to the heat, or had been doing some remarkably heavy work. Not that I had ever before seen a woman looking quite like that, not even my mother, when we were alone together. And there was a young girl sitting at her feet, with her head in the woman's lap, so that I could see only that she had dark hair, too, as if she had been the woman's daughter, which of course one would have supposed she was, particularly as the woman was all the time stroking and caressing the girl's hair.

The woman gazed across the cellar at me for some time before she uttered a word. Her eyes were as dark as everything else about her, but they looked very bright and luminous at the same time. Of course, I was little more than a kid, but that was how it all seemed to me. Immediately our eyes met, the woman's and mine, something stirred within me, something quite new and strong. This, although the light was so poor. Or perhaps at first it was *because* of the poor light, like what I said about sometimes seeing more when there is no definition than when there is.

I couldn't utter a word. I wasn't very used to the company of women, in any case. I hadn't much wished for it, as I have said.

So she spoke first. Her voice was as dark as her hair and her eyes. A deep voice. But all she said was: "How old are you?"

"Seventeen and a half, ma'am. A bit more than that, actually."

"So you are still a minor?"

"Yes, ma'am."

"Do you live in the City of London?"

"No, ma'am."

"Where then do you live?"

"In South Clerkenwell, ma'am."

"But you work in the city of London?"

"No, ma'am. I only come to the city on errands."

In those days, we were taught at school how to reply to cate-chisms of this kind. I had been taught such things very carefully. I must say *that* whatever else I might have to say about education in general. We were told to reply always simply, briefly, and directly. We used to be given exercises and practices.

I must add that the woman was well-spoken, and that she had a highly noticeable mouth. Of course, my faculties were not at their best in all that heat and after the series of odd things that had been happening to me: complete novelties, at that age.

"Whom do you visit on these errands?"

"Mostly people in the backstreets and side streets. We're only in a small way so far." It was customary for everyone who worked for a firm to describe that firm as "we," provided the firm was small enough, and sometimes not only then. With us, even the boozy women who cleaned everything up did it.

"Hardly heard of in the wider world, we might say?"

"I think that could be said, ma'am." I had learned well that boasting was always idle, and led only to still closer interrogation.

"Are your parents living?"

"My father is supposed to be dead, ma'am."

She transfixed me. I was mopping at myself all the time.

"I *think* he's dead, ma'am."

"Was he, or is he, a sailor, or a horsebreaker, or a strolling player, or a hawker?"

"None of those, ma'am."

"A Gay Lothario, perhaps?"

"I don't know, ma'am."

She was gazing at me steadily, but she apparently decided to drop the particular topic. It was a topic I specially disliked, and her dropping it so easily gave me the impression that I had begun to reach her, as well as she me. You know how it can happen. What hypnotism was then, telepathy is now. It's mostly a complete illusion, of course.

"And your mother? Was she pretty?"

"I think she still is pretty, ma'am."

"Describe her as best you can."

"She's very tiny and very frail, ma'am."

"Do you mean she's ill?"

"I don't think she's ill, ma'am."

"Do you dwell with her?"

"I do, ma'am."

"Could she run from end to end of your street, loudly calling out? If the need were to arise. Only then, of course. What do you say?"

At this strange question, the girl on the floor, who had hitherto been still as still, looked up into the woman's face. The woman began to stroke the girl's face and front, though from where I was I could see neither. Besides, it was so hot for caresses.

"I doubt it, ma'am. I hope the need does not arise." We were taught not to make comments, but I could hardly be blamed, I thought, for that one.

"Are you an only child?"

"My sister died, ma'am."

"The family diathesis seems poor, at least on the female side."

I know now that this is what she said, because since then I've worked hard at language and dictionaries and expressing myself, but I did not know then.

"Beg pardon, ma'am?"

But the woman left that topic, too.

"Does your mother know where you are now?"

At school, it might have been taken as rather a joke of a question, but I answered it seriously and accurately.

"She never asks how I spend the day, ma'am."

"You keep yourselves to yourselves?"

"I don't wish my mother to be fussed about me, ma'am."

Here the woman actually looked away for a moment. By now her doing so had a curious effect on me. I should find it difficult to put it into words. I suddenly began to feel queasy. For the first time, I became aware physically of the things that had been happening to me. I longed to escape, but feared for myself if I succeeded.

The woman's eyes came back to me. I could not but go out to meet her.

"Are you or your mother the stronger person?"

"My mother is, ma'am."

"I don't mean physically."

"No, ma'am."

The hot smell, familiar to me as it was, and for that reason all the more incongruous, seemed to have become more overpowering. It was perhaps a part of my newly regained faculties. I had to venture upon a question of my own. At home it was the customary question. It was asked all the time.

"Should not the oven be turned down a little, ma'am?"

The woman never moved a muscle, not even a muscle in her dark eyes. She simply replied "Not yet." But for the first time she smiled at me, and straight at me.

What more could be said on the subject? I knew that overheated ovens burned down houses.

The catechism was resumed.

"How much do you know of women?"

I am sure I blushed, and I am sure that I could make no reply. Our exercises had not included such questions, and I was all but dying of the heat and smell.

"How close have you dared to go?"

I could not withdraw my eyes, though there was nothing that part of me could more deeply wish to do. I hated to be mocked. Mockery was the one thing that could really make me lose control, go completely wild.

"Have you never been close even to your own mother?"

I must all the while have looked more like a turkey than most because my head was so small. You may not allow for that, because it's so much larger now.

You will have gathered that the woman had been drooling slightly, as women do when appealing in a certain way to a man. As I offered no response, she spoke up quite briskly.

"So much the better for all of us," she said, but this time without a trace of the smile that usually goes with remarks of that kind.

Then she added, "So much the better for the customers."

I was certainly not going to inquire what she meant, though I had no idea what I *was* going to do. Events simply had to take their course, as so often in life, though one is always taught otherwise.

Events immediately began to do so. The woman stood up. I could see that the chair, which at first seemed almost like a throne, was in feet hammered together from old sugar boxes and packing cases. The coloring on the outside of it, which had so impressed me, looked much more doubtful now.

"Let's see what you can make of Monica and me," said the woman.

At that the little girl turned to me for the first time. She was a moon-faced child, so pale that it was hard to believe so swarthy a woman could possibly be her mother.

I'm not going to tell you how I replied to what the woman had said. Old though I am, I should still hesitate to do so.

There was a certain amount of dialogue between us.

One factor was that heat. When Monica came to me and started trying to take off my jacket, I could not help feeling a certain relief, even though men, just as much as women, were then used to wearing far heavier clothes, even when it was warm.

Another factor was the woman's bright and steady gaze, though there you will simply think I am making excuses.

Another factor again was that the woman had unlocked something within me that my mother had said should please never be unlocked, never, until she herself had passed away. It was disloyal, but there's usually disloyalty somewhere when one is drawn in that way to a person, and more often than not in several quarters at once.

I did resist. I prevaricated. I did not prevail. I leave it there. I don't know how fond and dutiful you proved at such a time in the case of your own mother.

Monica seemed sweet and gentle, though she never spoke a word. It did, I fear, occur to me that she was accustomed to what she was doing; a quite long and complicated job in those days, which only married ladies and mothers knew about among women. Monica's own dress was made simply of sacking. It was an untrimmed sack. I realized at once that almost certainly she was wearing nothing else. Who could wonder in such heat? Her arms and legs and neck and round face were all skinny to the point of pathos, and white and slimy with the heat. But her hands were gentle, as I say. In the bad light, I could make nothing of her eyes. They seemed soft and blank.

The woman was just standing and gazing and waiting. Her arms rested at her sides, and once more she was quite like a queen, though her dress was still open all down the front to the waist. Of course that made an effect of its own kind too. It was a dark velvet dress, I should say, with torn lace around the neck and around the ends of the sleeves. I could see that she was as bare-footed as little Monica, but that by no means diminished her dignity. She was certainly at her ease, though she was certainly not smiling. She was like a queen directing a battle. Only the once had she smiled; in response to my silly remark about turning down the oven; when I had failed to find the right and unfunny words for what I had meant, and meant so well.

I could now see that the solitary lamp stood on a mere rough ledge rather than on any kind of desk. For that matter, the lamp itself was of a standard and very inexpensive pattern. It was equipped with a movable shade to direct the weak illumination. My mother and I owned a dozen lamps better than that, and used them too, on many, many occasions.

In the end, Monica had me completely naked. She was a most comfortable and competent worker, and, because there was nowhere else to put them; she laid out all my different things neatly on the rough floor, where they looked extremely foolish, as male bits and pieces always do, when not being worn, and often when being worn also.

I stood there gasping and sweating and looking every bit as ridiculous as my things. It is seldom among the most command-ing moments in the life of a man. One can see why so many men are drawn to rape and such. Otherwise, if the woman has any force in her at all, the man is at such an utter disadvantage. He is lucky if he doesn't remain so until the end of it. But I don't need to tell you. You'll have formed your own view.

There was no question of that woman lacking a thing. It was doubtless grotesque that I had assented to Monica stripping me, but as soon as Monica had finished, and was moving things about on the floor to make the total effect look even neater, the woman rotated the shade on the lamp, so that the illumination fell on the other end of the cellar, the end that had formerly been in the darkness behind her.

At once she was shedding her velvet dress (yes, it was velvet, I am sure of it) and, even at the time, it struck me as significant that she had put herself in the limelight, so to speak, in order to do so, instead of hiding behind a curtain as most women would have done, more then than now, I believe.

She too proved to be wearing no more than the one garment. Who could wear chemises and drawers and stays in that atmosphere?

The light showed that beneath and around the woman's feet, and I must tell you that they were handsome, well-shaped feet, was a tangle of waste hair, mingled with fur and hide, such as the rag and bone men used to cry, and refuse to pay a farthing for, however earnestly the women selling the stuff might appeal. By no stretch of drink or poetry could one call the heap of it a bed or couch. Our cat would have refused to go near it, let alone lie on it.

None of that made the slightest difference; no more than the heat, the smell, the mystery, or anything else.

The woman, with no clothes on, and with her unleashed hair, was very fine, though no longer a queen. "Let's see," she said, and half-extended her arms toward me.

A real queen might have expressed herself more temptingly, but being a queen is very much a matter of wearing the clothes, as is being a woman. The matter was settled by little Monica giving me a push from behind.

It made me look even more ridiculous, because I fell across the sugar-box throne. In fact, I cut my bare thigh badly. But a flow of blood made no difference in that company, and in a second or two I was wallowing egregiously amid the woman's dark hair and the soft mass of hair and fur from God knows where, and Monica had come in from behind, and begun to help things on.

Almost at once, I became aware of something about Monica, which is scarcely polite to talk about. I only mention it for a reason. The thing was that she herself had no hair, where, even at that time, I knew she should have had hair, she being, I was fairly certain, old enough for it. I refer to that personal matter because it gave me an idea as to who might be Monica's father. On Monica's round head, locks just hung straight around her face, as if they had stopped growing prematurely, and everyone was waiting for them to continue. I began to wonder if there were not some kind of stuck-on wig. I still doubted whether the woman who held me tight was Monica's mother, but for the moment there were other things to think about, especially by such a novice as I was.

There seems to be only one thing worth adding to a scene which you must find obvious enough.

It is that never since have I known a mouth like that woman's mouth. But the entire escapade was of course my first full experience—the first time I was able to go through the whole thing again and again until I was spent and done, sold and paid for.

I suppose I should also say that it was good to have Monica there as well, scrappy though she was, a bit like an undernourished fish. Monica knew many things that she should not have known, and which you can't talk most grown women into bothering about. You'll have come upon what I mean for yourself.

With the two of them, one didn't feel a fool. I even forgot about the heat. I simply can't remember how the woman and Monica managed about that. Perhaps I didn't even notice. I daresay there were creatures making a happy home for themselves in the vast pile of ancient warmth. I should have thought there would have been, but I didn't worry about it at the time. Over the heap, on the dirty wall, was a black-and-white engraving of an old man whose face I knew, because he had been hanged for political reasons. Every now and then, I could see him winking at me through the murk, though I was too pressed to recall his name just then. You remember my telling you that I couldn't keep my hands off the Newgate Calendar and all that went with it. I think his was the only picture in the room.

I keep calling it a room. What else can one call it? A gigantic rat hole, a sewage-overflow chamber, a last resting place for all the world's shorn hair? For me it was an abode of love. My first. Maybe my last.

The woman's hair just smelt of itself. The waste hair was drawn into one's nose and mouth and eyes, even into one's ears, into one's body everywhere. Monica, I believe, had no hair. The tatters of known and unknown fur insinuated themselves between her and me, as if they had been alive. They tickled and chafed but I never so much as tried to hold them back. Joy was all my care, for as long as the appointment lasted.

At the time, it seemed to last more or less for ever. But of course I had no comparisons. The woman and Monica set themselves to one thing after another. Sometimes in turn. Sometimes together. I was half-asphyxiated with heat and hair. I was wet and slimy as a half-skinned eel. I was dead to everything but the precise, immediate half-second. Like the Norseman, I had discovered a new world.

In the end, the woman began tangling her fragrant hair round my crop. I've told you that my neck was like a turkey's in those days. Stringy and very slender.

I am sure that the sweet scent of her hair came from nothing she put on it. In any case, the shop had not struck me as going out for the ladies. For what she was doing, she did not need to have especially long hair either. The ordinary length of hair among women would serve perfectly well. The ordinary length in those days. From what had gone before, I guessed that part of the whole point lay in the tangling process bringing her great mouth harder and tighter than ever against mine. Hair that was too long might have defeated that.

At first the sensation was enough to wake the dead. And by then, as you will gather, that was just about what was needed.

Then it was as if there was a vast shudder in the air. At which the entire spell broke. Nothing had ever taken me more completely by surprise.

It can always be one of the most upsetting experiences in

the world, as you may have learned for yourself. I don't know whether it comes worse when one is fully worked up or when the whole miserable point is that one is not.

But that time there was something extra. You won't believe this: I saw a vision of my mother.

She was just standing there, looking tiny and sad, with her arms at her sides, as the woman's had been, and with her own dignity, too. My mother was not wringing her hands or tearing at her wisps of hair or anything fanciful like that. She was just standing very still and looking as if she were a queen, too, a different sort of queen naturally, and this time on the scaffold. That idea of a queen on the scaffold came to me at once.

Until that moment, the huge dark woman had been powerful enough to do exactly what she liked with me. Now, at the first effort I exerted, I broke clean away from her and her hair, and rolled backward on top of Monica. I knew that I had, in fact, dragged a big hank of the woman's hair right away from her head. I could not be mistaken about that because the hank was in my hand. I threw it back among the rest.

I positively leapt to my feet, but even before that the woman was standing, her feet among the garbage, and with a knife in her hand. It was not one of the slim blades that in those days ladies carried in their garters for safety. This lady wore no garters. It was a massive working knife, of the kind employed by butchers who are on the heavier side of the trade. If there had been a little more light, its reflections would have flashed over the walls and ceiling as had happened with the hairdresser's razors.

Monica had climbed up too. She stood between us shuddering and shivering and fishy.

The woman did not come for me. She stepped elegantly across the room, across the place, to the door, and leaned back against it. That was her mistake.

When Monica had undressed me, she could easily have robbed me. I was soon to discover that she had taken nothing. That had been a mistake too.

My few sovereigns and half sovereigns were in a sovereign case, left behind by my father, and among the things given me by my mother when I was confirmed. My other coins were in a

purse that had been knitted for me with my name on it. A poor
orphan girl named Athene had done that. But there was something else that Monica might have found if she had been tricky
enough to look. Wherever I went in those days, I always carried a
small pistol. It had been the very first thing I bought with my own
money, apart from penny broadsheets and sticks of gob. Even my
mother had no idea I possessed it. I did not want her to grieve and
fret about what things were like for me in the highways of the
world.

She never knew I had it.

Down in that place, the pistol was in my hand more swiftly
than thought in my head.

The woman, for her part, gave no time to thinking, or to
trying to treat with me. She simply took a leap at me, like a fierce
Spanish bull, or a wild Spanish gypsy. There was nothing I could
do but allow the pistol to speak for me. I had never discharged it
before, except in play on the Heath at night.

I killed the woman. I suppose I am not absolutely certain of
that; but I think so. Monica began to whimper and squirm about.

The heat made dressing myself doubly terrible.

I had to decide what to do with Monica. I can truly say that I
should have liked very much to rescue her, but I had to drop the
idea as impracticable. Apart from everything else, quite a good
lot else, I could never have brought her to my home.

I never even kissed her good-bye, or tried in any way to comfort her. I felt extremely bad about that. I still do. It was terrible.

The door opened to me at once, though I had to step over the
woman's body to reach it.

Outside, a stone passage ran straight before me to another
door, through the glass panels of which I could see daylight. The
reek and savor of baking was overwhelming, and the heat, if possible, worse than ever. There were other doors on both sides of
the passage. I took it that they led to the different ovens, but I left
them unopened.

The door ahead was locked, but the key was on my side of it.
Turning it caused me considerable trouble. It called for a knack,
and my eyes were full of sweat and my hands beginning to tremble. Nor of course had I any idea what or who might be on the

other side of the door. The panels were of obscured glass, but it seemed to me that too little light came through them for the door to open onto the outer world.

Before long, I managed it, perhaps with the new strength I had acquired from somewhere or other. No one had as yet appeared at my rear. I think that, apart from Monica, I was alone down there; and, at that moment, I preferred not to think about Monica.

I flung the door open and found myself in a small, empty, base-ment shop. It had a single window onto an area; and, beside it, a door. When I say that the shop was empty (and just as well for me that it was), I mean also that it seemed to contain no stock. Nothing at all. There was a small, plain counter, and at the back of it tiers of wooden shelves, all made of dingy polished deal, and all bare as in the nursery rhyme. Brightly colored advertisements were coming in then for the different products, but there was not a bill or a poster in that shop. Nor was there anything like a list of prices, or even a chair for the more decrepit purchasers. I think there was a bit of linoleum on the floor. Nothing more.

I paused long enough to trail my finger down the counter. At least the place seemed to be kept clean, because no mark was left either on the counter or on my finger.

In the shop it was not so hot as in the rest of the establishment, but it was quite hot enough. When later I was allowed to look into a condemned cell, it reminded me of that shop.

But I now had the third door to tackle, the outer door, that might or might not lead to freedom. It looked as if it would, but I had been through too much to be at all sure of anything.

As quietly as I could, I drew the two bolts. They seemed to be in frequent use, because they ran back smoothly. I had expected worse trouble than ever with the lock, but, would you believe it? when the bolts had been drawn, the door simply opened of itself. The protruding part of the lock no longer quite reached into the socket. Perhaps the house was settling slightly. Not that there was any question of seeing much. Outside it was simply the usual, narrow, dirty street with high buildings, and a lot of life going on. A bit of slum, in fact. Most streets were in those days. That was before the concrete had taken everything over.

I couldn't manage to shut the door. As far as could be seen, one had to be inside to do that. I soon dropped it and started to creep up the area steps. The steps were very worn. Really dangerous for the older people.

For some reason it had never occurred to me that the area gate might be locked, but this time it was. And this time, naturally, there was no key on either side. The area railing was too spiky and too high for me to leap lightly across, even though I was a very long and lanky lad at that time. I was feeling a bit faint as well. For the third time.

A boy came up, dragging a handcart full of stuff from the builders' merchants. He addressed me.

"Come out from under the piecrust, have yer?"

"Which crust?"

The delivery boy pointed over my shoulder. I looked behind me and saw that over the basement door was a sign. It read "Mrs. Lovat's Pie Shop."

At once I thought of the man's name in the picture downstairs. Simon, Lord Lovat. Of course. But Lord Lovat hadn't been hanged, not even with a silken rope. He had been beheaded. Now I should have to think quickly.

"You're wrong," I said to the boy. "I went in to get my hair cut and by mistake came out at the back."

"You was lucky to come out at all." said the boy.

"How's that?" I asked, though I wasn't usually as ready as all this suggests. Not in those days.

"Ask no questions and you'll be told no fibs," said the boy.

"Well," I said, "help me to get out of it."

The boy looked at me. I didn't care for his look.

"I'll watch out for the bobby," said the boy. "He'll help you."

And I had to slip him something before he let me borrow four of his bricks to stand upon on my side of the railing and four to alight upon on the other side. I slipped him a whole five shillings; half as much as his wages for the week in those days. I had taken the place of the barber's assistant who would have had to stand on a box.

After I had helped the boy put the bricks back in his cart, I lost myself in the crowd, as the saying goes. Apart from everything else, I had aroused suspicion by overtipping.

I never heard another thing. Well, not for a very long time, and then not in a personal way.

But I had temporarily lost my appetite for criminal literature. I became out of touch with things for a while. I suffered not only for myself but for my mother. Fortunately, I knew few people who could notice whether I was suffering or not. They might have mocked me if they had, which I could never have endured.

It was a much longer time before I strolled down Fleet Street again. Not until after I was married. And by then Temple Bar had gone, which made a big difference. And manners and customs had changed. Sometimes for the better. Sometimes not. Only on the surface, I daresay, in either case.

I still sometimes break into a sweat when I think of it all. I don't commonly eat meat pies, either. And for a long time I had to cut my own hair, until my wife took over. Since she passed on, I've not bothered with it, as you can see. Why disfigure God's image? as the Russians used to put it. He'll disfigure you fast enough on his own. You can count on that.

The old man was beginning to drool, as, according to him, the woman had done; so that I shut my newly acquired pad and bound it with the still unstretched elastic.

If it had not been in a pub that I had met the old man, where then? I had met him in the auditorium of the Elephant, to which I had been sent as dramatic critic. That too is properly an old man's job, but, in case of need, the smaller papers had, and still have, a habit of sending the youngest person available. I had also to cover boxing matches, swimming matches, dance contests, the running at Herne Hill, and often political and evangelical meetings. Never football matches at one end, or weddings at the other; both of which involved specialists.

The programme for that evening is before me now. I kept it with my notes of the old man's tale, and I have just found the packet, one of hundreds like it.

"Order Tea from the Attendants, who will bring it to you in the Interval. A Cup of Tea and A Plate of Bread and Butter, Price 3d. Also French Pastries, 3d. each."

Wilfrid Lawson, later eminent, played the clean-limbed, over-involved young hero, Mark Ingestre, in the production we had seen.

There had been a live orchestra, whose opening number had been "Blaze Away."

There were jokes, there were adverts ("Best English Meat Only"), there were even Answers for Correspondents. The price of the programme is printed on the cover: Twopence.

On the other hand, there was a Do You Know? section. "Do You Know," ran the first interrogation, "that *Sweeney Todd* has broken all records for this theatre since it was built?"

"Making him wear a three-cornered hat!" the old man had exclaimed with derision. "And Mrs. Lovat with her hair powdered!"

"David Garrick used to play Macbeth in knee breeches," I replied. Dramatic critics may often, as in my case, know little, but they all know that.

ROSAMUND'S BOWER

"You don't find anything that matters by going out and looking for it."

Thus spoke Sir Louis Emanuel. It was typical of the tactless utterances that made him so unpopular with the other Fellows. Emanuel might be an historian, but he was perfectly prepared to apply his dogmas in quite other fields, such as seeking a cure for cancer or one for inflation. Nor could it be denied that his notion of leaving all that matters to Providence had done pretty well for him academically. The confidential chores he was believed occasionally to undertake for persons and families had led to his being offered a knighthood before he had become a British citizen. The haze of ambiguity that set off the angular, little man, undoubtedly appealed to a certain type of undergraduate, though the number was not large. Undergraduates in general are more cautious than before.

One could see how it worked in the respective responses of Michael Aylwin-Scott and Paul Tent when they first encountered the Bower, first set eyes on it.

For many generations of undergraduates there had been a project which called for volunteers: the search for Rosamund's Bower. Needless to say, most of the volunteers dropped out pretty soon, or faded away in promises; but a handful was always found to keep looking, through humid heat and sodden wind, either because they were mild obsessionals in embryo, or because it was a respectable device for minimizing more specific studies. A very few were perhaps held by the romance of the quest.

It is common knowledge that even if one discovers the Bower, one cannot find one's way to the heart of it. That was the whole point of the Bower.

Not, of course, that there seemed the slightest hope of doing more than unearth a few hypothetical, and almost certainly debatable, traces of where the Bower once was; and even that would be at the very best.

There were no acceptable arguments against those who questioned the worth of the whole enterprise. The unending, though intermittent, search either appealed or it repelled. That was all there was to it.

Aylwin-Scott and Tent, having walked up the towpath from Osney to Godstow, had embarked upon a vague ramble to the westward, through hedge and through briar. Improvisation, avoidance of any beaten track, was a great part of the fun. Indeed, having, while on the towpath, discussed country matters of one kind, they were now discussing country matters of another kind.

There had for some time been, not a path, not even the memory of a path, but occasional pointers to there once having been a path; gaps, not quite fully grown up, in hedges; irregular patches of ground where nothing would grow; a few fragments from skeletal stiles, and decaying planks across ditches.

"Don't trust yourself on that," said Paul Tent, who was the cautious one.

Michael Aylwin-Scott just flitted across it, in the manner of Harlequin. He was very tall and long-legged.

Considerably further on (particularly in terms of effort expended), they found a hand, or the partial and faded remains of a hand. It had been painted on wood; jacket sleeve, shirt sleeve, sleeve links, everything. Almost certainly the shirt-cuff depicted had been starched. Three fingers were clenched back, but the forefinger indicated imperiously, with the thumb in support. Now, however, the hand merely lay among the weeds. It was at the edge of a coppice, into which, or out of which, it had once pointed.

"If we could find the rest of it, we might discover where it was pointing to," observed Paul Tent.

"Does it matter?"

"Time spent in finding things out is seldom wasted."

Michael Aylwin-Scott helped quite loyally with the search, but they could find nothing more, though Paul Tent, who had red hair, was reluctant to give the order of release.

They entered the coppice and pressed straight ahead as best they could.

On the other side was a scrubby field. It looked long unused. It was also of irregular outline, the vaguest and apparently most pointless of polygons.

"The dung looks Ancient Egyptian," said Paul Tent.

"Does it indeed?"

"You see dung like that in the Cairo Museum. Ox-dung, I suppose. Or camel-dung."

"The whole field has rather a left-over appearance."

"That's exactly what it is. It's the bit left when all the other fields had been ruled out symmetrically."

"Yes, of course. The earth is hardly symmetrical automatically."

"Nor is the pattern of ownership."

"Where do we go now?"

"Across to that corner, wouldn't you say?"

Conversation flagged.

"Damned great moles on this side of the wood," complained Aylwin-Scott.

"No one's tried to keep them down. The whole area looks depopulated."

"Isn't that what we want?"

"You'd think that no one owns this land at all."

"In that case, the Crown owns it," remarked Aylwin-Scott.

"I don't suppose it's gone as far as that. It's just that it doesn't pay to farm it."

Aylwin-Scott stopped. "What do we think that is?" he asked, but quite casually.

The field rose somewhat at the centre, rather as if there were pressure beneath, vague forces soon to burst out. The two friends had surmounted the modest eminence, and could see over the unkempt hedge which wavered in and out, up and down, before and around them.

"We need the Archaeological Survey. I'll try to find where we are on the map we *have* got."

"*I* think it's Rosamund's Bower," declared Aylwin-Scott. "Anyway, it's exactly what I imagine it to look like."

"To *have* looked like," said Tent with a smile. He was on his knees, looking at the Ordnance Survey.

"Well, see for yourself!" patiently exclaimed Aylwin-Scott. "Have a good look."

"Can't see from down here."

Aylwin-Scott sat down beside him and waited. That often happened.

There were no birds in the sky, despite the nearness of the coppice. Perhaps only nightingales nested therein? What was more, there was no mooing or baaing or braying; no sound of diesel lorries or of midget radios or of light aircraft. Nothing, in fact, but gnats and mosquitoes flighting from the unkempt bushes.

Aylwin-Scott waited and waited; swatting and scratching intermittently.

In the end, Tent reluctantly summed up. "There are simply not enough landmarks. You'd have to use trigonometry."

"Well, why don't you?"

"Haven't got the Tables," Tent answered quite seriously.

"Can we find the way back?"

"Of course we can."

"That's always important."

"Of course we can find the way back," said Tent again.

"In that case, let's look at the Bower."

They rose and began to descend the slight slope ahead of them.

"We ought to be able to decide for ourselves what it really is," observed Tent.

"It's Rosamund's Bower," said Aylwin-Scott, unwaveringly. "It's obvious that it is."

The intervening hedge proved to be the most difficult of all to scramble through.

"Curse it," cried Tent. "I'm wounded."

But Aylwin-Scott, who had experienced less difficulty, had gone a little ahead.

Then, once more, he stopped. It was probably to enable the injured, and always more circumspect Tent to catch up.

"My God, Michael," said Tent in the end. "I've never seen anything like *that.*"

"Not many people have, it seems. The people who made the map, for instance."

"I think we ought to be careful," said Paul Tent.

"I'm going in," said Michael Aylwin-Scott, gazing at the object.

"It was a maze. You were supposed to need a key, or a guide of some kind."

"We haven't got either."

Paul Tent sat on the ground once more and again began to puzzle over the map. "Cry out, if you need help," he said.

Inside, all was as unkempt and unowned-looking as the surrounding fields. Nonetheless, there *were* faint tracks though the scrub and brush, and there was nothing whatever to do but to take one's chance, pushing, stumbling, persisting; arms above the head, hands before the face, eyes mostly shut, shoulders humped.

The air was neither dusty nor musty; if one choked at all, it would be on the universal sweet scent of honeysuckle. No blue songsters warbled. No leaden crows adjured. No kingfishers darted, even though the sound of rippling and cascading water became steadily less mistakable, sometimes coming, sometimes going, sometimes flowing, sometimes ebbing.

The dim track rounded angles, and each time one supposed it would end. Also there were choices to be made: at present there seemed nothing to do but leave things to chance or to instinct.

Upon traversing possibly the ninth or tenth turn, Aylwin-Scott saw, as it were, a vision before him.

The vision filled the whole oval ahead, so that this indeed seemed to be the end of the route, but it was a remarkably simple vision, in that it merely presented Paul Tent, recumbent upon the neglected hummocks outside, and fretting away at the map. There was, however, something else to be seen, standing at a little distance behind Tent, still fairly close to the thick, spiky, hedge, which cast a gloom that prevented Aylwin-Scott seeing what the thing was, in the very limited time available.

For the vision was gone almost as soon as come, and Aylwin-Scott could see that the faint track continued, after all, and much as hitherto, with the same vague splits or bifurcations.

Many minutes seemed to pass before he came upon a second vision. This time, it amounted to no more than a figure of about his own stature which suddenly appeared facing him, hardly even blocking the way, and was gone in a moment. All the same, it had been there long enough for Aylwin-Scott to know who it was: it was a figure of himself, a little older; possibly even twenty years older. He did not at all care for the look of the figure, just in itself; but, of course, there was more to the experience than that. Michael Aylwin-Scott was just the man to know very well that to meet one's double is to presage one's death.

He stood without breathing. Then the thought came to him that he had not seen his true double. The implication must be a little different from what he had at first supposed.

He released his breath very slowly, and plodded on. He suspected there could be no returning. Quite probably the Bower had by now closed in behind him. Tent would have looked, but Aylwin-Scott did not. The going was hard enough as it was.

But suddenly, and round only a few more of the blind turns, past a few more of the double entries, the prospect changed greatly: the going became half-mown grass, filtering between half-dead hedges partly clipped, it was true, but extremely high, so that they made the sky too distant to be easily visible, even by one so tall as Aylwin-Scott. There was even a lingering peacock, which screamed vindictively, and continued to scream. All its feathers were greying, so that it looked to be the oldest peacock Aylwin-Scott had ever come upon, and it seemed to be resenting to the full both that fact and his own presence. He reflected that it matters less how old and grey a peacock is when there is no observer; and that now an observer had quite irrationally intruded.

Aylwin-Scott hesitated, much as Paul Tent would have done. He feared to pass an angry bird with an eye of stone and a splinter beak. Moreover, its clawed, grey feet seemed to belong more to an eagle.

But as he tried to meet the ancient eye and stare it out, the creature was no longer there, and his way was blocked instead by a big woman; a grey sister of mercy perhaps, or to judge by her demeanour, a grey Abbess, one with uncounted souls dependent upon her. The peacock had been assuredly male, but the Abbess had the same eye as the peacock and a similarly shrivelled and pointed face, though her feet were lost in her long robe. Her garments were old and dirty. Beyond doubt, she had attained to a position in the convent where neatness and tidiness were no longer demanded.

Michael Aylwin-Scott could only sink to the ground before her. The words "a big woman" are frightening in themselves.

"Get up," she cried, in her peacock scream. "You know perfectly well who I am."

And so he did, though needless to say, she had been very differently arrayed, or would be, and not as a dingy peacock either. At that very moment, he could see her (of course, in his mind's eye) in that faded green scrap she wore day after day when Susannah and he were with her at Rocquebrune—or would so wear!

He lunged at her, without, however, quite touching her, taking care not to.

"Why can't you leave us alone?" he cried. "Just sometimes."

She positively hissed at him. "And what are we to suppose would happen in that case?"

There was so much to be said in reply that nothing could be said. "Everything would be different," was all he could offer.

"As it is, you are responsible for what happened to Charlotte. How many more people do you wish to destroy? Apart from me, of course."

"I was at no time a free agent." He managed a surprising level of dignity, at least in his own eyes; but, from first to last, the simple question had been, and still was, that if he were not responsible, then who was? Certainly not Susannah. Certainly not the woman confronting him, who was one that never in any matter strayed a single small step. Certainly not Ken Hunt, oaf though he was. Least of all, sweet Charlotte herself, so pale and frail.

"And what have you to offer an attractive woman in any case? You have never kept a job for more than six months, and you try to behave as if you were all the oil in Texas."

"Meeting you was the worst thing that has yet actually happened to me," he said, quite quietly; and still, as he thought, with dignity.

"Not as bad as what happened to you in the City, and again in Montreal, and yet again in wherever it was." She laughed like a foghorn. "You'd be the world's biggest loser, Michael, except that you're on far too small a scale to be a big anything."

"Filthy interloper," observed Aylwin-Scott; again quite quietly.

"I don't even believe your stories about Oxford. No one does."

"Hag," observed Aylwin-Scott, in much the same tone.

"Lies to women. Lies about money. Lies about your education. Lies about everything."

He flipped his hand at her cheek. It was far from an uncontrol-
lable assault, but he lacerated his fingers, none the less, so that
blood streamed over his trousers and was soon sprinkling a quite
large area of the sketchy grass. The Abbess's grimy habit was
much indued.

"Sacrilege!" screamed the Abbess. "Sacrilege! Sacrilege!"

Aylwin-Scott half expected the appearance of roughcast vil-
leins with choppers taller than themselves, but all that happened
was that instead of the grey Abbess, there was again the faded
peacock, and, this time, he was somehow on the far side of it.
The bird was eyeing him as stonily as ever, but had fallen silent.
Every few seconds it lifted its immense grey foot and snatched
away a lump of turf. It could of course also be added that the
deadly bird now stood between Aylwin-Scott and the notion of
retreat; though obviously there might be other routes.

As he snatched away his gaze and resumed his advance, he
perceived that the man he had seen earlier, his own near-double,
once more stood before him. Perhaps he had been there all the
time, listening and noting, and concealed from Aylwin-Scott by
the immense figure of the Abbess. Assuredly, there was now the
bird behind, and the double before.

Certainly there was no hint of a smile on the man's face, neither of delicate amusement, nor of ironical understanding. He
looked utterly inimical. Also, he looked twenty years or more
older than before. As far as Aylwin-Scott could see, his hair was
now grey completely, instead of merely streaked and patched. It
was also much sparser. The furrows on his face were wider and
deeper and more. There was even a scar across his left cheek continuing up the side of his brow, like the maquillage of a warrior
Indian. The mouth had changed shape perceptibly, and the hands
were those of a pugilist.

The theory relating to one's double had plainly taken on further complexity. Nothing in the content of life or death is ever simple: not even an omen.

"Well?" enquired Aylwin-Scott, his hands in his pockets.

But, of course, the man was no longer there, and all that Aylwin-Scott could do was go forward as if he never had been and never would be again.

Considering the total expanse of the Bower, not only as calculated by laboratory computers but as actually beheld by himself and, up to a point, witnessed by his friend, Aylwin-Scott thought that the particular alley seemed fantastically protracted.

He could hardly look behind him to confirm that impression, because he might then become reinvolved with the peacock. He could just imagine the bird leaving the ground at his first backward glance, and, with one swift trajectory, swooping to where he was and swiftly pecking away his head. The imagining of things like that was habitual to him, and, no doubt, he would not have been the man he was, part poet, part dreamer, part babe, had it been otherwise.

The long avenue might have been slightly less depressing had the hedges been less dizzying, and the whole presentation in more whole-hearted trim. But it had to be supposed that neither electronic hedge-cutters nor leviathan grass-mowers were at the service of those who maintained the place. An immemorial retreat and seclusion were best maintained by immemorial crafts. At least the dim web of alternative routes seemed so far to have been traversed with what might be called success.

Not that the fundamentals within the Bower were significantly distinct from those prevailing in the terrain surrounding it. The walk up which Aylwin-Scott was advancing might be half-heartedly under grass, but the ground was the same lumpy, furrowed, ancient earth that Tent and he had toiled across. In fact, the going was still so hard and rough that Aylwin-Scott even began to feel footsore, absurd though that seemed. Of course there were all those records of pilgrims and penitents having to struggle across actual sword-blades for years on end; suffocated and surfeited with honeysuckle sweetness; battling with their ever recurring selfdoms and other demons; lured by the distant promise of lapping water.

At the end of the walk, a certain relief might once have been available, because there were to be seen the remains, however scanty, of a small stone kiosk, or perhaps even shrine, which unmistakably had once offered a bench of a kind, long, long ago. Here the wanderer might sink exhausted, or enlist new strength for the trials ahead, or both. Aylwin-Scott even smiled slightly when contemplating the jagged remnants: after all, at the heart of the bower was the flower of life, the rose of love. He rounded the turn at the end of the long tramp.

A man stood there soberly, as if awaiting him. This fellow did not even trouble to stand in his path, as his near-double had twice done, and the bold woman who had always been so right about everything, or always would be.

The man was dressed as a Seneschal. His hair, if he had any, was hidden by his headdress.

"What now?" Aylwin-Scott enquired.

"Neglect and deprivation. Criminal charges, I'm afraid, master. You need a licence from the court to do things like that, and I admit it's not easily got."

"What *is*?" enquired Aylwin-Scott. An idle question, of course.

"The court likes grown people to be fully fed and clothed at all times, let alone their little children."

"How could an ordinary person possibly know *that*?"

"You've got an Oxford degree, master. Not everyone has a thing of that kind. A guiding star, we might put it."

"No such star. I failed to get a degree."

"Then I'm afraid I have to say that there's another charge. Wasting money that might have been spent on your fellow men. That matters, you know. I shall have to inform the court."

"I didn't even sit for my degree. I had to leave Oxford. I had to go down. It was circumstances."

"In that case, the provisions require that you applied for full-time work as a Merry Andrew. It's not an easy life, master, I admit, but there it is. It's the law. It always will be. You can count on that. It's obvious."

"You don't seem to realize that at the time I could read and write and split hairs and reap where I'd sown. I was as half-qualified as anyone."

"It's not for me to realize one thing. Now is it, master? I can safely leave that sort of thing to you. But, strictly off the record, I should put it like this: I should observe it's not much use having all that fancy stuff at your free disposal, unless you use it to cheer people up, and full time too, in accordance with our common nature."

"Most people are quite young when they leave a university, you know. They're often pretty ignorant."

"No doubt, master, but no one can say *that* lasts long, least of all a gentleman like yourself. Why, you don't look more than twenty-one or twenty-two at this moment. What exactly *did* you do next? That's the question, master. I ought to warn you that the court will want full details. They're entitled to demand the inside and outside of everything, and that's only the start of it. So what happened then?"

"I skipped and quipped and ripped. What do you suppose I did? I never entered a bed for years, good or bad. If that's not full time, then the law's an ass."

"Properly speaking, master, the law is more like a veil. Like the veil of the temple," said the Seneschal gravely. "You get to see that when you've been in the law's service for a long lifetime."

"A thousand years, perhaps?" ventured Aylwin-Scott. It was high time for him to take the initiative; though he must do it without sounding pert.

"Give or take a few double centuries, maybe," said the Seneschal, possibly meeting him halfway, as a man can sometimes do when he is secure within himself and within his worldly position. "But a full grown adult is expected to feed and clothe his own wife and tiny toddlers," the Seneschal continued, bringing the converse back to the starting-point.

"I lost the proper use of my eyes and ears, and of my arms and legs too, and of my brain and teeth, and of my spleen and pancreas."

"Did you submit yourself to the infirmary?"

"You can see that I did. That's why I'm as I am now."

"They can only give you the full treatment. It's useless to expect more. In fact, it's a sacrilege."

But Aylwin-Scott was staring at him. "We've met before, I think."

Quite clearly, he could see the brute coming up the crazy path (crazy concrete) from the dropped gate—or foresee him doing so: in either case, as distinctly as if it were that present moment, treacherous as all other moments. He suspected, indeed he knew, that it had happened, or would happen, again and again. There could be no excluding the man. Nothing would keep him out.

"And we shall meet again, master," the Seneschal confirmed. "It's the penalty for expecting too much if I may speak more confidentially."

"It was I who entered the Bower when Paul Tent was too afraid."

"Positively, my master. Unquestionably. And where is Mr. Tent now? Lord Mayor of London for eighteen consecutive years, a peer of the United Kingdom, a Companion of Honour, and still with the best of his life well ahead of him." The Seneschal smiled sentimentally. "Everyone loves Mr. Tent. Lord Ordnance, I should say. 'E knows every rule in the book." The Seneschal was so moved by majority emotion that for the first time he had neglected an aspirate.

"He's the best of chaps," said Aylwin-Scott. "Well, in many ways. Just about my closest friend, in fact."

"None better, master. Everyone agrees. You've read books, but you're not what we call quick, or you'd know it had all been said before. That won't excuse you when the time comes."

"There is nothing for which I need to apologize," affirmed Aylwin-Scott, stoutly, as he thought.

"It would make no difference if you did apologize, master. The court decides partly on the evidence, and you must admit it's dead against you. How often have you stood properly in a queue, like the others? Why aren't you wearing the correct socks? Can't you speak to your own children in a language they can understand? What made you think you could get away with eyes like that once you were grown up? Evidence, that's one thing the court asks for, and you seem to be dragging a wainload of it. You're a heretic. You're a lunatic. You're enrolled with the Father of Lies. You're moonstruck. It would be better for all of us if you had never been born."

As the Seneschal was plainly working himself up into some other form of life, Aylwin-Scott made a further demand on his stock of worldly experience, however sketchy.

"Good man," he said, and in very nearly the appropriate tone, "could you please tell me how far it is to the centre of the Bower?"

Through what could only be called an aperture (perhaps an alternative route, after all), emerged a page. Indeed there was even a small, alabaster door, which the page had opened from within. Aylwin-Scott had not observed the fitment, owing to the Seneschal's demanding converse. Now he could see at a glance that the small elaborate carvings were incredibly beautiful: lovers caressing, and saints suffering; or possibly the reverse.

"That depends upon whether you are sleeping or waking," said the page, who, though arrayed as a boy-page, was very obviously a girl-page.

"Which *am* I?" enquired Aylwin-Scott.

"Waking," said the page. "It's Saturday afternoon. Have you forgotten?"

"It's just possible to fall asleep on a Saturday afternoon," replied Aylwin-Scott with elegant sarcasm. "I've done it myself on several occasions."

"Don't you count upon *that* as a defence," growled the Seneschal. "Now I'm warning you, master. Remember your deathbed."

"Tell me about your deathbed, Michael," cooed the page.

"You lack the time to listen, boy," said the Seneschal. "Remember how long it went on. The people he cut off made a better end than he did. A cough, a prayer, and head-first into the ground. A blessing for them, really."

"That's what I've been saying all along," cried Aylwin-Scott, by now more confident than pleading. "Death in battle is glorious ever."

"Sir Michael!" piped the page in her small voice, and threw her arms tightly round him though, as her head hardly rose above his waist, it was his loins that she mainly encircled. He had never become entirely reconciled to his height being so absurdly above average.

"But, all the same, Michael, it's very important to make a good end," said the page, gurgling into Aylwin-Scott's midriff.

"Tell me about it," he managed to say, though talking made him feel slightly bilious, so close was her clasp. "Tell me how to do that."

The page flung away from him. "Rosamund will tell you," she said petulantly, and now with pink spots on her otherwise almost translucent cheeks.

"Then *take* me to Rosamund. How much further?"

"Life is what we make it," put in the Seneschal. "It's entirely up to us. I've told you already. You weren't compelled to do anything wrong. You weren't even hungry, though many are. You weren't thinking of your children, though many do. You were educated. You were dishonest deliberately. You were picked and then rejected."

For Aylwin-Scott, words such as these settled the matter. He knew very well who the Seneschal was: we may or may not love such a person, but we go badly astray without him. Not that what had been said was wholly true either; then or at any time, there was a quite enormous amount to be adduced on the other side. There always is.

Further fortified by that last consideration, and with the little page twitting him, challenging him, Aylwin-Scott managed positively to glare at the rumbustious Seneschal. To his relief, though not astonishment, the Seneschal slowly turned into a series of hideous stone figures, partly human, partly not, and mostly as much above ordinary lifesize, as was the neglected hedge behind them, to say nothing of Aylwin-Scott himself.

Standing afar, the little page half-winked at him, and executed a pretty caper.

Over the hard, lumpy ground, he ran towards her, intending to gather her up.

But she skipped aside. "No," she said. "You must remember Rosamund." He knew that equivocal tone.

Again he ran, but she merely ran ahead of him, and much faster. Now she wore a little plumed cap, which he had not observed before. He marvelled that with the swiftness of her motion the cap did not fall off, and become defeathered.

Here was another of those long walks between high hedges, one-third dead and brown. The expert estimates of the Bower's magnitude were proving characteristically void. Aylwin-Scott was well up in the debate as to whether it is better to derive knowledge imaginatively (even, sometimes, aesthetically) from books, or more casually from experience and adversity. This second long transit seemed virtually to range into the next county, though presumably the river ran between. Aylwin-Scott felt that he should latch on to that riparian aspect of local government topography.

"Come *on*!" called the little page. Her azure shirt managed to flash in the watery sun, as if it had been plumaged; otherwise so singularly absent, apart from one greying peacock.

Aylwin-Scott, however, saw no reason why he should continue especially to exert himself, since plainly he was not going to catch her in her present mood. On the other hand, he had no wish to suggest that he was in any way losing heart. He who enters the Bower must persevere to the centre of it, unless he be swept away, or willing to acknowledge himself a laggard. Aylwin-Scott would not cry Halt to his life for a long time yet. At the moment, a brisk walking pace seemed to him best adapted to all the circumstances he was informed of. The honeysuckle had never smelt more pungently.

Perhaps it was that very river he could all the time hear; the immemorial Isis, so dear to every swelling Oxford heart for more generations than a druid's oak has rings. Certainly the sound was no longer to be described as rippling. By now the word might perhaps be rumbling. There seemed to be more water, and swifter and less constrained.

"Oh—do—come—on."

"Stand still and I shall!"

She posed with legs far apart, a hand on each hip, and her eyes shadowed by the cap. She was staring straight at him, none the less; watching his minutest move, alert to dart ahead once more. Aylwin-Scott wondered what her name could be: Jocelyn, Amyas, Bosco Faucon? Perhaps Aylwin? It is what he would have called her, had she been his minion, instead of Rosamund's. He, Michael; she, Aylwin.

But suddenly, and as in one way or another seemed the way of the place, his view of her was blotted out by the apparition of a stumbling ancient, who filled the entire area of view, though it was quite illogical that he should do so, as he was bent with malady. It was equally illogical that he should be able for a single moment to keep ahead of the lanky Aylwin-Scott, as he could move at all only by the use of implements, and, by a sober standard, should have been confined to bed and virtually forgotten, years before. None the less, the old man managed it over a surprising distance; partly, perhaps, because, this time, Aylwin-Scott had no particular will to overtake him, knowing, this time, perfectly well who he was, even though he could discern merely the threadbare back, and no vestige of the accepted but totally unacceptable face. Well, well, a promise is always at the same time a threat or curse; and now precisely the same measure, neither more nor less. By now, Aylwin-Scott also knew in advance that when the intruding duffer took himself off, the ever-elusive page would be gone about her business also.

The sound of the water would in any case have drowned her words unless her cherub lips had been at his very ear. It would have had to be his left ear too, because, as with many young men, one of his ears was greatly more useful than the other. He had found *that* out when (how few years ago?) the wolfhounds had sprung at him in the perilous orchard; quite noiselessly, as it had seemed to him at the time, preoccupied, as he was, and always would be.

So he was alone once more; apart from the tumbling water, which was company enough for any single individual. At this farther end of the second walk, the standard of maintenance was better. There were fewer dead growths in the high hedges, and fewer dingy parasites. Underfoot, the grass was greener and more diffuse; the ground more level, even a little softer.

Aylwin-Scott forced his neck back in order to look up at the empyrean. It proved perfectly possible to glimpse it when one had made the required effort. In Oxfordshire, especially, of course, in Oxford herself and her near vicinity, it is ever raining or expected to rain. When the sky is not grey and watery, it is yellow and watery; nor is the yellow a beautiful yellow. Thus it was, high above the Bower that afternoon. Much is ever perfectly normal and predictable.

At last there were even birds; both hedge-hoppers and love-charmers; and not, as yet, a kestrel in sight. The ravellings of the Bower probably disheartened the aerial carnivores and droppers.

All the same, owing to the water noise, not a trill could be heard. It was strange to watch birds, some magical, some habitual, all hopping and flittering without a squeak or throb.

Aylwin-Scott perfectly well realized that, in a sense, he had outlived himself, and had managed to emerge, in some shape or form, on the other side of his existence. All those near-doubles! Paul Tent himself could not seriously question the firm evidence. It was a feat on Aylwin-Scott's part! And in a career which seemed unlikely to achieve all that much by mere worldly criteria. Of course there were no looking glasses to confirm one single thing.

But there was another of those corners ahead: blind turns, the officials (almost anywhere) would have called them; and, for the first time, all, truly all, was trimmed, edged, and smoothed. One could conceive of the Bower's inmost dweller fully sustaining the centre only; exactly as the dweller in a castle or palace sustains only the core, and sadly resigns the rest to vicissitude and all fiscal evils.

Round the next corner strolled a creature that Aylwin-Scott had never seen before. It had ears with points; a wispy, tufted tail; and very light blue eyes; but it seemed to ignore him. It neither bristled nor nuzzled. Rather, it proceeded by the laws of heraldry. Aylwin-Scott knew a little about those laws too.

Holding its head high, the creature ambled away along the alley he had just traversed. He suspected that it saw, and in every way sensed, infinitely more than he could.

He turned the corner finally; and then another and another and another, and these so quickly that his head spun stupidly, and the sound of water had become not rippling, not rumbling even, but roaring.

Somehow he was standing and moving within an immense

cascade, though there was nothing tactile beyond the unchanging Oxfordshire humidity upon his brow, neck, and girth.

Aylwin-Scott stood, stagnant, stunned.

For moments the noise was as shattering as birth itself, and then he was standing at the edge of a lawn the shape of a heart, or perhaps of a lyre, or perhaps of an Italian axe-head. Small pug-like dogs were dotted about, grazing; so that Aylwin-Scott apprehended at once what deficiency it was that led the dogs he had so far known occasionally to snuffle grass. Some of the pugs were ribboned; others belled. At the far end of the lawn was a pavilion. Aylwin-Scott was startled by its smallness. The attendance on the occupant could be scarcely more than notional. He walked onto the lawn.

The honeysuckle smell was gone; headachy in its intensity, far too much of a supposedly good thing. Here the smell was of the rampant roses on the trees and bushes; pure, elevating, ecstatic, akin to speech, Alas, Aylwin-Scott was hardly able to assimilate it, owing to the distracting din, which had lessened only very little, since its crisis.

He placed his hands on his ears, shut his eyes tightly, and crumpled into himself. He knotted himself so that it looked as if he would have to be straightened by helpers.

But almost at once a hand fell gently on his shoulder. There was nothing left that he could offer in response. He could not even open his eyes.

The hand gently drew at him and made as if to shift and turn him. He realized that it was behind him that the other was standing.

Then the hand was lifted, there was a pause, and then there could be no doubt that the noise was diminishing; evenly and steadily.

Aylwin-Scott half-opened his eyes, or perhaps one of his eyes.

He saw ramifying mulberry trees, and a woman in a mulberry-coloured dress, who was going through the motions of drawing a heavy curtain which he could not see. As she dragged, the noise of the water was proportionately cut off; but, plainly the curtain was difficult to move, so that, in ordinary courtesy, Aylwin-Scott should have taken his hands from his ears and applied them to her aid.

When he did remove them, there was no noise at all, other than a single plop-plop from some other source, which the noise of the waterfall had previously drowned into absurdity.

Aylwin-Scott realized at once that it was the slow dripping of blood, not of water. He found it hard to decide how soft or loud it was. It was more remorseless than any clock, or imaginable clock.

The woman stood among the mulberry trees regarding him. It was hard to decide whether or not she was smiling. Though she was a beautiful shape, she looked older than Aylwin-Scott (with many romancers) had assumed: a woman, not a girl; eminently maternal, some might say. She was breathing a little hard after her exertion (but very beautifully, so that Aylwin-Scott's heart plunged a little, youth that he was), and her arms now hung straight down her sides, with the palms of her hands towards him. It was almost as if she were an athlete who had momentarily stepped back in order to survey her opponent with a view to seeking a new advantage; but of course her mulberry-coloured form, of finest mulberry-tree silk, made that passing idea distinctly ridiculous.

She raised her right hand to the edge of the invisible curtain, and with her left pointed behind her to the seething flood which the curtain hushed. Unmistakably it was a monition, or at least a caution.

Aylwin-Scott shook his head in vigorous negation, and with his own arms and hands made towards her a gesture of mock-supplication. Often he had known it to prevail with females, at least in the momentary situation; until its use with them had become almost unconscious.

The woman appeared to relax a little, and, lowering her hand, took a few steps to the side. She was still watching him closely, and, he fancied, not smiling at all.

"Be friends," he said, dropping his arms and attempting no further gesture.

She spoke. But it was not in any tongue that Aylwin-Scott could identify. He took it to be Norman-French. Sensibly, he had been prepared for that from his first entrance into the Bower. One trouble was that he hardly excelled even at contemporary French, notwithstanding the fact that, when the time came, he would be living in France for years, and trying to make a proper livelihood there.

All he could distinguish was the one name, "Eleanor". Of course it was natural that he should be taken for some kind of spy or other hostile invader. It might well seem almost incredible to her that a man could attain to the centre of the Bower without aid; suspect aid, almost certainly; and proffered by the Queen's minions.

He could think only to shake his head once more, and to essay a reassuring smile.

Again she spoke. This time he understood no single word. It was accepted, he knew, that Norman-French was as unlike Larousse French as Chaucer's English was unlike that of a university sociologist, or Ancient Greek unlike the guttural babble of the jaded Piraeus.

For the moment, he could devise no further response,

She looked puzzled, then opened wide her mouth and pointed inside it interrogatively with her forefinger.

One smiling negative movement of his head would suffice, he hoped, to indicate that dumb he was not; a condition to which she was probably well accustomed. But he suspected that further words from him would increase her alarm. He might well be taken for a warlock. She must know much about warlocks too. A warlock would have no difficulty with the intricacies of the Bower.

He then recollected: she herself had been widely assumed to be a witch. Indeed, that had always been the official explanation of her and of all her mixed achievement. Good women en masse had even vacated a small nunnery because of its proximity to her recondite abode.

For what might pass as a long time, the two of them gazed at one another. The only sound was the slow drip which Aylwin-Scott knew was of blood. The pugs seemed to replenish themselves quite soundlessly, though unflaggingly. The birds had fallen silent again and were watching, waiting, withdrawing.

Then, on an instant, she drew a jewelled cross from the top of her dress. Presumably it had been hanging from a chain round her neck, though the chain was so fine that Aylwin-Scott could not see it. So much for the witchcraft hypothesis. It had vanished as soon as thought of, when one had found oneself alone with the nominated lady.

She pressed the cross to her lips tenderly, kissing it again and again. The splendid stones glinted in the watery sun. She carefully rebestowed the holy object within her bosom. Her touching feminine movements when doing this filled Aylwin-Scott with desire for her.

He could not but smile a little. She was so sweet, he felt. Almost all women have at moments that melting sweetness, he thought. It promised an illusion of total reconciliation; momentarily even with the universe.

She stepped, not this time crabwise, but actually towards him and with her right hand slightly advanced. He saw that the hand was adorned with strange rings. He would have preferred it bare, white, and girlish.

Now that she was closer to him, he could see that her eyes were blue pools to drown in. He could not have moved a muscle even if he had wished.

He could see that her feet were bare. The lawn was as green taffeta. To him its texture might have been a faint squirming embarrassment, had he been unshod. But the sight, the sound, and even the feel of her white feet advancing delicately across that faintly tinkling green would be with him for all his days. No terror, no lassitude, no deception would ever erase it.

It had been hard to decide how loud or soft was the unceasing knell. It was equally unclear how slowly or swiftly the woman was coming towards him. Her hair was golden. Aylwin-Scott had seen such hair painted on the walls of churches.

It seemed to him that within an instant she would be in touching distance. Even her lips were mulberry-coloured: either of their nature, or stained with the fruit; but perhaps by magic. The bone-structure of her face and head seemed as beneficent as that of the Virgin Mother.

Before the consummation of their proximity, a single,

mutually joyous touch, all that is ever necessary, a shadow fell. Despite the damp weakness of the sun, the shadow was black and huge.

The woman silently retreated.

At Aylwin-Scott's left hand had appeared a tall man, proportionately broad and more than proportionately muscular, from constant wielding of the axe, the bow, and the heavy lance or shaft. His beard and eyes were black, but Aylwin-Scott could see perfectly well that the beard had been crudely dyed. The hair on the man's head was too sparse to dye, and very short. He wore a single black garment, which left bare his arms and lower legs; very informal.

"Idling still?" enquired the man, in plain corrosive English. "*Still* idling, Michael?"

The voice of the world was achieving its final and crystallized oracle.

"This is the woman I love," said Aylwin-Scott, quietly but firmly; exactly as he had always intended and long planned.

"What difference do you suggest that makes?"

"That at last I am free."

"You perfect fool. For how long? Try to wake up."

"We shall start completely anew. In some other land. Any land but this."

"There's no *we*. I'm concerned only about *you*, Michael."

"We shall live together and we shall die together."

"Words, Michael. There's not a thing you can do."

"With her help, I mean to try."

Aylwin-Scott glanced at the woman, who now crouched at a distance: abject before the man and king. He could see a thick grey snake weaving slowly through her wondrous, fair hair. He realized that the pure and speaking perfume of the roses had strangely evaporated; that the heavy honeysuckle was in command once more. He looked back at the tall and burly man.

"I don't know what I'm supposed to do with you, Michael." The man's tone was entirely grim and serious; desperate, even.

"Just leave me alone," Aylwin-Scott responded half-jauntily. "That's all I ask of you."

"Everyone will do *that* soon enough, Michael. Before long,

you'll find out. When it's too late, of course. When you're done for finally."

Aylwin-Scott recollected the figure that had come shambling between his young and ardent self and the pretty page.

"That's not yet. Not now."

"Everything's now, Michael. Haven't you grasped even that?"

"Then the sweetness is now, too. You forget that."

The man went striding away towards the place where the woman had drawn the invisible curtain. He seemed merely to ignore the woman, which was what Aylwin-Scott would have expected of him, and which many chaps said was what women really liked; but, when he himself looked at her, obviously for the last time, as is everything, he realized that she had vanished, fled, or merely hidden. Quite probably she would re-emerge, seductive as a dream, when her majestic master had rid her Bower of an intruder, and had clapped his huge hands, hard as if they had been tanned by tanners, flattening every line and fold of the weakness he abhorred.

Also for the last time, as everything is, Aylwin-Scott glanced round the flowered and tended enclosure, the centre and heart of the Bower. Behind his back, there had been a new development. From the high, trim hedges had emerged fanged things which stood everywhere on guard; though the pretty, decorated pugs cropped on, regardless or inured. Flambeaux burned without and within the simple pavilion, though daylight remained, nor had excuse to depart for hours. It was a miracle that the small structure did not burn to ashes as he watched.

When Aylwin-Scott once more turned, he realized that more of the same guardians now edged that end of the pleasance also.

The mighty man, almost grotesque within his unrestrictive garment, was not going to draw back the invisible curtain himself. He had summoned a hideous buffoon for the task: shapeless, hairless, eyeless, almost noseless, for ever loveless.

The comical little entity had much labour with the heavy drapery. He gasped and grunted as he dragged, all the time stumbling across his own misshapen extremities. To Aylwin-Scott it mattered little, because as soon as the servitor had succeeded in moving the curtain at all, the din and crash of the immense cascade pounded through his being: and this time the cascade was visible as well as audible, sparkling as well as speaking, blinding as well as deafening. Possibly this explained why the presumed servant of the fall lacked organs of apprehension. And of course the first thing to be drowned was the tender plopping of the blood.

The mighty man urged Aylwin-Scott's advance with the single sweeping gesture of one who has defaulters slain upon the instant, and often upon every instant. Those lethal guardians of the place that had stood in an arc before Aylwin-Scott, were now arrayed in phalanxes to either side. He had not seen them stir, and, indeed, had no idea what locomotion they possessed.

The far greater number that had surrounded the larger area to his rear had similarly massed behind him. He knew this perfectly well, though, as ever, he did not look back. To them no doubt was allotted the task of compelling him into the flood, should the need for compulsion arise. Perhaps intrusion, even into the Bower's heart, truly occurred quite often.

Alone in the world, as are all men, Aylwin-Scott walked straight into the thunderous cascade. A third party, had one been conceivable, might have deemed his conduct heroic.

For moments the noise was as overwhelming as sudden death; and then Aylwin-Scott was not merely without the Bower, but right in the centre of the unkempt field, looking down on Paul Tent, who was asleep on his back, and with his mouth open, as if he were already a pensioner.

The shadow Aylwin-Scott had seen in his vision of Tent had instantly flitted. Aylwin-Scott's senses were fatigued, so that he hardly glimpsed its going.

After moments had passed, Aylwin-Scott gave Tent a slight kick.

"Hullo, Michael. Did you discover anything?"

"A perfectly bloody tangle. Nothing definite anywhere."

"Hardly to be expected after all this time." Tent sat himself up. He stared at Aylwin-Scott. "I say, Michael. You *are* all right?"

"The whole place stinks of honeysuckle. I never want to smell honeysuckle again." However, Aylwin-Scott then considered for a moment. "Well, not for some time."

At that, Tent glanced quite sharply. "So," he said, summing up everything. "So there it is."

Then he sprang to his feet, "I suppose we'd better wend."

"I suppose," agreed Aylwin-Scott. "You go first."

Life is so simple really. All our difficulties are in the mind.

CPSIA information can be obtained at www.ICGtesting.com
Printed in the USA
LVOW09*1454041016

507371LV00016B/155/P